SCARECROW

Also by Matthew Reilly

ICE STATION
TEMPLE
CONTEST
AREA 7

MATTHEW REILLY

SCARECROW

MACMILLAN
Pan Macmillan Australia

This is a work of fiction. Characters, institutions and organisations mentioned in this novel are either the product of the author's imagination or, if real, used fictitiously without any intent to describe actual conduct.

Reprinted 2003 (twice)

First published 2003 in Macmillan by Pan Macmillan Australia Pty Limited
St Martins Tower, 31 Market Street, Sydney

National Library of Australia
cataloguing-in-publication data:

Reilly, Matthew, 1974–.
Scarecrow.

ISBN 0 7329 1116 8 (hbk.).
ISBN 1 4050 3594 3 (pbk.).

1. Conspiracies – Fiction. 2. Assassins – Fiction. I. Title.

A823.3

Typeset in 11/14 pt Sabon by Post Pre-press Group
Printed in Australia by McPherson's Printing Group
Text design by i2i Design, Melanie Feddersen
Cartographic art by Laurie Whiddon, Map Illustrations

For Natalie, again

ACKNOWLEDGEMENTS

I don't know about you, but when I read a book, usually most of the names on the 'Acknowledgements' page mean very little to me. They're either friends of the author, or people who helped the author with research or getting published.

But let me tell you, profound and public thanks is exactly what these people deserve.

In my previous books, I have written on the 'Acknowledgements' page these words: 'to anyone who knows a writer, never underestimate the power of your encouragement.'

Believe me, writers—indeed, all creative people—live off encouragement. It drives us, propels us onward. One encouraging word can outshine a thousand critical comments.

And so while you, dear reader, may not recognise all of the following names, each in their own way *encouraged* me. This book is the richer for their help.

So.

On the friendship side:

Thanks, again, to Natalie Freer for her companionship and her smile and for reading the book in 60-page chunks once again; to John Schrooten, my mum and my brother, Stephen, for telling me what they really thought. And to my dad for his quiet support.

To Nik and Simon Kozlina for taking me out for coffee when I needed it and to Bec Wilson for those dinners every Wednesday night. And to Daryl and Karen Kay, and Don and Irene Kay, for being keen test subjects, hard-nosed engineers and good friends.

On the technical side:

Special thanks to the remarkable Richard Walsh from BHP Billiton for taking me on a fantastic tour of a coalmine down at Appin—the mine scenes in this book are so much more authentic for that experience! And thanks to Don Kay for arranging the introduction.

And of course, once again, sincere thanks to my amazing American military advisors, Captain Paul Woods, US Army, and

Gunnery Sergeant Kris Hankison, USMC (retired). It's incredible what these two guys know—as such, any mistakes in the book are mine and were made over their objections!

And again, to everyone at Pan Macmillan, thank you for another great effort. They're a wonderful crew at Pan Macmillan: from editorial to publicity to the sales reps out on the road.

To anyone who knows a writer, never underestimate the power of your encouragement.

M.R.

TURNING AND TURNING IN THE WIDENING GYRE,
THE FALCON CANNOT HEAR THE FALCONER;
THINGS FALL APART; THE CENTRE CANNOT HOLD;
MERE ANARCHY IS LOOSED UPON THE WORLD . . .

W. B. YEATS
The Second Coming

ALL OF THE BRAVE MEN ARE DEAD.

RUSSIAN MILITARY PROVERB

THE RULERS
OF THE WORLD

 LONDON, ENGLAND
20 OCTOBER, 1900 HOURS

There were 12 of them in total.

All men.

All billionaires.

Ten of the 12 were over 60 years of age. The other two were in their thirties, but they were the sons of former members, so their loyalty was assured. While membership of the Council was not strictly conditional on heredity, over the years it had become commonplace for sons to replace their fathers.

Otherwise membership was by invitation only and invitations were rarely given—as one would expect of such an august collection of individuals.

The co-founder of the world's largest software company.

A Saudi oil magnate.

The patriarch of a Swiss banking family.

The owner of the world's biggest shipping company.

The world's most successful stock trader.

The Vice-Chairman of the US Federal Reserve.

The newly-inherited heir to a military construction empire that built missiles for the United States Government.

There were no media barons on the Council—since it was widely known that their fortunes were largely based on debt and fluctuating share prices. The Council controlled the media simply by controlling the banks that fed the media barons their money.

Likewise, there were no national leaders—as the Council well knew, politicians possess the lowest form of power: transient power. Like media barons, they are beholden to others for their influence. In any case, the Council had made and unmade presidents and dictators before.

And no women.

It was the Council's view that there was—as yet—no woman on the planet worthy of a seat at the table. Not the Queen. Not even the French make-up heiress, Lillian Mattencourt, with her $26 billion personal fortune.

Since 1918, the Council had met twice a year, every year.

This year, however, it had been convened nine times.

This was, after all, a special year.

While the Council was a somewhat secretive group, its meetings were never held in secret. Secret meetings of powerful people create attention. No. It had always been the Council's opinion that the best-kept secrets existed out in the open, witnessed by the world but never actually *seen*.

As such, Council meetings were usually held during major international gatherings—the annual World Economic Forum in Davos, Switzerland; various World Trade Organisation meetings; the Council had even met once at Camp David, when the President wasn't there.

Today it met in the grand executive boardroom of the Dorchester Hotel in London.

The vote was taken and the decision was unanimous.

'Then it is agreed,' the Chairman said. 'The hunt will commence tomorrow. The list of targets will be released tonight through the usual channels, and bounties will be paid to those contractors who present to Monsieur J. P. Delacroix of AGM-Suisse the accustomed form of proof that a particular target has been eliminated.

'There are fifteen targets in total. The bounty for each has been set at US$18.6 million.'

An hour later, the meeting ended, and the members of the Council adjourned for drinks.

On the boardroom table behind them lay their meeting notes. Of the notes sitting in front of the Chairman's seat, one page lay face-up.

On it was a list of names.

	Name	Nat.	Org.
1.	ASHCROFT, William H.	UK	SAS
2.	CHRISTIE, Alec P.	UK	MI-6
3.	FARRELL, Gregory C.	USA	Delta
4.	KHALIF, Iman	AFGH	Al-Qaeda
5.	KINGSGATE, Nigel E.	UK	SAS
6.	McCABE, Dean P.	USA	Delta
7.	NAZZAR, Yousef M.	LEBN	HAMAS
8.	NICHOLSON, Francis X.	USA	USAMRMC
9.	OLIPHANT, Thompson J.	USA	USAMRMC
10.	POLANSKI, Damien G.	USA	ISS
11.	ROSENTHAL, Benjamin Y.	ISR	Mossad
12.	SCHOFIELD, Shane M.	USA	USMC
13.	WEITZMAN, Ronson H.	USA	USMC
14.	ZAWAHIRI, Hassan M.	SAUDI	Al-Qaeda
15.	ZEMIR, Simon B.	ISR	IAF

It was, to put it mildly, a singularly impressive list.

It featured members of the world's elite military units—the British SAS, the US Army's Delta Detachment and the Marine Corps.

The Israeli Air Force made an appearance, as did intelligence agencies like the Mossad and the ISS—the Intelligence and Security Service, the new name for the CIA. Plus members of the terrorist organisations HAMAS and Al-Qaeda.

It was a list of men—special men, brilliant at their chosen deadly professions—who had to be removed from the face of the earth by 12 noon, October 26, US Eastern Standard Time.

FIRST ATTACK

SIBERIA
26 OCTOBER 0900 HOURS (LOCAL TIME)
E.S.T. (NEW YORK, USA) 2100 HOURS (25 OCT)

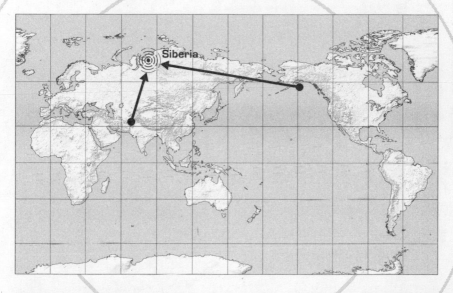

Modern international bounty hunters bear many similarities to their forebears in the Old American West.

There are the *lone wolf bounty hunters*—usually ex-military types, freelance assassins or fugitives from justice themselves, they are lone operators known for their idiosyncratic weapons, vehicles or methods.

There are the *organisations*—companies that make the hunting of fugitive human beings a business. With their quasi-military infrastructures, mercenary organisations are often drawn to participate in international human hunts.

And, of course, there are the *opportunists*—special forces units that go AWOL and undertake bounty hunting activities; or law enforcement officials who find the lure of a private bounty more enticing than their legal obligations.

But the complexities of modern bounty hunting are not to be discounted. It is not unknown for a bounty hunter to act in concert with a national government that wants to distance itself from certain acts. Nor is it unknown for bounty hunters to have tacit agreements with member states for sanctuary as payment for a previous 'job'.

For, in the end, one thing about them is clear: international borders mean little to the international bounty hunter.

United Nations White Paper: Non-Government Forces in UN Peacekeeping Zones,
OCTOBER 2001 (UN PRESS, NEW YORK)

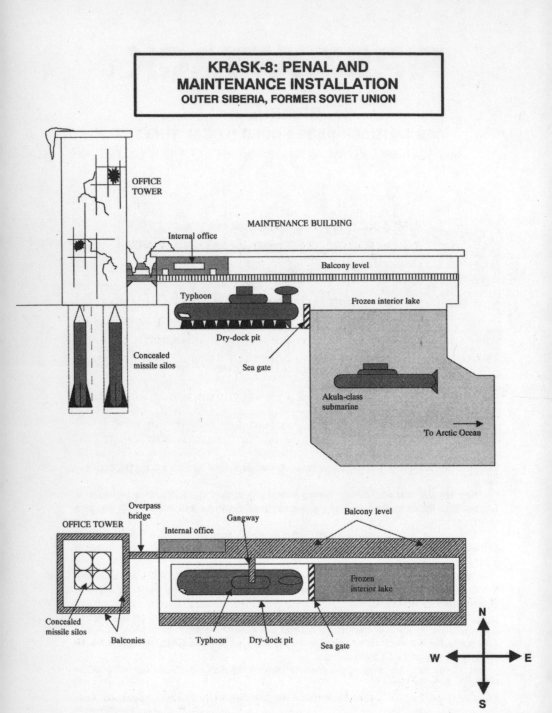

KRASK-8: PENAL AND MAINTENANCE INSTALLATION
OUTER SIBERIA, FORMER SOVIET UNION

OFFICE TOWER

MAINTENANCE BUILDING

Internal office

Balcony level

Typhoon

Frozen interior lake

Dry-dock pit

Concealed missile silos

Sea gate

Akula-class submarine

To Arctic Ocean

Overpass bridge

OFFICE TOWER

Internal office

Gangway

Balcony level

Frozen interior lake

Concealed missile silos

Balconies

Typhoon

Dry-dock pit

Sea gate

N
W — E
S

The aeroplane rocketed through the sky at the speed of sound.

Despite the fact that it was a large plane, it didn't show up on any radar screens. And even though it was breaking the sound barrier, it didn't create any sonic booms—a recent development in wave-negativing sensors took care of that.

With its angry-browed cockpit windows, its black radar-absorbent paint and its unique flying wing design, the B-2 Stealth Bomber didn't normally fly missions like this.

It was designed to carry 40,000 pounds of ordnance, from laser-guided bombs to air-launched thermonuclear cruise missiles.

Today, however, it carried no bombs.

Today its bomb bay had been modified to convey a light but unusual payload: one fast-attack vehicle and eight United States Marines.

As he stood in the cockpit of the speeding Stealth Bomber, Captain Shane M. Schofield was unaware of the fact that, as of six days previously, he had become a target in the greatest bounty hunt in history.

The grey Siberian sky was reflected in the silver lenses of his wraparound anti-flash glasses. The glasses concealed a pair of vertical scars that cut down across Schofield's eyes, wounds from a previous mission and the source of his operational nickname: Scarecrow.

At five-feet-ten-inches tall, Schofield was lean and muscular. Under his white–grey Kevlar helmet, he had spiky black hair and a creased handsome face. He was known for his sharp mind, his cool head under pressure, and the high regard in which he was held by lower-ranking Marines—he was a leader who looked out for his men. Rumour had it he was also the grandson of the great Michael Schofield, a Marine whose exploits in the Second World War were the stuff of Marine Corps legend.

The B-2 zoomed through the sky, heading for a distant corner of northern Russia, to an abandoned Soviet installation on the barren coast of Siberia.

Its official Soviet name had been 'Krask-8: Penal and Maintenance Installation', the outermost of eight compounds surrounding the Arctic town of Krask. In the imaginative Soviet tradition, the compounds had been named Krask-1, Krask-2, Krask-3 and so on.

Until four days ago, Krask-8 had been known simply as a long-forgotten ex-Soviet outstation—a half-gulag, half-maintenance facility at which political prisoners had been forced to work. There were hundreds of such facilities dotted around the former Soviet Union—giant, ugly, oil-stained monoliths which before 1991 had formed the industrial heart of the USSR, but which now lay dormant, left to rot in the snow, the ghost towns of the Cold War.

But two days ago, on October 24, all that had changed.

Because on that day, a team of thirty well-armed and well-trained Islamic Chechen terrorists had taken over Krask-8 and announced to the Russian government that they intended to fire four SS-18 nuclear missiles—missiles that had simply been left in their silos at the site with the fall of the Soviets in 1991—on Moscow unless Russia withdrew its troops from Chechnya and declared the breakaway republic an independent state.

A deadline was set for 10 a.m. today, October 26.

The date had meaning. October 26 was a year to the day since a

force of crack Russian troops had stormed a Moscow theatre held by Chechen terrorists, ending a three-day siege, killing all the terrorists and over a hundred hostages.

That today also happened to be the first day of the Muslim holy month of Ramadan, a traditional day of peace, didn't seem to bother these Islamist terrorists.

The fact that Krask-8 was something more than just a relic of the Cold War was also news to the Russian government.

After some investigation of long-sealed Soviet records, the terrorists' claims had proved to be correct. It turned out that Krask-8 was a secret that the old Communist regime had failed to inform the new government about during the transition to democracy.

It did indeed house nuclear missiles—*sixteen* to be exact; sixteen SS-18 nuclear-tipped intercontinental ballistic missiles; all contained in concealed underground silos that had been designed to evade US satellite detection. Apparently, 'clones' of Krask-8—identical missile-launch sites disguised as industrial facilities—could also be found in old Soviet client states like the Sudan, Syria, Cuba and Yemen.

And so, in the new world order—post-Cold War, post-September 11—the Russians had called on the Americans to help.

As a rapid response, the American government had sent to Krask-8 a fast-and-light counter-terrorist unit from Delta Detachment—led by Specialists Greg Farrell and Dean McCabe.

Reinforcements would arrive later, the first of which was this team, a point unit of United States Marines led by Captain Shane M. Schofield.

Schofield strode into the bomb bay of the plane, breathing through a high-altitude face-mask.

He was met by the sight of a medium-sized cargo container, inside of which sat a Fast Attack 'Commando Scout' vehicle. Arguably the lightest and fastest armoured vehicle in service, it looked like a cross between a sports car and a Humvee.

And inside the sleek vehicle, strapped tightly into their seats, sat seven Recon Marines, the other members of Schofield's team. All were dressed in white–grey body armour, white–grey helmets, white–grey battle dress uniforms. And they all stared intently forward, game faces on.

As Schofield watched their serious expressions, he was once again taken aback by their youth. It was strange, but at 33 he felt decidedly old in their presence.

He nodded to the nearest man. 'Hey, Whip. How's the hand?'

'Why, er, it's great, sir,' Corporal Whip Whiting said, surprised. He'd been shot in the hand during a fierce gun battle in the Tora Bora mountains in early 2002, but since that day Whip and Schofield hadn't worked together. 'The docs said you saved my index finger. If you hadn't told them to splint it, it would have grown in a hook shape. To be honest, I didn't think you'd remember, sir.'

Schofield's eyes gleamed. 'I always remember.'

Apart from one member of the unit, this wasn't his regular team.

His usual team of Marines—Libby 'Fox' Gant and Gena 'Mother' Newman—were currently operating in the mountains of northern Afghanistan, hunting for the terrorist leader and long-time No. 2 to Osama bin Laden, Hassan Mohammad Zawahiri.

Gant, fresh from Officer Candidate School and now a First Lieutenant, was leading a Recon Unit in Afghanistan. Mother, an experienced Gunnery Sergeant who had helped Schofield himself when he was a young officer, was acting as her Team Chief.

Schofield was supposed to be joining them, but at the last minute he'd been diverted from Afghanistan to lead this unexpected mission.

The only one of his regulars that Schofield had been able to bring with him was a young sergeant named Buck Riley Jnr, call-sign 'Book II'. Silent and brooding and possessed of an intensity that belied his 25 years, Book II was a seriously tough-as-nails warrior. And as far as Schofield was concerned, with his heavy-browed face and battered pug nose, he was looking more and more like his father—the original 'Book' Riley—every day.

Schofield keyed his satellite radio, spoke into the VibraMike strapped around his throat. Rather than pick up actual spoken words, the vibration-sensing microphone picked up the reverberations of his voice box. The satellite uplink system driving it was the brand-new GSX-9—the most advanced communications system in use in the US military. In theory, a portable GSX-9 unit like Schofield's could broadcast a clear signal halfway around the world with crystal clarity.

'Base, this is Mustang 3,' he said. 'Sitrep?'

A voice came over his earpiece. It was the voice of an Air Force radio operator stationed at McColl Air Force Base in Alaska, the communications centre for this mission.

'*Mustang 3, this is Base. Mustang 1 and Mustang 2 have engaged the enemy. Report that they have seized the missile silos and inflicted heavy casualties on the enemy. Mustang 1 is holding the silos and awaiting reinforcements. Mustang 2 reports that there are still at least twelve enemy agents putting up a fight in the main maintenance building.*'

'All right,' Schofield said, 'what about our follow up?'

'*An entire company of Army Rangers from Fort Lewis is en route, Scarecrow. One hundred men, approximately one hour behind you.*'

'Good.'

Book II spoke from inside the armoured Scout vehicle. 'What's the story, Scarecrow?'

Schofield turned. 'We're go for drop.'

Five minutes later, the box-shaped cargo-container dropped out of the belly of the Stealth Bomber and plummeted like a stone towards the Earth.

Inside the container—in the car resting inside it—sat Schofield and his seven Marines, shuddering and jolting with the vibrations of the terminal-velocity fall.

Schofield watched the numbers on a digital wall-mounted altimeter whizzing downwards:

50,000 feet . . .

45,000 feet . . .

40,000 . . . 30,000 . . . 20,000 . . . 10,000 . . .

'Preparing to engage chutes at five thousand feet . . .' Corporal Max 'Clark' Kent, the loadmaster, said in a neutral voice. 'GPS guidance system has us right on target for landing. External cameras verify that the LZ is clear.'

Schofield eyed the fast-ticking altimeter.

8,000 feet.

7,000 feet . . .

6,000 feet . . .

If everything went to plan, they would land about fifteen miles due east of Krask-8, just over the horizon from the installation, out of sight of the facility.

'Engaging primary chutes . . . *now*,' Clark announced.

The jolt that the falling container received was shocking in its force. The whole falling box lurched sharply and Schofield and his Marines all shuddered in their seats, held in by their six-point seat belts and rollbars.

And suddenly they were floating, care of the container's three directional parachutes.

'How're we doing, Clark?' Schofield asked.

Clark was guiding them with the aid of a joystick and the container's external cameras.

'Ten seconds. I'm aiming for a dirt track in the middle of the valley. Brace yourselves for landing in three . . . two . . . one . . .'

Whump!

The container hit solid ground, and suddenly its entire front wall just fell open and daylight flooded in through the wide aperture and the four-wheel-drive Commando Scout Light Attack Vehicle skidded off the mark and raced out of the container's belly into the grey Siberian day.

The Scout whipped along a muddy earthen track, bounded on both sides by snow-covered hills. Deathly grey tree skeletons lined the slopes. Black rocks stabbed upward through the carpet of snow.

Stark. Brutal. And cold as hell.

Welcome to Siberia.

As he sat in the back of the Light Attack Vehicle, Schofield spoke into his throat-mike: 'Mustang 1, this is Mustang 3. Do you copy?'

No reply.

'I say again. Mustang 1, this is Mustang 3. Do you copy?'

Nothing.

He did the same for the second Delta team, Mustang 2. Again, no reply.

Schofield keyed the satellite frequency, spoke to Alaska: 'Base, this is 3. I can't raise either Mustang 1 or Mustang 2. Do you have contact?'

'*Ah, affirmative on that, Scarecrow,*' the voice from Alaska said. '*I was just talking to them a moment ago—*'

The signal exploded to hash.

'Clark?' Schofield said.

'Sorry, Boss, signal's gone,' Clark said from the Scout's wall console. 'We lost 'em. Damn, I thought these new satellite receivers were supposed to be incorruptible.'

Schofield frowned, concerned. 'Jamming signals?'

'No. Not a one. We're in clear radio airspace. Nothing should be affecting that signal. Must be something at the other end.'

'Something at the other end . . .' Schofield bit his lip. 'Famous last words.'

'Sir,' the Scout's driver, a grizzled old sergeant named 'Bull' Simcox, said, 'we should be coming into visual range in about thirty seconds.'

Schofield looked forward, out over Simcox's shoulder.

He saw the black muddy track rushing by beneath the Scout's armoured hood, saw that they were approaching the crest of a hill.

Beyond that hill, lay Krask-8.

At that same moment, inside a high-tech radio receiving room at McColl Air Force Base in Alaska, the young radio officer who had been in contact with Schofield looked about himself in confusion. His name was Bradsen, James Bradsen.

A few seconds before, completely without warning, the power to the communications facility had been abruptly cut.

The base commander at McColl strode into the room.

'Sir,' Bradsen said. 'We just—'

'I know, son,' the CO said. 'I know.'

It was then that Bradsen saw *another* man standing behind his base commander.

Bradsen had never seen this other man before. Tall and solid, he had carrot-red hair and an ugly rat-like face. He wore a plain suit and his black eyes never blinked. They just took in the entire room with a cool unblinking stare. Everything about him screamed ISS.

The base commander said, 'Sorry, Bradsen. Intelligence issue. This mission has been taken out of our hands.'

The Scout attack vehicle crested the hill.

Inside it, Schofield drew a breath.

Before him, in all its glory, lay Krask-8.

It stood in the centre of a wide flat plain, a cluster of snow-covered

buildings—hangars, storage sheds, a gigantic maintenance ware-house, even one 15-storey glass-and-concrete office tower. A miniature cityscape.

The whole compound was surrounded by a 20-foot-high razor wire fence, and in the distance beyond it, perhaps two miles away, Schofield could see the northern coastline of Russia and the waves of the Arctic Ocean.

Needless to say, the post-Cold War world hadn't been kind to Krask-8.

The entire mini-city was deserted.

Snow covered the complex's half-dozen streets. Off to Schofield's right, giant mounds of the stuff slouched against the walls of the main maintenance warehouse—a structure the size of four football fields.

To the left of the massive shed, connected to it by an enclosed bridge, stood the office tower. Enormous downward-creeping claws of ice hung off its flat roof, frozen in place, defying gravity.

The cold itself had taken its toll, too. Without an anti-freeze crew on site, nearly every window pane at Krask-8 had contracted and cracked. Now, every glass surface lay shattered or spider-webbed, the stinging Siberian wind whistling through it all with impunity.

It was a ghost town.

And somewhere underneath it all lay sixteen nuclear missiles.

The Scout roared through the already blasted-open gates of Krask-8 at a cool 80 kilometres an hour.

It shot down a sloping road toward the complex, one of Schofield's Marines now perched in the 7.62mm machine-gun turret mounted on the rear of the sleek armoured car.

Inside the Scout, Schofield hovered behind Clark, peering at the young corporal's computer screen.

'Check for their locators,' he said. 'We have to find out where those D-boys are.'

Clark tapped away at his keyboard, bringing up some computer maps of Krask-8.

One map showed the complex from a side-view:

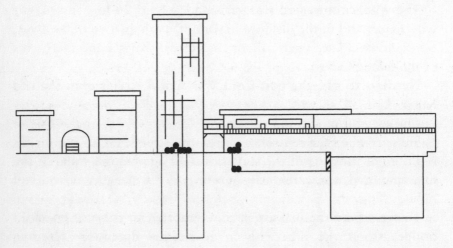

Two clusters of blinking red dots could be seen: one set on the ground floor of the office tower and a second set inside the massive maintenance shed.

The two Delta teams.

But something was wrong with this image.

None of the blinking dots was moving.

All of them were ominously still.

Schofield felt a chill on the back of his neck.

'Bull,' he said softly, 'take Whip, Tommy and Hastings. Check out the office tower. I'll take Book II, Clark and Rooster and secure the maintenance building.'

'Roger that, Scarecrow.'

The Scout rushed down a narrow deserted street, passing underneath concrete walkways, blasting through the mounds of snow that lay everywhere.

It skidded to a halt outside the gargantuan maintenance warehouse, right in front of a small personnel door.

The rear hatch of the Scout was flung open and immediately

Schofield and three snow-camouflaged Marines leapt out of it and bolted for the door.

No sooner were they out than the Scout peeled away, heading for the glass office tower next door.

Schofield entered the maintenance building gun-first.

He carried a Heckler & Koch MP-7, the successor to the old MP-5. The MP-7 was a short-barrelled machine pistol, compact but powerful. In addition to the MP-7, Schofield carried a Desert Eagle semi-automatic pistol, a K-Bar knife and, in a holster on his back, an Armalite MH-12 Maghook—a magnetic grappling hook that was fired from a double-gripped gun-like launcher.

In addition to his standard kit, for this mission Schofield carried some extra firepower—six high-powered Thermite-Amatol demolition charges. Each handheld charge had the explosive ability to level an entire building.

Schofield and his team hurried down a short corridor lined with offices, came to a door at its end.

They stopped.

Listened.

No sound.

Schofield cracked open the door—and caught a glimpse of wide-open space, *immense* wide-open space . . .

He pushed the door wider.

'Jesus . . .'

The work area of the maintenance warehouse stretched away from him like an enormous hangar bay, its cracked-glass roof revealing the grey Siberian sky.

Only this was no ordinary hangar bay.

Nor was it any ordinary old 'maintenance shed' for a penal colony.

Taking up nearly three-quarters of the floorspace of this massive interior space was a gigantic—*gigantic*—rectangular concrete pit in the floor.

And mounted at Schofield's end of the pit, raised off the floor on a series of concrete blocks, was a 200-metre-long submarine.

It looked awesome.

Like a giant on its throne, surrounded by a complex array of structures that belonged to people of a vastly smaller size.

And all of it covered in a crust of ice and snow.

Cranes and catwalks criss-crossed over the top of the sub, while thin horizontal walkways connected it to the concrete floor of the shed. A single vertiginous gangway joined the three-storey-high conning tower of the submarine to an upper balcony level.

Blinking away the strangeness of the sight, Schofield's mind processed this new information.

First, he recognised the submarine.

It was a Typhoon.

The Typhoon class of submarines had been the jewel in the crown of the USSR's ocean-going nuclear arsenal. Despite the fact that only six had ever been built, the long-nosed ballistic missile subs had been made famous in novels and Hollywood movies. But while the Typhoons looked sexy, they had been terribly unreliable, requiring constant upgrades and maintenance. They remain the largest submarines ever built by man.

This one, Schofield saw, had been having work done to its forward torpedo bays when Krask-8 had been abandoned—the outer hull around the Typhoon's bow torpedo tubes lay ripped open, taken apart plate-by-plate.

How a Typhoon-class sub came to be inside a maintenance shed *two miles* inland from the Arctic Ocean was another question.

A question that was answered by the remainder of the maintenance building.

Beyond the Typhoon's enormous dry-dock—indeed, cutting the dry-dock off from the rest of the pit—Schofield saw a large vertical plate-steel sea gate.

And beyond the sea gate was water.

A wide rectangular *indoor* expanse of partially-frozen water, held out from the dry-dock by the dam-like sea gate.

Schofield guessed that beneath that pool of water lay some kind of underground cave system that stretched all the way to the coast—allowing submarines to come into Krask-8 for repairs, away from the prying eyes of American spy satellites.

It all became clear.

Krask-8—two miles inland from the Arctic coast, listed on maps as a forced-labour facility—was a top-secret Soviet submarine repair facility.

Schofield, however, didn't have time to ponder that issue, because it was then that he saw the bodies.

They lay over by the edge of the dry-dock pit: four bodies, all dressed in US Army snow fatigues, body armour and . . .

. . . all shot to hell.

Blood covered everything. It was splashed across faces, splattered over chests, spread out across the floor.

'Motherfucker,' Clark breathed.

'Christ, man, these were friggin' D-boys,' Corporal Ricky 'Rooster' Murphy said. Like Schofield—and maybe in imitation of him—Rooster wore silver anti-flash glasses.

Schofield remained silent.

The uniforms on the corpses, he saw, had been customised: some of the men had removed their right-hand shoulderplates, others had cut off the sleeves of their snow gear at the elbows.

Customised uniforms: the signature of Delta.

Two more bodies lay down in the pit itself—30 feet below floor level—also shot to shit.

Hundreds of ejected shell casings lay in a wide circle around the scene. Fire from the Delta men. By the look of it, Schofield saw, the D-boys had been firing in nearly every direction when they'd gone down . . .

Whispered voices.

'How many in total?'

'Just the four in here. Blue Team reports four more in the office tower.'

'So which one is Schofield?'

'The one in the silver glasses.'

'Snipers ready. On my mark.'

One of the bodies caught Schofield's attention.

He froze.

He hadn't seen it at first, because the body's upper half had been hanging over the edge of the dry-dock pit, but now he saw it clearly.

Alone among the six dead bodies, *this man's head had been cut off*.

Schofield grimaced at the sight.

It was absolutely disgusting.

Ragged threads of flesh hung from the corpse's open neck; the twin pipes of the oesophagus and the windpipe lay exposed to the open air.

'Mother of God,' Book II breathed, coming up alongside Schofield. 'What the hell happened here?'

As the four tiny figures of Schofield and his Marines examined the death scene down on the floor of the dry-dock hall, no fewer than twenty pairs of eyes watched them.

The watchers were arrayed around the hall, at key strategic points—men dressed in identical snow fatigues but carrying a variety of weapons.

They watched in tense silence, waiting for their commander to give the kill signal.

Schofield crouched beside the headless body and examined it.

D-boys didn't wear ID tags or patches, but he didn't need to see a tag or a patch to know who this was. He could tell by the physique alone.

It was Specialist Dean McCabe, one of the Delta team leaders.

Schofield glanced around the immediate area. McCabe's head was nowhere in sight. Schofield frowned at that. The Delta man's head had not only been cut off, it had been *taken*—

'*Scarecrow!*' a voice exploded in his earpiece. '*This is Bull. We're over in the office tower. You're not going to believe this.*'

'Try me.'

'*They're all dead, all the Delta guys. And Scarecrow . . . Farrell's head has been fucking cut off.*'

An ice-cold charge zoomed up Schofield's spine.

His mind raced. His eyes scanned the hall all around him—its cracked glass windows and ice-faded walls blurring in a kaleidoscope of motion.

Krask-8. Deserted and isolated . . .

No sign of any Chechen terrorists since they'd got here . . .

Radio contact with Alaska lost . . .

And all the D-boys dead . . . plus the bizarre extra feature of McCabe's and Farrell's missing heads.

And it all crystallised in Schofield's mind.

'Bull!' he hissed into his throat-mike. 'Get over here right now! We've been set up! We've just walked into a trap!'

And at that moment, as he spoke, Schofield's searching eyes settled on a small mound of snow in a corner of the immense dry-dock hall—and suddenly a shape huddled behind the snow-mound came into sharp focus, revealing itself to be a carefully-camouflaged man dressed in snow-fatigues and pointing a Colt Commando assault rifle directly at Schofield's face.

Damn.

And with that the twenty assassins arrayed around the hall opened fire on Schofield and his men and the dry-dock facility became a battlefield.

Schofield ducked reflexively just as two bullets swooshed low over his head.

Book II and Clark did the same, diving in amongst the Delta bodies on the ground as a rain of bullets sparked against the floor all around them.

The fourth Marine, Rooster, wasn't so lucky. Perhaps it was the reflective glasses he wore—making him look like Schofield—or perhaps he was just unlucky. Nevertheless, a hailstorm of rounds pummelled his body, cut it to ribbons, making him dance even though he was dead.

'Into the pit! Now!' Schofield yelled, practically crash-tackling Clark and Book II out of the line of fire and rolling the three of them off the edge of the dry-dock pit just as it was assaulted by a thousand bullet sparks.

As Schofield and the others dropped down into the dry-dock pit, they did so under the watchful eye of the commander of the heavily-armed force surrounding them.

The commander's name was Wexley—Cedric K. Wexley—and in a previous life he had been a major in the elite South African Reconnaissance Commandos.

So this is the famous Scarecrow, Wexley thought, watching Schofield move. *The man who defeated Gunther Botha in Utah. Well, if nothing else, his reflexes are good.*

Before his own fall from grace, Wexley had been a shining star in the Reccondos, chiefly because he had been a devoted follower of apartheid. Somehow, he had survived the transition to democracy, his racist tendencies going unnoticed. And then he had killed a black soldier in boot camp, beat him to death during hand-to-hand training. He had done it before, but this time it was noticed.

And when soldiers like Cedric Wexley—psychopaths, sociopaths, thugs—were discharged from the legitimate armed forces, they invariably ended up in the illegitimate ones.

Which was how Wexley came to be in command of this unit: a Special Ops team belonging to one of the world's pre-eminent mercenary organisations—the highly corporate, South African-based 'Executive Solutions' or 'ExSol'.

While ExSol specialised in Third World security missions—like propping up African dictatorships in exchange for diamond-mining royalties—it also, when the logistics allowed, engaged in the more lucrative international bounty hunts that occasionally arose.

At nearly $19 million per head, this was the most lucrative bounty hunt ever, and thanks to a well-placed friend on the Council, Executive Solutions had been given the inside running to claim three of those heads.

Wexley's radio operator came up beside him. 'Sir. Blue Team has engaged the Marines in the office tower.'

Wexley nodded. 'Tell them to return to the dry-dock via the bridge when they're done.'

'Sir, there's another thing,' the radio man said.

'Yes?'

'Neidricht up on the roof says he's picked up two incoming signals on the external radar.' There was a pause. 'Judging by the signatures, he thinks it's the Hungarian and the Black Knight.'

'How far out are they?'

'The Hungarian's about fifteen minutes away. The Knight is further, maybe twenty-five.'

Wexley bit his lip.

Bounty hunters, he thought. *Fucking bounty hunters.*

Wexley hated bounty hunt missions precisely because he hated bounty hunters. If they didn't beat you to the target, the little fuckers would let you do all the dirty work, stalk you all the way back to the proof-station, *steal* the target out from under you and then claim the money for themselves.

In an up-front military exchange, the winner was the last man standing. Not so in a bounty hunt. In a bounty hunt, the winner was the one who presented the prize back at base—*however* he might have obtained it.

Wexley growled. 'The Hungarian I can handle, he's a brute. But the Black Knight . . . he'll almost certainly be a problem.'

The ExSol commander looked down at the submarine pit. 'Which means we'd better make this quick. Get this Schofield asshole, and bring me his fucking head.'

Schofield, Book II and Clark dropped down the wall of the dry-dock pit.

They fell for a full thirty feet, before—*whump*—they landed heavily on the two Delta bodies slumped at the bottom.

'Come on, move! Move! Move!' Schofield pulled the other two underneath the big black Typhoon sub, mounted on its blocks in the pit.

Each block was about the size of a small car and made of solid concrete. Four long rows of the blocks supported the massive submarine, creating a series of narrow right-angled alleyways underneath the Typhoon's black steel hull.

Schofield spoke into his throat-mike as he zig-zagged through the dark alleyways: 'Bull! Bull Simcox! Do you copy!'

Bull's voice, fast and desperate: '*Scarecrow, shit! We're under heavy fire over here! All of the others are down and I'm . . . I'm hit bad! I can't—oh, fuck—no!—*'

There was a brief crack of gunfire at the other end and then the signal cut to hash.

'Shit,' Schofield said.

Then, abruptly, there came several soft whumps from somewhere behind him.

He spun—MP-7 up—and through the forest of fat concrete blocks, saw the first set of enemy troops drop into the pit on ropes.

With Book II and Clark behind him, Schofield weaved his way through the shadowy alleyways under the Typhoon, ducking enemy fire.

Their pursuers had now entered the dark concrete maze as well—maybe ten men in total—and they were systematically moving forward, covering the long alleyways with heavy fire, herding Schofield and his men toward the sea-gate-end of the dry-dock.

Schofield watched his enemies as they moved, analysed their tactics, eyed their weapons. Their tactics were standard. Basic flushing stuff. But their weapons . . .

Their weapons.

'Who are these guys?' Book II said.

Schofield said, 'I have an idea, but you're not going to like it.'

'Try me.'

'Check out their guns.'

Book II took a quick look. Some of the white-masked men held MP-5s while others carried French-made FAMAS assault rifles or American Colt Commandos. Others still held old AK-47s, or AK-47 variants like the Chinese Type 56.

'See the guns?' Schofield said as they moved. 'They've all got different kinds of weapons.'

'Damn it,' Book II said. 'Mercenaries.'

'That's what I'm thinking.'

'But why?'

'Don't know. At least not yet.'

'What are we going to do?' Clark asked desperately.

'I'm working on it,' Schofield said, gazing up at the thick steel hull above them, looking for escape options.

With his back pressed against a concrete block, he poked his head around one of the outer corners and looked all the way down the dry-dock pit—and saw the high steel sea gate that separated the pit from the ice-covered pool of water at the eastern end of the hall.

The mechanics of the dry-dock leapt into his mind.

To get an enormous Typhoon into the dock, you lowered the sea gate, flooded the dry-dock, and sailed your sub into it. Then you *raised* the sea gate again and drained the dry-dock, lowering the sub onto the concrete blocks in the process and giving yourself a clean and dry environment to work on the submarine.

The sea gate . . .

Schofield eyed it closely, thought of all the water being held back behind it. Looked the other way: toward the bow of the sub, and saw it.

It was their only shot.

He turned to the others. 'You guys got Maghooks on you?'

'Er, yeah.'

'Yes.'

'Get ready to use 'em,' Schofield said, looking down at the great steel sea gate, three storeys high and 90 feet wide. He drew his own Maghook from his back-mounted holster.

'We going that way, sir?' Clark asked.

'Nope. We're going in the other direction, but to do that we need to blow open that sea gate.'

'*Blow open* the sea gate?' Clark gasped, looking at Book.

Book II shrugged. 'This is standard. He destroys things—'

Just then, an unexpected volley of bullets raked the concrete blocks all around them. It had come from the direction of the sea gate.

Schofield ducked for cover, peered out, and saw that ten more mercenary soldiers had dropped into the pit at that end.

Christ, he thought, now they were stuck in the pit between two sets of bad guys.

The new group of mercenaries began to advance.

'Screw this,' he said.

Cedric Wexley watched the dry-dock pit from high above.

He saw his two squads of mercenaries closing in on Schofield and his men from both sides.

A cold smile cracked his face.

This was too easy.

Schofield grabbed two Thermite-Amatol demolition charges from his combat webbing. 'Gentlemen. Maghooks.'

They all pulled out their Maghooks.

'Now do this,' Schofield moved to the port-side edge of the Typhoon, raised his Maghook and fired it at close range up into the hull of the sub.

Clangggggg!

Clark and Book II did the same.

Clangggggg! Clangggggg!

Schofield peered down the length of the submarine. 'When the wave hits, let your Maghook ropes play out, so we can move along the outside of the sub.'

'Wave?' Clark said. 'What wave . . . ?'

But Schofield didn't answer him.

He simply took the two demolition charges in his hands and selected the timer switch he wanted.

Timer switches on Thermite-Amatol charges come in three colours: red, green and blue. Depressing the red switch gives you five seconds. Green gives you thirty seconds. Blue: one minute.

Schofield chose red.

Then he hurled the two charges down the length of the dry-dock pit, over the heads of the advancing mercenary team, sending the two high-powered explosives bouncing into the plate-steel sea gate like a pair of tennis balls. They came to rest at the

gate's weakest point, at the spot where it met the pit's concrete right-side wall.

Five seconds. Four . . .

'This is going to hurt . . .' Book II said, wrapping the rope of his Maghook around his forearm. Clark did the same.

Three . . . two . . .

'One,' Schofield whispered, eyeing the dam. 'Now.'

Boom.

The twin blasts of the Thermite-Amatol demolition charges shook the walls of the entire dry-dock building.

A blinding-white flash of light lit up the sea gate. Smoke rushed up the length of the pit, filling the alleyways between the giant concrete blocks as it roared forward, consuming the nearest group of assassins, enveloping everything in its path, including Schofield's team.

There was a moment of eerie silence . . .

And then came the crack—an almighty, ear-splitting *craaaack*—as the wounded sea gate broke under the weight of the water pressing against it, and 100 million litres of water rushed into the pit, *bursting* through the smoke.

A wall of water.

The immense body of liquid created an incredible sound—it *roared* down the length of the dry-dock pit: foaming, roiling, bounding forward.

The nearest group of mercenaries were simply blasted off their feet by the wall of water, and hurled westward.

Schofield, Book II and Clark were next in line.

The wall of water just collected them where they stood—one second they were there, the next they were gone. It lifted them instantly off their feet, flinging them like rag dolls toward the bow-end of the Typhoon, bouncing them along the side of its hull.

The other team of mercenaries was also taken by the rushing wall of water. They were smashed into the solid concrete wall at the far end of the dry-dock, many of them going under as the waves of roiling water crashed against the edge of the 200-metre-long pit.

Schofield and his men, however, didn't hit the end of the pit.

As the roaring body of water had collected them, they'd held grimly onto their Maghook launchers as the ropes connected to their magnetic hooks unspooled at a phenomenal rate.

When they came alongside the bow of the Typhoon, Schofield had yelled, 'Clamp now!'

He had then jammed his finger down on a button on his Maghook's grip, initiating a clamping mechanism inside it that stopped the unspooling of its rope.

Book II and Clark did the same . . . and the three of them jolted to simultaneous halts right next to the bow of the Typhoon, the rushing water kicking up blast-sprays all around their bodies.

Next to them, exactly where Schofield had seen it before, was the yawning opening of the Typhoon's port-side torpedo tubes—the tubes which had evidently been undergoing repairs when Krask-8 had been abandoned.

At the moment, the torpedo tubes lay a foot above the surface of the inrushing water.

'Get into the tubes!' Schofield yelled into his mike. 'Into the sub!'

Book and Clark did as they were told, and squirming and struggling against the rushing water, entered the submarine.

Sudden silence.

Schofield wriggled out of the torpedo tube last of all and found himself standing inside a Soviet Typhoon-class ballistic missile submarine.

It was a world of cold steel. Racks that had once contained torpedoes occupied the centre of the room. Rows of pipes lined the ceiling. The stench of body odour—the smell of fear, the smell of submariners—filled the air.

Two fat waterfalls of seawater now gushed in through the sub's open torpedo tubes, rapidly filling the cramped room.

It was largely dark in here: the only light, the grey daylight that crept in through the now-flooding torpedo tubes. Schofield and the others flicked on their barrel-mounted flashlights.

'This way,' Schofield said, charging out of the torpedo room, his legs sloshing through the rising water.

The three Marines bolted through the Typhoon's imposing silo hall next—a long high-ceilinged chamber that contained twenty gigantic missile silos; tall tubular structures that rose from floor to ceiling, dwarfing them.

As he ran past the silos, Schofield saw that the access hatches on some of them were open, revealing hollow emptiness inside. The hatches on at least six of the silos, however, remained closed—indicating that they still contained missiles.

'Where to now?' Book II called forward.

Schofield said, 'The control room! I need information on these assholes!'

He hit the nearest rung-ladder on the fly.

Thirty seconds later, Shane Schofield entered the control room of the Typhoon.

Dust lay everywhere. Mould grew in the corners of the room. Only the occasional glinting reflection from his men's flashlights betrayed the shiny metallic surfaces under the dust.

Schofield hurried over to the command platform, to the periscope located there. He yanked the scope up out of the floor, turned to Book II.

'See if you can get some power up. This sub would've been connected to the base's geothermal supply. There might still be some residual power. Fire up the Omnibus central control system. Then get the ESM and radio antennas online.'

'Got it,' Book II said, hurrying away.

The periscope reached its full height. Schofield put his eye to it. A basic optical periscope, it didn't need any electric power to work.

Through it, Schofield saw the dry-dock hall outside—saw the

swirling water filling the pit around the Typhoon—saw a half-dozen mercenaries standing at the edge of the pit, watching it fill with seawater.

Pivoting the periscope, Schofield lifted his view, casting his gaze over the balcony level that overlooked the dry-dock pit.

There he saw more mercenaries, saw one man in particular gesticulating wildly, sending another half-dozen men running toward the gangway that connected the Typhoon's conning tower to the balcony level.

'I see you . . .' Schofield said to the man. 'Book? How's that power coming!'

'Just a second, my Russian's a bit rusty—wait, here it is . . .'

Book flicked some switches and suddenly—*vmmm*—a small collection of green lights burst to life all around Schofield.

'Okay, try it now,' Book said.

Schofield snatched up a pair of dusty headphones and engaged the sub's Electronic Support Measures antenna—a feature on most modern submarines, an ESM antenna is little more than a roving scanner, it simply trawls over every available radio frequency, searching for activity.

Voices came through Schofield's headset instantly.

'—*crazy bastard blew open the fucking sea gate!*'

'—*they went in through the torpedo tubes. They're inside the sub!*'

Then a calmer voice.

As he gazed through the periscope, Schofield saw that it was the commander-type individual up on the balcony level who was speaking.

'—*Blue Team, storm the sub via the conning tower. Green Team, find another gangway and use it as a bridge. Split up into two groups of two and enter the sub via the forward and rear escape hatches—*'

Schofield listened to the voice intently.

Crisp accent. South African. Calm, too. No sign of pressure or anxiety.

That wasn't a good sign.

Usually a commander who has just seen a dozen of his men swept away by a tidal wave would be somewhat rattled. This guy, however, was completely calm.

'—*Sir, this is radar. That first incoming aerial contact has been identified as a Yak-141 strike fighter. It's the Hungarian.*'

'—*ETA?*' the commander asked.

'—*Based on current speed, five minutes, sir.*'

The commander seemed to ponder this news. Then he said, '—*Captain Micheleaux. Send me every other man we've got. I'd like to finish this before our competitors arrive.*'

'—*It will be done,*' a French-accented voice replied.

Schofield's mind went into overdrive.

They were about to storm the Typhoon—through the conning tower and the forward and rear escape hatches.

And reinforcements were on their way . . . but from where?

All right, he caught himself. *Rewind. Think!*

Your enemy. Who are they?

They're a mercenary force of some kind.

Why are they here?

I don't know. The only clue is the missing heads. McCabe and Farrell's heads . . .

What else?

That South African guy spoke of 'competitors' who were on their way. But it was a strange word to use . . . competitors.

What options do you have?

Not many. We have no contact with our home base; no immediate means of escape; at least not until the Rangers arrive, and that's a minimum of thirty minutes away . . .

Damn it, Schofield thought, *a whole half-hour, at the very minimum. That was his enemies' biggest advantage.*

Time.

Aside from the 'competitors' they had mentioned, they had all the time in the world to hunt Schofield and his men down.

Then that's the first thing we have to change, Schofield thought. *We have to impose a time constraint on this situation.*

He looked about himself, assessing the constellation of pilot lights that illuminated the control room.

He had power . . .

Which meant maybe he could—

He thought of the six missile silos down below that had been firmly sealed, while all the others had been opened.

There might still be missiles in them. Sure, the Russians would have removed the warheads, but maybe the missiles remained.

'Here,' Schofield invited Clark to the periscope. 'Keep an eye on the bad guys outside.'

Clark seized the periscope, while Schofield dashed to a nearby console. 'Book. Give me a hand here.'

'What are you thinking?' Book II asked.

'I want to know if the missiles on this sub still work.'

The console came alive when he hit the power switch. A code screen came up and he entered an ISS-obtained all-purpose Soviet code that he had been given at the start of this mission.

Called the 'Universal Disarm Code' it was kind of like an electronic skeleton key, the *ultimate* skeleton key, designed for use by only the most senior Soviet personnel. It was an eight-digit code that worked on all Soviet-era keypad locks. It had been given to Schofield to overcome any digital keypads at Krask-8. Apparently, there was an American equivalent—known only to the President and a few very senior military figures—but Schofield didn't know that one.

'I can see six men on the balcony level heading for the gangway!' Clark called. 'Four more down on ground level, they're hauling a bridge into position so they can board us!'

Book II flicked some switches, brought up a screen that revealed, yes, there were indeed some missiles still sitting in their silos in the forward section of the Typhoon.

'Okay,' Book II said, reading the screen. 'The nuclear warheads have been removed but it seems that some of the missiles are still in their silos. There appear to be, let me see, six of them . . .'

'One is all I need,' Schofield said. 'Open the hatches for the six missiles, and then open one extra hatch.'

'An extra one?'

'Trust me.'

Book II just shook his head and did as he was told, hitting the hatch switches for seven of the sub's missile silos.

Cedric Wexley's eyes widened at the sight.

He saw the Typhoon, now surrounded by an enormous indoor pool of water, saw his own men converging on it . . .

. . . and now, to his astonishment, he saw seven of the submarine's forward missile hatches slowly and steadily opening on their hydraulic hinges.

'What on earth is he doing?' Wexley asked aloud.

'What on earth are you doing?' Book asked.

'Changing the timescale for this fight,' Schofield said.

He brought up another screen, saw the exact GPS co-ordinates of Krask-8: 07914.74, 7000.01. They matched the grid co-ordinates he had employed when his team had dropped in from the Stealth Bomber earlier.

Schofield punched in the necessary information.

He set the missiles to fire immediately—programmed them to fly for a duration of 20 minutes—and then he set the target co-ordinates as: 07914.74, 7000.01.

He didn't expect *all* of the missiles to work. The O-ring seals on their solid-fuelled rocket boosters would have degraded significantly over the past few years, possibly rendering all of them useless.

But then he only needed one to work.

The fourth one he tried did.

When its green 'Go' light blinked to life, a final approval-code screen came up. Schofield used the Universal Disarm Code. Authorisation granted.

Then he hit 'FIRE'.

Cedric Wexley heard the noise before he saw the spectacle.

An ominous deep-seated *thromming* emanated from within the submarine.

Then—with an ear-shattering explosive *shoom*—a 30-foot-long SS-N-20 ballistic missile blasted out from one of the sub's forward hatches!

It looked like the launch of a space shuttle: smoke billowed everywhere, expanding wildly, completely filling the dry-dock hall, shrouding the giant Typhoon in a misty grey fog, enveloping the mercenaries who had been converging on its entrances.

For its part, the missile shot straight upward, blasting right through the cracked glass roof of the hall and rocketing off into the grey Siberian sky.

Cedric Wexley was unperturbed. '*Men, continue your attack. Captain Micheleaux, where are those reinforcements?*'

If, at that same moment, one had been watching Krask-8 from the horizon, one would have witnessed an incredible sight: a single dead-straight column of smoke rocketing high into the sky above the mini-city.

As it happened, someone was indeed watching that sight.

A lone individual, sitting in the cockpit of a Russian-made Yak-141 fighter jet that was speeding towards Krask-8.

In the control centre of the sub, Schofield whirled around.

'Where are they?' he asked Clark at the periscope.

'It's too cloudy,' Clark said. 'I can't see anything.'

The view through the periscope now revealed a grey misty nothingness. Clark could only see the immediate area around the periscope itself—the small standing-room-only space on top of the sub's conning tower and the narrow gangway connecting the conning tower to the balcony level.

'I can't see a thi—'

A man's face brushed up against the periscope, large and clear, wearing a gas-mask.

'Yow!' Clark leapt back from the eyepiece. 'Jesus. They're right outside. Right above us!'

'Doesn't matter,' Schofield said, heading downstairs. 'It's time for us to go and we're not leaving that way.'

Schofield, Book II and Clark raced into the missile silo hall that they had passed through before. A foot-deep pool of rising water covered its floor.

They came to one of the empty silos—its little access hatch still lay open—and hustled inside it.

They were met by the sight of the empty missile silo: a towering 30-foot-high cylinder, at the top of which, looking very small, they could see the open outer-hull hatch—the *seventh* outer hatch that Schofield had opened. Some hand and foot indentations ascended the wall of the silo like a ladder.

The three Marines began climbing.

They reached the top of the silo, and Schofield peered out—

—and saw two mercenaries disappearing *inside* the submarine's forward escape hatch three metres further down the hull.

Perfect, Schofield thought. They were going in while he and his men were coming out.

In addition to this, the hall around the Typhoon was still enveloped in the cloudy white fog of the missile launch.

Schofield's eyes fell on the balcony level overlooking the

Typhoon and on the South African commander directing the mercenary operation.

That was the man Schofield wanted to talk to.

He charged toward the hand-rungs on the outside of the Typhoon's conning tower.

Schofield and the others climbed the submarine's conning tower and dashed across the gangway connecting it to the upper balcony level.

They saw a small internal office structure at the end of the elongated balcony.

Standing in a doorway there, barking into a radio mike while at the same time trying to peer through the fog at the Typhoon, was the mercenary commander, Wexley, flanked by a single armed bodyguard.

Under the cover of the smoke, Schofield, Book II and Clark side-stepped their way down the balcony, approaching Wexley fast.

They sprang on him: Schofield yelling 'Freeze!'—the bodyguard firing—Clark firing at the same time—the bodyguard dropping, hit in the face—Clark falling, too—then Wexley drew his pistol—only to see Schofield roll quickly and fire his Desert Eagle twice—*blam! blam!*—and Wexley was hit in both the chest and the hand and hurled backwards a full three feet, slamming into the outer wall of the office structure and slumping to the ground.

'Clark! You okay!' Schofield called, kicking Wexley's gun away.

Clark had been hit near the shoulder. He winced as Book II checked his wound. 'Yeah, he just winged me.'

Wexley was largely okay, too. He'd been wearing a vest under his snow gear, which saved him from the chest-shot. He lay slumped against the outer wall of the office, winded and gripping his wounded hand.

Schofield pressed the barrel of his Desert Eagle against Wexley's forehead. 'Who are you and why are you here?'

Wexley coughed, still gasping for air.

'I said, who the hell are you and why are you here?'

Wexley spoke in a hoarse whisper. 'My name . . . is Cedric Wexley. I'm with . . . Executive Solutions.'

'Mercenaries,' Schofield said. 'And why are you here? Why are you trying to kill us?'

'Not everyone, Captain. Just you.'

'Me?'

'You and those two Delta men, McCabe and Farrell.'

Schofield froze, remembering Dean McCabe's headless body. He also recalled Bull Simcox saying that the same thing had been done to Greg Farrell.

'Why?'

'Does it really matter?' Wexley sneered.

Schofield didn't have time for this. So he simply pressed his boot against Wexley's wounded hand, twisting it slightly.

Wexley roared with pain. Then he looked directly up at Schofield, his eyes filled with venom.

'Because there is a price on your head, Captain Schofield. Enough to entice just about every bounty hunter in the world to come after you.'

Schofield felt his stomach tighten. 'What?'

With his good hand Wexley withdrew a crumpled sheet of paper from his breast pocket, threw it dismissively at Schofield. 'Choke on it.'

Schofield snatched the piece of paper, glanced at it.

It was a list of names.

Fifteen names in total. A mix of soldiers, spies, and terrorists.

He quickly noticed that McCabe, Farrell and he himself were on it.

Wexley's South African accent dripped with grim delight as he spoke: 'I can imagine that you are about to meet quite a few of the world's crack bounty hunters, Captain. Your friends, too. Bounty hunters do so have a proclivity to hold friends and loved ones as bait to draw out a target.'

Schofield's blood went cold at the thought of his friends being held hostage by bounty hunters.

Gant . . . Mother . . .

He yanked his mind back to the present.

'But why do you have to cut off our heads?' he asked.

Wexley answered him with a snort. Schofield simply moved his boot towards Wexley's bloody hand again.

'Wait. Wait. Wait. Perhaps I haven't been specific enough,' Wexley said nastily. 'The price on your head, Captain, is *literally* a price on your head—18.6 million dollars to the person who brings *your head* to a castle in France. It's a worthwhile sum, the largest I've ever seen: enough to bribe the highest officials, enough to erase all evidence of a sham mission against some terrorists in Siberia, enough to ensure that your reinforcements, a company of Rangers out of Fort Lewis, *never even left the ground*. You're on your own, Captain Schofield. You're here . . . alone . . . with us . . . until we kill you and cut off your fucking head.'

Schofield's mind raced.

He'd never expected this. Something so targeted, so individual, so *personal*.

Then abruptly, he saw Wexley do something odd: he saw him look away again, only this time the South African was glancing out over Schofield's shoulder.

Schofield turned—and his eyes widened in horror.

Like the ominous precursor to an underwater volcanic eruption, a roiling mass of bubbles appeared in the ice-covered 'lake' that now extended out from the dry-dock pit. The thin layer of ice covering this body of water cracked loudly.

And then from out of the middle of the bubbling froth, like a gigantic whale breaching the surface, came the dark steel body of a Soviet Akula-class attack submarine.

While it could never attain the international sales of the smaller Kilo-class submarines, the Akula was rapidly gaining popularity on international arms markets—markets which the new Russian government was keen to exploit. Obviously, Executive Solutions was one of Russia's customers.

The Akula in the icy lake moved quickly. No sooner was it up than armed men were swarming out of its hatchways, extending exit gangways to the shore, and running across those gangways onto the floor of the dry-dock hall.

Schofield blanched.

It was at least *thirty more mercenaries.*

Wexley smiled wickedly.

'Keep smiling, asshole,' Schofield said. He looked at his watch. 'Because you don't have forever to catch me. In exactly sixteen minutes that missile from the Typhoon is going to return to this base. Till then, smile at this.'

Thwack!

Schofield punched Wexley in the nose with his Desert Eagle, knocking him out.

Then he hustled over to Book II and started helping him with Clark. 'Grab his other shoulder . . .'

They helped the young corporal up. Clark strained to get to his feet. 'I can do it—' he said just as his chest exploded in a sickening gout of blood. An involuntary bloody gob shot out from his mouth—direct from the lungs—and splashed all over Schofield's chestplate.

Clark just stared at Schofield, aghast, the life fading quickly from his eyes. He dropped to the balcony's grilled catwalk, dead—shot from behind—by the force of mercenaries now charging out of the newly-arrived sub and swarming down the length of the hall.

Schofield just looked down at his dead companion in horror.

He couldn't believe it.

Apart from Book II, his whole team was gone, dead, murdered.

And so here he was, stranded at a deserted Siberian base with close to forty mercenaries on his tail, one man by his side, no reinforcements on the way and no means of escape at all.

Schofield and Book II ran.

Ran for their lives as bullet-holes shredded the thin plasterboard walls all around them.

The new collection of ExSol mercenaries from the Akula had entered the battle with frightening intensity. Now they were climbing every rung-ladder they could find and sprinting down the dry-dock hall, with only one purpose: *to get Schofield's head*.

The mercs who had entered the Typhoon earlier were now also aware that Schofield had got away, and they re-emerged, guns blazing.

Schofield and Book II dashed westward, entering the concrete overpass bridge that connected the dry-dock hall with Krask-8's office tower.

As they had approached the bridge, Schofield had seen the movements of the Executive Solutions forces—some of them were scaling the balcony level, while others were paralleling his and Book's movements down on ground level, running along underneath them, also heading for the tower.

Schofield knew one thing: he and Book had to get over to the office tower and then down to the ground before the bad guys got there. Otherwise, the two of them would be stuck in the 15-storey building.

They bolted through the overpass bridge, whipped past its cracked concrete window frames.

Then they burst out the other end of the bridge, entered the office tower . . .

. . . and stopped dead.

Schofield found himself standing on a balcony—a tiny catwalk balcony, one of many that rose up and up for 15 floors, all connected by a network of ladders—overlooking a gigantic square-shaped chasm of open space.

This wasn't an office tower at all.

It was, in truth, a hollowed-out glass-and-steel structure.

A false building.

It was an amazing sight, kind of like standing in a gigantic greenhouse: the grey Siberian landscape could be seen beyond the cracked glass windows that formed the four sides of the building.

And at the base of this gigantic crystalline structure, Schofield saw its reason for being.

Four massive ICBM missile silos, half-buried in the wide concrete floor in a neat square-shaped formation. Covered by the false office tower, they could never have been spotted by US spy satellites. Schofield guessed that three more silo clusters could be found under the other 'buildings' in Krask-8.

On the ground beside the silos, one level below him, he saw ten slumped figures—the six members of Farrell's Delta team and Bull Simcox's four-man Marine squad.

Schofield glanced at his watch, at the countdown indicating when the Typhoon's missile would return to Krask-8: 15:30 . . . 15:29 . . . 15:28 . . .

'The ground floor,' Schofield said to Book. 'We have to get to the ground floor.'

They dashed for the nearest rung-ladder, started down it—

—just as it was assailed by a volley of gunfire.

Shit.

The mercenaries had got to the ground floor first. They must have run across the snow-covered road between the dry-dock warehouse and the tower.

'Damn it!' Schofield yelled.

'What now!' Book II called.

'Doesn't look like we have much choice! We go up!'

And so they went up.

Up and up, climbing rung-ladders like a pair of fleeing monkeys, dodging the mercenaries' fire as they went.

They were ten floors up when Schofield dared to stop and take a look down.

What he saw crushed any hope of survival he'd had until then.

He saw the whole mercenary force arrayed around the concrete missile silos on the ground floor of the tower—about 50 men in all.

And then the crowd of mercenaries parted as a lone man walked into the middle of their ranks.

It was Cedric Wexley, his nose all smashed up with blood.

Schofield froze.

He wondered what Wexley would do now. The mercenary commander could send his men up the ladders after Schofield and Book—and watch Schofield and Book pick them off one by one until the two Marines ran out of ammunition and became sitting ducks. Not exactly an appealing strategy.

'*Captain Schofield!*' Wexley's voice echoed up the wide shaft of the tower. '*You run well! But now there is nowhere else for you to go! Mark my words, very soon you will run no more!*'

Wexley pulled several small objects from his combat webbing.

Schofield recognised them instantly, and stopped dead.

Small and cylindrical, they were Thermite-Amatol demolition charges. Four of them. Wexley must have taken them from the bodies of Schofield's dead Marines.

And now he saw Wexley's plan.

Wexley passed the Thermite charges to four of his men who promptly scattered to the four corners of the ground floor and attached them to the tower's corner pillars.

Schofield snatched his field binoculars from his webbing, pressed them to his eyes.

He caught a glimpse of one of the Thermite charges affixed to its pillar, saw the coloured timer switches on it: red, green and blue.

'*Initiate the timers!*' Wexley called.

The man Schofield was watching hit the blue timer switch on his Thermite-Amatol charge.

Blue meant one minute.

The three mercenaries manning the other demolition charges did the same.

Schofield's eyes went wide.

He and Book II now had sixty seconds till the building blew.

He started his watch's stopwatch:

00:01 . . .

00:02 . . .

00:03 . . .

'*Captain Schofield! When this is over, we will sift through the rubble and we will find your body! And when we do, I will personally rip your fucking head off and piss down your throat! Gentlemen!*'

With that, the mercenaries scattered, dispersing like a flock of birds to every exit on the ground floor.

Schofield and Book II could only watch them go. Schofield pressed his face to the nearest window to see them appear on the snow-covered ground outside and spread out in a wide circle, covering every exit from the building with their weapons.

He swallowed.

He and Book were stuck in this building—a building which in 52 seconds was going to explode.

It was while he was peering out the window at the mercenary troops on the ground that Schofield heard it.

A deep reverberating *throbbing* sound.

The unmistakable sound of a fighter jet.

'The transmission from before,' Schofield breathed.

'What?' Book II asked.

'When we were inside the Typhoon, they picked up an incoming aerial contact: a Yak-141 strike fighter. Flown by someone they called "the Hungarian". On his way here.'

'A bounty hunter?'

'A competitor. But in a Yak-141. And a Yak-141 is a . . .' Schofield said. 'Come on! Quickly!'

They dashed for the nearest rung-ladder and climbed it—heading upwards—heading for the roof of the doomed office tower.

Schofield threw open the hatch to the roof. He and Book II climbed out—to be immediately assaulted by the bitter Siberian wind.

His stopwatch ticked upwards:

00:29

00:30

00:31

They cut a lonely sight indeed: two tiny figures on the roof of the tower, surrounded by the deserted buildings of Krask-8 and the stark Siberian hills.

Schofield hurried to the edge of the roof, searching for the source of the engine noise.

00:33
00:34
00:35
There!

It was hovering in the air over by a low dome-shaped building five hundred yards to the west: a Yakovlev-141 strike fighter.

The Russian equivalent of a Harrier jump-jet, the Yak-141 is potentially the ugliest fighter plane ever built; indeed with its squared edges and single fat afterburning engine, it was never meant to look beautiful. But a hinged rear nozzle allows it to redirect its afterburner so that it points downward, allowing the plane to take off and land vertically, and also hover like a helicopter.

00:39
00:40
00:41

Schofield drew his MP-7 and loosed a full clip of thirty rounds across the bow of the hovering Yak, desperately trying to get the pilot's attention.

It worked.

Like a T-rex disturbed from its meal, the Yak-141 pivoted in the air and seemed to gaze directly at Schofield and Book II. Then with an aerial lurch, it powered up and approached the glass tower.

Schofield waved at the plane like an idiot.

'Over *here*!' he yelled. 'Closer! Get closer . . . !'

00:49
00:50
00:51

The Yak-141 came closer, so that it now hovered about fifty yards out from the roof of the tower.

Still not close enough . . .

Schofield could see its pilot now—a wide-faced man wearing a flight helmet and a confused frown. Schofield waved frantically, calling him over.

00:53
00:54

00:55

The Yak-141 edged a fraction closer.

Forty yards away . . .

00:56

'Jesus, hurry up!' Schofield yelled, looking down at the roof beneath his feet, waiting for the Thermite charges to blow.

00:57

'Too late.' Schofield turned to Book and with a meaningful look, drew his signature weapon. Seeing him do so, Book did the same.

'Just do what I do,' Schofield said, 'and you'll stay alive. Now *run*!'

And so they ran—hard, together, side-by-side—rushing toward the edge of the 15-storey roof.

00:58

They hit the edge, moving fast, legs pumping—

00:59

—and as Schofield's stopwatch hit 1:00, he and Book II leapt out into the clear open sky, their feet stepping off the parapet just as the whole lower section of the building exploded in a billowing cloud of concrete and the entire office tower—all 200 feet of it, the roof, the glass walls, the concrete pillars—just fell away beneath them like a gigantic falling tree.

The pilot of the Yak-141 watched in absolute amazement as the 15-storey building in front of him just disintegrated, crumpling to the earth in eerie slow motion, collapsing into its own dustcloud.

A stocky bear of a man with a wide round face forever set in a heavy-browed Eastern European frown, his name was Oleg Omansky.

But no-one ever called him that.

A former major in the Hungarian Secret Police with a reputation for employing violence rather than brains, he was known in free-lance bounty-hunting circles simply as 'The Hungarian'.

Right now, however, the Hungarian was confused.

He had seen Schofield—whom he recognised immediately from the bounty list—and Book II leap off the roof a moment before the building had collapsed.

But he couldn't see either of them now.

A massive dustcloud rose up from the wreckage of the building, enveloping everything within a half-mile radius.

The Hungarian circled the site, looking for the spot where Schofield had landed.

He noticed a force of men forming a perimeter around the fallen building—a bounty-hunting force, no doubt—saw them rush forward when the collapse of the tower had ceased.

But still he saw no Schofield.

He readied his weapons, and made to land on the roof of a nearby building.

★ ★ ★

The Yak-141 landed lightly on the roof of one of Krask-8's smaller buildings, its downward-pointed rear thruster blasting the rooftop clear of any debris.

No sooner was it down than the fighter's canopy opened and the Hungarian climbed out, his body as heavy as his face, carrying an AMD assault rifle—the crude but effective Hungarian variant of the AK-47, notable for its extra forward handgrip.

He was four steps away from the plane when—

'Drop the gun, mister.'

The Hungarian turned . . .

. . . to see Shane Schofield emerge from the underside of the Yak-141, an MP-7 held in his hand and pointed right at the Hungarian's nose.

While the glass tower had smashed down into the earth, Schofield and Book II had launched themselves into the air above it, falling in matching arcs underneath the bow of the hovering Yak-141.

Before they'd started their run, Schofield had drawn his signature weapon—his Maghook—from his back-holster. Then as he had fallen through the air, he had aimed it at the underbelly of the Yak and fired. Book II had done the same.

Their Maghooks had shot into the air, unspooling wobbling tails of rope behind their hooks. With a pair of dull *clunks*, the two powerful magnetic heads had slammed into the underside of the Yak—and Schofield's and Book's respective falls had abruptly ceased as they were yanked up by their Maghooks' ropes.

As the Yak had made its way toward the nearest rooftop, they had initiated the internal spoolers on their Maghooks which had reeled them upwards, toward the safe forward underbelly of the hovering fighter jet—while at the same time they were hidden from the eyes of the mercenary force on the ground by the billowing dustcloud below.

The landing had been a little hairy, what with all the flying debris and the deflected heat-blast from the Yak's downward thruster, but they'd made it.

The Yak-141 had touched down, and Schofield and Book II had dropped down to the roof underneath it and rolled away.

Now Schofield had one simple plan for the Yak-141.

To steal it.

Schofield and Book II faced off against the Hungarian on the roof of the low building.

The Hungarian dropped his assault rifle. It clattered to the ground. Schofield scooped up the ugly gun.

'You another bounty hunter?' he demanded, yelling above the roar of the idling fighter.

'Da,' the Hungarian grunted.

'What's your name?'

'I am the Hungarian.'

'Hungarian, huh? Well, you're too late. The mercenaries beat you here. They got McCabe and Farrell.'

'But they did not get you.' The Hungarian's voice was entirely devoid of emotion.

Schofield's eyes narrowed. 'They told me that you have to bring my head to a castle in France to claim the money. Which castle?'

The Hungarian eyed Schofield's gun warily. 'Valois. The Forteresse de Valois.'

'The Forteresse de Valois,' Schofield said. Then he asked the money question. 'And who is paying for all this? Who wants me dead?'

The Hungarian held his gaze.

'I do not know,' he growled.

'You sure about that?'

'I said I do not know.'

There was something in his simple directness that made Schofield believe him. 'Right . . .'

Schofield headed for the Yak, walking backwards, his guns still up, but as he did so, he felt a twinge of pity for this chunky bounty hunter in front of him. 'I'm taking your plane, Hungarian, but I'm

also going to tell you something that I don't have to. Don't be here in eleven minutes.'

Schofield and Book II ascended the cockpit ladder of the Yak-141, their guns trained on the Hungarian.

'You know,' Book II said. 'One day your Maghook isn't going to work . . .'

'Shut up,' Schofield said.

They climbed in.

A former Harrier pilot, Schofield had little difficulty figuring out the Yak's controls.

He keyed the vertical take-off thruster and the Yak-141 lifted into the air above the rooftop.

Then he charged up the plane's afterburners and blasted off over the barren Siberian hills, leaving the lone figure of the Hungarian staring dumbly and helplessly after him.

Schofield and Book II left Krask-8 disappearing in their wake.

As he sat at the controls of the Yak-141, Schofield contemplated his next move.

Sitting in the back, Book II said, 'What are you thinking? We go to that castle?'

'The castle is important,' Schofield said. 'But it's not the key.'

He pulled Wexley's bounty list from his pocket.

'This is the key,' he said.

He looked at the names on the crumpled sheet and wondered what they all had in common.

In short, the list was a Who's Who of international warriors: crack commandos like McCabe and Farrell; British spies from MI-6; an Israeli Air Force pilot. Even Ronson Weitzman was on it—*Major General* Ronson Weitzman from the United States Marine Corps, one of the highest-ranking Marines in America.

And that wasn't even mentioning the Middle-Eastern terrorists on the list: Khalif, Nazzar and Hassan Zawahiri.

Hassan Zawahiri . . .

The name leapt out at Schofield.

He was the second-in-command of Al-Qaeda, Osama bin Laden's right-hand man.

And a man being hunted right now in the mountains of northern Afghanistan by the United States, by Schofield's Marine Corps friends: Elizabeth Gant and Mother Newman.

Wexley's voice invaded Schofield's thoughts: *'Bounty hunters do so have a proclivity to hold friends and loved ones as bait to draw out a target . . .'*

Schofield pursed his lips.

His friends, plus at least one target on the list—Zawahiri—were in the same place. It was the perfect starting point for any bounty hunter.

And so he made the decision.

He set the Yak's autopilot for south-south-west, destination: northern Afghanistan.

Eleven minutes after Schofield left Krask-8, a finger of white smoke blasted out of the clouds above the base—led by the point of the submarine-launched SS-N-20 missile that had been launched twenty minutes earlier.

It descended like a lightning bolt towards the remains of Krask-8, ready to do whatever damage it could.

The missile rushed downward at supersonic speed.

5,000 feet . . .

2,000 feet . . .

1,000 feet . . .

And then in a fleeting shocking instant . . .

. . . it *exploded* . . .

. . . a clear 800 feet off the ground.

The descending missile blasted out into a million fragments, bursting like a firecracker as it was hit by a smaller laser-guided missile from the side.

Glittering fragments of the submarine-launched missile rained down on Krask-8 harmlessly.

And when the smoke cleared, there, hovering in the sky above the mini-city, was the second fighter jet to arrive at Krask-8 that morning.

This one was far sleeker than the Hungarian's Yak-141, longer too, and it was painted almost entirely black. The only trace of another colour could be found in its white-painted nose cone. It was also possessed of rare forward-swept wings and a two-man cockpit.

It was a Sukhoi S-37—a Russian-made hover-capable fighter that was far more advanced than the old Yak-141.

The sleek S-37 hovered like a hawk above the destroyed Siberian base, surveying the scene. The streets were deserted. The members of ExSol were nowhere to be seen.

After a few minutes of aerial surveillance, the Sukhoi landed on a stretch of open ground not far from the enormous dry-dock warehouse.

Two men climbed out of its cockpit.

One was exceedingly tall, at least seven feet, and armed with a massive G-36 rifle.

The second man was shorter than the first but still tall, well-built, about six feet. He was dressed entirely in black—black combat fatigues, black body armour, black helmet—and he wore two short-barrelled Remington 870 pump-action shotguns in thigh holsters. Both shotguns were made of glistening silver steel.

He also had one other distinguishing feature.

He wore wraparound anti-flash glasses with black frames and yellow-tinted lenses.

Drawing one of his silver shotguns and holding it like a pistol, the man in black left his partner to guard the Sukhoi while he him-self strode toward the door that Schofield had used to enter the dry-dock hall earlier.

He stopped at the door, checked the snow-covered ground, touched it with a black-gloved hand.

He moved inside.

The dry-dock hall was deserted. The remnants of Schofield's smoke cloud lingered in the air. The Typhoon submarine towered in the middle of it all.

The ExSol mercenary force was long gone. Likewise its Akula submarine.

The man in black examined the Delta corpses on the ground next to the now-flooded pit—the spent ammo shells on the ground—the headless corpse of McCabe—and the still-warm body of Schofield's Marine corporal, Rooster, who had been snipered when the mercenary trap had revealed itself.

Some bodies were floating face-down in the flooded dry-dock.

Moving with calm measured steps, the man in black went over to the sea gate that had once separated the dry-dock from the lake—noticed its exploded-open side section.

A sign of the Scarecrow, the man in black thought. *After they shot one of his boys, they trapped him in the dry-dock. So he blew it open, flooding the dry-dock, killing the men who had followed him in . . .*

The man in black strode over to the edge of the indoor lake, crouched beside a series of wet footprints smeared on the concrete there: the fresh outlines of combat boots.

Different brands of combat boots. Which meant mercenaries.

And all of them stepping onto the dock from a *wet* surface.

A submarine. A second submarine.

So, Executive Solutions had been here.

But they had got here very quickly. Too quickly.

They must have been tipped off by someone behind the bounty hunt. Given a head-start to claim the American heads.

There came a sudden grunt and the man in black snapped around, gun up, quick as a mongoose.

It had come from the balcony level overlooking the warehouse.

The man in black dashed up a nearby rung-ladder and arrived at a small internal office up on the balcony.

In the doorway to the shack lay two figures: the first was the dead body of Corporal Max 'Clark' Kent; the second was another soldier—judging by his French-made assault rifle, a mercenary from ExSol—and he was still alive.

But only just. Blood gurgled from a gaping bullet wound to his cheek. Half of his face had been blown off.

The man in black stood over the wounded mercenary, gazed at him coolly.

The wounded mercenary extended a hand toward the man, pleading with his eyes, moaning, 'Aidez moi! S'il vous plait . . . aidez moi . . .'

The man in black looked over at the concrete overpass that had connected this hall to the collapsed office tower.

A destroyed 15-storey building: *another sign of the Scarecrow*.

The wounded mercenary switched to English. '*Please*, monsieur. Help me . . .'

The man in black turned to face him, looked coldly down at the distressed fellow.

After a long moment, he spoke.

'No.'

Then he shot the wounded mercenary in the head.

The man in black returned to his sleek Sukhoi, rejoined his massive companion.

They then climbed back into their fighter, took off vertically, and blasted off into the sky, heading south-south-west.

After the Sukhoi had gone, a lone figure emerged from one of the buildings of Krask-8.

It was the Hungarian.

He just stood there on the deserted street and watched the Sukhoi disappear over the hills to the south, his eyes narrowing.

SECOND ATTACK

AFGHANISTAN–FRANCE
26 OCTOBER 1300 HOURS (AFGHANISTAN)
E.S.T. (NEW YORK, USA) 0300 HOURS

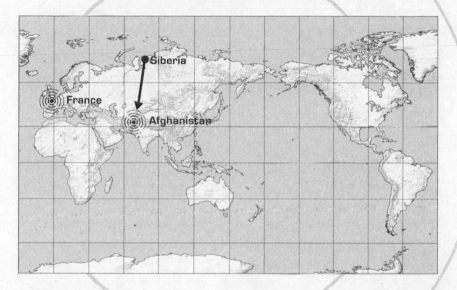

Think of a stretch limo in the potholed streets of New York City, where homeless beggars live. Inside the limo are the air-conditioned postindustrial regions of North America, Europe, the emerging Pacific Rim, and a few other isolated places ... Outside is the rest of mankind, going in a completely different direction.

—Dr Thomas Homer-Dixon,
DIRECTOR OF THE PEACE AND CONFLICT STUDIES PROGRAM,
DEPARTMENT OF POLITICAL SCIENCE, UNIVERSITY OF TORONTO

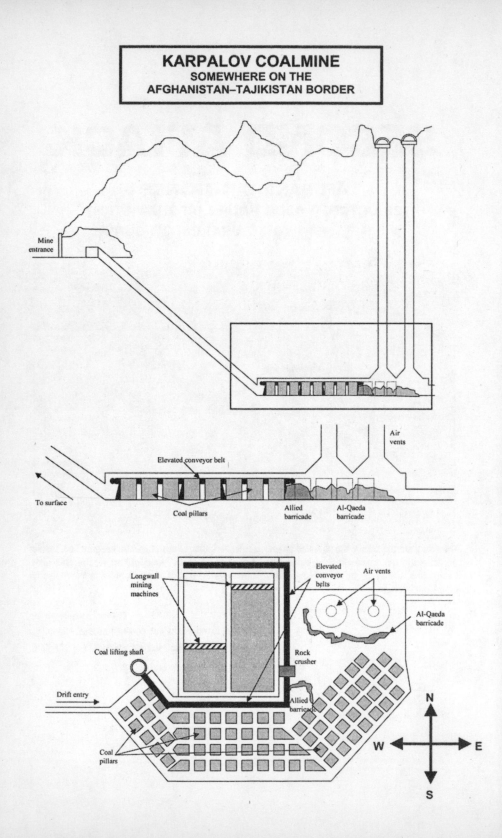

KARPALOV COALMINE
SOMEWHERE ON THE
AFGHANISTAN–TAJIKISTAN BORDER

Mine entrance

Air vents

Elevated conveyor belt

To surface

Coal pillars

Allied barricade

Al-Qaeda barricade

Longwall mining machines

Elevated conveyor belts

Air vents

Al-Qaeda barricade

Coal lifting shaft

Rock crusher

Drift entry

Allied barricade

Coal pillars

N

W E

S

FORTERESSE DE VALOIS
BRITTANY, FRANCE
26 OCTOBER, 0900 HOURS LOCAL TIME
(1300 HOURS IN AFGHANISTAN—0300 HOURS
E.S.T. USA)

The two bounty hunters crossed the drawbridge that gave entry to the Forteresse de Valois, a mighty castle that thrust out into the Atlantic Ocean from the rugged north-western coast of France.

Built in 1289 by the mad Compte de Valois, the Forteresse was not your typical French castle.

Whereas most fortified buildings in France put an emphasis on beauty, the Forteresse de Valois was far more utilitarian. It was a rock, a grim fortress.

Squat, fat and solid as hell, through a combination of sheer engineering audacity and the uniqueness of its location, in its time the Forteresse de Valois was all-but impregnable.

The reason: it was built on top of an enormous rock formation that jutted up from the ocean itself, about sixty yards out from the high coastal cliffs.

As they stretched downward, the fortress's colossal stone walls blended seamlessly with the vertical sides of the rocky mount, so that the whole structure stood 400 feet above the crashing waves of the Atlantic.

The castle's only connection with the mainland was a 60-metre-long spanning bridge of stone, the last twenty metres of which was a lowerable drawbridge.

The two bounty hunters crossed the drawbridge, dwarfed by the dark castle looming above them, the relentless Atlantic wind blasting their bodies.

They carried between them a large white box marked with a red cross and the words: 'HUMAN ORGANS: DO NOT OPEN—EXPRESS DELIVERY'.

Once across the bridge, the two men stepped underneath the fortress's 700-year-old portcullis, and entered the castle.

They were met in the courtyard by a dapper gentleman dressed in perfectly-pressed tails and wearing a pair of wireframed pince-nez.

'Bonjour, messieurs,' the man said. 'My name is Monsieur Delacroix. How may I help you?'

The two bounty hunters—Americans, dressed in suede jackets, jeans and cowboy boots—looked at each other.

The bigger one growled, 'We're here to collect the bounty on a couple of heads.'

The dapper gentleman smiled politely. 'But of course you are. And your names?'

The bigger one said, 'Drabyak. Joe Drabyak. Texas Ranger. This here is my partner, my brother, Jimbo.'

Monsieur Delacroix bowed.

'Ah, oui, the famous brothers Drabyak. Why don't you come inside.'

Monsieur Delacroix led them through a garage that contained a collection of rare and expensive automobiles—a red Ferrari Modena; a silver Porsche GT-2; an Aston Martin Vanquish; some race-ready rally cars, and taking pride of place in the centre of the showroom, a glistening black Lamborghini Diablo.

The two American bounty hunters eyed the array of supercars with delight. If their mission went according to plan, they'd be buying themselves some all-American muscle cars very soon.

'They yours?' Big Drabyak grunted as he walked behind Monsieur Delacroix.

The dapper gentleman snuffed a laugh. 'Oh, no. I am but a humble banker from Switzerland supervising this distribution of funds for my client. The cars belong to the owner of this castle. Not me.'

Monsieur Delacroix led them down some stone stairs at the end of the pristine garage, down to a lower level . . .

. . . and suddenly they entered medieval times.

They came to a round stone-walled ante-room. A long narrow tunnel branched off it to the left, disappearing into torch-lit subterranean gloom.

Monsieur Delacroix stopped, turned to the smaller of the two Texans. 'Young monsieur James. You will stay here, while your brother and I verify the heads.'

Big Drabyak gave his younger brother a reassuring nod.

Monsieur Delacroix then led Big Drabyak down the long torch-lit tunnel.

At the end of the passageway was a magnificent office. One entire wall of it was a picture window offering a stunning panoramic view of the Atlantic Ocean, stretching away to the horizon.

As they came to the end of the stone tunnel, Monsieur Delacroix stopped again.

'If I may have your case, please . . .'

The bounty hunter gave him the white medical transport box.

Monsieur Delacroix said, 'Now, if you would wait here.'

Delacroix entered the office, leaving the Texan bounty hunter standing just beyond the doorway, still inside the stone passageway.

Delacroix crossed to his desk, pulling a handheld remote from his coat as he did so, and pressed a button on it—

Wham! Wham! Wham!

Three steel doors came thundering down into the medieval passageway from slits concealed in its roof.

The first two doors sealed off the ante-room, imprisoning Little Drabyak in the circular stone room, cutting him off from both the upstairs garage and the narrow tunnel containing his older brother.

The third steel door sealed off the office from the passageway—separating Monsieur Delacroix from Big Drabyak.

Small perspex windows set into each steel door allowed the two bounty hunters to look out from their new prisons.

Monsieur Delacroix's voice came to them via speakers in the ceiling.

'Gentlemen. As you both would no doubt appreciate, a bounty hunt of this value attracts—how shall I put it—some rather *unscrupulous* individuals. You will stay where you are while I verify the identity of the heads that you have brought me.'

Monsieur Delacroix placed the medical delivery box on his desk, opened it with expert hands.

Two severed heads gazed up at him.

One was speckled in blood, its eyes wide with horror.

The other was in poorer condition. It had been badly burned.

Monsieur Delacroix was unperturbed.

Donning a pair of surgical gloves, he calmly extracted the blood-speckled head from the box and placed it on a scanning device beside his computer.

'And who do you claim this is?' Monsieur Delacroix asked Big Drabyak over the intercom.

'The Israeli, Rosenthal,' Drabyak said.

'Rosenthal,' Delacroix punched the name into his computer. 'Hmmm . . . Mossad agent . . . no DNA records. Typical of the Israelis, really. It is no matter. I have instructions on this. We shall have to use other means.'

Delacroix initiated the scanning device on which the severed head sat.

Like a CAT scan, the device ran a series of laser beams over the exterior of the severed head.

Once the device had finished scanning the head, Delacroix calmly opened the mouth of the blood-speckled face and exposed the head's *teeth* to the laser scanner.

Delacroix then pressed another button on his keyboard and compared the analysed head to a collection of records on his computer screen.

The computer beeped, and Monsieur Delacroix smiled.

'The cross-reference score is 89.337%. According to my instructions, a verification score of 75% or higher is enough to warrant payment of the bounty. Gentlemen, your first head has been successfully verified by cranial shape and known dental records as that of Major Benjamin Y. Rosenthal of the Israeli Mossad. You are now 18.6 million dollars richer.'

The two bounty hunters smiled in their respective stone cages.

Delacroix then pulled out the second head.

'And this one?' he asked.

Big Drabyak said, 'It's Nazzar, the HAMAS guy. Found him in Mexico. Buying M-16s from a drug lord.'

'How utterly fascinating,' Delacroix said.

The second head was blackened with burn-damage, and it appeared as if half its teeth had been blasted out with a gunshot wound . . . or a hammer.

Monsieur Delacroix performed the cranial and dental laser tests.

The two bounty hunters held their breath. They seemed to get increasingly apprehensive with Delacroix's examination of the two heads.

The skull and dental records returned a verification score of 77.326%.

Monsieur Delacroix said, 'The percentage is 77%, no doubt due to the extensive fire and bullet damage to this head. Now, as you know, according to my instructions, a verification score of 75% or higher is enough to warrant payment of the bounty . . .'

The bounty hunters grinned.

'. . . *unless* there is a DNA record of the individual at issue, in which case I am to consult it,' Delacroix said. 'And it appears from my records here that there *is* a DNA sample for this individual.'

The two bounty hunters whirled to face each other, shocked.

Big Drabyak said, 'But there can't be . . .'

'Oh, yes,' Delacroix said, 'according to my records here, Mister Yousef Nazzar was imprisoned in the United Kingdom in 1999 on minor weapons importation charges. A sample of his blood was taken in accordance with the UK's prisoner-intake DNA policy.'

As Big Drabyak shouted for him to stop, Monsieur Delacroix injected a hypodermic needle into the left cheek of the blackened head in front of him and extracted some blood.

The blood was then placed in an analyser attached to Delacroix's computer.

Another beep.

A bad one.

Delacroix frowned—and suddenly his face took on a far more dangerous complexion.

'Gentlemen . . .' he said slowly.

The bounty hunters froze.

The Swiss banker paused, as if he was *offended* by the indiscretion. 'Gentlemen, this head is a forgery. This is not the head of Yousef Nazzar.'

'Now wait a minute—' Big Drabyak began.

'Please be quiet, Mister Drabyak,' Delacroix said. 'The cosmetic surgery was quite convincing; you employed a good plastic surgeon, that much is certain. The burning of the head to remove visual identification, well, that is clever but old. And the restructured teeth were very well faked. But you didn't know there was a DNA record, did you?'

'No,' Big Drabyak growled.

'The Rosenthal head was also a fake, then?'

'It was obtained by an associate of ours,' Big Drabyak lied, 'and he assured us that it was—'

'But *you* have presented it to me, Monsieur Drabyak, therefore it is your responsibility. Let me be clear. Honesty, in this moment, may help you. Is the Rosenthal head also a fake?'

'Yes,' Drabyak grimaced.

'This is a grave offence against the rules of the hunt, Mister Drabyak. My clients will not tolerate attempts to deceive them, you do understand that?'

Big Drabyak said nothing.

'Fortunately, I have instructions on this,' Delacroix said. 'Monsieur Drabyak the Elder. The passageway in which you are standing, do you know what it is?'

'No.'

'Oh, yes. How silly of me to forget, you are American. You know nothing of world history except the name of every US President and the capital of every US state. A knowledge of medieval European warfare would be somewhat beyond you, no?'

Big Drabyak's face was blank.

Delacroix sighed. 'Monsieur Drabyak, the tunnel in which you now stand was once used as a trap to ensnare those who would attack this castle. When enemy soldiers came through that passageway, boiling oil would be flushed into it through the gutters in its walls, killing the intruders in a most painful way.'

Big Drabyak snapped to look at the walls of the stone passageway around him. They were indeed pockmarked with a series of basketball-sized holes high up near the ceiling.

'This castle, however, has been modified slightly,' Delacroix said, 'in keeping with modern technology. If you would observe your brother.'

Big Drabyak spun, and stared wide-eyed through the perspex window in the steel door that separated him from his younger brother.

'Now. Say goodbye to your brother,' Monsieur Delacroix's voice said over the speakers.

In the office, Delacroix lifted his handheld remote again and pressed another button on it.

Immediately, an ominous mechanical humming noise emanated from the stone walls of Little Drabyak's circular ante-room.

MATTHEW REILLY

The humming noise gathered intensity, getting faster and faster and faster.

At first Little Drabyak seemed unaffected.

Then with frightening suddenness, he convulsed violently, snapping a hand to his chest, to his heart. Then he clutched his ears—a moment before they spurted hideously with blood.

He screamed.

Then, as Big Drabyak watched, the most horrifying thing of all happened.

As the humming noise hit fever-pitch, his little brother's *chest* just burst open, his whole rib cage blurting outward in a disgusting spray of blood and gore.

Little Drabyak dropped to the floor of the ante-room, his eyes vacant, his rib cage blasted apart. Dead.

Delacroix's voice: 'A microwave defence system, Monsieur Drabyak. Très effective, no?'

Big Drabyak was thunderstruck.

He spun where he stood, powerless to escape.

'You little fuck! I thought you said honesty would help!' he yelled.

Delacroix laughed. 'Americans. You think you can plea-bargain your way out of anything. I said it might help. But on this occasion, I have decided that it will not.'

Drabyak glanced at his brother's grisly remains. 'Is that what you're going to do to me?'

Monsieur Delacroix smiled. 'Oh, no. Unlike you, I am an admirer of history. Sometimes, the old ways are the most satisfying.'

And with that the Swiss banker hit a third and final button on his remote . . .

. . . and 1,000 litres of boiling oil sprayed out from the wall-holes in the tunnel containing Joe Drabyak.

Any exposed flesh was burned on contact—all the skin on his face was scalded in a second. Wherever the boiling oil touched his clothes, it simply melted them to his body.

And as the oil felled him, Drabyak screamed. He would

shriek and cry and wail until he was dead, but no-one would hear him.

Because the Forteresse de Valois, mounted on its high rocky pinnacle overlooking the Atlantic Ocean, hanging off the edge of the Brittany coast, lay 20 miles from the nearest town.

**DEEP IN THE HINDU KUSH MOUNTAINS
AFGHANISTAN–TAJIKISTAN BORDER
26 OCTOBER, 1300 HOURS LOCAL TIME
(0300 HOURS E.S.T USA)**

It was like storming the gates of hell.

Lieutenant Elizabeth Gant's eight-wheeled Light Armoured Vehicle kicked up a tornado of dust and dirt as it sped across the 200 yards of open ground that protected the entrance to the terrorist cave system.

An absolute storm of bullets hammered the ground all around the speeding LAV as it wended its way toward the cave entrance, covered by an overhead artillery barrage of its own.

This was the Allies' fifth attempt to get troops into the cave system—a converted Soviet mine known to be harbouring Osama bin Laden's second-in-command, Hassan Zawahiri, and about two hundred heavily-armed Al-Qaeda terrorists.

More than a year after the Taliban regime had been ousted from Kabul—and even though a far more public war had since been waged and won against Saddam Hussein in Iraq—Operation Enduring Freedom still raged in the darkest places of Afghanistan: the caves.

For the final annihilation of Al-Qaeda could not be achieved until all the terrorist caves had been cleared, and that involved a kind of warfare not suitable for viewing on CNN or Fox. A down-and-dirty variety of fighting. Hand-to-hand, man-on-man cave-hunting.

And then just this week, US and UK forces had found this cave

system far in the north of the country, straddling the Afghan–Tajikistan border—the most important terrorist cave base in Afghanistan.

It was the core of the Al-Qaeda network.

An abandoned Soviet coalmine once known as the Karpalov Mine, it had been converted by Osama bin Laden's construction company into a labyrinthine network of hiding caves: caverns in which terrorists lived and worked and in which they'd stored a veritable arsenal of weapons.

It also came with an extra defence mechanism.

It was a methane trap.

Coal gives off methane—a highly flammable gas—and methane levels of 5% are explosive. One spark and it all goes up. And while the inner sections of the abandoned mine were supplied with fresh air from chimney-like vents, its outer extremities were filled with methane.

In other words: invading soldiers couldn't use guns until they arrived at the core of the mine.

One thing was certain: the terrorists who had withdrawn to this cave system were not going to give up without a fight. Like Kunduz the previous year and the bloodbath at Mazar-e-Sharif, this was going to be a fight to the death.

It was Al-Qaeda's last stand.

The mine's entrance was a reinforced concrete archway wide enough for large trucks to pass through.

The sharply-sloping mountainside above it was pockmarked with dozens of tiny snipers' nests, from which the terrorists covered the wide expanse of open ground in front of the entrance.

And somewhere up in the tangle of mountain peaks covering the mine were the openings to two air vents—twin 10-metre-wide shafts that rose like chimneys from the bottom of the mine, allowing fresh air into it. The terrorists had long ago covered the tops of these vents with camouflaged lids, so that they were invisible to spy planes.

Those vents were Gant's objective.

Capture a vent from inside the mine, blow its lid from below, and then send up a targeting laser that would be picked up by an over-flying C-130 bomber, giving it a bull's-eye that it wouldn't miss.

The only thing left to do then was to get the hell out of the mine before a devastating 21,000-pound Massive Ordnance Air Burst (more commonly known as MOAB, the Mother Of All Bombs) was dropped down the chimney.

The first three attempts that morning to storm the tunnel system had been successful.

In each attempt, a pair of LAV-25s—eight-wheeled Light Armoured Vehicles—filled with Marines and SAS troopers had sur-vived the hail of bullets and entered the cave.

The fourth attempt, however, had been a disaster.

It had ended with a terrible cross-fire of Russian-made rocket-propelled grenades—known to many as 'LAV-Killers'—slamming into the two inrushing vehicles, killing all the men inside them.

Gant's was the fifth attempt, and it had entailed sending two high-speed decoy buggies into the gauntlet first, to attract the enemy's fire, after which Gant's two eight-wheelers had zeroed in on the cave entrance under cover of mortar fire targeted at the enemy's emplacements.

It had worked.

The speeding decoy buggies caught all manner of shit—automatic gunfire, RPGs that smashed into the ground all around them—while Gant's LAV-25 had burst forth from cover, closely followed by a sec-ond eight-wheeled beast.

The mountainside above the cave entrance had erupted in mortar impacts while the two LAVs had shot across the open plain before whipping into the entrance of the cave system, disappearing into darkness, out of the rain of gunfire and into a whole new kind of hell.

★ ★ ★

Elizabeth 'Fox' Gant was 29 years old and a newly-minted First Lieutenant, fresh from Officer Candidate School.

Now, it wasn't often that a brand-new lieutenant was given command of a prized Recon Unit, let alone a stand-alone one, but Gant was something special.

Compact, blonde and fitter than many triathletes, she was a natural leader. Behind her sky-blue eyes lay a razor-sharp mind. Plus she already had two years' experience in a Recon Unit as an NCO.

She also, it was said in whispers, had friends in high places.

Some said that her rapid rise to Recon command had been the result of a recommendation from no less than the President of the United States himself. It had something to do, they said, with an incident at the US Air Force's most secret base, Area 7, during which Gant had shown her worth in the presence of the President himself. But that was conjecture.

The greatest recommendation, in the end, had come from a highly-respected Marine Gunnery Sergeant named Gena 'Mother' Newman who had vouched for Gant in the best possible way: if Gant were put in command of a Recon Unit, Mother had said, then she herself would act as Gant's Team Chief.

At six-feet-two, with a fully-shaven head, one artificial leg and some of the most ruthless skills in the killing trade, Mother's word was gold. Her nickname said it all. It was short for 'Motherfucker'.

And so Gant took command of Marine Force Reconnaissance Unit 9 one month before it shipped out for Afghanistan.

There was one other thing about Libby Gant worth noting.

For almost a year now, she had been the girlfriend of Captain Shane M. Schofield.

Schofield's newly acquired Yak-141 shot through the air at close to Mach 2.

It had been nearly five hours since his battle at Krask-8, and now, spread out before him and Book II, were the formidable Hindu Kush mountains.

And somewhere in them was Libby Gant—Potential Hostage No. 1 for anyone wanting Schofield's head.

Their Yak was almost out of gas. A quick pit-stop at an abandoned Soviet airfield in rural Kazakhstan had allowed them to refuel, but now they were running low on fuel again. They needed to find Gant soon.

Since he didn't trust anyone in Alaska any more, Schofield tuned his plane's radio to a very obscure US satellite frequency—the frequency of the US Defense Intelligence Agency.

After his identity had been verified, he asked to be put through to the Pentagon, to David Fairfax in the Cypher and Cryptanalysis Department.

'*This is Fairfax,*' a young male voice came in over his earpiece.

'Mr Fairfax, this is Shane Schofield.'

'*Hey, Captain Schofield. Nice to hear from you. So, what have you destroyed today?*'

'I've flooded a Typhoon-class submarine, levelled a building, and launched a ballistic missile to destroy a maintenance facility.'

'*Slow day, huh.*'

'Mr Fairfax, I need your help.'

'*Sure.*'

Schofield and Fairfax had formed an unlikely alliance once

before, during the incident at Area 7. Both had received (classified) medals for their bravery and afterwards had become good friends.

Now, as he and Book II blasted over the mountains of Tajikistan in the Yak-141, Schofield could picture Fairfax—sitting at his computer in an underground room at the Pentagon, dressed in a Mooks T-shirt, jeans, glasses and Nikes, munching on a Mars Bar and looking pretty much like Harry Potter as a graduate student. A code-cracking genius of a graduate student.

'*So what do you need?*' Fairfax asked.

'Four things,' Schofield said. 'First, I need you to tell me where Gant is stationed in Afghanistan. Exact GPS location.'

'*Jesus, Scarecrow, that's operational information. I don't have clearance for that. I could get arrested just for accessing it.*'

'Get clearance. Do whatever you have to do. I just lost six good Marines because my mission to Siberia was compromised by someone back home. It was a set-up designed to put me in the hands of some bounty hunters. I can't trust anybody, David. I need you to do this for me.'

'*Okay, I'll see what I can do. What else?*'

Schofield pulled out the list of names he'd taken from Wexley, the ExSol leader. 'I need you to look up the following names for me . . .'

Schofield read out the names on the bounty list, including his own.

'Find out what these names have in common. Career history, sniper skills, hair colour, anything. Cross-check them on every database you've got.'

'*Got it.*'

'Third, look up a base in Siberia called Krask-8. Find out whatever you can about it. I want to know why it was chosen as an ambush site.'

'*Okay. And the last impossible task?*'

Schofield frowned, thinking—thinking about one of the names he had heard mentioned on the radio at Krask-8.

At last he said, 'This is going to sound weird, but can you look up a guy called the "Black Knight"? Check the mercenary databases in particular, anything ex-military. He's a bounty hunter—and so far as I know, a very good one—and he's after me. I want to know who he is.'

'It will be done, Scarecrow. I'll get back to you as soon as I can.'

Gant's armoured eight-wheeler skidded to a halt inside the darkened cave entrance.

Its double rear doors were flung open from within and the six-man team of Marines thundered out of it, boots slamming against the ground, guns up.

Gant stepped out of the LAV and scanned the area, the gigantic Mother Newman by her side. Both were dressed in sand-coloured fatigues, helmets and body armour, and held MP-7s and pistol-sized crossbows in their hands.

The cave here was wide and high and completely concrete-walled. A wide set of train tracks disappeared down a very steep tunnel in front of them. The tunnel was called a drift and it was how you entered the mine.

'Sphinx, this is Fox,' Gant said into her throat-mike. 'We're in. Where are you?'

A British-accented voice came in: '*Fox, this is Sphinx. Christ, it's bedlam down here! We're at the eastern extremity of the mine! About two hundred metres from the drift! They're bunkered down in front of the two vents, in an air pock—*'

The signal cut off.

'Sphinx? Sphinx? Damn,' Gant turned to two of her men. 'Pokey. Freddy. Flush out those RPG foxholes upstairs. There's gotta be some internal tunnels giving access to them. Nail those suckers so we can open a safe corridor into this mine.'

'Yes, ma'am.' The two young Marines took off.

'The rest of you,' Gant said, 'follow me.'

★ ★ ★

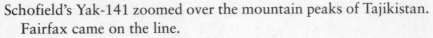

Schofield's Yak-141 zoomed over the mountain peaks of Tajikistan.

Fairfax came on the line.

'Okay, you listening. I found Gant for you. Her unit is working out of Mobile Command Station California-2, under the command of Colonel Clarence W. Walker. California-2 is located at GPS co-ordinates 06730.20, 3845.65.'

'Got it,' Schofield said, punching the co-ordinates into his trip computer.

Fairfax went on. *'I also got a couple of hits on that list of yours. Seven of the fifteen names matched up immediately on the NATO personnel database: Ashcroft, Kingsgate, McCabe, Farrell, Oliphant, Nicholson and you are all mentioned in something called the "NATO Joint Services MNRR Study". It's dated December 1996. Looks like some kind of joint medical study we did with the Brits.'*

'Where is it kept?'

'USAMRMC—Army Medical Research and Matériel Command.'

'Think you can get it?'

'Of course.'

'And the other hit?' Schofield asked.

'One of our Echelon spy satellites caught a voice transmission from an unknown aircraft flying over Tajikistan only this morning. Several of the names on your list were mentioned. I'll read you the transcript:

' "BASE, THIS IS DEMON. WE HAVE **WEITZMAN**, ALIVE, AS INSTRUCTED. HEADING FOR THE KARPALOV MINE SYSTEM NOW. IT'S THE MONEY SHOT—THE BIGGEST CONCENTRATION OF TARGETS ON THE LIST. FOUR OF THEM IN THE ONE PLACE: **ASHCROFT, KHALIF, KINGSGATE** AND **ZAWAHIRI**. PLUS **SCHOFIELD**'S GIRL IS THERE, TOO." '

Schofield felt his insides tighten.

Fairfax said, *'There's a notation here. It says that the voice on the intercept had a British accent, and that its owner is—whoa . . .'*

'Keep talking.'

Fairfax started reading: *'Voice identified as that of Damon F.*

Larkham, call-sign "The Demon", former colonel in the British SAS.' Fairfax paused. *'He was big in the '90s, but was court-martialled in '99 because of his links with the former head of the SAS, a real bad dude named Trevor J. Barnaby.'*

'Yeah, I've met Barnaby,' Schofield said.

'Larkham was sentenced to eleven years' jail but he escaped en route to Whitemoor Prison, killing nine guards in the process.

'Now alleged to be a principal in the freelance bounty hunting organisation known as the Intercontinental Guards, Unit 88, or "IG-88", based in Portugal. Jesus, Scarecrow, what the hell have you got yourself into?'

'Something that could lose me my head if I'm not careful.' Schofield swapped a look with Book II.

'As for that place you mentioned, Krask-8,' Fairfax said, *'the only thing I could find was this: in June 1997, the whole town of Krask, plus its surrounding maintenance facilities, was sold to an American company, the Atlantic Shipping Corporation. In addition to its shipping businesses, Atlantic also has oil interests. It got Krask-8 when it purchased about 10,000 hectares of northern Siberia for oil exploration.'*

Schofield thought about that. 'Nope. Doesn't help me.'

Fairfax said, *'Oh, and I haven't found anything on that Black Knight guy on the regular ex-military databases. I'm running a search program now on some of the classified intelligence databases.'*

'Thanks, David. Keep at it. Let me know when you find something. I've got to go now.'

He hit the afterburners.

Nine minutes later, the Yak-141 landed vertically in a cloud of dust in a clearing not far from a large gathering of American desert vehicles and command tents.

Schofield had heard that the campaign in Afghanistan had become like Vietnam all over again—principally because Afghanistan, even in war, was one of the world's foremost producers of heroin.

Not only did the Afghan mountain-men have the uncanny ability to vanish into hidden cave systems, but every now and then, when they *were* cornered, they would try to bribe Allied soldiers with bricks of 100% pure heroin. And when one such brick was worth about a million dollars on the street, it sometimes worked.

Why, only last week, Schofield had heard of a Russian unit going AWOL. A whole unit of special forces Spetsnaz soldiers—24 men in total, supposedly there as an observer unit—just stole an Mi-17 Russian-made transport helicopter and disappeared in search of a cavern reputedly filled with thirty *pallets* of heroin bricks.

Welcome to Afghanistan.

Schofield's plane was met by a ring of heavily-armed Marines who didn't take kindly to an unauthorised Russian fighter landing in their midst. But within seconds they recognised Schofield and Book II and escorted them to the tent of the base commander, Colonel Clarence Walker, USMC.

The command tent stood at the bottom of a low hill, beyond which lay the entrance to the Al-Qaeda mine.

Colonel Walker was standing at a map table yelling into a radio when Schofield and Book entered: 'Well, find a way to restore radio signals down there! Lay an antenna cable! Use fucking cups and a piece of string if you have to! I need to talk to my men down in that mine before the bombers arrive!'

'Colonel Walker,' Schofield said, 'I'm sorry to barge in on you like this, but this is very important. My name is Captain Shane Schofield and I have to find Lieutenant G—'

Walker spun, glowering. 'What? Who the fuck are you?'

'Sir, my name is Captain Shane Schofield, and I think there's more in that cave than just Islamist terrorists. There are probably also bounty hu—'

'Captain, unless you're flying a C-130 Hercules with a laser-guided MOAB bomb on board, I don't want to talk to you right now. Take a seat and take a fucking number—'

'Hey! What the hell is that!' someone yelled.

Everyone charged out of the tent and peered out into the gauntlet just in time to see a huge Russian transport helicopter swoop down in front of the mine entrance and land in the dust.

About twenty masked men leapt out of the chopper and disappeared inside the mine under fire from the terrorist emplacements on the mountainside.

No sooner were the men inside the mine than the chopper lifted off, blasting the sniper holes with its side-mounted cannons before disappearing over a hill to the north.

'What in God's name was that?' Colonel Walker yelled.

'It was an Mi-17! With Russian insignia on its flanks!' a spotter called. 'It was that rogue Spetsnaz unit!'

'This place is nuts, fucking nuts . . .' Walker muttered. He turned. 'Okay, Captain Schofield. Do you know anything about this—?'

But Schofield and Book II were nowhere to be seen.

Indeed, the only thing Walker saw was a nearby Light Strike Vehicle skidding off the mark and speeding into the gauntlet with Schofield and Book II inside it.

The Light Strike Vehicle whipped across the stretch of no-man's-land in front of the mine entrance, kicking up a billowing cloud of dust behind it.

Gunfire erupted from the slopes above the mine entrance, smacking into the dirt next to its wheels.

A Light Strike Vehicle is like a dune buggy. It has no windscreens and no armour. It consists merely of a series of roll bars which form a cage around the driver and passenger. It is light, it is fast and it is supremely agile.

Schofield swung his LSV in a wide circle, raising a billowing dustcloud around himself, hiding his car from view. The snipers' shots began to miss by a larger margin.

Then he zeroed in on the mine entrance.

The bullet-fire became more intense—

—before suddenly there came several explosions from the mountainside above the mine's entrance, six sniper emplacements blasting outward in simultaneous showers of dirt.

And in an instant there was no more gunfire. Someone had blown up the emplacements from within the mine itself.

Schofield jammed the accelerator to the floor and zoomed into the darkness of the mine.

Six hundred metres below the surface, Libby Gant hurried on foot down a long rocky tunnel guided by flashlights attached to her helmet and MP-7.

She was followed by her three Marines, and she constantly checked her methanometer, a device that measured the levels of methane in the atmosphere.

At the moment, it read 5.9%.

That was bad. They were still in the mine's outer protective ring.

It was a maze down here—a series of low square-shaped tunnels, each about the width of a train tunnel, and all possessed of rigidly right-angled corners. Some tunnels seemed to go off into the darkness forever, others ended in abrupt dead-ends.

And everything was grey. The rock walls, the low horizontal ceilings, even the creaky wooden posts that supported the roof—all were covered in a ghostly grey powder.

Nothing escaped the powder. It was limestone dust, an inert substance designed to prevent highly flammable coal dust from flaking out from the walls and creating an even greater firetrap.

When Gant and her team had reached the bottom of the steep drift tunnel, they'd been met by an SAS commando. After the radio comms had dropped out, he'd been sent back as a verbal messenger.

'Turn left here, then go straight until you hit the conveyor belt! Then follow the belt to the barricade! Don't stray from the belt, because it's easy to get lost!' he'd said.

Gant's team had followed his instructions to the letter, jogging for about 200 metres down a bending rock-walled tunnel that housed an elevated conveyor belt.

Methanometer: 5.6% . . . 5.4% . . .

The methane levels were getting lower as they ventured further into the mine.

5.2% . . . 4.8% . . . 4.4% . . .

Better, Gant thought.

'You know,' Mother said as they jogged, 'I think he's gonna pop the question in Italy.'

'Mother . . .' Gant said.

After this mission, Mother and Gant—together with Schofield and Mother's nuggetty little husband, Ralph—were going on a group holiday to Italy. They were going to rent a villa in Tuscany for two weeks before taking in the famous 'Aerostadia Italia' airshow in Milan—the centrepiece of which were two very rare X-15s, the famous NASA-built rocket planes, the fastest aircraft ever built. Mother was really looking forward to it.

'Think about it,' she said. 'Tuscan hills. An old villa. A classy guy like the Scarecrow wouldn't miss an opportunity like that.'

'He told you he was going to ask, didn't he?' Gant said, eyes forward.

'Yep.'

'He's such a chicken,' Gant said as they rounded a bend and all of a sudden, heard gunfire. 'To be continued,' she said, giving Mother a look.

Up ahead in the darkness, they saw the beams of helmet-mounted flashlights and the shadows of running Allied soldiers, all moving behind a makeshift barricade constructed of old mining equipment—barrels, crates, empty steel mini-skips.

And beyond the barricade, Gant saw the all-important air vents.

In this tight, low-ceilinged, square-edged world, the air vent cavern was a welcome stretch of open space. Six storeys high and lit by brilliant white phosphorus flares, it shone like a glowing underground cathedral.

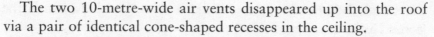

The two 10-metre-wide air vents disappeared up into the roof via a pair of identical cone-shaped recesses in the ceiling.

And underneath the air vents, one of the fiercest battles in history was underway.

The members of Al-Qaeda had prepared well.

They had built a blockade of their own in this high-ceilinged cavern—a barricade that was infinitely superior to the ad hoc creation of the Allied soldiers.

It was made of the larger mining equipment that had been left in the mine: big vehicles featuring gigantic hemispherical drill bits, front-end loaders, some old white Humvee-like trucks called 'Driftrunners', and tip-trays filled with bullet-absorbing coal.

As Gant reached the Allied barricade, she saw the terrorists on the other side of the cavern: over a hundred of them, all dressed in brown leather waistcoats, white shirts, and coiled black turbans.

They were also armed to the teeth. AK-47s, M-16s, RPGs. Bathed in the fresh air of the vents, gunfire was clearly safe inside this subterranean hall.

Gant linked up with the Allied soldiers on the scene.

There were about twenty of them, a mix of United States Marines and British SAS troops.

She arrived at the side of the Allied commander, an SAS major named Ashcroft, call-sign: Sphinx.

'It's a bloody nightmare!' the English commando shouted. 'They're dug in around those vents for the long term! And then every few minutes, one of them—*shit!* Here comes another one! Shoot him! *Shoot* him!'

Gant snapped round to look over the Allied barricade.

With shocking suddenness, a bearded Arab terrorist had burst forth from a gap in the Al-Qaeda barricade *on a motorcycle*, firing an AK-47 one-handed and yelling to Allah.

Strapped to his chest were four wads of C4.

Three SAS soldiers nailed him with their automatic rifles, blasting the suicide bomber from his saddle, sending him crashing to the ground behind his speeding motorbike.

The Arab hit the ground in a clumsy puff of dust—

—and then he exploded.

One second he was there. The next he was simply gone.

Gant's eyes widened.

Madness . . .

The SAS leader, Ashcroft, turned to her. 'It's absolute bedlam, darlin'! Every now and then, the bastards launch a suicide run and we have to cut them down before they reach our barricade! The problem is they must have a supply cave somewhere back there! Generators, gasoline and enough ammo, food and water to see them through to the year 3000! It's a stand-off!'

'What if we went around?' Gant said, indicating the series of tunnels off to their right.

'No. It's booby-trapped! Trip-wires. Landmines. I've already lost two good men going that way! These ragheads have been waiting for a fight in this place for a long time! This is going to take a frontal assault. What I need is more men!'

At that moment, as if on cue, a collection of about twenty more barrel-mounted flashlights appeared in the tunnel that led back to the mine's entrance.

'Ah, reinforcements,' Ashcroft said, heading down the tunnel to meet them.

Gant watched him go, saw him meet the leader of this new squad and shake the man's hand.

Funny, she thought. *Colonel Walker had said that the next team wouldn't be coming in for at least another twenty minutes. How did these guys get in so quickly—*

She watched Ashcroft wave his hand toward the barricade, explaining the situation, turning his back on his new acquaintance for a split second, during which moment the leader of this new group of soldiers smoothly and fluidly drew something from his belt and swiped it hard across Ashcroft's neck region.

At first Gant didn't know what had happened.

Ashcroft didn't move.

Then, to her absolute horror, Gant saw Ashcroft's head tilt at an impossible angle and just drop off his body.

Her eyes went wide with disbelief.

What—?

But she didn't have time for shock, for no sooner was Ashcroft down than the submachine-guns of this new force of men burst to life, raining fire on the Allied troops gathered behind their barricade.

Quick as a flash, Gant dived over and *into* one of the steel mini-skips that formed her barricade, just as bullets impacted all around her. She was joined a second later by Mother and her other two Marines.

The rest of the Allied troops weren't so lucky.

Most of them were caught out in the open . . . and they were pummelled mercilessly by this unexpected storm of bullets from behind. Their bodies exploded with bloody holes, convulsed horribly.

'Goddamnit! What the hell is this!' Gant pressed herself close to a mini-skip's rusty steel walls.

Now they were caught between *two* sets of enemies: one in front of their barricade, one behind.

A lethal sandwich.

'What do we do, Chickadee?' Mother yelled.

Gant's face set into a determined expression. 'We stay alive. Come on, this way!'

And with that, Gant led her team in the only direction they could go—she leapt over the *forward* side of the mini-skip and landed, cat-like, on the dusty section of open ground *in between* the two facing barricades.

At that very same moment, Schofield and Book's Light Strike Vehicle skidded to a halt in the upper entrance cave of the mine.

Schofield saw the roller-coaster-like tracks of the drift diving down into the mine, took a step toward them, just as two figures burst out from a nearby side-tunnel.

Schofield and Book whipped around together, MP-7s up. The two dark figures did the same and—

'Pokey?' Schofield said, squinting. 'Pokey de Villiers?'

'Scarecrow?' one of the figures lowered his gun. 'Man, I almost shot you dead.'

It was Corporal Paul 'Pokey' de Villiers, just returned from cleaning out the Al-Qaeda sniper holes on the mountainside with his partner, a lance-corporal nicknamed Freddy.

'I need to find Gant,' Schofield said. 'Where is she?'

'Down there,' Pokey said.

Thirty seconds later, Schofield was sliding down the steep drift tunnel at the wheel of the Light Strike Vehicle with Book II riding shotgun and the two extra Marines, Pokey and Freddy, sharing the rear gunner's seat.

The LSV's headlights blazed as it rocketed down the 30-degree slope, straddling the train tracks that ran down the centre of the tunnel.

Nearing the bottom, Schofield jammed the LSV into reverse, causing its wheels to spin wildly backwards as the speeding car skidded *forwards* down the tunnel.

The strategy worked: they slowed, if only slightly. But it was enough and with a few yards to go, Schofield slipped the dune

buggy out of reverse and the LSV blasted out of the bottom of the drift tunnel and shot into the maze, swinging left past the dead body of the SAS messenger who had been stationed there.

Gant was completely exposed.

Out on the forward side of the Allied barricade—with only thirty yards of open ground between her and about 200 murderous holy warriors.

If the terrorist forces wanted to kill her and her three Marines, then this was their chance. Gant waited for the hail of bullets that would end her life.

But it never came.

Instead she heard gunfire—from somewhere *behind* the Al-Qaeda blockade.

Gant frowned. It was a type of gunfire that she had never heard before. It sounded too fast, way too fast, like the whirring of a six-barrelled mini-gun . . .

And then she saw something that took her completely by surprise.

She saw the Al-Qaeda blockade get absolutely *raked* with internal gunfire—its walls blew out, assaulted by a million hypervelocity bullets—and suddenly a whole crowd of terrorists were leaping *over their own barricade* out into no-man's-land, fleeing some unseen force behind their own blockade . . . exactly as Gant had done herself.

Another thing was clear.

The terrorists were fleeing something far worse than Gant was.

As they leapt desperately over their barricade, they were shot in mid-air—from behind—and all but ripped apart, their limbs exploding from their bodies.

A split-second before one such Al-Qaeda warrior was ripped to pieces as he clambered over the barricade, Gant caught a glimpse of a *green* targeting laser zeroing in on him.

A green laser . . .

'Er, Lieutenant!' Mother yelled from beside her. 'What the hell happened to this fight! I thought wars were supposed to be fought between *two* competing forces!'

'I know!' Gant called. 'There are more than two forces down here! Come on, follow me!'

'Where!'

'There's only one way to solve this problem, and that's to do what we came here to do!'

With that, Gant made a break across no-man's-land, ducking underneath the overhead conveyor belt that ran up its left-hand side, and headed towards the left-hand air vent.

Gant came to the northern end of the elevated conveyor belt just as four Al-Qaeda terrorists came running out from behind their barricade, chased by gunfire.

The first three holy warriors scrambled up some boxes that had been arranged like stairs and jumped up onto the conveyor belt while the fourth hit a fat green button on a console.

The conveyor belt roared to life—

—and the three men on it were instantly whisked out of sight at tremendous speed, heading towards the Allied barricade. The fourth man jumped onto the belt after them and—*whoosh*—he was swept southward as well.

'Whoa. Fast belt . . .' Mother said.

'Come on!' Gant yelled as she dashed behind the Al-Qaeda barricade.

She burst into open space—the high-ceilinged area underneath the air vents. It did look like a cathedral here. Dim white light from electric lamps partially illuminated the area.

She also saw the reason why the Al-Qaeda terrorists had bolted from the safety of their barricade.

A team of maybe 15 black-clad commandos—dark wraiths wearing green-eyed night-vision goggles and motorcross-style Oakley anti-flash glasses—was fanning out from a small tunnel located behind the Al-Qaeda barricade, tucked into the north-eastern corner of the cavern.

It was, however, the weapons in their hands that seized Gant's attention. The weapons which had unleashed hell on the Al-Qaeda troops.

These new soldiers were equipped with MetalStorm M100 assault rifles. A variety of rail gun, the MetalStorm range of weapons do not use conventional moving parts to fire their bullets. Rather, they employ rapid-sequential electric shocks to trigger each round, and as such, are able to fire at the unbelievable rate of 10,000 rounds per minute. It amounts to a literal storm of metal, hence the name.

The MetalStorm guns of this new force of men were equipped with ghostly green laser-sighting devices—so in her mind, until she found out their real name, Gant just labelled them 'the Black-Green Force'.

One thing about them was truly odd. This Black-Green Force didn't seem to care about her at all. They were pursuing the fleeing terrorists.

In the midst of all this confusion, Gant slid to the dusty ground underneath the left-hand air vent and started erecting a vertical mortar launcher.

When the launcher was ready, she yelled, 'Clear!' and hit the trigger. With an explosive *whump!*, a mortar round shot up into the air vent, disappearing up it at rocket speed before . . .

. . . *BOOM!!!!*

Six hundred metres above them, the mortar round hit the camou-flaged lid that capped the air vent, blasting it to smithereens. Debris rained down the vent, smacking to the ground, at the same time as a shaft of natural grey light flooded into the cavern from above.

When the rain of debris had cleared, Gant stepped forward again, and surrounded by her team, erected a new device, a much smaller one: a compact laser-emitting diode.

She flicked a switch.

Immediately, a brilliant red laser beam shot up into the vent from the diode, disappearing up the chimney, shooting into the sky.

'All units, this is Fox,' Gant said into her radio mike. 'If you're still alive, pay attention. The laser is set. Repeat, the laser is set. According to mission parameters, the bombers will be here in ten minutes! I don't care what else is happening in here, let's clear out of this mine, people!'

At the Marine compound outside the mine, a communications officer abruptly sat up straight at his console.

'Colonel! We just picked up a targeting laser coming from inside the mine! It's Gant's beam. They did it.'

Colonel Walker stepped forward. 'Call the C-130s, tell them they have a laser. And get evac crews to that mine entrance to pick up our people as they come out. In ten minutes that mine is going to be history and we can't wait for any stragglers.'

Gant and Mother and the two Marines with them turned together.

They were still behind the Al-Qaeda barricade and now they had to get back to the Allied one and then beyond it to the sloping entry shaft.

They didn't get more than a few yards.

No sooner had they started moving than they saw a stand-off taking place just in front of the Al-Qaeda barricade, at the edge of no-man's-land.

Four Al-Qaeda holy warriors stood surrounded by a six-man squad of the Black-Green Force, caught in the beams of their MetalStorm rifles.

Gant watched from behind the barricade.

The Black-Green Force's squad leader stepped forward, pulled down his ski-mask to reveal a male model's square jaw and hand-some blue-eyed features. He addressed the terrorists. 'You're Zawahiri? Hassan Zawahiri . . .'

One of the Al-Qaeda men raised his chin defiantly.

'*I* am Zawahiri,' he said. 'And you cannot kill me.'

'Why not?' the Black-Green squad leader said.

'Because Allah is my protector,' Zawahiri said evenly. 'Do you not know? I am His chosen warrior. I am His Chosen One.' The terrorist's voice began to rise. 'Ask the Russians. Of the captured mujahideen, I alone survived the Soviets' experiments in the dungeons of their Tajik gulag. Ask the Americans! I alone survived their cruise missile attacks after the African embassy bombings!' Now he started shouting. 'Ask the Mossad! They know! I alone have survived over a dozen of their assassination attempts! No man born of this earth can kill me! I am the One. I am God's messenger. I am *invincible*!'

'You,' the squad leader said, 'are wrong.'

He fired a burst from his MetalStorm rifle into Zawahiri's chest. The terrorist was hurled backwards, his torso torn to mush, his body all but cut in half.

Then the handsome squad leader stepped forward and did the most gruesome thing of all.

He stood over Zawahiri's corpse, drew a machete from behind his back, and with one clean blow, sliced Zawahiri's head from his shoulders.

Gant's eyes went wide.

Mother's mouth opened.

They watched in horror as the Black-Green commando then grabbed Zawahiri's severed head and casually placed it in a white medical box.

Mother breathed: 'What kind of fucked-up shit is going on here?'

'I don't know,' Gant said. 'But we're not gonna find out now. We have to get out of this place.'

They turned—

—just in time to see a crowd of about thirty Al-Qaeda terrorists *stampeding* toward them—toward the conveyor belt, screaming, shouting, their empty machine-guns useless—pursued by more Black-Green commandos.

Gant opened fire—smacked down four terrorists.

Mother did too—took down four more.

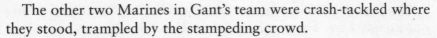

The other two Marines in Gant's team were crash-tackled where they stood, trampled by the stampeding crowd.

'There are too many of them!' Gant yelled to Mother. She dived left, out of the way.

For her part, Mother stepped back onto the boxes leading up to the conveyor belt, firing hard, before she was overwhelmed by the sheer numbers of the terrorists and was herself flung backwards onto the speeding conveyor belt in their midst.

The Black-Green men who had killed Zawahiri seemed amused by the sight of the Al-Qaeda warriors fleeing desperately onto the conveyor belt.

One of them strode over to the conveyor belt's control console and hit a fat yellow button.

A mechanical *roar* filled the cavern, and from her position on the dusty floor, Gant spun to see its source.

Over by the Allied barricade, at the far end of the conveyor belt, a giant rock crusher had been turned on. It was composed simply of a pair of massive rollers that were each covered in hundreds of conical rock-crushing 'teeth'.

Gant gasped as she saw the Al-Qaeda terrorists now jumping for their lives *off* the speeding conveyor belt. She watched for Mother to jump, too, but it never happened.

Gant didn't see anyone resembling Mother leap off.

Shit.

Mother was still on the conveyor belt, rushing headlong toward the rock crusher.

Mother was indeed still on the belt—shooting down its length toward the rotating jaws of the rock crusher sixty yards away.

The problem was she was wrestling with two Al-Qaeda terrorists as she went.

While the other Al-Qaeda troops had decided to leap off the conveyor belt, these two had decided to die in the rock crusher . . . and they were going to take Mother with them.

The conveyor belt rushed down the length of the cavern, racing toward the rock crusher at about thirty kilometres an hour—eight metres per second.

Mother had lost her gun when she'd hit the conveyor belt and now she struggled with the two terrorists.

'You suicidal ratfuckers!' she yelled as she fought. At six feet two, she was as strong as an ox—strong enough to hold off her two attackers but not overpower them.

'Think you're gonna take me down, huh!' she shouted in their faces. 'Not fucking likely!'

She kicked one of them in the balls—hard—and he yelped. She flipped him over her head, toward the rock crusher, now only twenty yards away and approaching fast.

Two-and-a-half seconds away.

But the second guy held on. Tight. He was a dogged fighter and he wouldn't let go of her arms. He was travelling backwards, feet-first. Mother was now travelling forwards, on her belly, head-first.

'*Let—go—of—me!*' she yelled.

The first Al-Qaeda man entered the rock crusher.

A shriek of agony. An explosion of blood. A wash of it splattering all over Mother's face.

And then, in an instant of clarity, Mother realised.

She wasn't going to make it.

It was too late. She was dead.

Time slowed.

The terrorist holding her arms went into the jaws of the rolling rock crusher feet-first.

It swallowed him whole and Mother saw it all up close: a six-foot man chewed in an instant. *Shluck-splat!* Another blood explosion assaulted her face from point-blank range.

Then she saw the rolling jaws of the crusher inches away from her own face, saw each individual spoked tooth, saw the blood on each one, saw her hands disappear into the—

—and then suddenly she was lifted into the air above the yawning maw of the rock crusher.

Not far into the air, mind you.

Just a couple of inches, enough to take her off the swiftly moving conveyor belt, enough to stop her forward movement.

Mother frowned, snapped her head round.

And there above her, hanging one-handed from a steel overhead beam, gripping the collar of her body armour with his spare hand, was Shane Schofield.

Five seconds later, Mother was on solid ground again, standing with Schofield and Book II and their new offsiders, Pokey and Freddy. The Light Strike Vehicle was parked nearby, behind the Allied barricade.

'Where's Gant!' Schofield yelled above the mayhem.

'We got separated over at the other barricade!' Mother shouted back.

Schofield glanced that way.

'Scarecrow! What the fuck is going on! Who are all these people?'

'I can't explain it yet! All I know is that they're bounty hunters! And at least one of them is after Gant!'

Mother grabbed his arm. 'Wait. I got bad news! We've already set the targeting laser for the bombers. We got exactly'—she checked her watch—'eight minutes before this mine is hit by a 21,000-pound laser-guided bomb!'

'Then we'd better find Gant fast,' Schofield said.

After the Al-Qaeda stampede had passed her by, Libby Gant leapt to her feet—only to find several green laser beams immediately zero in on her chest armour.

She looked up.

She was surrounded by another sub-group of the Black-Green Force, six men, their MetalStorm rifles trained on her.

One of the black-clad soldiers held up his hand, stepped forward.

The man took off his helmet—at the same time removing his protective Oakley goggles, revealing his face.

It was a face Gant would never forget.

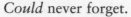

Could never forget.

He looked like something out of a horror movie.

At some point in the past, this man's head must have been caught in a raging fire—his entire skull was completely hairless and horribly wrinkled, with flash-burned skin that was blistered and scarred. His earlobes had *melted* into the side of his head.

Beneath this scarring, however, the man's eyes glistened with delight.

'You're Elizabeth Gant, aren't you?' he said amiably, taking her guns.

'Ye—Yes,' Gant said, surprised.

Like the other Black-Green squad leader, the bald man had a British accent. He looked about 40. Experienced. Cunning.

He pulled Gant's Maghook out of her back-holster and threw it to the ground far away from her.

'Can't let you keep that either, I'm afraid,' he said. 'Elizabeth Louise Gant, callsign: Fox. Twenty-nine years old. Recent graduate of OCS. Graduated second in your class, I believe. Former member of Marine Force Reconnaissance Unit 16 under the command of then-Lieutenant Shane M. Schofield. Former member of HMX-1, the Presidential Helicopter Detachment, again under the command of Captain Shane M. Schofield.

'And now . . . now you are no longer under the command of Captain Schofield because of Marine Corps regulations about troop fraternisation. Lieutenant Gant, my name is Colonel Damon Larkham, callsign: Demon. These are my men, the Intercontinental Guards, Unit 88. I hope you don't mind, but we just need to borrow you for a while.'

And with that, one of Larkham's men grabbed Gant from behind and clamped a rag soaked in trichloromethane over her mouth and nose and in an instant Gant saw nothing but black.

A moment later, the handsome young squad leader whom Gant had seen cut off Zawahiri's head arrived at Demon Larkham's side, holding three head-sized medical transport containers.

'Sir,' the squad leader said, 'we have the heads of Zawahiri, Khalif and Kingsgate. We found the body of Ashcroft, but his head was already missing. I believe the Skorpions are here and that they got to him first.'

Larkham nodded thoughtfully. 'Hmmm, Major Zamanov and his Spetsnaz Skorpions. Thank you, Cowboy. I think we have gained more than enough from this incursion already.' He looked down at Gant's prone body. 'And we might have just added to our catch. Tell everybody to head for the back door. Time to get back to the planes. This mine has been lased for an airstrike and the bombers are on their way.'

Two minutes later, Schofield's Light Strike Vehicle slid around the conveyor-belt end of the Al-Qaeda barricade and skidded to a dusty halt.

Schofield, Book II, Mother and the two junior Marines piled out of it, guns up, searching for Gant.

'Mother. Time to the bomb?' Schofield called.

'Six minutes!'

Gant was nowhere to be seen. As was the Black-Green force. The area behind the Al-Qaeda barricade was deserted, the battle over.

Mother stood at the near end of the barricade, not far from the conveyor belt. 'This is where I last saw her. We saw a good-looking guy from that black-and-green group cut some terrorist dude's head off and then suddenly a whole bunch of Al-Qaeda chumps came stampeding at us from over there.'

She indicated the far north-eastern corner of the cavern, beyond the air vents. There Schofield saw a small tunnel about the size of a garage door.

And then he saw something else—on the floor.

A Maghook.

He went over to it and picked it up, saw the words 'Foxy Lady' written in white marker on its side. Gant's Maghook. He clipped it to his belt.

When he rejoined the others, Mother was saying: '. . . and don't forget the fourth force that's down here.'

'A *fourth* force?' Schofield said. 'What fourth force?'

'There are four separate forces in this mine,' Mother said. 'Us, Al-Qaeda, those black-and-green fuckers who took my little

Chickadee, and a fourth force: that bunch of guys who killed Ashcroft and took out the Allied barricade from behind.'

'They killed Ashcroft?' Schofield said.

'Fuckin'-A. Cut off his goddamn head.'

'Jesus. It's another group of bounty hunters,' Schofield said. 'So where is this fourth force now?'

'I, uh, think they're already here . . .' Book II said ominously.

They materialised from within and around the Al-Qaeda barricade—about twenty armed troops dressed in tan desert fatigues, caramel ski-masks and yellow Russian combat boots. They stepped out of the Driftrunner vehicles and tip-trays that made up the Al-Qaeda barricade.

Most of them held sinister-looking short-barrelled VZ-61 Skorpion machine pistols: the signature weapon of Russia's elite special forces unit, the Spetsnaz. It was from this gun that they had garnered their bounty hunting nickname: *the Skorpions*.

They'd been waiting.

A man wearing major's bars stepped forward from the group. 'Drop your weapons,' he said crisply, curtly.

Schofield and the other four Marines did so. Two Spetsnaz soldiers immediately rushed to his side and held him firmly.

'Captain Schofield, what a pleasant surprise,' the Spetsnaz major said. 'My intelligence did not mention that you would be at this site, but your appearance is a welcome bonus. Your head may pay exactly the same price as the others, but there is no doubt a certain *prestige* that goes with being the bounty hunter who brings in the famous Scarecrow.'

The major seemed to appraise Schofield down his long aquiline nose. He snorted. 'But perhaps your reputation is unwarranted. Kneel, please.'

Schofield remained standing. He nodded at Gant's laser-emitting diode on the ground. 'You see that device down there. That diode is leading a 21,000-pound laser-guided bomb to this mine. It'll be here in five minut—'

'I said kneel.'

One of the guards whacked Schofield behind the knees with his rifle butt. Schofield dropped to the ground underneath one of the cathedral-like domes of the air vents.

With a sharp slicing noise, the major then withdrew a glistening sword from his back-holster: a short-bladed Cossack fighting sword.

'Really,' the major said as he approached Schofield, rotating the sword lazily in his hand, 'I am somewhat disappointed. I had thought killing the Scarecrow would be more *difficult* than this.'

He raised the sword and, gripping it with both hands, started to swing it . . . just as a pair of blue laser dots appeared on the chests of Schofield's guards. The next instant, the two guards were blown away.

Schofield snapped up—

The Spetsnaz major whirled around—

And they all saw him.

He was standing out in the open, underneath the other air vent, two silver Remington shotguns in his hands, held like pistols. High-tech blue laser-sighting devices were attached to the shotguns' stainless steel barrels.

Erected next to him on collapsible tripods were two remote-operated FN-MAG machine-guns—also equipped with blue laser sights. One of the robot guns was now illuminating the Spetsnaz major's chest with its blue targeting laser, the other gun just roved randomly among the Russian troops.

Whoever this man was, he was dressed entirely in black.

Black fatigues.

Black body armour, scratched with battle scars.

Black hockey helmet.

And on his face—a rugged face, weathered and hard, unshaven—he wore a pair of wraparound anti-flash glasses with yellow lenses.

Schofield caught a glimpse of a thick rope hanging vertically from the air vent above the man, before—*whoosh*—it whiplashed up into the vent, disappearing like a spooked snake.

'Why hello, Dmitri,' the man in black said. 'Gone AWOL again have you?'

The Spetsnaz major didn't look at all pleased to see the man in black. Nor was he thrilled at the blue laser dot now lighting up his own chest.

The Russian major snarled. 'It is always easier to disappear on these international missions. As I'm sure *you* of all people would know, Aloysius.' He pronounced the name: *allo-wishus*.

The man in black—Aloysius—stepped forward, walking casually in amongst the heavily-armed Spetsnaz unit.

Schofield noticed his black utility vest. It was equipped with a bizarre array of *non*-military devices: handcuffs, mountain-climbing pitons, a small hand-held scuba tank called a Pony Bottle, even a miniature welding torch—

The man in black strode past a Russian trooper, and suddenly the trooper whipped his gun up.

Muzzle flash. Gunfire.

The trooper was riddled with bullets, nailed.

The roving robot machine-gun whizzed back to pin its laser sights on the other Spetsnaz troops.

Unperturbed, the man in black stopped before Schofield and the Spetsnaz major.

'Captain Schofield, I presume?' he said as he lifted Schofield to his feet. 'The Scarecrow.'

'That's right . . .' Schofield said guardedly.

The man in black smiled. 'Knight. Aloysius Knight. Bounty hunter. I see you've met the Skorpions. You'll have to excuse Major Zamanov. He has this really bad habit of cutting off people's heads as soon as he meets them. I saw the laser signal from the air—when is the bomb due?'

Schofield glanced at Mother.

'Four minutes, thirty seconds,' she said, eyeing her watch.

'If you take his head, Knight,' the Russian major hissed, 'we will hunt you down to the ends of the earth, and we will kill you.'

'Dmitri,' the man named Knight said, 'you couldn't do that if you tried.'

'I could kill you right now.'

'But then you'd die, too,' Knight said, nodding at the blue dot on Major Dmitri Zamanov's chest.

'It would be worth it,' Zamanov spat.

'I'm sorry, Dmitri,' Knight laughed. 'You're a good soldier, and let's be honest, a fucking psychotic asshole. But I know you too well. You don't want to die. Death scares the shit out of you. Me, on the other hand . . . well, I couldn't give a fuck about dying.'

Zamanov froze.

This Knight character, Schofield saw, had called Zamanov's bluff.

'Come on, Captain,' Knight said, handing Schofield his MP-7 from the ground. 'Grab your boys and girls and follow me.'

With that, Knight led Schofield and the other Marines through the ranks of Spetsnaz troops without another shot being fired.

'Who *are* you?' Schofield asked as they walked.

'Never mind,' Knight said. 'The only thing you need to know right now, Captain, is that you have a guardian angel. Someone who doesn't want to see you killed.'

They reached the eastern end of the Al-Qaeda barricade, a short distance from the tunnel in the corner of the cavern.

Knight yanked open the door to a wide-bodied Driftrunner truck that formed the end section of the Al-Qaeda barricade.

'Get in,' he said.

Schofield and the others climbed inside—under the baleful glares of the Skorpions.

Aloysius Knight jumped into the front seat of the Driftrunner, keyed the ignition.

'Now,' he turned to Schofield, 'are you ready to run? Because as soon as we leave the cover of my remote guns, those cocksuckers are gonna be really pissed.'

'I'm ready.'

'Good.'

Then Knight gunned the accelerator and the Driftrunner shot off the mark, disappearing into the small tunnel in the corner of the cavern.

No sooner was it out of sight than the 20-odd members of Zamanov's Spetsnaz team were moving, jumping into other Driftrunners, three men even leaping into Schofield's abandoned Light Strike Vehicle.

Their engines roared and the chase began.

Headlights in darkness.

Bouncing, jouncing, carving sabre-like beams through the dust-filled air.

The Black Knight's Driftrunner roared down the narrow tunnel.

The Driftrunner was about the size of a Humvee and essentially just an oversized pick-up truck, with a long rear tray and a partially-enclosed driver's compartment. There was, however, no dividing wall or window between the driver's compartment and the rear personnel tray: one could traverse between the two simply by climbing over the seats.

The tunnel around it was almost perfectly square, with sheer granite walls and a flat hardstone ceiling held up by wooden support beams. It was also practically dead straight, stretching away into darkness like an arrow.

And it was tightly—tightly—fitted around the Driftrunner. There were only about 12 inches to spare on either side of the speeding truck. Above the vehicle's roof the gap was about four feet.

The Skorpions were close behind them.

The three Russian commandos who had commandeered Schofield's LSV were now speeding along the tunnel right behind the Driftrunner—the smaller, more nimble little vehicle catching up to it easily. The driver drove hard while his partners fired at the Driftrunner with their VZ-61 machine pistols.

Bathed in the glare of the LSV's bouncing headlights, Mother and Book and Pokey and Freddy returned fire.

Behind the speeding LSV came three other Driftrunners, packed with the other seventeen members of Zamanov's rogue Spetsnaz unit.

A mini-convoy, racing at dangerously high speed through the tight stone passageway.

'Mother! Time!' Schofield yelled from the passenger seat of the front-running truck.

'Three minutes!'

'How long is this tunnel?' he asked Knight.

'About four miles.'

'This is going to be close.'

Book and Mother and Pokey and Freddy's guns blazed, firing at the speeding LSV behind their truck. They alternated their fire, so that while two of them fired, the other two were reloading.

Following this pattern, Mother and Book ducked to reload; Pokey and Freddy took their places—and were hit by a shocking wave of gunfire. Freddy's face disappeared, transformed to pulp. Pokey was hit in the throat and he fell, teeth clenched. Book II dived forward to stop him falling off the back of the truck, caught him—

—but that was all the Skorpions needed.

Still reloading, Mother spun to see what was happening. She turned in time to see the two passengers from the LSV leaping off the front of the Light Strike Vehicle *up onto the rear tray of the Driftrunner!*

Book had his hands full with Pokey.

The two Skorpions landed on their feet, brought their guns up to kill Book and Pokey.

Lacking a loaded gun, Mother just hurled herself into them, crash-tackling them *both*, and the three of them fell to the floor of the tray, the walls of the tunnel rushing past them in a blur of rocky grey.

Knight and Schofield saw it all.

Schofield got up to help.

'Here!' Knight yelled, tossing him one of his silver Remingtons. 'While you're back there, nail that car!'

Schofield dived back into the open rear tray of the Driftrunner.

He saw Mother on the floor, fighting—saw Book II lifting Pokey back up into the tray—saw the LSV whipping along the tunnel behind them, its headlights illuminating the confined space.

He raised the silver Remington and, two-handed, fired it at the LSV.

The recoil from the shotgun was enormous.

The effect was even bigger. Whatever shells this Knight guy used, they packed one hell of a punch.

The LSV was literally blasted off its wheels.

Hit by the shotgun shell, it was lifted clear into the air and tumbled sideways. Such was its velocity in the close confines of the stone tunnel, the speeding Light Strike Vehicle flipped and rolled and tumbled, banging off the walls and the ceiling before it came to a skidding halt on its crumpled roof.

Miraculously, its driver was still alive.

Not for long.

A split-second after it had stopped, the LSV was ripped apart from behind, blasted into a million pieces as the first Skorpion Driftrunner *exploded* right through it, followed by the second Spetsnaz truck, then the third.

Within seconds, the Skorpion Driftrunners were travelling *right behind* Schofield's truck, headlights ablaze, rushing forward in the dusty tunnel.

The first Russian truck sped up, banged its bullbar against the rear bumper of Schofield's Driftrunner.

Both vehicles rocked with the impact.

Then the Skorpions kicked out the windscreen of the first Russian Driftrunner and clambered out onto its bonnet and before Schofield could do anything about it, in the confined space of the dark tunnel, three of them leapt over into the rear tray of his Driftrunner.

They completely ignored Book II and Mother—instead they headed straight for Schofield, their machine pistols drawn.

Knight saw them in the rear-view mirror, slammed down on the brakes.

The Driftrunner lurched, and everyone was thrown forward, including Schofield, Mother, Book and Pokey in the back.

Like dominoes falling, the three other trucks in the convoy all rammed into each other, thumping nose-to-tail, nose-to-tail, nose-to-tail.

Up in Schofield's Driftrunner, the three Skorpions attacking him were all flung forward.

One dropped his gun as he reached for a handhold; another tumbled to the floor next to Schofield; the third was thrown all the way forward into the driver's compartment where he slammed into the dashboard and looked up to find himself staring into the barrel of a silver shotgun, a blue laser dot illuminating his nose.

Boom!

Knight fired.

The trooper's head exploded like a can of tomato soup.

Knight jammed the accelerator back down and the Driftrunner shot forward again.

The other two Spetsnaz guys, however, their balance now restored, only had eyes for Schofield.

The gunless one drew a Warlock hunting knife, the other brought his VZ-61 machine pistol around fast—

—and at that very same moment, Knight snapped round and saw them, and something in his eyes ignited, a look that said that Schofield could never *ever* be touched.

Schofield reacted quickly.

He parried the machine pistol away, karate-style, pushing its barrel to the side just as his enemy fired.

But he couldn't hold off the two of them.

The knife-wielding Skorpion lunged at him, swiping at his throat—

—and suddenly Aloysius Knight was there—

—and with incredible strength, Knight yanked *both* the knife-wielder and the VZ-61 man away from Schofield, down into the driver's compartment—

—at precisely the same moment as their Driftrunner was rammed hard by the truck behind it.

Knight and the two Spetsnaz commandos were hurled forward, and they smashed right through the windshield of their Driftrunner, went tumbling onto its bonnet.

Truth be told, they didn't actually *smash* the windscreen. Constructed of shatterproof glass, the windscreen just burst into a spiderweb of cracks and popped out of its frame, landing on the bonnet as an intact but crumpled rectangular mat.

The four Driftrunners continued to rocket down the narrow tunnel.

Schofield now saw that Knight had wisely wedged a steel bar against the gas pedal, keeping their Driftrunner moving down the dead-straight tunnel, its steering corrected by the tunnel's close stone walls.

Out on the bonnet of the first Driftrunner, Knight struggled with the two Skorpions.

The knife-wielder was trying desperately to get back to Schofield, while the VZ-61-armed one had lost his gun in the scramble to get a handhold.

Knight, however, had caught the worst of the smash through the windscreen—he lay with his legs dangling off the front of the speeding Driftrunner, hanging onto its bullbar for dear life.

He saw the knife-wielder clawing his way back towards Schofield, grabbed the man's boot and yanked hard on it, dragging the knife-wielder toward the front of the bonnet . . . and off it!

With a horrified scream, the Russian trooper went under the front of the Driftrunner, under its roaring tyres. He tumbled and smacked underneath the wheels of the *whole convoy of Driftrunners* before he was spat out the back of the fourth truck, crumpled and mangled and dead.

The other Skorpion saw this and started kicking at Knight's hands, but Knight got a grip on the man's belt and started pulling on it too.

'No!' the Skorpion yelled. 'Noooo!'

'You can't have him!' Knight called, dragging the Spetsnaz trooper toward the front of the bonnet.

The Skorpion came alongside Knight. He was a big guy, with a fierce angry face. He clutched Knight's throat.

'If I go, Black Knight, you go too . . .' he growled.

Knight looked him in the eye. 'Fine.'

And with that Knight kicked himself clear of the front of the Driftrunner—dragging the aghast Russian commando with him—and dropped to the dusty roadway in front of the speeding truck . . .

The Spetsnaz trooper hit the ground and rolled and—*splat!*—was flattened under the wheels of the lead Driftrunner.

Unlike Knight, he hadn't grabbed the mat-like windscreen of the Driftrunner on his way down.

As he'd fallen off the front of the Driftrunner, Knight had snatched the cracked-glass mat and thrown it to the rushing ground beneath him.

The mat hit the ground—and Knight landed on it, cat-like—and the mat slid along the dusty ground, at first sliding forward, before *whoosh* the first Driftrunner roared over the top of it, and over the top of Knight, too!

The convoy of Driftrunners—all four of them—rumbled quickly forward, *over* the tiny figure of Aloysius Knight sliding on his back on his makeshift mat.

Whoosh—whoosh—whoosh . . .

Knight shot underneath the quartet of trucks and was about to blast out behind the last Driftrunner when he drew his second shotgun, held it by the barrel . . . and hooked its pistol-grip on the underside of the rear bumper of the fourth and last Driftrunner.

The mat swished out from under him, tumbled away into the darkness of the tunnel, and Knight was dragged along behind the Driftrunner, his flailing legs bouncing on the roadway.

Then he reached up and hauled himself up into the tray of the last Driftrunner, ready to rejoin the fight.

★ ★ ★

Up in the first Driftrunner, Schofield was now sitting in the driver's seat. After Knight had gone flying out through the windshield and under the front of the truck, Schofield had kicked away the steel bar pinned to the gas pedal and taken the wheel.

In the rear-view mirror, he saw Mother and Book II fighting hand-to-hand with their two Spetsnaz assholes—saw two *more* Skorpion troopers make the leap forward from the second Driftrunner onto his one.

These two new guys charged straight for Schofield in the driver's compartment.

There are just too many of them, Schofield's mind screamed.

He saw the two new Skorpions rushing forward, guns drawn. They'd be on him in seconds.

And then he remembered something about mining vehicles. He hurriedly reached for his seatbelt.

'*Book! Mother!* Hang on to something!'

Then he reached across the driver's compartment . . . and kicked open the passenger door of the Driftrunner.

The response was instantaneous.

The Driftrunner's handbrake immediately activated itself and the speeding truck came to a sudden bone-jarring halt. It was a safety feature on all mining vehicles—to prevent miners from being hurt, if the passenger door was opened, the vehicle was instantly disabled, its park-brake initiated.

Caught by surprise, the second Driftrunner *slammed* into the back of the first one. The third and fourth trucks did the same, running into each other like a collapsing accordion.

As for the two Skorpions who had been coming for Schofield, one went flying *through* the now-empty windscreen, hurled at least 15 feet clear of the vehicle, the other caught his chin on the roof of the driver's cabin and while his legs flew forward, his head stayed still, and with a sickening *snap!* his neck broke.

Mother and Book II, on the other hand, had done as they'd been told and instead of fighting their assailants, had grabbed onto the nearest handholds, so that when the truck stopped, their attackers

had been thrown forward, smacking into the back of the driver and passenger seats.

One was knocked unconscious by the fall.

The other was only bruised, and he rose—only to be headbutted viciously by Mother, a blow that put his lights out for good.

The damage done, Schofield reached over and closed the passenger door and hit the gas and soon they were speeding again.

There was less damage and mayhem in the other Driftrunners. They sped along behind the first truck once more—still with at least ten men on board.

But then the damage came.

In the form of Aloysius Knight.

When the impact had occurred, Knight had been in the process of climbing into the rear tray of the last Driftrunner, so it hadn't really affected him.

Now that the Driftrunners were racing along again, however, he moved quickly through the last vehicle, dispatching the Skorpions in it with brutal—*brutal*—efficiency.

The Russians tried to resist, tried to raise their own weapons and kill him first.

But Knight was like a killing *machine*.

Two Skorpions in the rear tray: he shot one in the head with his shotgun, while at the same time he shoved the other one's head *above* the roof of the driver's compartment . . . allowing it to be hit by a speeding overhead support beam, an impact that removed the soldier's head from his body.

He came to the driver's compartment—levelled his short-barrelled Remington at the passenger and without so much as a blink, fired.

Boom.

The driver turned, surprised, just as Knight—ignoring him— blasted the windscreen out of its frame and climbed through it, leaping forward onto the tray of the third truck.

Zamanov was on this truck.

He dived for cover as Knight moved forward through the Driftrunner, blasting men left and right. Several of the Skorpions tried to return fire, but Knight was too fast, too fluid, too good. It was as if he anticipated their moves, even the order in which they would shoot.

On his way through the driver's cabin, Knight glimpsed Zamanov cowering under the dash, but he only saw him momentarily and since Knight's first priority was to get forward, back to Schofield, he didn't stop to kill the Russian. He was only killing anyone who was in his way.

He leapt over onto the second truck.

Up in the first Driftrunner, Schofield was now driving hard—with only friends not foes on his truck.

He could also now see a small white speck in the distance in front of him—the end of the tunnel.

Mother climbed into the passenger seat beside him. 'Scarecrow! Who the fuck are these people! And who is that dude in black?'

'I don't know!' Schofield yelled.

He looked in his rear-view mirror and saw Aloysius Knight step out onto the bonnet of the Driftrunner immediately behind his own.

'But he seems to be the only one around here who *isn't* trying to kill me.'

'He could be planning to kill you later,' Book II suggested from the rear tray. 'I say we ditch him.'

'I agree—' Mother began before cutting herself off.

They had reached the end of the tunnel.

Brilliant white light streamed in through a small square entryway. It was about 200 metres away.

What had silenced her, however, was the enormous demonic object that had apparated in the air beyond the tunnel's exit.

A jet fighter.

A black Sukhoi S-37 fighter, hovering in the air just outside the tunnel.

Seen from head-on, with its sharply-pointed nose and downward-swept wings dripping with missiles, the S-37 looked like a gigantic evil hawk, *staring right at them*.

There came a loud thump from behind Schofield as Knight landed in the tray of their Driftrunner and came up behind them.

'It's okay,' he said, nodding at the fighter, 'he's with us.'

Knight pressed a button on his wrist guard, initiating a radio on it. 'Rufus, it's me! We're coming out and we're coming out hot, with three enemy vehicles on our tail. I need a Sidewinder. Just one. Aim low and to your right; arm at two hundred metres. Just like we did in Chile last year.'

'*Copy that, Boss*,' a deep voice said in Knight's earpiece.

'May I?' Knight nodded at Schofield's steering wheel.

Schofield let him take it.

Knight immediately yanked the steering wheel hard over and drove the Driftrunner up against the left-hand wall of the tunnel.

The big four-wheel-drive rode up against the wall, grinding against it until . . . *whump* . . . it jolted upwards, and suddenly was speeding along at a 45-degree angle, riding with two wheels on the ground and two on the wall itself.

'Okay, Rufus! Now!' Knight yelled into his wrist mike.

Immediately, a horizontal finger of smoke shot out from the right wing of the hovering black fighter, and with a resounding *phoom!* a Sidewinder missile streaked into the tunnel system, rocketing at tremendous speed, hugging the ground.

From Schofield's point of view, the missile stayed close to the left-hand wall, zooming fast and low before—

—*shooooooooom!*—

—it whizzed underneath his Driftrunner's 45-degree-tilted body and *slammed* into the truck immediately behind it.

The explosion ripped through the tunnel. The first Spetsnaz Driftrunner was blasted into a million pieces. With no way to avoid it, the two mine trucks behind the first one smashed into the back of it, driving their noses into the wreck, slamming to a halt.

At the same time, Schofield's Driftrunner blasted out into glaring

daylight, shooting onto a wide flat turnaround area carved into the side of the mountain. Beyond the turnaround—directly underneath the hovering fighter jet—was a sheer thousand-foot drop.

Knight turned to Mother. 'You. How long till the bomb?'

Mother checked her watch. 'Thirty seconds.'

'That'll hurt Dmitri.' Knight then spoke into his wrist mike: 'Rufus. Meet us on the next turnaround down the mountainside.' He looked over at Schofield. 'I've got three passengers with me, including our man.'

'*Any problems?*'

Knight said, 'Nah, it was pretty light this time.'

Thirty seconds later, the sleek Sukhoi landed in a cloud of dust on another turnaround area further down the precarious cliff-side roadway. Flat and round, the turnaround looked like a natural landing platform jutting out from the cliff-face.

Schofield's Driftrunner skidded to a halt beside it.

At that very same moment, guided by Gant's laser diode down in the mine, a 21,000-pound MOAB bomb was dropped out the back of a C-130 Hercules and angled in toward the mine's air vents.

The precision guidance system worked perfectly.

The bomb rushed toward the earth, hitting terminal velocity, its fins controlling its flight-path, before—*whump*—the giant weapon disappeared into the mine's now-open chimney.

One, one thousand . . .

Two, one thousand . . .

Three . . .

Detonation.

The entire mountain shuddered.

A volcanic *boooom!* echoed out from within the mine.

Standing next to the Sukhoi's two-man cockpit, pushing Mother up into it, Schofield had to grab onto its ladder just to keep his balance.

He glanced up at the mountain peak above them—at the layer of snow resting on top of it—and realised.

'Oh no,' he breathed. 'Avalanche . . .'

Then he snapped round to look back up the roadway, in time to see two bent-over figures stagger out of the mine tunnel on foot— a bare moment before a *shocking* blast of air came rocketing out of the tunnel, expelling the crumpled remains of the Skorpion Driftrunners that had been left in it.

The three Driftrunners were catapulted clear off the edge of the upper turnaround—shooting horizontally out into the sky, past the two hunched figures—after which the three trucks fell a thousand feet straight down into the ravine below.

It was then that an ominous rumbling came from somewhere above Schofield.

The gigantic body of snow resting on the mountain above the Sukhoi's perch was shifting, cracking, starting to . . .

Slide.

'*Move!*' Schofield yelled, climbing up the ladder.

The sliding body of snow began to gather speed.

'Quickly! Into the bomb bay!' Knight yelled.

Book and Mother squeezed through the small cockpit and into the tight space behind it: a bomb storage bay that had been con-verted into a . . . holding cell.

'Just get in!' Knight yelled from behind them. 'I'll be joining you!'

Knight squeezed in with them. Schofield jumped into the cockpit last of all, climbed into the rear gunner's seat, looked up.

The vertically-sliding snowdrift had taken on the appearance of a crashing ocean wave: blasting explosions of white preceding the full weight of the avalanche.

Knight called forward, 'Er, Rufus . . . !'

'Already on it, Boss!' the large man in the front seat hit the throt-tles and the Sukhoi rose.

'Faster . . .' Schofield said.

The avalanche came rushing down at them, tumbling, rumbling, smashing, crashing.

The Sukhoi lifted higher, hovering for a moment before it powered out over the edge of the cliff *just as* the avalanche rushed past it, the falling wall of snow rushing by with a colossal roar, gobbling up the turnaround in a single enormous bite before rumbling past the floating black fighter jet and disappearing into the abyss below.

'Now *that* was close,' Knight said.

Three minutes later, the Sukhoi S-37 landed in a clearing on the Afghan side of the mountain, about a mile away from Schofield's parked Yak-141.

Schofield, Knight, Book and Mother all climbed out, while the pilot—an enormous bushy-bearded individual whom Knight introduced simply as 'Rufus'—killed the engines.

Schofield walked a few yards away to regather his thoughts. A lot had happened today and he wanted to clear his head.

His earpiece crackled.

'Scarecrow, it's me, Fairfax. You there?'

'Yeah, I'm here.'

'Listen. I got a couple of things for you. A few facts on those USAMRMC guys on your list, and some big stuff on that Black Knight guy, most of it from the FBI and ISS Most Wanted lists. You got a moment?'

'Yeah,' Schofield said.

'Jesus, Scarecrow, this Knight guy is bad news . . .'

In his office deep beneath the Pentagon, Dave Fairfax sat bathed in the glow of his computer screen. In the eastern United States, it was just hitting 4 a.m., October 26, and the office was quiet.

On Fairfax's screen were two photos of Aloysius Knight: the first was a portrait shot of a clean-shaven young man in US Army dress uniform, smiling. The second was a blurred long-distance shot of Aloysius Knight holding a shotgun in each hand and running hard.

'All right,' Fairfax said, reading. 'His real name is Knight,

Aloysius K. Knight, 33 years old, 6 feet 1 inch tall, 185 pounds. Eyes: brown. Hair: black. Distinguishing features: known to wear amber-tinted anti-flash glasses because of an eye abnormality known as acute retinal dystrophy. It means that his retinas are too sensitive to handle natural light, hence the need for tinted glasses.'

As Fairfax's voice came through his earpiece, Schofield gazed over at Knight, standing over by the Sukhoi with the others, with his two holstered shotguns, his yellow glasses, his all-black fighting uniform.

Fairfax went on: *'Former member of Delta Team 7 which is regarded as the best within Delta, an elite within an elite. Reached the rank of captain, but found guilty of treason against the United States in absentia in 1998 after he betrayed a mission he was leading in Sudan. Intelligence sources say that Knight was paid $2 million by a local Al-Qaeda cell to inform them of an impending US assault on their arms depot. Thirteen Delta operatives died as a result of the forewarning Knight gave.*

'He disappeared after that, but was rediscovered eighteen months later living in Brasilia. A team of six Navy SEAL commandos was sent in to liquidate him. Knight killed them all, then mailed their heads back to the SEAL training facility at Coronado Naval Base in San Diego.

'Now known to be working as a freelance international bounty hunter. Get this. Apparently, insurance companies keep track of these things for kidnap scenarios: he's rated by Carringtons of London as the second-best bounty hunter in the world.'

'Only second? Who's the best?'

'That Demon Larkham guy I told you about before. Wait a second, I'm not finished with Knight yet. ISS believes that in 2000, Knight tracked down and killed twelve Islamic terrorists who'd kidnapped the daughter of Russia's Deputy President, cut off four of her fingers, and demanded a ransom of US$100 million. Knight traced them to a terrorist training camp in the Iranian desert, went

there, razed the whole frigging camp to the ground, grabbed the girl—minus the fingers—and returned her to Moscow without the media getting a whiff of it. In return, it says here, the Russian government gave him . . . wait for it . . . a test-damaged Sukhoi S-37 jet fighter, plus refuelling privileges at any Russian base in the world. Apparently, the plane is known in bounty hunting circles as the Black Raven.'

'*Black Raven*, huh,' Schofield turned to look at the black Sukhoi S-37 standing nearby . . . and saw that Aloysius Knight was walking towards him.

'*I tell you, Scarecrow,*' Fairfax said, '*this is not the kind of guy you want hunting you.*'

'Too late,' Schofield said. 'He's standing right in front of me.'

Schofield and Knight rejoined the others underneath the *Black Raven*.

Book II and Mother came up to Schofield.

'You all right?' Mother asked softly. 'Book told me what happened in Siberia. Excuse my French, Scarecrow, but what the fuck is happening here?'

'It's been a tough morning,' Schofield said, 'and a lot of people have died. Any idea what happened to Gant?'

'The last time I saw her was when those cocksuckers with the green laser sights came rocking in and I was knocked onto that conveyor belt—'

'She was taken,' a voice said from behind Mother.

It was Aloysius Knight.

'Taken by a bounty hunter named Demon Larkham and his men from IG-88.'

'How do you know that?' Book II asked.

'Rufus,' Knight nodded to his partner, the mountainously tall pilot.

With his great bushy beard, Rufus had a wide smiling face and earnest eyes. He hunched slightly, as if trying to diminish his seven-foot height. When he spoke, he spoke quickly and matter-of-factly, report-style.

'After I lowered Aloysius down the air vent,' he said, 'I went to hover over by the back entrance. I dropped a MicroDot aerosol charge onto the turnaround outside the exit tunnel—just like you told me to, Boss. Then I took up a hovering pattern about a mile away—again just like you told me to.

'About five minutes before you all came charging out, a great big Chinook helicopter flanked by a couple of Lynx attack choppers landed on that turnaround. Then two LSVs and a Driftrunner came speeding out of the mine tunnel and shot straight up the ramp of the Chinook and into its belly. Then the Chinook lifted off and headed out over the hills, back toward Afghanistan.'

Schofield said, 'How do you know Gant was with them?'

'I got photos,' Rufus said simply. 'Aloysius told me that if anything unusual happened while he was inside the mine, I was to take photos of it, so I did.'

Schofield assessed Rufus as the big man spoke. For a guy who could manoeuvre a hover-capable Russian fighter with incredible skill—something which required an almost innate knowledge of physics and aerodynamics—his speech seemed oddly formal and direct, as if he took comfort in military formality.

Schofield had seen men like Rufus before: often the most gifted pilots (and soldiers) had great difficulty in social situations. They were so focused on their area of expertise that they often had trouble expressing themselves, or missed conversational nuances like irony and sarcasm. You just had to be patient with them. You also had to make sure their fellow troops were equally patient. Direct but not stupid, there was more to this Rufus than met the eye.

Knight pulled a handheld monitor from the cockpit of the Sukhoi, showed it to Schofield.

On the monitor was a series of digital photos showing three speeding vehicles blasting out of the mine's rear entrance, out onto the turnaround and up the ramp of a waiting Chinook helicopter.

Knight flicked a switch, blowing up several of the photos, zooming in on the lead Light Strike Vehicle.

Knight said, 'See the three white boxes on the passenger seat. Medical transport cases. Three cases: three heads.'

He clicked to another photo, which showed a blurry zoomed-in image of the Driftrunner racing along behind the two LSVs.

'Check out the rear tray on the truck,' Knight said. 'Notice that all of Larkham's guys are dressed in black. One person, however . . . that one . . . the one without the helmet . . . is wearing sand-coloured Marine fatigues.'

And Schofield saw her.

Although the figure was blurred and out-of-focus, he recognised her shape, the fall of her short blonde hair.

It was Gant.

Slumped unconscious in the rear tray of the Driftrunner.

Schofield's blood ran cold.

The greatest bounty hunter in the world had Gant.

More than anything else, Schofield wanted to go after her—

'No. That's exactly what the Demon wants you to do, Captain,' Knight said, reading his thoughts. 'Don't rush into anything. We know where she is. And Larkham won't kill her. He needs her alive if he's going to use her to flush *you* out.'

'How can you be sure of that?'

'Because that's how I'd do it,' Knight said evenly.

Schofield paused, holding Knight's gaze. It was almost like looking in a mirror—Schofield with his silver anti-flash glasses masking his scars, Knight with his yellow-lensed wraparounds covering his defective eyes.

A tattoo on Knight's forearm caught Schofield's eye. It showed an angry bald eagle and the words:

SLEEP WITH ONE EYE OPEN.

Schofield had seen that image before: on posters that had come out soon after September 11. On them, the American eagle said, 'Hey terrorists, sleep with one eye open.'

Underneath Knight's eagle tattoo was another one which simply read: BRANDEIS. Schofield didn't know what that one meant.

He locked eyes with Knight.

'I've heard about you, Mr Knight,' he said. 'Your loyalty isn't exactly something to brag about. You sold out your unit in the Sudan. Why should I think you won't sell me out, too?'

'Don't believe everything you read in the papers,' Knight said, 'or what you read in US Government files.'

'Then you're not going to kill me?'

'Captain, if I was going to kill you, you'd already have a bullet in your brain. No. My job is to keep you alive.'

'Keep me alive?'

Knight said, 'Captain, understand. I am not doing this because I *like* you or because I think that you are in any way *special*. I am being paid to do this, and paid well. The bounty on your head is 18.6 million dollars. Rest assured, I am being paid considerably more than that to make sure that you don't get killed.'

'Okay, then,' Schofield said. 'So who's paying you to keep me alive?'

'I can't say.'

'Yes, you can.'

'I won't say.' Knight's eyes didn't waver.

'But your employer—'

'—is not a subject for discussion,' Knight said.

Schofield chose another tack.

'All right, then, so why is this all happening? What do you know about this bounty hunt?'

Knight shrugged, looked away.

Rufus answered for him. Released from straight reportage, his tone was simple, honest. 'Bounty hunts happen for all kinds of reasons, Captain Schofield. Catch and kill a spy who goes AWOL with a secret in his head. Catch and retrieve a kidnapper who's *been paid* his ransom—mark my words, hell hath no fury like a rich guy who wants payback. Some of those rich assholes prefer to pay us two million dollars so they can catch some kidnapper who took them for one. It ain't often, though, that you get a list worth ten million dollars in total, let alone almost twenty million dollars *per head*.'

'So what do you know about this hunt then?' Schofield asked.

'The ultimate sponsor is unknown,' Rufus said, 'as is the reason for staging it, but the assessor—a banker from AGM-Suisse named Delacroix—is experienced at this sort of thing. We've run into him before. And so long as the assessor is legitimate, most bounty hunters don't care about the reason for a hunt.'

Rufus turned to Knight.

Knight just cocked his head. 'Big hunt. Fifteen targets. All have

to be dead by 12 noon today, New York time. 18.6 meg per head. That's 280 million dollars in total. Whatever the reason for staging this hunt is, it's worth paying over a quarter of a *billion* dollars for.'

'You say that we all have to be dead by 12 noon, New York time?' Schofield said. This was the first he'd heard of the time limit placed on the hunt. He looked at his watch.

It was 2:05 p.m. here in Afghanistan. That made it 4:05 a.m. in New York. Eight hours till crunch time.

He fell silent, thinking.

Then abruptly he looked up.

'Mr Knight, now that you've found me, what are your instructions from here?'

Knight nodded slowly, impressed that Schofield had asked this question.

'My instructions are very clear on this point,' he said. 'From now on, I am to keep you alive.'

'But you haven't been told to keep me imprisoned, have you?'

'No . . .' Knight said. 'I have not. My instructions are to allow you complete freedom of action to go wherever you please—but under my protection.'

And with that a piece of the puzzle fell into place in Schofield's mind.

Whoever was paying Knight to protect him not only wanted Schofield kept alive, that person also wanted Schofield to be active, to do whatever this bounty hunt was designed to stop him doing.

He turned to Knight. 'You said you knew where Gant is. How?'

'The MicroDot aerosol charge that Rufus dropped onto the turnaround area before the Demon's boys got there,' Knight said.

Schofield had heard about MicroDot technology. Apparently, it was the Next Big Thing in nanotechnology.

MicroDots were microscopic silicon chips, each about the size of a pinhead but with enormous computing power. While many believed that MicroDots would be the basis for a new series of liquid-based supercomputers—imagine a liquid ooze filled with supercomputing particles—at the moment they were mainly used

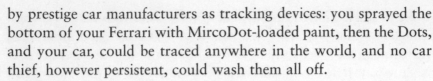

by prestige car manufacturers as tracking devices: you sprayed the bottom of your Ferrari with MircoDot-loaded paint, then the Dots, and your car, could be traced anywhere in the world, and no car thief, however persistent, could wash them all off.

The MicroDot charge that Rufus had detonated on the turn-around area had released an aerosol cloud of about a billion MicroDots over the area.

'The Demon, his men, his vehicles and your girl are all covered in MicroDots,' Knight said. He pulled a jerry-rigged Palm Pilot from his belt. It bristled with home-made attachments and anten-nas, and looked a little chunkier than a regular PDA, as if it were waterproof.

On its screen was a map of the world and superimposed on that map, over Central Asia, was a set of moving red dots.

Demon Larkham's team.

'We can trace them to any point in the world on this,' Knight said.

Schofield started thinking, tried to order his thoughts, to weigh up his options so he could arrange a plan of action.

Then at last he said, 'The first thing we have to do is find out why all this is happening.'

He pulled out the bounty list, analysed it for the hundredth time.

Mother and Book II read it over his shoulder.

'The Mossad,' Mother said softly, seeing one entry:

```
11.   ROSENTHAL, Benjamin Y.          ISR      Mossad
```

'What about it?' Schofield said.

'That Zawahiri guy said something about the Israeli Mossad down in the mine, before he lost his head. He was crazy, shouting about how he'd survived Soviet experiments in some gulag, and then the US cruise-missile attacks in '98, and then about how the Mossad knew he was invincible, since they'd tried to kill him a dozen times.'

'The Mossad . . .' Schofield mused.

He keyed his sat-comm. 'David Fairfax, you still there?'

'*So long as there's coffee around, I'm still here,*' came the reply.

'Mr Fairfax, look up Hassan Mohammad Zawahiri and Benjamin Y. Rosenthal. Any cross-matches?'

'*Just a second,*' Fairfax's voice said. '*Hey, got something already. A match from some US–Israeli intelligence swap. Major Benjamin Yitzak Rosenthal is Hassan Zawahiri's "katsa", or case officer, the guy who monitors him. Rosenthal is based in Haifa, but it seems that only yesterday he was recalled to Mossad's London headquarters.*'

'London?' Schofield said.

A plan was beginning to form in Schofield's mind.

And all of a sudden he started to feel alive.

He'd been on the back foot all morning, *reacting*—now he was getting *proactive*.

'Book, Mother,' he said, 'how would you like to pay Major Rosenthal a visit in London? See if he can shed some light on this situation.'

'Be happy to,' Mother said.

'Sure,' Book II said.

Aloysius Knight watched this exchange casually, uninterested.

'*Oh, hey, Scarecrow,*' Fairfax's voice said, '*I was going to mention this before but I didn't get a chance. You remember that US Army Medical Research and Matériel Command paper I mentioned earlier, the "NATO MNRR Study". Well, that thing is out of my reach from here. It was deprioritised two months ago and deleted from the USAMRMC's files. An archive copy exists in some warehouse in Arizona, but otherwise all other copies have been shredded or deleted.*

'*But I did find something on the two guys who wrote it, those two fellas on your list who worked for Medical Research Command: Nicholson and Oliphant. Nicholson retired a couple of years ago and is now living at some retirement village in Florida. But Oliphant quit USAMRMC only last year. He's now chief physician in the ER at St John's Hospital, Virginia, not far from the Pentagon.*'

'Is that so?' Schofield said. 'Mister Fairfax, would you like to be a field officer for a day?'

'*Anything to get out of this office, man. My boss is the biggest asshole on the planet.*'

'When you get a chance, then, why don't you go down to St John's and have a chat with Doctor Oliphant.'

'*You got it.*' Fairfax signed off.

'What about you?' Mother said to Schofield. 'You're not going to stay with this bounty hunter, are you?' She shot Knight a withering glare. Knight just raised his eyebrows.

'He says I can go wherever I like,' Schofield said. 'It's up to him to protect me.'

'So where are you going?' Book II asked.

Schofield's eyes narrowed. 'I'm going to the source of this bounty hunt. I'm going to that castle in France.'

Book II said, 'What are you going to do? Knock on the front door?'

'No,' Schofield said. 'I'm going to collect a bounty.'

'A bounty?' Mother said. 'I, er, don't mean to be devil's advocate, but don't you need a . . . *head* . . . to collect the reward?'

'That's right,' Schofield said, looking at Knight's modified Palm Pilot, the mini-computer that depicted Demon Larkham's progress. 'And I know just where to get some. And at the same time, I'm going to get Gant back.'

THIRD ATTACK

FRANCE–ENGLAND–USA
26 OCTOBER 1150 HOURS (FRANCE)
E.S.T. (NEW YORK, USA) 0550 HOURS

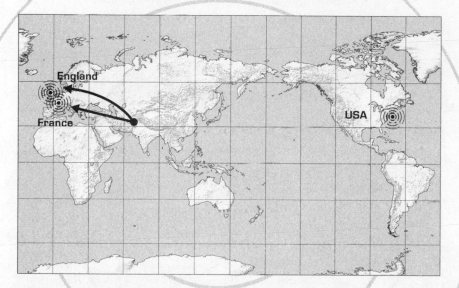

Over the next fifty years the earth's population will soar from 5.5 billion to more than 9 billion . . . 95 percent of the population increase will be in the poorest regions of the world.

From: *The Coming Anarchy* by Robert D. Kaplan

(VINTAGE, NEW YORK, 2001)

The Camp of the Saints, Jean Raspail's 1972 novel about an invasion of France by an armada of destitute Third World people . . . appears to have been prophetic . . . In the 19th century, Europe invaded and colonised Africa. In the 21st century, Africa invades and colonises Europe.

From: *The Death of the West* by Patrick J. Buchanan

(ST MARTIN'S PRESS, NEW YORK, 2002)

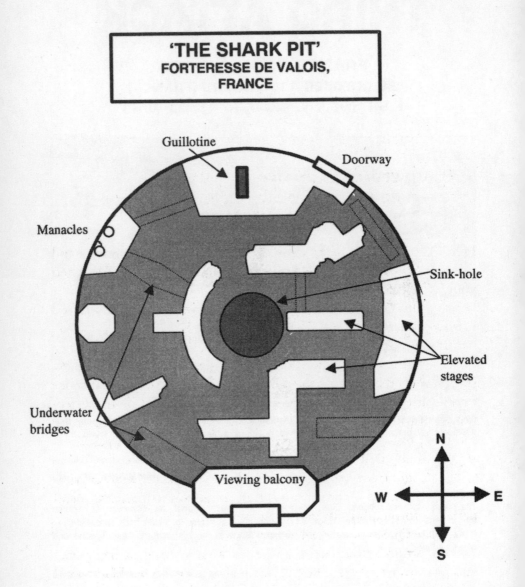

BERLIN, GERMANY
22 OCTOBER, 2300 HOURS

He liked to fuck girls from behind, pumping like a jackhammer and calling out cowboy shouts. And he was an ass man, too. He loved young twenty-somethings with tight little bottoms.

She'd discovered these facts from the prostitutes of Berlin's red light district, whose services he engaged often.

Damien Polanski's career had seen better days.

An Eastern Bloc expert during the Cold War, he was now stationed in the ISS's Berlin field office, growing older and more irrelevant every day. His daring conquests of the '80s—the defection of Karmonov, the discovery of the Soviet 'Cobra' files—long forgotten by an intelligence agency that didn't love you back.

An old dog in a new world.

She caught his eye easily enough. It wasn't hard. She was stunning to look at—long slender legs, muscular shoulders, small perfectly-formed breasts and those cool Eurasian eyes.

The Ice Queen, some called her.

She'd stood at the bar opposite his booth, dropped her purse, and bent over to get it, offering him a clear view up her black-vinyl mini-skirt. No panties.

Within 15 minutes, he was hurriedly taking off his trousers in a hotel room, thinking, *Giddy-up, baby! Giddy-up!*

She emerged from the bathroom wearing nothing at all, her hands hidden behind her back. Polanski's eyes widened with delight. He dived onto the bed, and turned—just as the short-bladed samurai sword that she gripped in her hands sliced clean through his neck.

7.   NAZZAR, Yousef M.   LEBN   HAMAS

BEIRUT, LEBANON
23 OCTOBER, 2100 HOURS

Witnesses would say it was one of the most professional hits they had ever seen in Beirut—which was saying something.

They saw Yousef Nazzar, a senior HAMAS commander known to have been trained by the Soviets, enter the apartment building.

Not a moment later, two sedans skidded to a halt outside the lobby and eight commandos piled out of them, rushed into the building. One of them carried a white box with a red cross on its side.

One thing was common to all the witnesses' accounts: the guns the assassins used. They were either identified or described as VZ-61 Skorpion machine pistols.

And then suddenly the assassins were out and, with a squeal of tyres, were gone.

Yousef Nazzar's body was found later, spreadeagled on the floor of his apartment, the head missing.

8.   NICHOLSON, Francis X.   USA   USAMRMC

CEDAR FALLS RETIREMENT VILLAGE
MIAMI, FLORIDA
24 OCTOBER, 0700 HOURS

The front-desk nurse couldn't have known he was a killer.

When she'd asked, 'Can I help you?' he had replied politely that he was from the hospital, come to collect the personal effects of a recently-transferred resident of Cedar Falls.

He was tall and thin, with deep black skin and a high forehead. More than one witness would describe him as 'African' in appearance. They didn't known that in the global bounty hunting community he was known by a very simple name: 'the Zulu'.

Dressed in a white labcoat, he strode calmly through the home, carrying a white organ-delivery box in his hand.

He found the room quickly, found the old man, Frank Nicholson, lying in his bed asleep.

Without missing a beat, the Zulu drew a machete from under his coat and . . .

The police found his car two hours later, abandoned in the long-term carpark at the airport.

By that time, however, the Zulu was sitting in the first-class section of United Airlines Flight 45 bound for Paris, the white organ-delivery box resting on the seat beside him.

Frank Nicholson was missed at the retirement village. He'd been a popular resident, friendly and outgoing.

The management had liked him too. Since he'd been a doctor in his career days, he'd saved more than one elderly resident who had collapsed on the golf course.

It was funny, though, unlike many others, he'd never really spoken about his glory days.

If asked he would say he'd been a scientist at the US Army Medical Research and Matériel Command at Fort Detrick, 'just doing some medical tests for the armed forces' before he'd retired the previous year.

And then came that night when the assassin had come and cut off his head.

FORTERESSE DE VALOIS
BRITTANY, FRANCE
26 OCTOBER, 1150 HOURS LOCAL TIME
(0550 HOURS E.S.T USA)

He'd always loved anarchy.

Loved the idea of it, the concept of it: the complete and utter loss of control; society without order.

He particularly loved the way people—common people, average people, ordinary people—responded to it.

When soccer stadiums collapsed, they stampeded.

When earthquakes struck, they looted.

During anarchic warfare—Nanjing, My Lai, Stalingrad—they raped and mutilated their fellow human beings.

The teleconference with the other members of the Council wouldn't begin for another ten minutes, which gave Member No. 12 enough time to indulge his passion for anarchy.

His real name was Jonathan Killian.

Jonathan James Killian III, to be precise, and at 37 he was the youngest member of the Council.

Born into wealth—his father had been American, his mother French—he had the supercilious bearing of a man who was accustomed to having everything he desired. He was also possessed of a cold level stare that could give the most combative negotiator pause. It was a powerful gift, one that was accentuated by an

unusual facial feature: Jonathan Killian had one blue eye and one brown.

He was worth $32 billion, and by virtue of a labyrinthine network of companies, was the ultimate owner of the Forteresse de Valois.

Killian had always disliked Member No. 5.

While wealthy beyond measure thanks to an inherited Texan oil empire, No. 5 was of low intellect and prone to tantrums. At 58, he was still essentially a spoilt brat. He had also been a continually stubborn opponent of Killian's ideas in Council meetings. He was very irritating.

Right now, however, Member No. 5 stood in a wide stone dungeon on the lowest level of the Forteresse de Valois, deep within the castle's stone mount, accompanied by his four personal assistants.

The dungeon was called the Shark Pit.

Sixteen feet deep with sheer stone walls, it was perfectly circular; and wide too, about 50 yards across. It was also filled with an irregular array of elevated stone stages. One thing about it was clear: once a person was placed inside it, escape was impossible.

In the pit's centre, plunging vertically down into the earth, was a 10-foot-wide 'sink-hole' that led directly to the ocean.

Right now, the tide was coming in, so the water entering the Pit via the sink-hole was rising fast, spilling out into the wider pit, *filling it*, turning the irregular collection of elevated stages into a series of small stone islands—much to the horror of Member No. 5 and his assistants.

Adding to their fear, two dark shapes could be glimpsed swimming through the alleyways between the islands, just beneath the surface of the water—shapes featuring dorsal fins and bullet-shaped heads.

Two large tiger sharks.

In addition to all this, the Shark Pit came with two other features worth noting.

First, a viewing balcony situated on its southern side. Before the

Revolution, the French aristocracy were known to hold gladiatorial contests in their dungeons—usually pitting peasants against peasants, or in the more elaborate dungeons like the one at the Forteresse de Valois, peasants against animals.

The second noteworthy feature of the Shark Pit could be found on the largest of its elevated stone platforms, over by the northern wall. On this stage sat a truly terrifying device: a 12-foot-high guillotine.

Tall and brutal, the guillotine was an addition made by Jonathan Killian himself. At its base was a crude wooden block with slots carved into it—slots for a person's head and hands. A crank handle on the guillotine's side raised its steeply-angled blade. A simple release lever dropped it.

Killian had been inspired by the acts of Japanese soldiers during the sack of the Chinese city of Nanjing in 1937.

During three horrific weeks, the Japanese had subjected the Chinese to unspeakable torture. Over 360,000 people were murdered *by hand* during that time. Horror stories emerged of Japanese soldiers conducting beheading contests; or worse, giving fathers a choice: rape their own daughters or watch them be raped; or telling sons to have sex with their own mothers or die.

Killian was intrigued. Usually, the Chinese men would take the honourable way out and accept death rather than perform such hideous acts.

But some did not.

And that was what had amused Killian. Just how far people would go in pursuit of self-preservation.

And so he'd had the guillotine inserted into the Shark Pit.

It was designed to give those who were placed in the pit a similar choice.

Die a terrifying death at the mercy of the tiger sharks, or die quickly and painlessly by their own hand on the guillotine.

Sometimes, when he had a group of people in the pit (as he did today), Killian would offer them Faustian bargains: 'Kill your boss on the guillotine, and I will release the rest of you'; 'Kill that hysterical screaming woman, and I will release the rest of you.'

Of course, he never released anyone. But the prisoners never knew that, and on many occasions they themselves died with blood on their hands.

The five people in the pit scratched desperately at the walls, the incoming water rising rapidly around them.

One of No. 5's female assistants made it a few feet up the wall—making for a tiny stone handhold there—but she was quickly pulled down by a bigger man who saw the handhold as his chance at life.

Killian watched them from the southern viewing balcony, utterly fascinated.

One of these people is worth $22 billion, he thought. *The others earn about $65,000 a year in salaries. Yet now they are all truly equal.*

Anarchy, he thought. *The great equaliser.*

Soon the water level rose five feet above the floor—chest height—and the two tiger sharks now roamed the pit more freely in a rush. At first the people cowered on the stone islands, but soon those islands also went sufficiently under the surface.

Five people. Two sharks.

It wasn't pretty.

The sharks rushed the hapless people—ramming them into the water, taking them under, ripping them open. Blood stained the churning waves.

After a male assistant went under in a froth of spraying blood, No. 5's two female assistants killed themselves on the guillotine.

So, too, No. 5 himself.

In the end, rather than face the sharks, he preferred to cut off his own head.

Then abruptly it was over and the rising water enveloped the guillotine stage, washing it clean of evidence, and the sharks gorged themselves on the headless corpses too, and Jonathan Killian III turned on his heel and headed up to his office for the noon tele-conference.

★ ★ ★

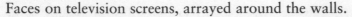

Faces on television screens, arrayed around the walls.

The faces of the other members of the Council, tuning in from around the world.

Killian took his seat.

Five years previously, he had inherited his father's vast shipping and defence-contracting empire—a maze of companies known as the Axon Corporation. Among other things, Axon Corp constructed destroyers and long-range missiles for the US Government.

In each of the first three years after his father's death, Jonathan Killian had increased Axon's annual profits fivefold.

His formal invitation to join the Council had come soon after.

'Member No. 12,' the Chairman said, addressing Killian. 'Where is Member No. 5? He is staying with you, is he not?'

Killian smiled. 'He pulled a muscle in the swimming pool. My personal physician is looking at him now.'

'Is everything in place?'

'Yes,' Killian said. 'The Kormoran ships are in position all around the world, fully armed. DGSE delivered the corpses to America last week and my facility in Norfolk has been liberally stained with their blood—ready for the US inspectors. All systems are in place, merely awaiting the go signal.'

Killian paused. Took the plunge.

'Of course, Mr Chairman,' he added, 'as I've said before, it's not too late to initiate the extra step—'

'Member No. 12,' the Chair said sharply, 'the course of action has been decided upon and we will *not* deviate from it. I'm sorry, but if you raise this "extra step" matter again, penalties will be imposed.'

Killian bowed his head. 'As you wish, Mr Chairman.'

A Council penalty was something to be avoided.

Joseph Kennedy had lost two of his famous sons for disobeying a Council directive to cease doing business with Japan in the '50s.

Charles Lindbergh's infant son was kidnapped and killed, while Lindbergh himself had been forced to endure a smear campaign suggesting he admired Adolf Hitler—all because he had defied a Council edict to *keep* doing business with the Nazis in the 1930s.

More recently, there was the impertinent Enron board. And everyone knew what had happened to Enron.

As the teleconference went on, Jonathan Killian remained silent. On this issue, he felt he knew better than the Council.

The Zimbabwe Experiment—his idea—had more than proved his point. After decades of economic repression at the hands of Europeans, poverty-stricken African majorities no longer cared for the white man's property rights.

And the Hartford Report on global population growth—and Western population *decline*—had only further bolstered his argument.

But now was not the time to argue.

The formal business of the teleconference concluded, and several of the Council members stayed online, chatting among themselves.

Killian just watched them.

One member was saying, 'Just bought the drilling rights for a flat billion. I said take it or leave it. These stupid African governments just don't have a choice . . .'

The Chairman himself was laughing: '. . . I ran into that Mattencourt woman at Spencer's the other night. She certainly is an aggressive little filly. She asked *again* if I would consider her for a seat on the Council. So I said, "What are you worth?" She said, "26 billion." "And your company?" "170 billion." So I say, "Well, that's certainly enough. What do you say, you give me a blow job in the men's room right now and you're in." She stormed off!'

Dinosaurs, Killian thought. *Old men. Old ideas. You'd expect better from the richest businessmen in the world.*

He pressed a button, cutting the signal, and all of the televisions on the walls around him shrank to black.

AIRSPACE ABOVE TURKEY
26 OCTOBER, 1400 HOURS LOCAL TIME
(0600 HOURS E.S.T USA)

The MicroDots that had attached themselves to Demon Larkham's IG-88 team told a peculiar tale.

After leaving the Karpalov coalmine, Larkham's team had flown to a British-controlled airfield in Kunduz—a fact which had immediately rung alarm bells in Schofield's head.

Because it meant that Larkham was working with the tacit approval of the British government on this matter.

Not a good sign, Schofield thought, as he ripped through the sky in the back of Aloysius Knight's *Black Raven*.

So the British knew what was going on . . .

At the airfield in Kunduz, the IG-88 men had divided into two sub-teams, one getting on board an aircraft and heading in the direction of London, the other boarding a second plane and heading for the northwestern coast of France.

The aircraft flying toward London—a sleek Gulfstream IV executive jet—was pulling rapidly away from the second one, a lumbering Royal Air Force C-130J Hercules cargo plane.

Right now, Knight's Sukhoi was paralleling Larkham's planes, flying just beyond the horizon, its stealth features on full power.

'Common tactic for the Demon,' Knight said. 'Dividing his men into a delivery team and a strike team. The Demon takes the strike team to liquidate the next target while his delivery team ferries the heads to the verification venue.'

'Looks like the strike team is going to London,' Schofield said. 'They're going after Rosenthal.'

'Likely,' Knight said. 'What do you want to do?'

Schofield could think of nothing else but Gant, sitting in the belly of the Hercules.

'I want that plane,' he said.

Knight punched some keys on his computer console.

'All right, I'm accessing their flight data computer. That Hercules is scheduled for a mid-air refuelling over western Turkey in ninety minutes.'

'Where's the tanker plane taking off from?' Schofield asked.

'A VC-10 aerial tanker is scheduled for lift-off from the Brits' Akrotiri air force base on Cyprus in exactly forty-five minutes.'

'Okay,' Schofield said. 'Book and Mother, Rufus here will take you to London. Find Benjamin Rosenthal before Larkham's strike team does.'

'What about you?' Mother asked.

'Captain Knight and I are getting off in Cyprus.'

Forty-five minutes later, a British Vickers VC-10 air-to-air refuelling tanker lifted off from its island runway on Cyprus.

Unbeknownst to the plane's four-man crew, it contained two stowaways in its rear cargo bay—Shane Schofield and Aloysius Knight—whom Rufus had dropped off, under the curtain of active stealth, in the shallows three miles away.

For their part, Rufus, Mother and Book II had powered off immediately in the *Black Raven*, cutting a beeline for London.

Soon the VC-10 was zooming through Turkish airspace, pulling alongside the RAF Hercules coming from Afghanistan.

The tanker moved in front of the Hercules, rose a little above it. Then it extended a long swooping fuel hose—or 'boom'—from its rear-end. The boom was about 70 metres long and at its tip was a circular steel 'drogue', which would ultimately attach itself to the receiving aircraft.

Controlled by a lone operator, or 'boomer', lying on his stomach in a glassed-in compartment at the rear of the tanker plane, the boom angled in toward the receiving probe of the Hercules.

The Hercules' receiving probe—essentially, it was just a horizontal pipe—was located just above the cargo plane's cockpit windows.

The aerial ballet went perfectly.

The tanker's boom operator extended the boom, manoeuvred it into place, just as below and behind it the Hercules flew forward and—*kerchunk*—the Hercules' receiving probe locked into the drogue at the end of the boom and fuel started pumping between the two moving planes.

While this was happening, Knight started loading his H&K pistol with some odd-looking 9mm rounds. Each bullet had an orange band painted around it.

'Bull stoppers,' he said to Schofield. 'Every Delta man's best friend. Gas-expanding nine-millimetre rounds. Better than hollow points. They enter the target and then blow big.'

'How big?'

'Big enough to cut a man in half. Want some?'

'No thanks.'

'Here, then,' Knight placed some of the orange bullets in a pocket on Schofield's combat webbing. 'For when you reconsider.'

Schofield nodded at Knight's utility vest, at the peculiar array of devices hanging from it—the Pony Bottle, the mini blowtorch, the mountaineering pitons. There was even a very small pouch-like rollbag which Schofield recognised.

'Is that a *body bag*?' he asked.

'Yeah. A Markov Type-III,' Knight said. 'Gotta hand it to the Soviets. Nobody ever built a better one.'

Schofield nodded. The Markov Type-III was a chemical body bag. With its double-strength ziplock and poly-coated nylon walls, it could safely hold a body infected with the worst kind of

contamination: plague, chem weapons, even superheated radio-active waste. The Russians had used a lot of them at Chernobyl.

It was the pitons, however, that intrigued Schofield the most. He could understand a bounty hunter carrying a portable body bag with him, but pitons?

Pitons are small springloaded scissor-like devices that mountain climbers jam into tiny crevices. The piton springs open with such force—pinioning itself against the walls of a crevice—that climbers can attach ropes to it and hold up their bodyweight. Schofield wondered what a bounty hunter might use them for.

'Question,' he said. 'What do you use pitons for?'

Knight shrugged casually. 'Climb over walls. Up the sides of buildings.'

'Anything else?' Schofield asked. *Like torture, perhaps.*

Knight held Schofield's gaze. 'They do have . . . other uses.'

When the refuelling was almost complete, Schofield and Knight sprang.

'You take the boomer,' Knight said, drawing a second 9mm pistol. 'I'll take the cockpit crew.'

'Right,' Schofield said, before adding quickly: 'Knight. You can do whatever you want on the Hercules, but how about using non-lethal force here.'

'What? Why?'

'This crew didn't do anything.'

Knight scowled. 'Oh, all right . . .'

'Thanks.'

And they moved.

With its fifteen wraparound cockpit windows, the C-130 cargo plane provided its pilots with exceptional visibility, and right now the two pilots of the British Hercules could see the bird-like rear-end of the VC-10 high above them, the long swooping fuel hose

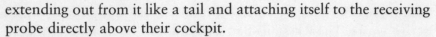

extending out from it like a tail and attaching itself to the receiving probe directly above their cockpit.

They'd done this sort of mid-air refuelling a hundred times before. Once the two planes were connected, the pilots had switched over to automatic pilot and become more concerned with observing the fuel pumping stats than with watching the amazing view outside.

Which was probably why they didn't notice when—twenty-two minutes into the refuelling—a lone black-clad figure came *whizzing* down the length of the fuel hose like a death-defying stuntman and their cockpit windows exploded under his withering assault of gunfire.

The sight was truly spectacular.

Two gigantic planes flying in tandem at 20,000 feet, connected tail-to-nose by the long swooping fuel hose . . .

. . . with a tiny man-shaped figure sliding down the hose as if it were a zipline, hanging onto a makeshift flying-fox one-handed, an H&K pistol held in his free hand, firing at the cockpit of the Hercules plane!

The two pilots of the Hercules went down in a hail of smashing glass.

Wind rushed into the cockpit. But the plane, under automatic pilot, remained steady.

For his part, Aloysius Knight slid down the fuel hose at incredible speed, hanging onto a seatbelt that he had lashed over the hose—his face covered in a high-altitude breathing mask, an ultra-compact MC-4/7 attack parachute strapped to his back.

Since the Hercules' receiving probe was situated directly above its cockpit, Knight's slide ended with him blasting *right through* the shattered glass windows of the Hercules and landing inside its wind-assaulted cockpit.

He keyed his radio mike. 'All right, Scarecrow! Come on down!'

A few seconds later, a second figure—also wearing a breathing mask and a small attack parachute—swung down from the tanker plane, shooting down the length of the fuel hose before disappearing inside the shattered windows of the Hercules.

★ ★ ★

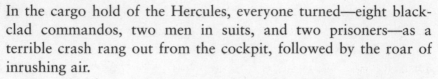

In the cargo hold of the Hercules, everyone turned—eight black-clad commandos, two men in suits, and two prisoners—as a terrible crash rang out from the cockpit, followed by the roar of inrushing air.

The eight commandos were members of the IG-88 delivery team. The two men in suits had no names that anyone knew but they did possess MI-6 identity badges: British Intelligence.

And the two prisoners were Lieutenant Elizabeth 'Fox' Gant and General Ronson H. Weitzman, both from the United States Marine Corps, both captured by the Demon's forces in Afghanistan.

Just before the mid-air attack had commenced, Gant had regained consciousness—to find herself seated in the wide cargo hold of the Hercules, her hands flex-cuffed behind her back.

A few feet away from her, Ronson Weitzman—one of the most senior officers in the entire US Marine Corps—lay spreadeagled on his back, on the bonnet of a Humvee parked in the cargo bay, tied down, his arms stretched wide as if he had been crucified horizontally, his wrists attached by two separate pairs of handcuffs to both of the Humvee's side mirrors.

The right sleeve of Weitzman's uniform had been torn off and a rubber tourniquet was tied tightly around his exposed arm.

Flanking the General were the two MI-6 men. Gant had awoken just as the shorter one had been removing a hypodermic needle from Weitzman's arm.

'Give it a couple of minutes,' the short one had said.

The General had raised his head, his eyes glazed.

'Hello, General Weitzman,' the taller intelligence officer smiled. 'The drug you are feeling right now is known as EA-617. I'm sure a man of your rank has heard of it. It's a neural disinhibitor—a drug that retards the release of the neurotransmitter "GABA" in your brain—a drug that will make answering our questions truthfully just that little bit easier.'

'Wha—?' Weitzman looked at his arm. '. . . 617? No . . .'

Watching the scene from a discreet distance were the members of the IG-88 bounty hunting team—led by the tall and strikingly

handsome soldier Gant had seen in the caves in Afghanistan. She had heard the other IG-88 men calling him 'Cowboy'.

'All right, General,' the tall MI-6 man said. 'The Universal Disarm Code. What is it?'

Weitzman frowned, squinting hard, as if his brain was trying to resist the truth drug.

'I . . . I don't know of any such code,' he said unconvincingly.

'Yes you do, General. The United States Universal Disarm Code. The code that overrides any and every security system in the US armed services. You oversaw its entry into a secret US military project called the "Kormoran Project". We know about Kormoran, General. But we don't know the code, and the code is what we want. What is it?'

Gant was completely shocked.

She'd heard rumours about the Universal Disarm Code. It was the stuff of legend: a numerical code that overrode *every* US military security system.

Weitzman blinked, fighting the drug. 'It . . . it doesn't . . . exist . . .'

'No, General,' the tall man said. 'It does exist, and you are one of five people in the US military establishment who know it. Maybe I will have to increase the dosage here.'

The tall man pulled out another syringe, inserted it into Weitzman's exposed arm.

Weitzman groaned, '*No* . . .'

The EA-617 serum went into his arm.

And that was when the cockpit windows had exploded under Knight's hailstorm of gunfire.

Schofield dropped into the cockpit of the Hercules, landed next to Knight.

'*Now* can I use lethal force?' Knight shouted.

'Be my guest!'

Knight pointed to a TV monitor on the cockpit dashboard—it showed a high-angle view of the Hercules' rear cargo hold.

Schofield saw about a dozen large wooden crates near the cockpit steps, one Humvee with Weitzman crucified on the bonnet, eight bad guys in black combat uniforms, two bad guys in suits and on the floor, up against the wall of the cargo hold, on the left-hand side of the Humvee, her hands cuffed behind her back . . .

. . . Libby Gant.

'Too many to take out with guns,' Schofield said.

'I know,' Knight said. 'So we take guns out of the equation.'

He pulled two small grenades from his combat webbing—small hand-held charges painted pale yellow.

'What are—?' Schofield asked.

'British AC-2 charges. Adhesive-chaff grenades.'

'Anti-firearm charges,' Schofield said, nodding. 'Nice.'

The British SAS, experts in counter-terrorist ops, had developed the AC-2 for operations against armed hostage takers. They were basically standard flash-bang grenades, but with one very special extra feature.

'You ready? Just remember, you get one shot before your gun jams,' Knight said. 'Okay, let's rock this joint.'

At which point, he cracked open the cockpit door and hurled his two AC-2 charges into the cargo hold beyond it.

★ ★ ★

The two pale yellow grenades flew into the hold, skipping across the tops of the wooden cargo crates before landing on the floor beside the Humvee and—

—*flash-bang!*

The standard explosion came first: blinding white flashes of light followed by ear-crashing bangs, designed to deafen and disorient.

And then came the AC-2 grenades' extra feature.

As they exploded, the two grenades sent brilliant starbursts of tiny white-grey particles shooting out in every direction, completely *filling* the enclosed space of the cargo bay.

The particles looked like confetti, and after they dispersed, they floated in the air, infinitesimally small, forming a white-grey veil over the scene, making it look like a snowglobe that had just been shaken.

Only this wasn't confetti.

It was a special form of adhesive chaff—a sticky stringy compound that stuck to *everything*.

The cockpit door burst open, and Knight and Schofield charged into the cargo hold.

The nearest IG-88 commando reached for his rifle, but received an arrow-bolt in his forehead—care of the mini-crossbow attached to Knight's right forearm guard.

A second-nearest man also spun quickly, and—*shlip!*—received an arrow from Knight's *left*-arm crossbow square in the eye.

It was the third IG-88 commando who actually managed to pull the trigger on his Colt Commando assault rifle.

The machine-gun fired—once. One bullet only. Then it jammed.

It had been 'chaffed'. The sticky adhesive chaff of Knight's grenades had got into its barrel, its receiver, all its moving parts, rendering it useless.

Schofield nailed the man with the butt of his Maghook.

But the other IG-88 men learned quickly, and within seconds, two Warlock hunting knives slammed into the wooden cargo crates beside them.

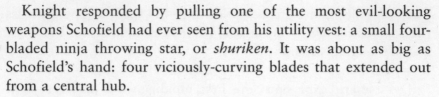

Knight responded by pulling one of the most evil-looking weapons Schofield had ever seen from his utility vest: a small four-bladed ninja throwing star, or *shuriken*. It was about as big as Schofield's hand: four viciously-curving blades that extended out from a central hub.

Knight threw the shuriken expertly, side-handed, and it sliced laterally through the air, whistling, before—*shnick! shnick!*—it cut the throats of *two* IG-88 commandos standing side-by-side.

Five down, Schofield thought, *three to go, plus the two guys in suits . . .*

And then suddenly a hand grabbed him—

—a *stunningly* strong grip—

—and Schofield was hurled back toward the cockpit doorway.

He hit the floor hard, and looked up to see an enormous IG-88 trooper stalking toward him. The IG-88 man was huge: at least six feet nine, black-skinned, with bulging biceps and a face that bristled with unadulterated *fury*.

'Wot *the fuck* d'you fink you're doin'?' the giant black man said.

But Schofield was already moving again—he quickly jumped to his feet and unleashed a thunderous blow with his Maghook's butt at the black trooper's jaw.

The blow hit home.

And the big man didn't even flinch.

'Uh-oh,' Schofield said.

The giant black trooper punched Schofield, sending him flying back into the wind-blasted cockpit like a rag doll. Schofield slammed into the dashboard.

Then the big black trooper picked him up easily and said, 'You came in froo that window. You go out froo that window.'

And without so much as a blink, the gigantic trooper hurled Shane Schofield out through the broken cockpit windows of the Hercules and into the clear open sky.

In the particle-filled cargo hold, Aloysius Knight—charging forward, hurling throwing stars—spun around to check on Schofield . . .

. . . just in time to see him get thrown out through the cockpit windows.

'Holy shit,' Knight breathed. Like himself, Schofield was wearing a parachute, so he'd be okay, but his sudden disappearance didn't help the mathematics of this fight at all.

Knight keyed his radio mike. 'Schofield! You okay?'

A wind-blasted voice replied: '*I'm not gone yet!*'

Seen from the outside, the Hercules was still cruising steadily at 20,000 feet, still behind and below the VC-10 tanker plane . . . only now it was possessed of a tiny figure hanging off its nose cone.

Schofield clung to the bow of the speeding Hercules, his body assaulted by the speeding wind, 20,000 feet above the world but thanks to his Maghook, now magnetically affixed to the nose of the cargo plane.

His big black attacker—the man's IG-88 nickname was, appropriately, 'Rocko'—stood peering out the cockpit windows above him.

Then Rocko ducked inside and suddenly reappeared with a Colt .45 pistol which had been kept in the cockpit and as such had been unaffected by Knight's chaff grenades.

'Whoa, shit!' Schofield yelled as the first shot went flying over his head.

He'd been hoping that Rocko would just assume he'd fallen to his death and then head back inside the plane, giving Schofield a chance to climb back in through the cockpit windows.

But not now . . .

And so Schofield did the only thing he *could* do.

He unclipped Gant's Maghook from his belt, and now moving downward with *two* Maghooks, affixed it to the hull of the Hercules below him—*clunk!*—and swung down *below* the nose-cone of the massive plane, out of the line of Rocko's fire, so that he was now hanging from the underbelly of the cargo plane, 20,000 feet above the earth.

He spoke into his voice-activated throat-mike.

'Knight! I'm still in the game! I just need you to open an external door for me!'

Inside the cargo bay, Knight ducked a flying knife and threw one of his shurikens into the chest of one of the suit-wearing bad guys.

He heard Schofield's call, saw the big red control button that opened the Hercules' cargo ramp, hurled a shuriken at it.

Thwack!

The multi-bladed throwing knife hit the button, pinned it to its console and with a low *vmmmmm*, the rear cargo ramp of the Hercules began to open.

'*All right, Captain! The cargo ramp is open!*' Knight's voice said in Schofield's earpiece.

Schofield moved as quickly as he could along the underbelly of the Hercules, manoeuvring the two Maghooks above him, alternately magnetising and demagnetising them, and then swinging from them like a kid on a jungle gym, making his way along the 60-foot length of the cargo plane's belly, toward its now-open rear ramp.

★ ★ ★

Wind blasted into the cargo bay, rushing in through the plane's open rear loading ramp, sending the chaff particles suspended in the air whizzing into swirls. An indoor blizzard.

Inside the cargo hold, Knight slid to Gant's side.

'I'm here to help you,' he said quickly, bringing his knife toward her flex-cuffs—

—just as two great black hands grabbed him and yanked him backwards.

Rocko.

The big IG-88 trooper banged Knight against the side of the Humvee. Knight's knife flew from his grip.

The IG-88 leader, Cowboy, stepped out from his cover position on the right side of the Humvee.

'His glasses!' he called.

Rocko let fly with a savage punch that cracked the bridge of Knight's yellow-tinted glasses, and also broke his nose. The cracked glasses fell from his face, exposing his eyes to the light.

'Ahh!' Knight squeezed his eyes shut.

Another crunching blow from Rocko knocked the wind out of him.

'Put him in front of the car,' Cowboy said, unclasping the Humvee's flight restraints before jumping behind the wheel. 'Knees in front of the tyres.'

Rocko did as he was told—lay the limp Knight in the path of the Humvee's tyres and stepped out of the way.

Cowboy fired up the engine, thrust the Humvee into gear, jammed down on the gas pedal.

The Humvee rushed forward, heading *straight for* Aloysius Knight's kneecaps.

And Cowboy felt a small satisfying bump as the big jeep ran over the bounty hunter and slammed into the side of a cargo crate.

'Damn it! Fuck!' Rocko yelled.

'What?' Cowboy called.

'The other one is back!'

None of the British men had seen Schofield re-enter the Hercules.

Not Cowboy or Rocko or the only other remaining bad guy in the hold—the surviving suited man from British Intelligence.

Hadn't seen him climb up into the hold behind the Humvee, via the rear cargo ramp, clutching onto his Maghooks.

Nor had they seen him slink down the right side of the Humvee and race across in front of it, tackling Aloysius Knight out of the way . . . while at the same time dragging the other remaining IG-88 commando to the ground in front of the speeding vehicle, causing it to bump over him instead.

Schofield and Knight fell against the side wall of the hold, right next to Gant.

Knight clutched his eyes. Schofield didn't even stop for breath.

He sliced open Gant's flex-cuffs, gave her the knife. 'Hey there, babe. Missed you in Afghanistan. Quickly, help me free the General.'

General Weitzman was still spreadeagled on the bonnet of the Humvee, his wrists handcuffed to the car's mirrors.

Gant scooped up a set of keys from the run-over IG-88 man, found a handcuff key.

In the meantime, Schofield rose, just as beside him Cowboy emerged from the driver's door of the Humvee—while at the *forward* end of the vehicle, Schofield saw the British Intelligence guy remove a knife embedded in a wooden crate.

A bad guy sandwich.

Schofield extended his arms in both directions, raising his two Maghooks simultaneously. In the chaff-filled environment of the cargo hold, he'd only get one shot from each.

He fired.

The first shot didn't hit Cowboy—but it wasn't meant to. Rather, it hit the car door that Cowboy had been opening. From such close range, the Maghook thundered into the armoured door, banging it shut, knocking Cowboy back into the car.

The suit-wearing Intelligence man was hit square in the chest by the other Maghook. He just folded in half, his ribs cracked, and went crashing back into the crate behind him.

For her part, Gant was busy unlocking General Weitzman's left hand. The cuff around his wrist came free.

'Okay,' she said. 'Other wrist. Other side . . .'

But on the other side of the Humvee stood . . .

Rocko.

Just standing there. Towering above Weitzman's prone body.

Schofield appeared at Gant's side, locked eyes with Rocko.

'Take care of the General,' he said, not taking his eyes off the gigantic commando. 'And get ready for my signal.'

'What signal?'

But Schofield didn't answer her. He just crouched down and withdrew two of Knight's evil-looking shurikens from a dead body. Across the Humvee from him, Rocko did the same.

Then the two of them strode around to the area of open space behind the Humvee, a small space which adjoined the rear loading ramp and looked out over the wide blue sky beyond it.

They stood opposite each other for a moment—the tall and bulky Rocko, and the smaller, more evenly proportioned Schofield—each holding two four-pointed throwing blades in his hands.

And they engaged.

Flashes of silver, the clang of clashing knives.

Rocko lunged, Schofield fended. Rocko lashed, Schofield parried.

As Schofield and Rocko fought at the aft end of the cargo hold, Gant unclasped Weitzman's right handcuff, freeing the General but leaving the open cuff still attached to the side mirror. She slid Weitzman off the Humvee, rolled him to the floor.

All while the General mumbled incoherently: 'Oh, God, the code . . . the universal code . . . all right, all right, it does exist, but only a few people know it . . . It's based on a mathematical principle . . . and yes, I inserted it into Kormoran, but there was . . . there was another project involved . . . Chameleon . . .'

Schofield and Rocko danced around the back of the cargo hold, their shurikens flashing and clanging.

They came down the right-hand side of the Humvee—towards Gant and Weitzman—Schofield leading the way, moving backwards, fending off Rocko's slashes.

'Gant!' Schofield called. 'You ready for the signal!'

'Sure! What is it!'

'This!'

And then, brilliantly, Schofield *caught* Rocko's next swing, and with lightning speed, he shifted his weight and slammed Rocko's knife-hand down into the bonnet of the Humvee, *right next to* the open handcuff that only moments before had bound Weitzman.

'Now!'

Gant responded instantly, dived up onto the bonnet of the Humvee and clasped the cuff around Rocko's knife-wrist.

Rocko's eyes boggled.

He was now shackled to the side mirror of the Humvee!

Schofield dived away from him, over toward General Weitzman on the floor.

'Sir! Are you okay?' he asked quickly, leaning close.

But the General was still babbling. 'Oh, no . . . it wasn't just Kormoran. It was Chameleon, too . . . oh God, Kormoran and Chameleon together. Boats and missiles. All disguised. *Christ* . . . But the Universal Disarm Code, it changes every week. At the moment, it's . . . the sixth . . . oh my God, the sixth m . . . m . . . mercen . . . mercen—'

A sudden whoosh. The flash of steel. And abruptly the General's head jolted slightly, a line of red appearing across his neck . . .

. . . and then, right in front of Schofield's eyes, General Ronson H. Weitzman's head tipped off his shoulders.

The head bounced on the floor, rolled to a stop at Schofield's feet. After beheading, the human head actually lives for up to 30 seconds. As such, Weitzman's disembodied face stared gruesomely up at Schofield from the floor, eyelids fluttering for a few moments before, mercifully, the facial muscles at last relaxed and the head went still.

Schofield snapped to look up, and saw Demon Larkham's handsome young deputy, Cowboy, standing on the other side of the Humvee, brandishing a long-bladed machete, fresh blood dripping from its blade.

His eyes were wide with bloodthirsty madness, and he made to hurl the machete at Schofield—

—just as a hand gripped his wrist from behind and slammed it down on the bonnet of the Humvee, causing the machete to spring out of Cowboy's grasp, at the same time as this unseen assailant quickly snapped the Humvee's *other* handcuff around Cowboy's now-exposed wrist.

Cowboy spun: to see Aloysius Knight standing behind him, now wearing a new pair of amber-lensed glasses.

'Not bad, Cowboy. You remembered my Achilles heel.'

Then Knight grabbed the machete and smiled at the IG-88 assassin. 'And I remember yours. Your inability to fly.'

Knight then walked to the driver's door of the Humvee, leaned inside and shifted the car into reverse. He nodded to Schofield and Gant: 'Stand clear.'

Cowboy and Rocko—cuffed to opposite sides of the Humvee— stared at Knight in horror.

'Goodbye, boys.'

And with that, Knight stabbed the Humvee's gas pedal to the floor with the machete.

The Humvee shot off the mark, racing backwards, toward the open rear cargo ramp.

It hit the edge doing twenty, before it tipped off it, rear-end first, and to Cowboy and Rocko's absolute terror, dropped out of sight and fell 20,000 feet straight down.

After the Humvee had disappeared out the back door of the Hercules, Schofield rushed over to Gant and held her tightly in his arms.

Gant returned his grip, her eyes closed. Others might have cried at such a reunion, but not Gant. She felt the emotion of the moment, but she was not one to shed tears.

'What the hell is going on?' she asked when they separated.

'Bounty hunters,' Schofield said. 'My name is on a list of people who have to be exterminated by noon today, New York time. They grabbed you to get to me.'

He told Gant about his experience in Siberia and then in Afghanistan, about the bounty hunters he had met—Executive Solutions, the Hungarian, the Spetsnaz Skorpions, and of course, Demon Larkham's IG-88. He also showed her the bounty list.

'What about him?' Gant nodded at Knight as he disappeared inside the cockpit to disengage their plane from the tanker. 'Who is he?'

'He,' Schofield said, 'is my guardian angel.'

There came a pained groan from over by the wooden crates.

Schofield and Gant spun quickly . . .

. . . and saw one of the suit-wearing British agents lying on the floor, clutching his broken ribs. It was the man Schofield had hit in the chest with his Maghook.

They went over to him.

The suited man was wheezing desperately, coughing blood.

Schofield bent down, examined him. 'His ribs are smashed. Punctured lungs. Who is he?'

Gant said, 'I only caught part of it. He and the other suit were interrogating the General with some disinhibiting drug, asking him about the American Universal Disarm Code. They said Weitzman oversaw the code's incorporation into something called the Kormoran Project.'

'Is that so?' Schofield said. 'A disinhibiting drug.' He looked around the hold, saw a medical kit on the floor. It had spilled out some syringes, needles and serum bottles. He grabbed one of the serum bottles, checked its label.

'Then let's see how he handles a dose of his own medicine.'

Aloysius Knight returned from the cockpit to find the suit-wearing British agent seated up against the wall of the cargo hold, his sleeve rolled up, and with 200 mg of EA-617 coursing through his veins.

Knight touched Schofield on the shoulder.

'I've disengaged us from the tanker plane,' he said. 'We're currently on autopilot, staying on the course they already set: heading for a private airstrip in Brittany, on the French Atlantic coast. And Rufus just called. He's going to drop your people at an abandoned airfield about forty miles outside of London.'

'Good,' Schofield said, thinking of Book II and Mother heading for the Mossad's headquarters in London.

Then he turned his attention to the captured British agent.

After a few vain efforts to resist the disinhibiting drug, it soon emerged that the man's name was Charles Beaton and he was a member of MI-6, British Intelligence.

'This bounty hunt. What do you know about it?' Schofield asked.

'Nearly twenty million per head. Fifteen heads. And they want you all out of the picture by 12 noon today, New York time.'

'Who are *they*? Who's paying for all this?'

Beaton snorted derisively. '*They* go by many names. The

Bilderberg Group. The Brussels Group. The Star Council. The Majestic-12. M-12. They are an elite group of private industrialists who rule this planet. Twelve of them. The richest men in the world, men who *own* governments, men who bring down entire economies, men who do whatever they want . . .'

Schofield leaned back, his eyes widening.

'O-*kay* . . .' Knight said drily.

'Give me names,' Schofield said.

'I don't know their names,' Beaton said. 'That's not my area. My area is the American military. All I know is that Majestic-12 exists and that it's bankrolling this bounty hunt.'

'All right, then. Do you know what they hope to achieve by staging this hunt?'

'No,' Beaton said. 'My job was to get the Universal Disarm Code from Weitzman and then give him to the bounty hunter, Larkham. To take advantage of this bounty hunt. I don't know about the hunt itself or Majestic-12's reasons for staging it.'

'So who at MI-6 does know?'

'Alec Christie. He's our man on the inside. He knows everything about Majestic-12 and presumably, this bounty hunt. But the problem is MI-6 doesn't know where Christie is anymore. He disappeared two days ago.'

Christie.

Schofield remembered the name from the list:

```
2.   CHRISTIE, Alec P.            UK      MI-6
```

'But this Christie guy must have blown his cover,' he said, 'because Majestic-12 put him on the list as well.'

He tried a new angle. 'What are these Kormoran and Chameleon Projects that you were interrogating Weitzman about?'

Beaton winced, still trying to resist the drug. 'Kormoran is a US Navy project. Deep black. In World War II, the German Navy disguised some of their strike vessels as commercial freighters. One of these was called the *Kormoran*. We believe that the US Navy is doing the same thing but on a modern scale: building warships capable of launching intercontinental ballistic missiles, only these warships don't look like warships. They're disguised as super-tankers and container ships.'

'Whoa,' Gant whispered.

'Okay. That's Kormoran,' Schofield said. 'What about the Chameleon Project?'

'I don't know about Chameleon.'

'You sure?'

Beaton groaned. 'We know it's linked to Kormoran, and we know it's big—it has the highest US security classification. But at this stage, we don't know exactly what Chameleon entails.'

Schofield frowned, thinking.

This was like building a jigsaw puzzle, piece by piece, until slowly a picture emerged. He had some pieces, but not the whole picture. Yet.

He said, 'So who does know, Mr Beaton? Where has MI-6 been getting all this top secret US information from?'

'The Mossad,' Beaton breathed. 'They have a field office in London at Canary Wharf. We managed to bug it for a few weeks last month. Trust me, the Mossad knows *everything*. They know about Majestic-12. They know about Kormoran and Chameleon. They know about every name on that list and why they are on it. They also know one other thing.'

'What's that?' Schofield said.

'The Mossad knows Majestic-12's plan for October the 26th.'

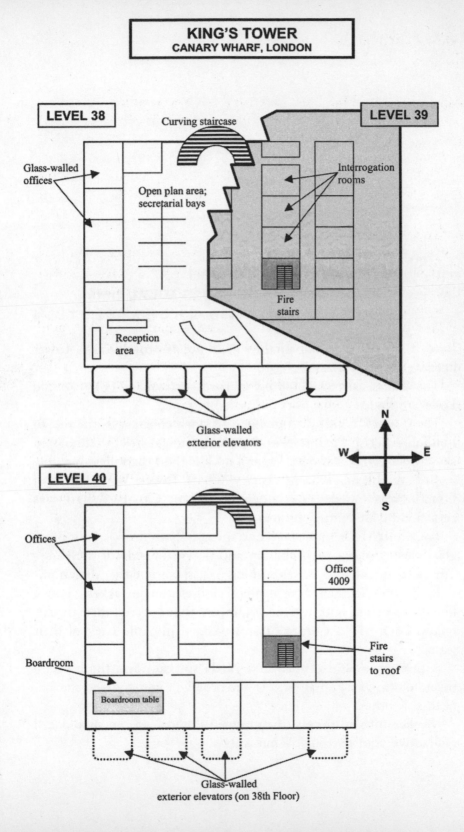

**KING'S TOWER,
CANARY WHARF, LONDON
26 OCTOBER, 1200 HOURS LOCAL TIME
(1300 HOURS IN FRANCE—0700 HOURS E.S.T USA)**

Book II and Mother rode up the side of the 40-storey King's Tower inside a speeding glass elevator.

The Thames stretched out before them, brown and twisting. Old London receded to the horizon, veiled in rain.

The Canary Wharf district stood in stark contrast to the rest of London—a crisp clean steel-and-glass business district that boasted skyscrapers, manicured parks, and no less than the tallest building in Britain: the magnificent Canary Wharf Tower. While much of London was faded 19th-century Victorian, Canary Wharf was crystal-cut 21st-century futurism.

Book and Mother rose high into the grey London sky. Four other glass elevators ferried people up and down the side of the King's Tower, identical glass boxes rushing past them in either direction.

Book and Mother wore civilian clothes: suede jackets, boots, blue-denim jeans and turtleneck jumpers that covered their throat-mikes. Each had a Colt .45 pistol wedged into the back of their jeans.

A pretty young executive in a Prada suit stood in the lift with them, looking very small next to the broad-shouldered and shaven-headed Mother.

Mother inhaled deeply, then tapped the girl on the shoulder. 'I really love your perfume. What is it?'

'Issey Miyake,' the girl replied.

'I'll have to get some,' Mother smiled.

They'd made good time.

After entering British airspace under active stealth, Rufus had dropped them off at an abandoned airfield not far from London City Airport. From there they'd hitched a ride on a charter helicopter, piloted by an old friend of Rufus's. He'd dropped them at Canary Wharf's commercial heliport 15 minutes later.

Ping.

Their elevator stopped on the 38th floor. Book II and Mother stepped out into the enormous reception area for Goldman, Marcus & Meyer, Lawyers. Goldman Marcus occupied the top three floors of the tower—the 38th, 39th and 40th floors.

It *looked* like the reception area of a big city law firm—plush, spacious, great view. And indeed to the casual visitor Goldman Marcus was a full-service legal provider.

Only this wasn't just a law firm.

In amongst its many offices, meeting rooms and open-plan areas, Goldman Marcus's offices contained three rooms on the 39th floor that all the lawyers were forbidden to enter—rooms that were kept for the sole and exclusive use of the Mossad, the notorious Israeli Secret Service.

The Mossad.

The most ruthless intelligence service in the world, protecting the most targeted nation in history: Israel.

No other nation has experienced such a continued threat of terrorism. No other nation has been surrounded by so many openly hostile enemies—Syria, Egypt, Jordan, Lebanon, not to mention the Palestinians inside its borders. No other nation has seen eleven of its Olympic athletes killed on international television.

So how has Israel dealt with this?

Easy. It finds out about foreign threats first.

The Mossad has people everywhere. It knows about international upheaval before anyone else does, and it acts according to an immovable policy of 'Israel First, Last, Always'.

1960. The kidnap of the Nazi war criminal Adolf Eichmann in Argentina.

1967. The pre-emptive strikes on Egyptian air bases during the Six Day War.

August 31, 1997. There had been a Mossad agent in the bar at the Ritz Hotel in Paris on the night Princess Diana died. He had been shadowing Henri Paul, Diana's driver.

It has even been said that the Mossad knew about the September 11 attacks on America before they happened—and *didn't* tell the Americans. Because it suited Israel to have the US enter the war on Islamist terrorism.

In global intelligence communities, there is one golden rule: the Mossad always knows.

'May I help you?' the receptionist's smile was polite.

'Yes,' Book II said. 'We'd like to speak to Benjamin Rosenthal, please.'

'I'm afraid there is no-one here by that name.'

Book II didn't miss a beat. 'Then please call the Chairman of Partners and tell him that Sergeants Riley and Newman are here to see Major Rosenthal. Tell him we're here on behalf of Captain Shane Schofield of the United States Marines Corps.'

'I'm terribly sorry, sir, but—'

At that moment, as if by magic, the receptionist's phone rang and after a short whispered phone call, she said to Book: 'The Chairman is sending someone down to collect you.'

One minute later an internal door opened and a burly man in a suit appeared. Book and Mother both registered the Uzi-sized bulge under his jacket—

Ping.

An elevator arrived.

Ping.

Then another one.

Book II frowned, turned.

The doors to the two elevators opened—

—to reveal Demon Larkham and his ten-man IG-88 assault squad.

'Oh, *shit*,' Book II said.

They came charging out of the elevators, dressed in their charcoal-black battle uniforms, their high-tech MetalStorm guns blazing.

Book and Mother flew over the reception desk together, just as the whole area around them was raked with whirring hyper-machinegun fire.

The burly man at the internal door convulsed under the barrage of gunfire and fell. The receptionist took a bullet in the forehead and snapped backwards.

Demon's team rushed inside, one man lagging behind to take care of the two civilians who had dived over the reception desk.

He rounded the counter and—

—*blam!-blam!*—

—received two bullets in the face from two separate guns. Book and Mother leapt to their feet, pistols smoking.

'They're here for Rosenthal,' Book said. 'Come on!'

It was like following in the path of a tornado.

Book and Mother entered the main office area.

Men and women in suits lay draped over desks, their bodies riddled with bloody wounds, their workstations smashed.

Up ahead, the IG-88 force stormed through the open-plan office area, their MetalStorm guns blazing.

Glass shattered. Computer monitors exploded.

A security guard drew an Uzi from beneath his jacket—only to be cut down by hypervelocity MetalStorm bullets.

The IG-88 men raced up a beautiful curving internal staircase, up to the 39th floor.

Book and Mother gave chase.

They reached the top of the staircase just in time to see three members of the IG-88 team break away from the others and enter an interrogation room, where they promptly killed two senior Mossad men and dragged a third—a young man who could only be Rosenthal—from the room. Rosenthal was thirty-ish, olive-skinned and handsome; he wore an open-necked shirt and he looked tired beyond belief.

Book and Mother wasted no time. They bounded off the stairs and took out the three bounty hunters, working perfectly as a pair—Book dropped the man on the left, Mother the one on the right, and both of them nailed the man in the middle, blowing him apart with their guns.

Rosenthal dropped to the floor.

Book and Mother raced to his side, scooped him up, draped his arms over their shoulders.

'You Rosenthal?' Book demanded. 'Benjamin Rosenthal?'

'Yes . . .'

'We're here to help you. Shane Schofield sent us.'

A glint of recognition appeared on Rosenthal's face. 'Schofield. From the list . . .'

Blam!

Mother dropped another IG-88 man as he emerged from the next room and saw them.

'Book!' she yelled. 'No time for chit-chat! We have to keep moving! You can debrief him as we run! Up the stairs! Now!'

They swept further up the internal staircase, heading for the 40th floor, running past a set of curving picture windows that looked out over London—before the view of the city was abruptly replaced by that of an evil-looking assault helicopter swinging into position, hovering right outside the windows, staring in at Book and Mother and Rosenthal!

It was a Lynx gunship, the British equivalent of a Huey, equipped with side-mounted TOW missiles and a six-barrelled mini-gun.

'*Go!*' Mother yelled, hauling them upward. '*Go-go-go-go-go!*'

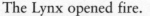

The Lynx opened fire.

There came a cataclysmic shattering of glass as the picture windows encasing the curving staircase collapsed under the weight of the helicopter's fire.

Glass rained down all around Book and Mother as they scampered up the stairs carrying Rosenthal between them, a whole section of the staircase itself falling away behind them, ripped clear from its mountings by the barrage of fire, just as they dived off it to the safety of the 40th floor.

Demon Larkham strode through the wreckage of the 39th floor, listening as reports came in over his headset radio.

'—*This is Airborne One. They're up on 40. Two contacts in civilian clothing. They appear to have Rosenthal with them*—'

'—*Airborne Two, landing on the roof now. Offloading second unit*—'

'—*This is Airborne Three. We're coming round the north-east corner. Heading for 40*—'

'—*This is Tech Team. Elevators are locked down. Four elevators are frozen on 38, the fifth is down in the lobby. No-one's going anywhere now*—'

'Gentlemen,' Demon said, 'exterminate these pests. And get me Rosenthal.'

Seen from a distance, the three IG-88 Lynx choppers buzzing around the peak of the King's Tower looked like flies harassing a picnicker.

One had landed on the roof, while the other two prowled around the upper floors, peering in through the windows.

At the sound of the windows being blasted to oblivion, a few local businesses called the police.

Book II and Mother charged down a hallway on the 40th floor, dragging Benjamin Rosenthal with them.

'Talk to me!' Book said to Rosenthal as they ran. 'The list. Why are you and Schofield on it?'

Rosenthal heaved for breath. 'Majestic . . . Majestic-12 put us on it . . . I'm on the list because I know who the members of Majestic-12 are, and I can expose them when they carry out their plan.'

'And Schofield?'

'He's different. He's a very special individual. He's one of the few who passed the Cobra tests . . . one of only nine men in the world who can disarm CincLock-VII, the security system on the Chameleon missiles—'

Just then, a fire stairwell door *right next to them* burst open, revealing four IG-88 mercenaries brandishing MetalStorm rifles and green laser sights.

Book and Rosenthal had no time to react, but Mother did.

She pushed them round a nearby corner, into another corridor,

while she herself dashed the other way down a long hallway, inches ahead of a wave of hypermachinegun fire.

Book and Rosenthal ran northward down their corridor, burst into a small office branching off it.

Dead end.

'Shit!' Book yelled, racing over to the window and looking out just as a Lynx helicopter shoomed past.

And then, outside the window, he saw it.

The four IG-88 bounty hunters who had burst out of the fire stair-well had split into two pairs—two going after Book and Rosenthal, the other pair going after Mother.

The two commandos pursuing Book and Rosenthal saw them enter the side-office twenty yards down the corridor.

They approached the office's door, flanked it silently on either side. The door was marked '4009'.

'Tech Team, this is Sterling Five,' the senior commando whispered into his headset. 'I need a floor schematic. Office number four-zero-zero-niner.'

The response came back. *'It's a dead end, Sterling Five. They've got nowhere to go.'*

The senior man nodded to the trooper beside him—and the junior trooper kicked open the door, blazing away with his MetalStorm rifle.

He hit nothing.

The office was empty.

Its single floor-to-ceiling window was *already* shattered, the pouring London rain sweeping in through it.

No Book.

No Rosenthal.

★ ★ ★

The two IG-88 men rushed to the broken window, looked down.

Nothing. Only the sheer glass side of the tower and a grassy park below.

Then they looked up—just as a mechanical whirring came to life above them—and they saw the steel underside of a window-washer's platform rising up the side of the building, heading for the roof.

Book and Rosenthal stood on the window-washer's platform as it rose quickly up the side of King's Tower.

The long rectangular platform hung from two sturdy winch-cranes that stuck out from the tower's roof.

Moments before their attackers had stormed the office, Book had blasted open the window, and with Rosenthal in front of him, leapt up and grabbed its catwalk.

He'd pushed Rosenthal up, and then hauled himself onto the platform, yanking his feet out of view just as the two IG-88 men had burst into the office.

A wave of hypercharged bullets chased Mother as she dashed westward down her hallway with two IG-88 bounty hunters on her tail.

Just as the bullets caught up with her, she dived sharply left, into an office—and found herself standing in a beautifully appointed boardroom.

It had a polished wooden floor, deep leather chairs, and the most gigantic boardroom table she had ever seen. It was easily 30 feet long.

'Fucking lawyers,' Mother breathed. 'Always overcompensating for their teeny-weeny dicks.'

It was a corner office, with floor-to-ceiling windows lining one side, providing a breathtaking view of London. The other side backed onto the exterior elevators.

Mother knew that her Colt pistol didn't stand a chance against the MetalStorm guns of the IG-88 men, so she waited behind the door.

Bang!

They kicked it in, rushed inside.

Mother shot the first man in the side of the head before he even saw her, turned her gun on the second man—

Click.

'Fuck!'

Out of ammo.

She crashtackled the second man instead, sending the two of them flying onto the boardroom table, the bounty hunter's MetalStorm rifle firing wildly in every direction.

The floor-to-ceiling windows of the boardroom took the brunt of the gunfire and spontaneously cracked into a million spiderwebs.

Mother grappled with her attacker on top of the boardroom table. He was a big guy, strong. He unsheathed a knife just as Mother did too and the two blades clashed.

Then, suddenly, as they fought, Mother caught sight of two shapes in the doorway.

Men.

But not IG-88 men.

Rather, two burly Israelis in suits, with Uzis slung over their shoulders and bloodstains on their shirts.

Mossad security men.

The two Israelis saw the fight taking place on the long boardroom table.

'Bounty hunters!' one of them spat.

'Come on!' the other yelled, looking back down the hallway. 'They're coming!'

The first man sneered at Mother and her attacker—then he quickly pulled a high-powered RDX grenade from his pocket, popped the cap and threw it into the boardroom.

Then he and his partner dashed off.

Still fending off her attacker's blows with her knife, Mother saw the grenade fly into the room in a kind of detached slow motion.

It bounced on the floor, disappearing underneath the gigantic

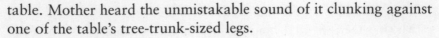

table. Mother heard the unmistakable sound of it clunking against one of the table's tree-trunk-sized legs.

And then it detonated.

The blast was monstrous.

Despite its solidity, the corridor-end of the massive table just disintegrated, shattering instantly into a thousand splinters.

As for the rest of the table—still a good 25 feet long—something very different happened.

The concussive force of the grenade *lifted* the elongated table clear off the floor and—like a railroad car being shunted forward on its tracks—sent it sliding at considerable speed down the length of the boardroom, *toward* the bullet-cracked windows at the western end of the room.

Mother saw it coming an instant before it happened.

The table exploded through the cracked glass windows, blasting through them like a battering ram, and shot out into the sky, forty storeys up.

Then with a sickening lurch, the table tipped downwards, and Mother suddenly found herself sliding—fast, down the length of the table, rain pounding against her face—toward four hundred feet of empty sky.

It looked totally bizarre: the elongated boardroom table jutting out from the top floor of the tower.

The table tilted sharply—passing through 45 degrees, then steeper—with the two tiny figures of Mother and the IG-88 commando sliding down its length.

Then—completely without warning—the falling table jolted to a halt.

Its uppermost edge had hit the *ceiling* of the 40th floor and wedged against it, while two of its thick legs had locked against the *floor* right on the precipice—causing the whole table to stop suddenly, suspended at a vertiginous angle 40 storeys above the ground!

Mother slid fast, before at the very last moment she jammed her knife deep into the surface of the table—and using the knife's brass fingerholes as a handgrip, swung to a halt, hanging from the embedded knife, her feet dangling off the lower edge of the almost-vertical table.

Her attacker wasn't as quick-thinking.

In an attempt to get a handhold, he'd dropped his knife as they'd fallen. As it turned out, he hadn't been able to find a handhold, but luckily for him he'd been *above* Mother as the table had burst out through the window. As such, he'd fallen into her, his feet slamming into her embedded knife.

He now hung above her, one foot crushing her knife-hand, smiling.

Gripping the edges of the table with his hands, he started kicking her fingers, hard.

Mother clenched her teeth, held on grimly despite his blows, the brass fingerholes of her knife deflecting some of them.

And then she heard the noise.

Thump-thump-thump-thump-thump-thump . . .

The sound of helicopter rotors.

She glanced around and saw a Lynx chopper hovering *right beside her* like a giant flying hornet.

'Oh, fuck . . .' she moaned.

The IG-88 man above her waved to the chopper pilot, directing him to go down, *below* them.

The pilot complied and the chopper swung below Mother, its speed-blurred rotor blades forming a hazy white circle beneath her dangling feet.

Then the bounty hunter above her resumed his kicking, only harder.

Crack!

She heard one of her fingers break.

'You mother*fucker*!' she yelled.

He kicked again.

The rotor blades roared like a buzzsaw ten feet below Mother's boots.

Her attacker raised his foot for one last blow. He brought it down hard—

—just as Mother did a most unexpected thing.

She withdrew the knife from the table, causing *both of them* to slide quickly downward, off the table's lower edge, toward the blurring blades of the helicopter!

Her attacker couldn't believe it.

Without the knife to lean on, he rocketed downward, sliding off the lower edge of the boardroom table!

They slid off the bottom end of the table together—but unlike her attacker, Mother had been prepared. As she went off the edge, she stabbed her knife into the underside of the table, and swung in underneath it, her fall halted.

The IG-88 man shot right past her, off the edge of the table and out into space . . .

. . . and the world went slow as Mother watched his horrified face—eyes wide, mouth open—falling, falling, dropping away from her.

Then he hit the rotor blades—*splat-choo!*—and his entire human shape just disappeared, spontaneously erupting into a star-shaped burst of blood.

A wash of red liquid splattered the windscreen of the chopper and the Lynx peeled away from the building.

Mother didn't even have time to sigh with relief.

For just then, as she hung from the downward-pointing boardroom table, pelted by the London rain, *the whole table shifted slightly*.

A sudden jolt.

Downward.

Mother snapped to look up: saw that the legs pinioning the table to the 40th floor were buckling.

The table was going to fall.

'Oh, damn it all to fucking hell!' she yelled to the sky. 'I am not going to die!'

She gauged her position.

She was at the corner of the building—the south-west corner—on the western side.

Just around the corner, slightly below her, she could see one of the glass elevators, stopped on the 38th floor on the southern face of the building.

'Okay,' she said to herself. 'Stay calm. What would the Scarecrow do?'

Maghook, she thought.

She drew her Maghook, aimed it up at the interior ceiling of the 40th floor, and fired.

Nothing happened.

The Maghook didn't fire.

Its trigger just clicked and its barrel emitted a weak fizzing noise. It was out of gas propellant.

'Oh, come on!' Mother yelled. 'That never happens to the Scarecrow!'

Then suddenly the table lurched again, dropped another two feet.

Mother started unspooling the Maghook manually—with her teeth—muttering as she did so. 'Not fair. Not fair. Not *fucking* fair . . .'

The table teetered on the edge of the 40th floor, its legs groaning under the weight, about to snap—

Mother felt she had enough rope and with her free hand, hurled the Maghook's grappling hook up at the 40th floor.

It landed on the edge of the shattered windowsill, its claws catching . . .

. . . just as the table tipped wholly out of the window . . .

. . . and Mother let go of her knife, swung away from the falling boardroom table . . .

. . . and the table fell through the rainy sky, all twenty-five feet of it dropping down the side of the building . . .

. . . while Mother swung on her rope, swooping around the corner of the building, before she slammed into the glass wall of the elevator just around the corner, and grabbed hold of its roof rim.

Seven whole seconds later, the gigantic boardroom table of Goldman, Marcus & Meyer hit the sidewalk and smashed into a billion tiny pieces.

Book and Rosenthal arrived at the roof on the window-washer's platform.

They ducked behind an exhaust stack, peered out to see one of Demon Larkham's Lynx helicopters resting on the rooftop helipad, it rotors turning, veiled in the pouring rain.

'Keep talking,' Book said to Rosenthal. 'This Majestic-12 wrote the list. And they want Schofield dead because . . .'

'Because of the Cobra tests,' Rosenthal said. 'Because *he passed* the Cobra tests. Although in NATO they were called something else: Motor Neuron Rapidity of Response tests. "Cobra" was the Russian name.'

'Motor Neuron Rapidity of Response?' Book II said. 'You mean reflexes.'

'Yes. Exactly,' Rosenthal said. 'It's all about reflexes. Superfast reflexes. The reflexes of the men on that list are the best in the world. *They passed the Cobra tests*, and only someone who passed the Cobra tests can disarm the CincLock-VII missile security system, and CincLock-VII is at the core of Majestic-12's plan. That's why Majestic-12 needs to eliminate them.'

'A missile security system . . .'

'Yes, yes, but don't be fooled. This bounty hunt is but one element of Majestic-12's larger plan.'

'And what is that plan?'

'Smashing the existing world order. Creating worldwide warfare. Scorching the earth so that it can regrow afresh,' Rosenthal said. 'Listen, I have a whole file on this downstairs. The Mossad has been debriefing me on it for the last two days. It's a file on this bounty hunt, on Majestic-12, its members, and, most importantly, what its overall plan is—'

Rosenthal's head exploded. Burst like a blood-filled water balloon.

There was no warning.

Rosenthal's face was simply ripped to pieces by a lethal 20-round burst from a MetalStorm rifle somewhere behind Book II.

Book spun—

—and saw Demon Larkham himself standing in the doorway to the fire stairs, thirty yards away, his MetalStorm rifle pressed against his shoulder.

Book looked down at Rosenthal, bloodied and broken. The Mossad man would tell no more tales—not without his face.

And so Book ran.

For the helicopter parked nearby, his pistol up and firing.

The glass wall of the elevator shattered and Mother swung inside it.

She was now on the south face of the tower, on the 38th floor. She saw the other glass elevators sitting silently in position, level with her own.

If the elevators were numbered 1-through-5 going across the face of the building, then Elevators 1, 2, 3 and 5 were stopped on Level 38. A gap existed where the fourth elevator should have been. It must have been on a lower floor. Mother stood in Number 1, on the far left-hand side of the southern face.

She hammered the 'DOOR OPEN' button.

It was like standing in a fishbowl and Mother knew that the Lynx helicopter that had terrorised her before would come searching for her soon and she didn't want to be a sitting duck when it di—

Thump-thump-thump-thump-thump-thump . . .

The Lynx.

Mother turned.

It was right there!

Hovering just out from her glass elevator, off to the western side, seemingly staring at her.

Mother kept hitting DOOR OPEN. 'Damn it, fuck! Is this button actually wired to anything?'

And then she saw the puff of smoke from one of the Lynx's side-mounted missile pods.

They were firing a missile at her!

A TOW missile blasted out of the pod, carving a horizontal line *straight at* Mother's glass elevator.

The elevator doors started to open.

The missile roared toward Mother's eyes.

Mother squeezed through the doors and dived out of the lift just as the TOW missile pierced her elevator's shattered western wall, entering it from the side, its superhot tail-flame charring the whole interior of the elevator before—*clash!*—it shot out the other side and rocketed into the next glass elevator beside it.

The sight was truly amazing.

The TOW missile shot across the southern face of the King's Tower, blasting through *all four* of the glass elevators parked there—*clash!-clash!-clash!-clash!*—causing sequential explosions of glass as it penetrated each lift's walls, one after the other—before in a final glorious shower of glass, it shot out of the last elevator and peeled off into the Thames where it exploded in a gigantic geyser of spray.

For her part, Mother landed in a clumsy heap inside the reception area on the 38th floor, the door of her glass elevator open behind her.

Lying flat on the floor, she looked up.

And saw four IG-88 bounty hunters standing in the destroyed reception area, right in front of her. They looked just as shocked to see her as she was to see them.

'Talk about out of the frying pan . . .' Mother breathed.

The IG-88 men whipped up their MetalStorm rifles.

Mother pounced to her feet and leapt in the only direction she could: back out onto her elevator.

Into the elevator, ducking behind its control panel just as a wave of hypermachinegun fire rushed in through the open doorway.

Rain and wind whipped all around Mother, the semi-destroyed elevator now little more than an open-air viewing platform that looked out over London.

Mother looked across the southern face of the tower.

The three other glass elevators faced her, lined up in a row, their glass walls all shattered by the TOW.

'Live or die, Mother,' she said aloud. 'Fuck it. Die.'

And so she ran.

Thirty-eight floors up, charging hard, across the southern face of the building, leaping across the three-foot gaps between the semi-destroyed elevators.

As soon as she landed on the second elevator, the Lynx helicopter returned, swooping in fast, now firing with its mini-gun, razing the side of the building with a storm of bullets.

But Mother kept running, outstripping the chopper's brutal rain of fire by centimetres, hurdling over onto the third elevator platform.

The gap where Elevator Number 4 should have been yawned before her.

Mother didn't miss a step.

The gap was wide—twelve feet—but she jumped anyway, diving forward, arms outstretched, 38 storeys up, hoping to catch the floor of the fifth and final elevator with her hands.

No dice.

She knew as soon as she jumped that she wasn't going to make it.

Her hands missed the floor of the fifth elevator by inches and Mother dropped below it.

But the clawed grappling hook of the Maghook in her hand didn't miss the edge of the elevator.

The damn Maghook might not have been working anymore, but by holding its hook in her outstretched hand, Mother had added another twelve inches to her reach.

Which was just what she needed.

The steel claws of the hook caught the floor of the elevator and Mother swung to a halt beneath it. She had just started climbing up into it when—

Thump-thump-thump-thump-thump-thump-thump . . .

The Lynx.

It was back. Hovering menacingly in front of her as she hung from the destroyed elevator's floor. A second IG-88 Lynx chopper swooped in behind it, checking out the action.

This time the Lynx was so close that Mother could see the pilot's smiling face.

He waved at her, then gripped his gun trigger.

Hanging from the elevator platform, dead for all money, Mother just shook her head.

'No . . .'

The Lynx's gunbarrels began to roll, just as another glimpse of movement caught Mother's eye—a grey smoketrail shooting through the air behind the Lynx—a *missile* smoketrail that seemed to come from . . .

The second Lynx helicopter.

The missile slammed into the Lynx that had been threatening Mother.

A colossal explosion rocked the air, and in the blink of an eye the Lynx was gone. In the face of the blast wave, it was all Mother could do to hold on.

The wreckage of the first Lynx tumbled down the side of the tower—flaming, smoking.

It landed on a grassy strip at the base of the tower with a massive metal-crushing *whump!*

Mother looked over at the second Lynx helicopter, the one that had shot its buddy out of the sky . . . and saw its pilot.

Book II.

His voice came over her earpiece. '*Hey there. I picked this baby up on the roof. Unfortunately, the pilot was a reluctant seller. I was wondering where you'd got to.*'

'Ha-de-fucking-ha, Book,' Mother said, hauling herself up into the fifth elevator. 'How about getting me off this damn tower.'

'*Be happy to. But can you get something for me first?*'

Mother charged through a corridor on the 39th floor, leading with her Colt.

The place was a mess. Bullet holes lined the walls. Anything made of glass had been shattered.

If the IG-88 team was still here, they weren't showing themselves.

'*It's back near that internal staircase,*' Book's voice said in her ear. '*The room where we found Rosenthal. It must be some kind of interrogation facility.*'

'Got it,' Mother said.

She could see the doorway near the top of the curving stairs, hurried into it.

She was confronted by a two-way mirror that looked into an adjacent interrogation room. Two video cameras peered through the mirror. Thick manila folders and two digital video tapes lay on a table nearby.

'It's an interrogation centre, all right,' Mother said. 'I got files. I got DV tapes. What do you want?'

'*All of it. Everything you can carry. Plus anything with Majestic-12 or CincLock-VII on it. And grab the tapes, including any that are still in the cameras.*'

Mother grabbed a silver Samsonite suitcase lying on the floor and stuffed it with the files and digital video tapes. The two cameras also had tapes in them, so she grabbed them, too.

And then she was out.

Out the door and up the fire stairs to the roof.

She hit the roof running, dashed out into the rain, just as Book landed his Lynx on it. She climbed inside and the chopper lifted off, leaving the smoking ruins of the King's Tower smouldering in its wake.

OFFICES OF THE DEFENSE INTELLIGENCE AGENCY,
SUB-LEVEL 3, THE PENTAGON
26 OCTOBER, 0700 HOURS LOCAL TIME
(1200 HOURS IN LONDON)

Dave Fairfax's boss caught him as he was leaving his office to go to St John's Hospital and find Dr Thompson Oliphant.

'And just where do you think you're going, Fairfax?' His name was Wendel Hogg and he was an asshole. A big guy, Hogg was ex-Army, a two-time veteran of war in Iraq, a fact which he never failed to tell people about.

The thing was, Hogg was stupid. And in the tradition of stupid managers worldwide, he (a) clung rigidly and inflexibly to rules, and (b) despised talented people like David Fairfax.

'I'm going out for coffee,' Fairfax said.

'What's wrong with the coffee here?'

'I've tasted hydrofluoric acid that was better than the coffee here.'

Just then, a small waif-like young woman entered the office. She was the mail clerk, a quiet mousy girl named Audrey. Fairfax's eyes lit up at the sight of her—unfortunately, so did Hogg's.

'Hey, Audrey,' Fairfax said, smiling.

'Hi, Dave,' Audrey replied shyly. Others might have said she was plain, but Fairfax thought she was beautiful.

Then Hogg said loudly, 'Thought you said you were leaving, Fairfax. Hey, while you're doing a Starbucks run, why don't you

get us a couple of grande frappacinos. And make it snappy, will ya.'

A million witty retorts passed through Fairfax's brain, but instead he just sighed. 'Whatever you say, Wendel.'

'*Hey*,' Hogg barked. 'You will address me as Sergeant Hogg or Sergeant, young man. I didn't take a bullet in Eye-raq to be called *Wendel* by some spineless little keyboard-tapper like you, Fairfax. 'Cause when the time comes, boy, to stand up and stare into the enemy's eyeballs,'—he threw a cocksure grin at Audrey—'who would you want holding the gun, you or me?'

Fairfax's face reddened. 'I'd have to say you, Wendel.'

'Damn straight.'

And with an embarrassed nod to Audrey, Fairfax left the office.

EMERGENCY WARD, ST JOHN'S HOSPITAL, ARLINGTON, USA
26 OCTOBER, 0715 HOURS

Fairfax entered the ER of St John's, went over to the reception counter.

It was quiet at this time of the morning. Five people sat slumped like zombies in the waiting area.

'Hi, my name is David Fairfax. I'm here to see Dr Thompson Oliphant.'

The desk nurse chewed bubble gum lazily. 'Just a second. *Dr Oliphant!* Someone here to see you!'

A second nurse appeared from one of the curtained-off bed-bays. 'Glenda, shhh. He's out back catching some shut-eye. I'll go get him.'

The second nurse disappeared down a back hallway.

As she did so, an exceedingly tall black man stepped up to the reception counter beside Fairfax.

He had deep dark skin and the high sloping forehead common to the inhabitants of southern Africa. He wore big fat Elvis sun-glasses and a tan trenchcoat.

The Zulu.

'Good morning,' the Zulu said stiffly. 'I would like to see Dr Thompson Jeffrey Oliphant, please.'

Fairfax tried not to look at the bounty hunter—tried not to betray the fact that his heart was now beating very very fast.

Tall and lanky, the Zulu was gigantic—the size of a professional basketball player. The top of Fairfax's head was level with his chest.

The desk nurse popped a bubble-gum bubble. 'Geez, old Tommy's popular this morning. He's out back, sleeping. Someone's just gone to get him.'

At that moment, a bleary-eyed doctor appeared at the end of the long 'Authorized Personnel Only' corridor.

He was an older guy: grey-haired, wrinkled face. He wore a white labcoat and he rubbed his eyes as he emerged from a side room putting on his glasses.

'Dr Oliphant?' the Zulu called.

'Yes?' the old doctor said as he came closer.

Fairfax was the first to see the weapon appear from under the Zulu's tan trenchcoat.

It was a Cz-25, one of the crudest submachine-guns in the world. It looked like an Uzi only meaner—the ugly twin brother—with a long 40-round magazine jutting out of its pistol grip.

The Zulu whipped up the gun, levelled it at Oliphant, and oblivious to the presence of at least seven witnesses, pulled the trigger.

Standing right next to the big assassin, Fairfax did the only thing he could think to do.

He lashed out with his right hand, punching the gun sideways, causing its initial burst to strafe a line of bullet holes along the wall next to Oliphant's head.

People ducked.

Nurses screamed.

Oliphant dived to the floor.

The Zulu backhanded Fairfax, sending him crashing into a nearby janitor's trolley.

Then the Zulu walked—just walked—around the reception desk and into the staff-only corridor, toward Oliphant, his Cz-25 extended.

He fired ruthlessly.

The nurses scattered out of the way.

Oliphant scrambled on his hands and knees into a supply room that branched off the corridor, bullet-sparks raking the ground at his toes.

Fairfax lay among the shattered janitorial supplies from the trolley he'd slammed into. He saw a bag of white powder that had been on the trolley: 'ZEOLITE-CHLORINE—INDUSTRIAL-STRENGTH CLEANING AGENT—AVOID SKIN CONTACT'. He grabbed it.

Then he leapt to his feet and ran forward—while everyone else ran *away* from the action—and peered down into the staff-only corridor where he saw the Zulu stop in front of an open doorway and raise his Cz-25.

Fairfax hurled the bag of powdered chlorine through the air. It hit the Zulu square in the side of the head and exploded in a puff of white dust.

The Zulu screamed, staggering away from the doorway, swatting at his powder-covered head, trying desperately to remove the burning zeolite on his skin. His Elvis sunglasses now bore a layer of white powder on their lenses. His flesh had started bubbling.

Fairfax dashed forward, slid on the floor underneath the Zulu, peered in through the doorway—and saw Dr Thompson Oliphant cowering underneath some supply shelves, covering his face.

'Dr Oliphant! Listen to me! My name is David Fairfax. I'm with the Defense Intelligence Agency. I'm not much of a hero, but I'm all you've got right now! If you want to get through this, you'd better come with me!'

Oliphant extended his hand and Fairfax grasped it, lifting the doctor to his feet. Then they ducked under the swatting Zulu and raced out past the reception counter into the early morning air.

The automatic sliding doors opened for them—just as the doors themselves shattered under Cz-25 bullet-fire.

The Zulu was moving again and coming after them with a vengeance.

An ambulance was parked right outside the Emergency Ward's entrance.

'Get in!' Fairfax yelled, throwing open the driver's side door. Oliphant jumped in the passenger side.

Fairfax fired her up and hit the gas. The ambulance peeled off the mark, but not before the two of them heard an ominous *whump!* from somewhere at the back of the vehicle.

'Uh-oh . . .' Fairfax said.

In his side mirror he saw the tall dark figure of the Zulu standing on the rear bumper, his hands clinging to the ambulance's roof rails.

The Zulu was on the ambulance!

The ambulance's tyres squealed as Fairfax gunned it out of the undercover turning bay and into the parking lot proper.

He bounced the white van over a gutter and a nature strip hoping to dislodge the Zulu from its bumper. The ambulance rocked wildly as it jounced down another gutter and Fairfax was certain that no-one could have held on after all that.

But then the rear doors of the ambulance were hurled open from the outside and the Zulu stepped into the rear compartment!

'Shit!' Fairfax yelled.

The Zulu no longer had his Cz-25, having discarded it in favour of holding onto the ambulance with both hands.

But now, safely inside the speeding ambulance, he withdrew a

long-bladed machete from his trenchcoat and stared at Fairfax and Oliphant with blazing fury in his bloodshot eyes.

Fairfax eyed the machete. 'Oh, man . . .'

The Zulu swept forward through the rear compartment, clambering quickly over a locked-down wheeled gurney.

Fairfax had to do something fast.

He saw the road up ahead divide—one lane heading left for the exit, the other sweeping to the right, up a curving concrete ramp that gave access to the hospital's multi-storey parking lot.

He chose right, and yanked the steering wheel hard over, hitting the gas as they charged up the spiralling ramp—the centrifugal force of their high-speed turn causing the Zulu in the back to lose his balance and slam against the outer wall, his forward progress momentarily halted.

But they could only go up for so long, Fairfax thought. The parking structure was only six storeys high.

He had five floors to think of something else.

At the same time, someone else was watching the ambulance's wild rise up the tightly curving ramp from across the street.

A strikingly beautiful woman with long legs, muscular shoulders and cool Japanese eyes.

Her real name was Alyssa Idei, but in the bounty hunting world she was known simply as the Ice Queen. She'd already collected the bounty on Damien Polanski and now she was after Oliphant.

She wore only black leather—tight hipster pants, biker jacket and killer boots. Her long black hair was tied back. Under her jacket, tucked into a pair of shoulder holsters, were two high-tech Steyr SPP machine pistols.

She started up her Honda NSX and pulled out from the kerb, and headed for the multi-storey parking lot.

Tyres squealing, Fairfax's ambulance wound its way up the curving ramp, its open rear doors flailing wildly.

They hit Level 3.

Three floors to go before they reached the roof—before the Zulu in the back would be able to move freely again.

But now Fairfax knew what he was going to do.

He was going to drive the ambulance off the top level of the parking structure—leaping out of it at the last moment with Oliphant, leaving the Zulu inside.

'Dr Oliphant!' he yelled, glancing back at the Zulu. 'Listen up and listen fast because I don't know if we'll get another chance to talk about this! You're a target in an international bounty hunt!'

'What!'

'You have an eighteen-million-dollar price on your head! I think it has something to do with a NATO study that you did back in 1996 with a guy named Nicholson at USAMRMC! The MNRR Study. What was that study about?'

Oliphant frowned. He was still in shock, and trying to assimilate this line of questioning with the ongoing attempt on his life was hard.

'MNRR? Well, it was . . . it was . . .'

The ambulance continued its dizzying ascent.

Level 4 and rising.

'It was . . . it was like the Soviet Cobra tests, a test of—'

As Oliphant spoke, Fairfax stole a glance back at the Zulu—and suddenly saw that the demonic figure of the bounty hunter was far closer than he had expected him to be and was now *swinging his machete right at Fairfax's head!*

No defence.

No escape.

The machete whistled forward.

And slammed into the headrest of Fairfax's seat, its steel blade stopping—dead—a millimetre from Fairfax's right ear.

Jesus!

But now the Zulu was on them. Somehow, he had managed to manoeuvre his way forward, despite the powerful inertia of the turning-and-rising ambulance.

Level 5 . . .

And now Fairfax's eyes narrowed, focused.

He slammed his foot down on the gas pedal.

The ambulance responded, increased its speed.

They hit the top of the curving ramp doing 40, the ambulance almost tipping over sideways, all-but travelling on two wheels.

Then they raced out onto the rooftop—at this hour, it was completely empty—and Fairfax straightened the steering wheel and the ambulance, coming out of its hard turn, bounced back down onto all four wheels, the abrupt change of direction causing the Zulu to fly to the *other* side of the rear compartment and bang into the wall . . . leaving his machete wedged in Fairfax's headrest.

Fairfax gunned the ambulance, aimed it directly at the edge of the deserted rooftop parking area.

'Dr Oliphant! Get ready to jump!' he yelled.

They rocketed toward the edge of the roof, toward the pathetic little fence erected there.

Fairfax shifted in his seat. 'Get ready . . . on three. One . . . two . . . thr—'

The Zulu lunged into the driver's seat from behind and grabbed both Fairfax *and* Oliphant!

Fairfax was stunned.

Now none of them could get out!

He saw the edge of the rooftop rushing at him at phenomenal unavoidable speed, so in desperation he yanked the steering wheel hard over and for what it was worth, slammed on the brakes.

The ambulance fishtailed, skidded wildly.

And so rather than hitting the fence head-on as Fairfax had intended it to, it did a screeching four-wheel skid, spinning a full 180 degrees so that instead, it slammed into the rooftop's fence *rear-end first*.

The ass end of the ambulance blasted through the fence and with Fairfax, Oliphant and the Zulu inside it, the whole ambulance went shooting off the edge of the roof, six storeys above the world, and fell—

—only about ten feet.

As the backward-travelling ambulance passed over the edge of the roof and blasted through the little fence, its front bumper bar caught hold of a surviving fence post and anchored the ambulance to the roof.

As such, the ambulance's fall was cut dramatically short. No sooner was most of its bulk over the edge than the whole vehicle jolted to a sudden halt.

And so now it hung vertically from the top floor of the parking structure, hanging by its nose, its rear doors flailing open beneath it.

Inside the ambulance, everything that should have been horizontal was now vertical.

Oliphant still sat in the passenger seat, only now facing upwards, his back pressing into his seat.

Fairfax hadn't been so lucky.

As they had hit the fence, he had been yanked from his seat by the Zulu and hurled into the rear section of the ambulance.

But then the ambulance had gone vertical, sending both of them tumbling ass over head.

And with its rear doors swinging open beneath them—revealing the six-storey drop—Fairfax and the Zulu had clutched at anything they could find.

The big Zulu had grabbed the locked-down gurney. Fairfax had clutched a shelf on the wall.

And so they hung there, inside the vertical ambulance, with a clear drop through the vehicle's rear doors yawning beneath them.

But the Zulu wasn't finished.

He *still* wanted to get to Oliphant.

He stretched upward, reaching for his machete, still wedged in the headrest of the driver's seat.

'No!' Fairfax yelled, lunging forward.

But he was too late.

Hanging onto the wheeled gurney with one hand, the Zulu lashed his fingers around the machete's grip and yanked it free.

He turned his bloodshot eyes on Fairfax, and his mouth widened into a sinister yellow-toothed grin.

'Bye-bye!' he said, drawing the machete back for the final blow.

'Whatever you say, asshole,' Fairfax said, seeing it.

The Zulu swung.

The blade whistled towards Fairfax's head.

Just as Fairfax lashed out with his foot and kicked open the locks that held the gurney in place.

The response was instantaneous.

The wheeled gurney dropped like a stone, out through the open doors at the bottom of the vertical ambulance . . .

. . . with the Zulu on it!

Fairfax watched as the big man fell with the gurney, his wide eyes receding to specks as he fell and fell and fell.

The gurney flipped on the way down, causing the Zulu to hit the ground first. He impacted against the concrete with a sickening thud, his internal organs shattering. But he was still alive.

Not for long. A second later, the leading edge of the gurney came slamming down against his head, crushing it like a nut.

It took a few minutes for Fairfax and Oliphant to negotiate their way out of the vertical ambulance, but they made it by climbing out through the front windshield and hauling themselves up over the bonnet.

The two of them slumped on the roof of the parking structure, breathless.

Fairfax peered down at the ambulance still hanging from the edge of the rooftop.

For his part, Oliphant was jabbering, overwhelmed with shock:

'It stood for . . . Motor Neuron . . . Motor Neuron Rapidity of Response . . . we were testing American and British soldiers for response times, response times to certain stimuli . . . all kinds of stimuli: visual, aural, touch . . . *reflexes* . . . it was all about reflexes.

'Christ, we must have tested over three hundred soldiers, and they all had different response times . . . some were super fast, others clumsy and slow.

'But our superiors never told us what the study was for . . . of course, we all had a theory. Most of us thought it was for commando-team selection, but some of the techs said it was for a new security system, some *amazing* new security system for ballistic missiles called CincLock . . . and then all of a sudden, the study was cancelled, the official reason being that the Department of Defense had canned the primary project, but we all thought it was because they'd got the information they needed—'

Shwat!

Still looking down at the ambulance, Fairfax heard the noise behind him.

He turned.

To see the now-headless body of Dr Oliphant kneeling beside him, swaying in position before—*whump*—it dropped to the concrete floor.

Standing over the corpse, holding a glistening short-bladed samurai sword in one tight fist, was a young leather-clad Japanese woman.

Alyssa Idei.

Bounty hunter.

She grabbed Oliphant's head by the hair and held it casually

by her side. Then in one fluid movement, she sheathed her sword and drew one of her Steyr machine pistols and pointed it at Fairfax.

She gazed at him over the gun. Eyes unblinking. Ice cold.

But then, strangely, a confused frown creased her perfect features, and she jerked her chin at Fairfax.

When it came her voice was as smooth as honey. 'You are not a bounty hunter, are you?'

'No . . .' Fairfax said tentatively. 'No, I'm not.'

'And yet you battle with the Zulu. Why?'

'I . . . I've a friend on your bounty list. I want to help him.'

Alyssa Idei seemed to have trouble grasping this. 'This man was your friend?'

'Well, not this guy. One of the other guys on the list.'

'And you do battle with the Zulu to help your friend?'

'Yes,' Fairfax said. 'I do.'

Her frown vanished, replaced by genuine curiosity. 'What is your name, friend-helper?'

'Er, David Fairfax.'

'Fair Fax. David Fair Fax,' she said slowly, rolling his name around in her mouth. 'I do not see such displays of loyalty often, Mr Fair Fax.'

'No?' Fairfax said.

She eyed him sexily. 'No. Your friend must be quite a man to inspire this bravery in you. Such bravery, Mr Fair Fax, is rare. It is also alluring. Intoxicating.'

Fairfax gulped. 'Oh.'

Alyssa said, 'And so I shall let you live. So that you may further help your friend—and so that we might meet again in fairer circumstances. But understand this, David Fair Fax, if we find ourselves together again, in a situation where you are protecting your friend, you will receive no such favour again.'

Then she holstered her gun and spun on the spot, sliding her lithe body into her low-slung sports car.

And she was gone.

Fairfax just watched the high-speed Honda whiz out of sight, shooting down the ramp, the headless body of Thompson Oliphant lying on the concrete beside him, the sun rising in the distance, and the sound of police sirens cutting through the dawn.

FOURTH ATTACK

FRANCE–ENGLAND
26 OCTOBER 1400 HOURS (FRANCE)
E.S.T. (NEW YORK, USA) 0800 HOURS

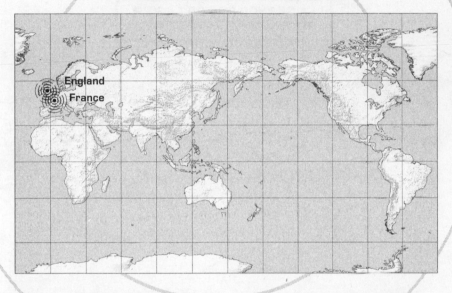

We live in a double world: carnival on the surface, consolidation underneath, where it counts.

From: *No Logo* by Naomi Klein

(HARPER COLLINS, LONDON, 2000)

Bread and circuses. That is all the people desire.

—Juvenal, Roman satirist

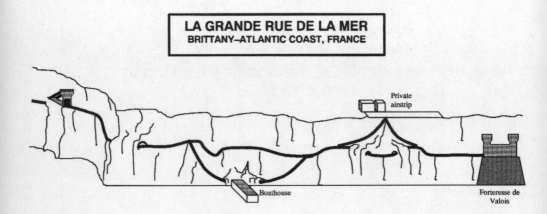

LA GRANDE RUE DE LA MER
BRITTANY—ATLANTIC COAST, FRANCE

Private airstrip

Boathouse

Forteresse de Valois

**FORTERESSE DE VALOIS
BRITTANY, FRANCE
26 OCTOBER, 1400 HOURS LOCAL TIME
(0800 HOURS E.S.T USA)**

The three tiny figures crossed the mighty stone bridge that connected the Forteresse de Valois to mainland France.

Shane Schofield.

Libby Gant.

Aloysius Knight.

They each carried a white medical transport box.

Three boxes. Three heads.

Owing to the fact that Schofield was one of the most wanted men in the world—and the fact that they were about to enter the inner sanctum of this bounty hunt—Schofield and Gant were partially disguised.

They now wore the charcoal battle uniforms and helmets of IG-88, taken from the men on the Hercules. In addition to their own weapons—now cleaned of chaff—they also carried MetalStorm rifles. For extra effect, Schofield wore several bloodstained bandages across his jaw and normal sunglasses over his eyes, just enough to cover his features.

In his thigh pocket, however, he also carried one of Knight's chunky modified Palm Pilots.

Knight pressed the doorbell to the castle. 'Okay, since I'm the only one of us who's done this before, I'll take the heads in to the assessor. You'll be asked to wait behind, in a secure area of some sort.'

'A secure area?'

'Assessors don't take kindly to bounty hunters who try to storm their offices and steal their money. It's happened before. As such, assessors usually have rather nasty protective systems. And if this assessor is who I think he is, then he's not a very nice person.

'In any case, just keep your eye on your Pilot. I'm not sure how much information I'll be able to syphon out of his computer, but hopefully I can pull enough so that we can find out who's paying for this hunt.'

Knight had an identical Palm Pilot in his own pocket. Like many such devices, it came with an infra-red data transfer feature, so you could send documents from your computer to your Palm Pilot wirelessly.

Knight's modifications to his Pilot, however, included a search program that allowed his device to access—wirelessly—*any* computer that he could get within ten feet of.

Which meant he could do something very special indeed: he could hack into standalone computers. If he could get close enough.

The castle's gates opened.

Monsieur Delacroix appeared, dapper as always.

'Captain Knight,' he said formally. 'I was wondering if I might be seeing you.'

'Monsieur Delacroix,' Knight said. 'I had a feeling you'd be the assessor. I was just saying to my associates here what a charming fellow you were.'

'But of course you were,' Delacroix said drily. He eyed Schofield and Gant in their IG-88 gear. 'New helpers. I did not know you had been recruiting from Monsieur Larkham's fold.'

'Good help is hard to find,' Knight said.

'Isn't it just,' Delacroix said. 'Why don't you come inside.'

They passed through the castle's showroom-like garage, filled with its collection of expensive cars: the Porsche GT-2, the Aston Martin, the Lamborghini, the turbo-charged Subaru WRX rally cars.

Delacroix walked in the lead, pushing a handcart with the three head boxes stacked on it.

'Nice castle,' Knight said.

'It is rather impressive,' Delacroix said.

'So who owns it?'

'A very wealthy individual.'

'Whose name is—'

'—something I am not authorised to divulge. I have instructions on this matter.'

'You always do,' Knight said. 'Guns?'

'You may keep your weapons,' Delacroix said, uninterested. 'They won't be of any use to you here.'

They descended some stairs at the rear of the garage, entered a round stone-walled anteroom that preceded a long narrow tunnel.

Delacroix stopped. 'Your associates will have to wait here, Captain Knight.'

Knight nodded to Schofield and Gant. 'It's okay. Just don't be shocked when the doors lock.'

Schofield and Gant took a seat on a leather couch by the wall.

Delacroix led Knight down the narrow torch-lit tunnel.

They came to the end of the forbidding passageway, to a well-appointed office. Delacroix entered the office ahead of Knight, then turned, holding a remote in his hand.

Wham! Wham! Wham!

The three steel doors in the tunnel whomped down into place, sealing Schofield and Gant in the ante-room and Knight in the tunnel.

Knight didn't even blink.

Delacroix set about examining the heads—heads that were originally captured by Demon Larkham in the caves of Afghanistan: the heads of Zawahiri, Khalif and Kingsgate.

Laser scans, dental exams, DNA . . .

★ ★ ★

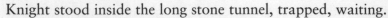

Knight stood inside the long stone tunnel, trapped, waiting.

He noticed the boiling oil gutters set into its walls. 'Hmmm,' he said aloud. 'Nasty.'

Through a small perspex window set into the steel door, he could see into Delacroix's office.

He saw Delacroix at work, saw the immense panoramic window behind the Swiss banker's desk revealing the glorious Atlantic Ocean.

It was then, however, that Knight noticed the ships outside.

On the distant horizon he saw a cluster of naval vessels: destroyers and frigates, all gathered around a mighty aircraft carrier that he instantly recognised as a brand-new, nuclear-powered Charles de Gaulle-class carrier.

It was a Carrier Battle Group.

A French Carrier Battle Group.

Schofield and Gant waited in the ante-room.

A whirring sound from up near the ceiling caught Schofield's attention.

He looked up—and saw six strange-looking antennas arrayed around the ceiling of the round ante-room, embedded in the stone walls. They looked like stereo speakers, but he recognised them as deadly microwave emitters.

He also saw the source of the whirring sound: a security camera.

'We're being watched,' he said.

In another room somewhere in the castle, someone was indeed watching Schofield and Gant on a black-and-white monitor.

The watcher was gazing intently at Schofield, as if he was peering right through Schofield's bandages and sunglasses.

Monsieur Delacroix finished his tests.

He turned to Knight, still captive in the tunnel.

'Captain Knight,' Delacroix said over the intercom. 'Congratulations. Each of your heads has carded a perfect score. You are now $55.8 million richer.'

The Swiss banker pressed his remote and the three steel doors whizzed up into their slots.

Knight stepped into Delacroix's office just as the banker sat down behind his enormous desk and started tapping the keys on his standalone laptop computer.

'So,' Delacroix said, hands poised over the keyboard. 'To which account would you like me to wire the bounty? Am I to assume you are still banking with Alan Gemes in Geneva?'

Knight's eyes were glued to Delacroix's computer.

'Yes,' he said as he hit the 'TRANSMIT' button on the Palm Pilot in his pocket.

Instantly, the Pilot and Delacroix's computer began communicating.

In the stone-walled ante-room, Schofield saw his Palm Pilot spring to life.

Data whizzed up the screen at dizzying speed. Documents filled with names, numbers, diagrams:

Source	Delivery Sys.	W-H	Origin	Target	Time
Talbot	Shahab-5	TN76	35702.90	00001.65	1145
			5001.00	5239.10	
	Shahab-5	TN76	35702.90	00420.02	1145
			5001.00	4900.25	
	Shahab-5	TN76	35702.90	01312.15	1145
			5001.00	5358.75	
Ambrose	Shahab-5	TN76	28743.05	28743.98	1200
			4104.55	4104.64	

MV HOPEWELL
Class: Kormoran-class supertanker
Length: 1,040 feet
Displacement: 190,456 gross tons

SUBJECT: PAYMENT OF ASSESSOR'S COMMISSION

PAYMENT OF THE ASSESSOR'S COMMISSION WILL BE MADE BY
INTERNAL ELECTRONIC FUNDS TRANSFER WITHIN AGM-SUISSE FROM
ASTRAL-66 PTY LTD'S PRIVATE ACCOUNT.

Executive Itinerary

The proposed order of travel is as follows: Asmara (01/08),
Luanda (01/08), Abuja (05/08), N'djamena (07/08) and Tobruk
(09/08).

01/08—Asmara (embassy)
03/08—Luanda (stay with M. Loch, R's nephew)

	Name	Nat.	Org.
1.	ASHCROFT, William H.	UK	SAS
2.	CHRISTIE, Alec P.	UK	MI-6
3.	FARRELL, Gregory C.	USA	Delta
4.	KHALIF, Iman	AFGH	Al-Qaeda
5.	KINGSGATE, Nigel E.	UK	SAS
6.	McCABE, Dean P.	USA	Delta

Schofield saw the last document, recognised it.

The bounty list.

The Pilot continued to download other documents. Careful to
keep it concealed, Schofield clicked on the list, opening it.

This list was slightly different to the one he had taken from
the leader of Executive Solutions, Cedric Wexley, in Siberia.

Some of the names on it had been shaded in. The full document read:

<u>ASSESSOR'S MASTER LIST</u>

VERIFIED REPORTS.
INFORMATION CORRECT AS AT:
26 OCTOBER, 1412 HOURS

	Name	Nat.	Org.
1.	ASHCROFT, William H.	UK	SAS
2.	CHRISTIE, Alec P.	UK	MI-6
3.	FARRELL, Gregory C.	USA	Delta
4.	KHALIF, Iman	AFGH	Al-Qaeda
5.	KINGSGATE, Nigel E.	UK	SAS
6.	McCABE, Dean P.	USA	Delta
7.	NAZZAR, Yousef M.	LEBN	HAMAS
8.	NICHOLSON, Francis X.	USA	USAMRMC
9.	OLIPHANT, Thompson J.	USA	USAMRMC
10.	POLANSKI, Damien G.	USA	ISS
11.	ROSENTHAL, Benjamin Y.	ISR	Mossad
12.	SCHOFIELD, Shane M.	USA	USMC
13.	WEITZMAN, Ronson H.	USA	USMC
14.	ZAWAHIRI, Hassan M.	SAUDI	Al-Qaeda
15.	ZEMIR, Simon B.	ISR	IAF

The dead, Schofield thought with a chill. *It's a list of the targets who have already been eliminated.*

And verified as dead.

Schofield could have added Ashcroft and Weitzman to that list—Ashcroft had been beheaded in Afghanistan by the Spetsnaz bounty hunters, the Skorpions, and Weitzman had been killed on the cargo plane.

Which meant that, at the very best, only five of the original 15 names remained alive: Christie, Oliphant, Rosenthal, Zemir and Schofield himself.

Schofield frowned.

Something bothered him about this list, something he couldn't quite put his finger on . . .

Then he glimpsed the word 'ASSESSOR' on one of the other documents.

He retrieved it.

It was an email:

SUBJECT: PAYMENT OF ASSESSOR'S COMMISSION

PAYMENT OF THE ASSESSOR'S COMMISSION WILL BE MADE BY INTERNAL ELECTRONIC FUNDS TRANSFER WITHIN AGM-SUISSE FROM ASTRAL-66 PTY LTD'S PRIVATE ACCOUNT (NO. 437-666-21) IN THE AMOUNT OF US$3.2 MILLION (THREE POINT TWO MILLION US DOLLARS) PER ASSESSMENT.

THE ASSESSOR IS TO BE **M. JEAN-PIERRE DELACROIX** OF AGM-SUISSE.

Schofield gazed at the words.

'ASTRAL-66 PTY LTD.'

That was where the money was coming from. Whatever it was, Astral-66 was paying for this bounty hunt—

'Good afternoon,' a pleasant voice said.

Schofield and Gant looked up.

A very handsome young man stood at the base of the stone stairs that led up to the garage. He was in his late thirties and clad in designer jeans and a Ralph Lauren shirt which he wore open over a T-shirt in the manner of the very wealthy. Schofield immediately noticed his eyes: one blue, one brown.

'Welcome to my castle,' the handsome young man smiled. His smile seemed somehow dangerous. 'And who might you be?'

'Colton. Tom Colton,' Schofield lied. 'This is Jane Watson. We're with Aloysius Knight, seeing Monsieur Delacroix.'

'Oh, I see . . .' the handsome man said.

He extended his hand.

'Killian. Jonathan Killian. You both look like you've seen a fair

amount of action today. May I get you a drink, or something to eat? Or perhaps my personal physician could give you some clean bandages for your wounds.'

Schofield shot a glance down the tunnel, searching for Knight.

'Please . . .' Killian guided them up the stairs. Not wanting to attract unnecessary attention, they followed him.

'I've seen you before,' Schofield said as they walked up the stone stairway. 'On TV . . .'

'I do make the odd appearance from time to time.'

'Africa,' Schofield said. 'You were in Africa. Last year. Opening factories. Food factories. In Nigeria . . .'

This was all true. Schofield recalled the images from the news— footage of this Killian fellow shaking hands with smiling African leaders amid crowds of happy workers.

They came up into the classic car garage.

'You've a good memory,' Killian said. 'I also went to Eritrea, Chad, Angola and Libya, opening new food processing plants. Although many don't know it yet, the future of the world lies in Africa.'

'I like your car collection,' Gant said.

'Toys,' Killian replied. 'Mere toys.'

He guided them into a corridor branching off the garage. It had dark polished floorboards and pristine white walls.

'But then I enjoy playing with toys,' Killian said. 'Much as I enjoy playing with *people*. I like to see their reactions to stressful situations.'

He stopped in front of a large wooden door. Schofield heard laughter coming from behind it. Raucous male laughter. It sounded like a party was going on in there.

'Stressful situations?' Schofield said. 'What do you mean by that?'

'Well,' Killian said, 'take for instance the average Westerner's inability to comprehend the Islamic suicide bomber. Westerners are taught since birth to fight "fair": the French duel at ten paces, English knights jousting, American gunslingers facing off on a Wild

West street. In the Western world, fighting is fair because it is presumed that both parties actually *want* to win a given battle.'

'But the suicide bomber doesn't think that way,' Schofield said.

'That's right,' Killian said. 'He doesn't want to win the *battle*, because the battle to a suicide bomber is meaningless. He wants to win a far grander war, a psychological war in which the man who dies *against his will*—in a state of distress and terror and fear— loses, while he who dies when he is spiritually and emotionally ready, wins.

'As such, a Westerner faced with a suicide bomber goes to pieces. Believe me, I have seen this. Just as I have seen people's reactions to other stressful situations: criminals in the electric chair, a person in water confronted by sharks. Oh, to be sure, I love to observe the look of pure horror that crosses a man's face when he realises that he is, without doubt, going to die.'

With that, Killian pushed open the door—

—at the same moment that something dawned on Schofield:

His problem with the master list.

On the master bounty list, McCabe and Farrell's names had been shaded in.

McCabe and Farrell, who had died in Siberia that morning, had been officially listed as dead.

And paid for.

Which meant . . .

The great door swung open—

—and Schofield and Gant were met with the sight of a dining room filled with the members of Executive Solutions, twenty of them, eating and drinking and smoking. At the head of the table, his broken nose wrapped in a fresh dressing, sat Cedric Wexley.

Schofield's face fell.

'And *that*,' Killian said, 'is the look I'm talking about.' The billionaire offered Schofield a thin, joyless smile. 'Welcome to my castle . . . Captain Schofield.'

Schofield and Gant ran.

Ran for all they were worth.

They bolted away from the dining room, dashed down the splendid corridor, Jonathan Killian's scornful laughter chasing them all the way.

The ExSol men were out of their seats in seconds, grabbing their weapons, the sight of another $18.6 million too good to resist.

Killian let them hustle past him, enjoying the show.

Schofield and Gant burst into the classic car garage.

'Damn. So many choices,' Schofield said, ripping off his bandages and gazing at the multi-million-dollar selection of cars before him.

Gant looked over her shoulder, saw the Executive Solutions mercenaries thundering down the hallway in pursuit. 'You've got about ten seconds to choose the fastest one, buster.'

Schofield eyed the Porsche GT-2. Silver and low, with an open targa top, it was an absolute beast of a car.

'Nah, it just isn't me,' he said, leaping instead toward the equally-fast rally car beside it—an electric blue turbo-charged Subaru WRX.

Nine seconds later, the men of ExSol burst into the garage.

They got there just in time to see the WRX blasting down the length of the showroom, already doing sixty.

At the far end of the showroom, the garage's external door was opening—thanks to Libby Gant standing at the controls.

The ExSol men opened fire.

Schofield stopped the rally car on a dime, right next to Gant.

'Get in!'

'What about Knight?'

'I'm sure he'll understand!'

Gant dived in through the Subaru's passenger window, just as the garage door opened fully to reveal the castle's sundrenched internal courtyard . . .

. . . and the surprised face of Major Dmitri Zamanov.

Accompanied by six of his Skorpions, and holding a medical transport box in his hands.

A pair of Russian Mi-34 high-manoeuvre helicopters stood in the gravel courtyard behind the Spetsnaz commandos, their rotor blades still turning.

'Oh, man,' Schofield breathed. 'Could this get any worse?'

Down in Monsieur Delacroix's office, Aloysius Knight spun at the sound of gunfire up in the garage.

He looked for Schofield in the ante-room at the other end of the tunnel.

Not there.

'Damn it,' he growled, 'can't this guy stay out of trouble for more than five minutes?'

He bolted out of the office.

Monsieur Delacroix didn't even bother to look up.

Schofield's turbo-charged WRX stood before Zamanov in the entry to the garage.

The two men locked eyes.

The look of surprise on Zamanov's face quickly transformed into one of sheer hatred.

'Floor it!' Gant yelled, breaking the spell.

Bam. Schofield hit the gas pedal.

The rally car shot off the mark, exploding through the doorway, scattering the Skorpions as they dived out of the way.

The WRX zoomed across the castle's courtyard, kicking up gravel, before it shot like a rocket out through the giant portcullis and sped across the drawbridge, heading for the mainland.

Dmitri Zamanov clambered to his feet just as *shoom!-shoom!-shoom!-shoom!-shoom!* five more cars whipped past him, blasting out of the garage after the WRX. There was a red Ferrari, a silver Porsche GT-2, and three yellow Peugeot rally cars with 'AXON' sponsorship logos on their sides.

ExSol.

In hot pursuit.

'Fuck!' Zamanov yelled. 'It's him! It's Schofield! *Go!* Go, go, go! Catch him and bring him to me! Before Delacroix gets his head, I am going to skin him alive!'

Four of the Skorpions immediately leapt to their feet and dashed for their two choppers, leaving Zamanov and two others at the castle with their head.

The chase was on.

WHITMORE AIRFIELD (ABANDONED)
40 MILES WEST OF LONDON
1230 HOURS LOCAL TIME
(1330 HOURS IN FRANCE¹)

Thirty minutes *earlier*—at the time Schofield, Gant and Knight had been arriving at the Forteresse de Valois—Book II and Mother had been landing their stolen Lynx helicopter at the abandoned airfield where Rufus had dropped them off.

They didn't expect to find Rufus still there. He'd said that after unloading them, he would head to France to catch up with Knight.

But when they landed, they saw the *Black Raven* parked inside an old hangar, surrounded by undercover police cars with strobe lights on their roofs.

Rufus stood sadly by his plane, helpless, covered by six trenchcoat-wearing undercover types and a platoon of heavily-armed Royal Marines.

Mother and Book were grabbed as soon as they landed.

One of the trenchcoat-wearing men approached them. He was young, clean-cut, and he held a cellphone in his hand as if he was halfway through a call.

When he spoke his accent was American.

'Sergeants Newman and Riley? My name is Scott Moseley, US State Department, London Office. We understand you're helping

---

¹Even though some areas in France, including Brittany, are significantly west of London, the whole of France adheres to a single time zone, one hour ahead of England.

Captain Shane M. Schofield of the United States Marine Corps in his efforts to avoid liquidation in an international bounty hunt. Is that correct?'

Book and Mother blanched.

'Uh, yeah . . . that's right,' Book II said.

'The United States Government has become aware of the existence of this bounty hunt. From the information available to us at this time, we have assessed the presumed reason for it and have come to the conclusion that the issue of keeping Captain Schofield alive is one of supreme national importance. Do you know where he is?'

'We might,' Mother said.

'So what's this all about then?' Book II asked. 'Tell us the grand conspiracy.'

Scott Moseley's face reddened. 'I don't personally know the details,' he said.

'Oh, *come on*,' Book II groaned, 'you've gotta give us more than that.'

'Please,' Moseley said. 'I'm just the messenger here. I don't have the clearance to know the full story. But believe me, I'm *not* here to hinder your efforts. All I have been told is this: the person or persons behind this bounty hunt have the capacity and perhaps the desire to destroy the United States of America. That is all I've been told. Beyond that, I know nothing.

'What I do know is this: I am here at the direct orders of the President of the United States and my orders are these: to help you. In any way I can. Anywhere you want to go. Anything you need to help Captain Schofield stay alive, I am authorised to give you. If you want weapons, they're yours. If you need money, I have it. Hell, if you want Air Force One to take you anywhere in the world, it is at your disposal.'

'Cool . . .' Mother breathed.

'How do we know we can trust you?' Book II said.

Scott Moseley handed Book his cellphone.

'Who's there?' Book said into it.

'Sergeant Riley?' a firm voice at the other end said. Book II recognised it instantly—and froze.

He'd met the owner of that voice before, during the mayhem at Area 7.

It was the voice of the President of the United States.

This was real.

'Sergeant Riley,' the President said. 'The full resources of the United States Government are entirely at your command. Anything you need, just tell Undersecretary Moseley. *You have to keep Shane Schofield alive*. Now I have to go.'

Then he hung up.

'*Right*,' Book II whistled.

'So,' Scott Moseley said. 'What do you need?'

Mother and Book exchanged a look.

'You go,' Book said. 'Save the Scarecrow. I'm going to find out what this is all about.'

'Ten-four,' Mother said.

She turned quickly, pointing at Rufus, but addressing Moseley. 'I need him. And his plane, fully fuelled. Plus free passage out of England. We know where the Scarecrow is and we have to get to him fast.'

'I can arrange the fastest possible—' Moseley said.

'Yeah, but I don't trust you yet,' Mother growled. 'Rufus, I trust. And he's just as fast as anyone else.'

'Okay. Done.' Scott Moseley nodded to one of his men. 'Fuel the plane. Clear the skies.'

Moseley turned to Book. 'What about you?'

But Book wasn't finished with Mother. 'Hey, Mother. Good luck. Save him.'

'I'll do my best,' Mother said. Then she dashed off to join Rufus at the Sukhoi. After a few minutes, its tanks replenished, the *Raven* rose into the sky and blasted off into the distance, afterburners blazing.

Only when it was gone did Book II turn to face Scott Moseley. 'I need a video player,' he said.

Schofield's rally car boomed along the coast of north-western France.

The road leading away from the Forteresse de Valois was known as La Grande Rue de la Mer—the Great Ocean Road.

Carved into the cliffs overlooking the Atlantic Ocean, it was a spectacular coastal highway, a twisting turning blacktop that featured low concrete guard-fences perched over sheer 400-foot drops, treacherous blind corners and the occasional tunnel that carved through rocky outcroppings.

In truth, since the fifteen miles of land surrounding the Forteresse de Valois belonged to Jonathan Killian, it was actually a private road. At two points along its length, side-roads branched off it—one headed upward, to Killian's private airstrip, while a second by-road plunged steeply downward, plummeting to the water's edge, providing access to an enormous boatshed.

Schofield's electric blue WRX ripped along the spectacular ocean road at 180 kilometres per hour. Its engine didn't so much roar as *whizz*, its turbocharger engaged. With its powerful all-wheel-drive system, the rally car was perfect for the Great Ocean Road's short tight bends.

Behind it, moving equally fast, were the five supercars of ExSol— the Porsche, the Ferrari and the three Peugeots—all in hot pursuit.

'Knight!' Schofield called into his throat-mike. 'You out there? We're . . . ah . . . in a little trouble here.'

'*I'm on my way*,' came the calm reply.

★ ★ ★

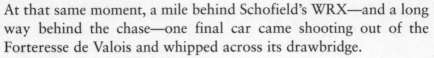

At that same moment, a mile behind Schofield's WRX—and a long way behind the chase—one final car came shooting out of the Forteresse de Valois and whipped across its drawbridge.

It was a Lamborghini Diablo.

V-12. Rear spoiler. Super low. Supercool. Superfast.

And painted black, of course.

Schofield keyed his satellite radio system.

'Book! Mother! Do you read me?'

Mother's voice answered him immediately. '*I'm here, Scarecrow.*'

'We're no longer at the castle,' Schofield said. 'We're on the road leading away from it. Heading north.'

'*What happened?*'

'Started out okay, but then just about every bad guy in the world arrived.'

'*Have you destroyed everything yet?*'

'Not yet, but I'm thinking about it. Are you on the way?'

'*Almost there. I'm with Rufus in the* Raven. *Book stayed in London to find out more about this hunt. I'm about thirty minutes away from you.*'

'Thirty minutes,' Schofield said grimly. 'I'm not sure we're gonna last that long.'

'*You have to, Scarecrow, because I've got a lot to tell you.*'

'Executive summary. Twenty-five words or less,' Schofield said.

'*The US Government knows about the bounty hunt and they're throwing everything behind keeping you alive. You just became an endangered species. So get your ass to US soil. An embassy, a consulate. Anything.*'

Schofield threw the WRX round a tight bend—and was suddenly presented with a vista of the road ahead of him.

The Great Ocean Road stretched away into the distance, twisting and turning like a flat black ribbon, hugging the coastal cliffs for miles.

'The US Government wants to *help* me?' Schofield said. 'In my

experience, the US Government only looks after the US Government.'

'Uh, Scarecrow . . .' Gant said, interrupting. 'We have a problem.'

'What?' Schofield snapped to look forward. 'Damn. ExSol must have called ahead . . .'

Half a mile in front of them the Ocean Road forked, with a side-road branching off it to the right, heading up the cliff-face. It was the side-road that led up to the airstrip, and right now two big semi-trailer rigs—minus their long trailers—were rushing down its steep slope at considerable speed, rumbling toward Schofield and Gant's fleeing car.

Hovering in the air above the two rigs was a sleek Bell Jet Ranger helicopter with 'AXON CORP' written on its flanks, also coming from the direction of the airfield.

ExSol has radioed ahead, Schofield thought, *and sent everyone they could from the airfield.*

'Those rigs are coming straight for us!' Gant said.

'No,' Schofield said. 'They're not going to ram us. They're going to block the road.'

Sure enough, the two semi-trailer rigs arrived at the junction of the airstrip road and the Great Ocean Road and promptly turned sideways, skidding to simultaneous halts, splaying their combined bulk across the road.

Blocking it completely.

'Mother,' Schofield said into his radio. 'We have to go. Please get here as soon as you can.'

The WRX whipped along the winding cliff-side road, rapidly approaching the two semi-trailer rigs.

Then, two hundred yards short of the road block, Schofield hit the brakes and the WRX squealed to a stop in the middle of the road.

A stand-off.

Two rigs. One rally car.

Schofield checked his rear-view mirror—the gang of five ExSol supercars was shooting along the Ocean Road behind him.

Beyond the ExSol cars loomed the giant stone castle, dark and sombre, before suddenly two helicopters dropped in front of the fortress, blasting through the air in pursuit as well.

Zamanov's two Skorpion Mi-34 choppers.

'Between a rock and a hard place,' Schofield said.

'A very hard place,' Gant said.

Schofield whirled back to face the road in front of him.

His eyes swept the scene—two rigs, the Axon helicopter, sheer rock wall to the right, 400-foot drop to the left, protected by a low concrete fence.

The fence, he thought.

'Pursuit cars are almost on us . . .' Gant warned.

But Schofield was still gazing at the concrete guard-rail fence. The Axon chopper hovered just out from it, almost at road level.

'We can do that,' he said aloud, his eyes narrowing.

'Do *what*?' Gant turned, alarmed.

'Hang on.'

Schofield slammed his foot down on the gas pedal.

The WRX roared off the mark, racing toward the rigs.

The rally car picked up speed fast, all four of its wheels giving power, its turbocharger screaming—*tzzzzzzzzz!*

60 kilometres an hour became 80 . . .

100 . . .

120 . . .

The WRX rushed toward the road block.

The two drivers of the rigs—ExSol men who had been waiting up at the airfield—swapped looks. *What was this guy doing?*

And then, very suddenly, Schofield cut left . . . bringing the rally car close to the concrete guard-rail fence.

Screeeeeeech!

The WRX hit the fence, its left-side wheels scraping against the concrete barrier, pressing against it, pinching against it, causing the whole left-hand side of the car to lift a little off the road . . .

. . . before abruptly—*ka-whump!*—the WRX mounted the fence!

Its left-hand wheels lifted clear off the asphalt, now riding *along the top of the fence*, so that the car was travelling at a 45-degree angle.

Schofield and Gant's world tilted sideways.

'There's still not enough room!' Gant yelled, pointing at the rig parked closest to the fence.

She was right.

'I'm not done yet!' Schofield yelled.

And with that he yanked the steering wheel hard to the *right*.

The response was instantaneous.

The WRX lurched sideways, its front half going right, its tail section going left—swinging dangerously out toward the ocean until finally its tail section slid . . .

. . . *off the edge of the concrete guard-rail.*

The WRX's rear wheels now hung 400 feet above the ocean!

But the rally car was still moving fast, still skidding wildly forward, its underside *sliding* along the top of the guard-rail fence—its front tyres hanging over the landward side of the fence, its rear wheels hanging above the ocean—so that now *none* of its wheels was touching the ground.

'*Ahhhhhhh!*' Gant yelled.

The WRX slid laterally along the guard-rail, its weight almost perfectly balanced, its underside scraping and shrieking and kicking up a firestorm of sparks until, to the amazement of the rig drivers, *it slid right past their road block*, squeezing through the gap between the outermost rig and the fence, a gap that until now had been too narrow for a car to pass through.

But then the inevitable happened.

With a fraction more of its weight hanging over the ocean side of the fence, the car—despite its forward momentum—began to tilt backwards.

'We're going to drop!' Gant shouted.

'No we're not,' Schofield said calmly.

He was right.

For just at that moment, the tail of the sliding car smacked at tremendous speed *against the nose of the Axon chopper* hovering just out from the fence.

The rear section of the car bounced off the chopper's nose at speed—ricocheting off it like a pinball—the impact powerful enough to punch the sliding WRX *back* over the fence and back onto the road . . . on the other side of the road block.

Just as Schofield had planned.

The WRX's tyres caught bitumen again, regained their traction, and the rally car shot off down the road once more.

Not a moment too soon.

Because a second later, the two rigs backed up, allowing the five ExSol pursuit cars to shoot between them like bullets out of a gun and catch up to Schofield's car.

The ExSol cars were all over them.

The two European sports cars that ExSol had 'borrowed' from Jonathan Killian—the red Ferrari and the silver Porsche, both low and sleek and brutally fast—were right on Schofield's tail.

The two mercenaries inside the Porsche made full use of its open-air targa roof—it allowed one man to stand up and fire at Schofield's WRX. The gunman in the Ferrari had to lean out of its passenger window.

As the rear window of the WRX shattered under a hail of gunfire, Gant turned to Schofield.

'Can I ask you a question!' she yelled.

'Sure!'

'Is there, like, some secret *school* where they teach you stuff like that? Death-defying driving school?'

'Actually, they call it "Offensive Driving",' Schofield said, glancing over his shoulder. 'It was a special course at Quantico given by a retired Gunnery Sergeant named Kris Hankison. Hank left the Marines in '91 and became a stunt driver in Hollywood. Makes a bundle. But every second year, as a kind of payback to the Corps, he offers the course to Marines assigned to Marine Security Guard Battalion. I got invited last year. You think that was good, you wouldn't believe what Hank can do on four wheels—'

Brrrrrrrrrrrrr!

A line of bullets razed the road beside Schofield's WRX, chewing up the bitumen, smacking against his driver's door. A split-second later one of the nimble Skorpion Mi-34 choppers roared by overhead.

But then the road bent right, hugging the cliff-face—and the chopper continued straight while the WRX whipped out of its line of fire just as—

SLAM!

—a colossal gout of earth exploded out from the rock wall on the right-hand side of the road, sending a starburst of dirt spraying out spectacularly behind the speeding rally car.

'What the—?' Schofield spun, searching for the source of the massive explosion.

And he found it.

'Oh, this cannot be happening . . .' he breathed.

He saw a *warship* powering in toward the coast, separating itself from a larger group of naval vessels on the horizon.

It was a French Tourville-class destroyer and its powerful 3.9-inch forward-mounted guns were firing, each shot accompanied by a belch of smoke and a noise so loud that it reverberated right through one's chest: *Boom! Boom! Boom!*

Then a second later . . .

SLAM!

SLAM!

SLAM!

The shells *rammed* into the cliff-side roadway, raining dirt all around Schofield's speeding car. Explosions of asphalt and dirt flew high into the air, leaving lethal craters in their wake—craters that took up nearly half the roadway.

After the first shellburst hit, Schofield's WRX screamed over the edge of its crater, blasting through the dustcloud above it and, looking down, Schofield saw that the shell had gouged a semi-circular hole in the Ocean Road that led all the way down to the sea.

The other shells rained down on the Great Ocean Road, striking it left and right. Schofield responded by flinging the rally car right and left, avoiding the newly-created craters by centimetres.

The Axon helicopter behind him banked and swayed, also trying to avoid the destroyer's deadly rain.

But the two more nimble Skorpion Mi-34 choppers didn't care, they just continued to pursue Schofield with a vengeance, their side-mounted cannons shredding the road.

And then Schofield's WRX rounded a bend and zoomed into a cliff-side tunnel and the two Russian choppers rose quickly, swooping over the jagged cliffs, and suddenly Schofield and Gant were enveloped by silence.

Not for long.

Into the tunnel behind them rushed the two ExSol sports cars— the Ferrari and the Porsche—their engines roaring, each car's gunner firing at the fleeing WRX.

Schofield swung left, toward the ocean side of the tunnel and abruptly discovered that this tunnel wasn't technically a tunnel— precisely because its entire seaward wall wasn't a wall at all. It was a series of thin columns that rushed by in a fluttering blur, allowing drivers to take in the view as they passed through the tunnel.

Schofield caught this information just as he saw a Skorpion chopper appear outside the blurring line of pillars and start firing *into* the exposed tunnel!

Bullets slammed into the road, his car, and against the far wall.

Schofield weaved right, away from the barrage, pressed his WRX up against the right-hand wall of the curving tunnel, losing speed . . .

. . . and in a second the pursuit cars were on him, the Porsche ramming into his rear bumper, the Ferrari boxing him in on the left, their two ExSol shooter-passengers letting fly.

Automatic gunfire ripped into the WRX.

Schofield's side window shattered—

—just as a deadly shape appeared at the end of the tunnel.

The second Skorpion Mi-34 chopper, rising above the roadway, its side-mounted missile pods poised and ready to fire.

'We're dead,' Schofield said matter-of-factly.

A flare of yellow backblast issued out from the back of one of the chopper's missile pods just as without warning the chopper itself exploded in mid-air—hit by a shell from the French destroyer off the coast. The Mi-34's missile exploded too, having never cleared its pod.

The massive naval shell hit the Skorpion helicopter so hard that the chopper was hurled against the edge of the roadway, where it crumpled like an aluminium can before falling 400 feet straight down. It hadn't been a deliberate strike, Schofield felt. The chopper had just got in the way.

'Close,' Gant said.

'Just a little,' he said as their car blasted out of the tunnel, racing past the spot where the Mi-34 had fallen, still boxed in against the rock wall by the two ExSol cars.

The three cars whipped along a short stretch of road. But then Schofield saw another tunnel yawning before them, 200 yards awa—

Bang!

The Ferrari rammed into the WRX's left side, forcing it closer to the rock wall.

Schofield grappled with his steering wheel.

The Porsche, meanwhile, pushed up against his rear bumper.

At first Schofield didn't know why they had done this, then he looked forward and saw that the arched entrance to the upcoming tunnel was *not* flush against the rock wall—it jutted out about six feet.

And so long as the Ferrari and the Porsche kept Schofield and Gant's car pressed up against the rock wall and travelling forward, the WRX would slam right into the protruding archway.

Schofield guessed they had about five seconds.

'This is very bad . . .' Gant said.

'I know, I know,' Schofield said.

Four seconds . . .

The three cars raced in formation along the narrow cliff-side roadway.

Three seconds . . .

The Ferrari pushed them up against the rocky wall on their right. The WRX's right wheels lifted slightly, rubbing against the hard stone wall. But the Porsche behind it kept pushing it forward fast.

'Please do something,' Gant said.

Two seconds . . .

The stone archway of the tunnel rushed toward them.

'Okay . . .' Schofield said. 'You want to play nasty? Let's play nasty.'

One . . .

Then, just as the WRX was about to slam at tremendous speed into the arched entrance of the tunnel, Schofield allowed the Ferrari to push him *closer* to the wall, driving him further up it, making the WRX rise up to about 60 degrees, its right-hand wheels riding clear up onto the wall itself.

And then time slowed and Schofield did the impossible.

He let the WRX ride so high up the rocky wall that, five metres short of the tunnel's archway, the electric blue rally car went too high . . . and *rolled* . . . to the left, turning completely upside down . . . so that it landed, on its roof . . . *on the roof of the low-slung Ferrari travelling beside it.*

And so, for a brief instant in time, the WRX and the Ferrari were travelling rooftop-to-rooftop, the WRX's wheels pointing skyward, its roof resting momentarily on the roof of the lower red Ferrari!

And then time sped up again and the WRX rolled off the Ferrari, bouncing back down to earth, now safely on the ocean side of the scarlet red supercar, and blasted into the tunnel with the Ferrari on its right.

The Porsche, unfortunately, had no options.

Travelling right behind Schofield it had intended to pull away at the last moment. Its driver, however, had never imagined that Schofield might *roll over the top of* the Ferrari. When Schofield did so, the Porsche driver stared at his feat for a split second too long.

As such, it was the Porsche that hit the archway at colossal speed. Instant fireball.

The Ferrari was only slightly more fortunate.

Having rolled over the top of it, Schofield now started ramming *it* into the wall of the tunnel. He did a better job than they had, cutting across the bow of the Ferrari, causing it to jackknife against the tunnel's right-hand wall and flip and tumble—spinning over and over like a toy flung by a child—bouncing down the confined space of the tunnel, skimming off its walls, before it stopped on its roof, wrecked and crumpled, its occupants deader than disco.

Schofield and Gant blasted out of the tunnel, just as the second Skorpion Mi-34 attack chopper swooped in alongside them, flying parallel to the cliff-side roadway with a sniper in its right-side doorway firing viciously.

One thing was clear—while Schofield was driving as fast as he could, the nimble chopper was merely cruising.

'Fox!' Schofield called. 'We have to get rid of that chopper! Nail that sniper!'

'Gladly,' Gant said. 'Lean back!'

Schofield did so as Gant raised her Desert Eagle pistol and fired it across his body, out through his window at the chopper.

Two shots. Both hit their mark.

And the sniper dropped . . . out of the chopper's door.

But he was buckled to a safety rope, so after about 40 feet of falling, his rope snapped taut and his fall abruptly stopped.

'Thanks, honey babe!' Schofield called, watching the suspended figure when suddenly Gant shouted, 'Scarecrow! Look out! Another fork!'

He snapped forward and saw a new fork in the road, this one with a side-road branching left and downward, while the Ocean Road continued flat to the right.

Left or right, he thought. *Pick a side.*

A shellburst from the incoming French destroyer hit the right-hand road.

Left it is.

He swung the car left, tyres squealing, and careered down the steeply sloping side-road.

The chopper followed.

Half a mile behind Schofield, Aloysius Knight was shooting along the Great Ocean Road in his shiny black Lamborghini Diablo.

The two semi-trailer rigs that had formed the road block before now rumbled along directly in front of him, while beyond them, he saw the three yellow Axon-sponsored Peugeots that ExSol had taken from the castle.

And about fifty yards beyond the Peugeots, he saw Schofield's blue WRX reach a fork in the road, hounded by the remaining Skorpion Mi-34 helicopter.

Knight stole a glance left at the destroyer out on the ocean, just as two bird-like shadows shot through the air over the warship, heading directly for the coastal road.

They looked decidedly like *fighter jets*, originating from the French aircraft carrier on the horizon.

Uh-oh, Knight thought.

He faced forward again just in time to see Schofield's car cut left at the fork in the road, disappearing down a side-road set into the cliff-face.

At which point, he saw Schofield's pursuers do a strange thing.

They split up.

Only one of the Axon Peugeots followed Schofield down the side-road. The other two went right, following the Ocean Road, skirting a newly-formed crater in the roadway.

Then the two trailer rigs came to the fork and went left, charging *down* the hill after Schofield.

Co-ordinated movement, Knight thought. *They've got a plan.*

And then Knight himself reached the fork and without any hesitation, he gunned the Lamborghini down the left-hand roadway, shooting down the hill after Schofield.

★ ★ ★

Schofield's WRX whizzed down the steep boathouse road, burning around blind corners, skidding around tight bends.

As it sped along, a storm of bullets hammered its flanks and the rock walls all around it—it was still under heavy fire from the Mi-34 chopper flying low through the air behind it, firing at the WRX with its side-mounted machine-guns.

The chopper's dead sniper still hung limply from its open side door, his body swaying wildly, occasionally bouncing on the road, leaving blood on the asphalt.

More fire came from the yellow Peugeot rally car that had followed Schofield down the boathouse road, from the shooter poking out of its passenger-side window with a Steyr.

Two hundred yards behind this speeding gun battle, Knight was also driving hard.

His Lamborghini easily hauled in the two semi-trailer rigs, and he whizzed past them in a fluid S-shaped move before they even knew he was there.

Knight came up behind the yellow Peugeot, tried to get around it on the right, but the Peugeot blocked him. Tried left and gunned it hard—very hard—and in a daring move, overtook the Peugeot on the ocean side of the road.

The Lamborghini shot past the yellow rally car, the driver of the Peugeot looking left just in time to see the Diablo rocket by in a blur of black—at the same time as an M-67 grenade came lobbing in through his open driver's window.

The Lamborghini shot down the road as the Peugeot erupted in a ball of flames. The flaming Peugeot promptly missed the next curve and blasted right through the guard-rail fence there and fell—a long, slow drop that ended in the Atlantic Ocean far, far below.

Knight's Lamborghini was now twenty yards behind Schofield's WRX and the Mi-34 chopper above it.

Knight saw that Schofield was now racing down a long straight stretch of road that ended at a tunnel at the very base of this side-road—a tunnel that gave access to an enormous boatshed.

'Schofield!' Knight called into his radio. 'Don't shoot behind you, okay! The Lamborghini is me!'

'*The Lamborghini. Why doesn't that surprise me,*' said Schofield's voice. '*Nice of you to join us. Anything you can do about this damn helicopter?*'

Knight took in the scene: saw Schofield's blue WRX up ahead, rapidly approaching the tunnel—saw the underbelly of the Mi-34 directly above and behind the WRX, saw the swaying Russian sniper dangling from it, banging and bouncing on the road right in front of his speeding Diablo.

Chopper—sniper—tunnel, he thought.

All he needed was an escape vehicle.

Knight glanced at his rear-view mirror: it was filled by the grille of the first rig—it was a Mack rig, with a distinctive long-nosed bon-net—rumbling down the road behind him.

Thank you very much.

'Hang on, Schofield. I've got this sucker.'

He powered forward, bringing the Lamborghini under the Mi-34 chopper, out of its sight. Then with a rather morbid bang, he charged his car right *into* the dangling sniper's corpse, so that the body bounced up onto his bonnet and then dropped in through the Diablo's open targa roof.

Knight whipped out a pair of handcuffs—the bounty hunter's most valuable tool—and cuffed the dead sniper's safety harness to the steering wheel of his Lamborghini.

He then hit the cruise control and jumped out of his seat, climbing up and out through the targa roof.

At that moment, the big Mack rig caught up with him and rammed into the back of the Lamborghini.

But Knight was ready for the impact, and as the two vehicles touched, he made his move—dashing across the flat rear section of the Lamborghini, firing his pistol into the windshield of the Mack

as he did so, killing its driver, and then leaping from the rear of the Lamborghini onto the long nose of the Mack!

Within seconds, he was through the rig's shattered windscreen and in its driver's seat, in control of the big rig—and with a front row seat for what was about to happen.

Schofield's WRX shot into the tunnel at the base of the hill.

The Skorpion chopper—knowing it had to go over the tunnel and recapture Schofield on the other side—lifted, or rather, tried to lift.

But the lightweight Mi-34 chopper *couldn't* rise, owing to the weight of the Lamborghini now anchored to it.

The Skorpion pilot realised the implications of this a second too late.

The driverless Lamborghini rushed into the tunnel's arched entrance, while the chopper rushed *over* it, and to the pilot's horror, the vertical rope connecting the two vehicles went taut and . . . folded . . . as it hit the archway.

The Skorpion chopper and the Lamborghini came together like a pair of scissor blades.

The Diablo was lifted completely off the ground, flying upwards, crunching into the ceiling of the tunnel, crumpling in an instant, bringing down a rain of tiles as it did so.

For its part, the Mi-34 was yanked *downward* by the rope, and it slammed down into the rocks above the tunnel and exploded in a shower of fire and rubble.

Knight shot under it all—at the wheel of the Mack rig—roaring into the tunnel, shooting past the fiery remains of his discarded Lamborghini.

Up ahead, Schofield blasted out the other end of the same tunnel, started zooming up the hill.

He rounded a corner, saw the upwardly-sloping road ahead—lots of sweeping bends and blind corners, and at the top of the road, the two other yellow Peugeots that had taken the high road.

They'd gone ahead, taking the shorter route, and doubled back, so that now they were shooting *down* this road, on a collision course with him and Gant.

Schofield's WRX powered up the hill, now trailed by only two vehicles, the two rigs: Knight's long-nosed Mack and the second rig, a snub-nosed Kenworth.

But then the WRX swept around a blind corner and was abruptly confronted by another unexpected sight:

A fighter jet had swung into a hover just out from the bend, its nose pointed menacingly downward, an arsenal of missiles hanging from its wings.

Schofield recognised it instantly as a Dassault Mirage 2000N-II, the French equivalent of the Harrier jump-jet. Converted from the regular Mirage 2000N, the 'II' was a hover-capable fighter stationed only on France's newest and biggest aircraft carriers. It looked a lot like a Harrier, stocky and hunchbacked, with semi-circular air intakes on either side of a two-man cockpit.

The Mirage's guns erupted and a swarm of laser-like tracer bullets tore into the rock walls above Schofield's car.

Schofield floored it, whipping past the hovering plane as it

wheeled around heavily in the air, its bullet-storm chasing him, but he shot around another bend just as some of its tracers sheared off his rear bumper.

'Here, quickly, take the wheel,' Schofield said to Gant.

She slipped over into the driver's seat while he dipped into a pocket on his combat webbing and removed some bullets—Knight's orange-banded rounds. Bull-stoppers.

'People, no. Fighter planes, yes,' he said as he loaded the orange bullets into his Desert Eagle's magazine, finishing at the same time as a second Mirage swooped down over the road right in front of the WRX, its guns blazing.

But now, Schofield was ready to respond.

He lifted himself out the passenger window, sat on its sill, and pointed his Desert Eagle dead ahead.

The Mirage's bullets tore up the road in front of the WRX just as Schofield started firing repeatedly at the hovering plane—*blam!-blam!-blam!-blam!-blam!-blam!-blam!-blam!-blam!*—hitting it in both of its air intakes at the same time as some of the fighter's tracers sizzled in through the windscreen of his WRX.

Schofield's gas-expanding bullets did their job.

As the first bullets hit the Mirage's intake fans, their internal gases blasted outward, tearing the fans' blades to pieces, warping them, causing them to jam and the plane to stall and also to allow the following bullets to race fully *into* the jet engines themselves and detonate within the plane's highly volatile fuel injection chambers.

Two small bullets was all it took to destroy a $600 million warplane.

Its engines failing, the Mirage wheeled wildly around in the sky, spraying tracer bullets everywhere, before—*boom!*—the French fighter blasted out into a thousand pieces, showering liquid fire, before it just dropped out of the sky, landing in a crumpled smoking heap on the road 50 yards in front of the speeding WRX.

Schofield dropped back inside the passenger window . . .

. . . to see Gant slumped against her door, blood gushing from a giant wound to her left shoulder. A two-inch-wide hole could be seen in the driver's seat behind her, matching the location of her wound.

She'd been hit by one of the Mirage's tracer bullets.

'Oh, no . . .' Schofield breathed. He dived across the seat, hit the brakes.

The WRX squealed to a halt, just short of the wreckage of the Mirage.

'Fox!' Schofield yelled. 'Libby!'

Her eyes opened, heavy-lidded. 'Ow, that hurts . . .' she groaned.

'Come on,' Schofield kicked open the door and lifted her out, carrying her in his arms. Then, into his radio: 'Knight! Where are you!'

'*I'm in the first rig. With another one close behind me. Where are—hang on, I see you.*'

'Fox has been hit. We need a ride.'

'*When I pull up, get in fast, 'cause that other rig is going to be right on my ass.*'

And then Schofield saw Knight: saw the long-nosed Mack rig rumbling up the slope, moving quickly.

With a loud shriek of its brakes, the Mack shuddered to a stop beside the WRX.

Knight threw open the door, and Schofield lifted Gant and himself in. Knight jammed the truck back into gear and hit the gas a bare moment before the snub-nosed Kenworth rig appeared around the bend behind them, coming at full speed, its engine roaring.

The Mack jounced and bounced over the wreckage of the Mirage fighter strewn across the road, picking up speed. The second rig just barged right through the Mirage's remains before ramming hard into the back of Knight's still-accelerating rig.

Knight, Schofield and Gant were all thrown forward by the impact.

Knight and Schofield turned to each other and said at exactly the same time: 'There are two rally cars coming at us from in front!'

They both paused. Mirror images.

'What happened to her!' Knight said.

'She got shot by a fighter plane,' Schofield said.

'Oh.'

The two trucks charged up the hill, their exhaust stacks belching black smoke.

Then suddenly the two yellow rally cars that had gone ahead came into view, rounding a wide bend *right in front of* Knight and Schofield's rig, roaring *down* the same slope—both cars featuring men leaning out their passenger windows, holding AK-47 machine-guns.

They might as well have been firing pea-shooters.

The giant Mack rig blasted right through the left-hand Peugeot, blowing it to smithereens, while the second Axon rally car just fishtailed out of the way, side-swiping the rock wall on the landward side of the roadway before skidding to a jarring halt, the two rigs rumbling past it.

The Mack reached the top of the hill and rejoined the flatter main road at a fork junction.

The snub-nosed Kenworth was right behind it, closely followed by the last-remaining Peugeot. Rejoining the chase, the rally car leapt up onto the main road a split second before—*SLAM!*—the entire fork junction erupted in a cloud of dirt, hit by a shell from the ever-present French destroyer.

The two big rigs flew around a bend, the ocean dropping away to their left, when suddenly they were confronted by the yawning entrance to another cliff-side tunnel. This tunnel bent away in a long curve to the right, hugging the cliff-face, and was clearly longer than any of the previous tunnels.

The Mack thundered into the tunnel doing ninety, just as behind it, the Peugeot pulled alongside the Kenworth and the gunman in the rally car's window unleashed a volley of fire at the Mack's rearmost tyres.

The Mack's tyres were blasted apart, started slapping against the roadway, and the big rig's rear-end started fishtailing wildly.

Which was when the Kenworth rig made its move, and powered forward.

'They're coming alongside us!' Schofield yelled.

In the confines of the tunnel, the snub-nosed rig pulled up next to the Mack's right-hand flank.

'I'll take care of it,' Knight said. 'Here, take the wheel.'

With that, Knight jumped out of the driver's seat and charged aft into the Mack's sleeping compartment where he quickly fired two shots into its rear window, a window which opened onto the rig's flat trailer-connection section. Within seconds he had disappeared out through the window, into the roaring wind.

The two rigs rushed through the curving tunnel side-by-side, whipping past its ocean-side columns.

Schofield drove, glancing at the wounded Gant beside him. She was hit badly this time.

There came a loud aerial boom from somewhere nearby, and Schofield snapped round to see the second Mirage fighter whip past the blurring columns on his left, shooting ahead of the chase.

Not a good sign, he thought.

And then the snub-nosed rig came fully alongside his own on the right. He saw two ExSol men inside its cabin, and as it drew level with the Mack, he saw the gunner climb quickly across the driver and throw open the door closest to the Mack.

He was going to come across.

Schofield raised his Desert Eagle pistol in response—*click.*

No ammo left.

'Crap!'

The Executive Solutions man leapt across the gap between the two speeding semi-trailer rigs, landing on the passenger step of Schofield's Mack. He raised his machine-gun, pointing it in through the window, an unmissable shot—

—at the same time as Schofield drew his Maghook from his thigh holster, aimed it at the thug and pulled the trigger—

Ppp-fzzz . . .

The Maghook didn't fire. It just emitted a weak fizzing sound. It was out of propulsion gas.

'Goddamn it!' Schofield yelled. 'That never happens!'

But now he was out of options: he and Gant were sitting ducks.

The ExSol man in the window saw this, and he leered, his finger squeezing on his trigger.

At which moment he was squashed like a pancake as the Kenworth rig—his rig—rammed viciously into the Mack, hitting it so hard that both trucks were lifted momentarily off the road!

The hapless mercenary simply exploded, his body popping in a burst of red, his eyes bugging before he dropped out of Schofield's view and fell to the rushing roadway beneath the two rigs.

And as the man dropped from sight, he revealed the new driver of the snub-nosed Kenworth rig—Aloysius Knight.

For when the ExSol mercenary had jumped over from the doorway of the Kenworth to the doorway of the Mack, another figure had crossed over *in the other direction*, from the rear section of the Mack to the rear section of the Kenworth rig.

Knight.

Now the two rigs raced side-by-side through the long curving tunnel, pursued only by the last yellow Peugeot.

But with its blown-open rear tyres, Schofield's Mack was dangerously unstable. It slipped and slid wildly, trying to get traction.

Schofield keyed his radio. 'Knight! I can't hold this truck! We have to come over to you!'

'*All right, I'll come in closer. Send your lady over.*'

The Kenworth swung in next to the Mack, rubbing up against its side.

Schofield quickly secured the Mack's steering wheel in place with his seatbelt. Then he shuffled over, kicked open the passenger door, and started to help Gant move.

At the same time, Knight opened his driver's side door and extended his spare hand.

Abruptly, gunfire.

Smacking into both trucks' frames. But it was just wild fire from the trailing Peugeot.

Schofield made the transfer, handed Gant over to Knight—who pulled her across the gap into the Kenworth's cab, before laying her gently on the passenger seat.

With Gant safely across, Schofield started to step across the gap—

—just as a shocking burst of a zillion tracer bullets ripped horizontally through the air in front of him, creating a lethal laser-like barrier, cutting him off from Knight and Gant's rig.

Schofield snapped to look forward and saw the source of this new wave of gunfire.

He saw the end of the curving tunnel, saw the road bend away to the right beyond it, and saw, rising ominously into the air just out from the turn, the second Mirage 2000N-II fighter, its six-barrelled mini-gun blazing away.

And then, to Schofield's horror, the line of sizzling tracer rounds swung in toward his rig and—*bam!-bam!-bam!-bam!-bam!-bam!-bam!-bam!-bam!-bam!*—an unimaginable barrage of bullets slammed into the metal grille of the Mack, hammering it with a million pock-marks.

The Mack's engine caught fire, hydraulic fluid sprayed everywhere, and suddenly Schofield could see nothing through his windshield. He pumped the brakes—no good; they were history. Tried the steering wheel—it worked only slightly, enough for him to say to the fighter plane:

'If I'm going down, you're going down with me.'

The Mack careered down the length of the tunnel, together with the Kenworth.

And still the Mirage's withering fire didn't stop.

The two rigs hit the end of the tunnel—separated now—and Aloysius Knight had no choice but to take the bend to the right, while Schofield's Mack—its bonnet blazing, its rear tyres sliding—could do nothing but rush *straight ahead*, ignoring the corner.

Schofield saw it all before it happened.

And he knew he could do nothing.

'Good God . . .' he breathed.

A second later, the speeding Mack truck missed the corner completely and blasted *right through* the guard-rail fence and shot out into the clear afternoon sky, heading straight for the hovering Mirage fighter.

The Mack truck soared through the air in a glorious arc, nose high, wheels spinning, its path through the sky traced by the line of black smoke issuing out from its flaming bonnet.

But its arc stopped abruptly as the massive trailer rig slammed at tremendous speed into the Mirage fighter hovering just out from the cliff-side roadway.

The truck and the plane collided with astonishing force, the Mirage lurching backwards in mid-air under the weight of the mighty impact.

Already on fire, the Mack completely blew up now, its flaming bonnet driving into the nose of the hovering French fighter. For its part, the Mirage just rocked—then swayed—and then *exploded*, blasting out in a brilliant blinding fireball.

Then it dropped out of the sky, falling four hundred feet straight down the cliff-face with the remains of the Mack truck buried in its nose, before it smashed into the waves below with a single gigantic splash.

And in the middle of it all, in the middle of the tangled mechanical mess, without a rope or a Maghook to call on, was Shane M. Schofield.

Knight and Gant saw it all from their rig as they sped away along the winding cliff-side road.

They saw Schofield's Mack blast through the guard-rail and crash into the hovering Mirage after which came the fiery explosion and the long drop to the ocean below.

No-one could have survived such an impact.

Despite her wounds, Gant's eyes widened in horror. 'Oh God, no. Shane . . .' she whispered.

'Son of a bitch,' Knight breathed.

A flurry of thoughts rushed through his mind: Schofield was dead—a man worth millions to Knight *if* he could have kept him alive—what did he do now—and what did he do with this wounded woman who was worth absolutely nothing to him?

The first thing you do is get out of here alive, a voice said inside him.

And then suddenly—*shoom!*—the last-remaining Peugeot rally car whizzed past his rig, heading quickly down the road.

Surprised, Knight looked ahead and saw the road before him.

It contained a strange but impressive feature: at the next curve, a small castle-like structure arched over the roadway.

Made of stone and topped with tooth-like battlements, it was a two-storey gatehouse which must have been as old as the Forteresse de Valois itself. Presumably, it marked the outer boundary of the Forteresse's land.

On the far side of this gatehouse, however, was a compact drawbridge, spanning a 20-foot section of empty space in the roadway. You only got over the gap if the drawbridge was lowered, and at the moment, it was.

But then the Peugeot arrived at the gatehouse and disgorged one of its occupants who ran inside—and suddenly, before Knight's eyes, the drawbridge slowly began to rise.

'No . . .' he said aloud. 'No!'

He floored it.

The Kenworth rig roared toward the medieval gatehouse, picking up speed.

The drawbridge rose slowly on its iron chains.

It was going to be close.

The big rig rushed forward.

The bridge rose slowly: *one foot, two feet, three feet* . . .

The men in the Peugeot opened fire as Knight's rig thundered over the last fifty yards.

Knight ducked. His windshield shattered.

The drawbridge kept rising . . .

. . . and then the rig roared in through the gatehouse's archway, whipping past the Executive Solutions men . . .

. . . and raced up the ramp-like drawbridge, easily doing a hundred, before—*voom!*—it launched itself off the leading edge of the bridge, shooting high into the sky, soaring over the vertiginous gap in the road beneath it and . . .

Whump!

. . . the big rig hit solid ground again, banging down on the roadway, bouncing once, twice, three times, before Knight regained control.

'Phwoar,' he sighed, relieved. 'That was—'

SLAM!

The road in front of the rig erupted in a mushroom cloud of dirt.

A shellburst from the destroyer.

Knight hit the brakes and his rig skidded sharply, lurching to a halt inches away from a newly-created hole in the road.

Knight groaned.

The *entire* road in front of him had simply vanished—the whole

width of it vaporised—the distance across the chasm to the other side at least thirty feet.

He and Gant were trapped—perfectly—on the vertical cliff-face, bounded both in front and behind by sheer voids in the roadway.

And at that moment, as if right on cue, the Axon corporate helicopter—which had watched the entire chase from a safe distance high above the road—hovered into view beside them, its pilot speaking into his helmet radio.

'Fuck,' Knight said.

FIFTH ATTACK

ENGLAND–FRANCE–USA
26 OCTOBER 1400 HOURS (ENGLAND)
E.S.T. (NEW YORK, USA) 0900 HOURS

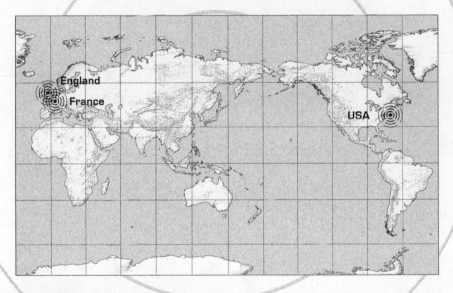

We must guard against the acquisition of unwarranted influence, whether sought or unsought, by the military–industrial complex.

President Dwight D. Eisenhower,
Farewell address to the nation, JANUARY, 1961

**UNITED STATES EMBASSY
LONDON, ENGLAND
1400 HOURS LOCAL TIME
(0900 HOURS E.S.T USA)**

'In their opinion, the war on terror isn't going far enough. While the members of Majestic-12 didn't plan the September 11 attacks, make no mistake, they are taking full advantage of them . . .'

The man talking on the television screen was Benjamin Y. Rosenthal, the Mossad agent who had been killed on the roof of the King's Tower an hour ago.

Book II watched the TV intently. Behind him stood the State Department guy, Scott Moseley.

Arrayed on the desks around them were documents—hundreds of documents. Everything Benjamin Rosenthal knew about Majestic-12 and this world-wide bounty hunt.

Book scanned the pile of documents again:

Surveillance photos of men in limousines arriving at economic summits.

Secretly-taped phone transcripts.

Stolen US Department of Defense files.

Even two documents taken from the French central intelligence agency—the notorious DGSE. One was a DGSE dossier on several of the world's leading businessmen who had been invited to a private dinner with the French President six months ago.

The second document was far more explosive. It outlined the recent capture by the DGSE of 24 members of the terrorist organisation Global Jihad, who had been planning to fly a tanker plane into the Eiffel Tower. Like Al-Qaeda, Global Jihad was a truly world-wide terrorist group, made up of fanatical Islamists who wanted to take the concept of holy war to a whole new global level.

The document that Book now saw was especially notable because one of Global Jihad's leading figures, Shoab Riis, had been among those caught. Normally the capture of such a high-profile terrorist would have been publicised worldwide. But the French had kept Riis's arrest to themselves.

Rosenthal had added a comment in the margin: *'All were taken to DGSE headquarters in Brest. No trial. No newspaper reports. None of the 24 was ever seen again. Possible connection to Kormoran/ Chameleon. Is France working with M-12? Check further.'*

But the most revealing evidence of all was in the Mossad video-tapes of Rosenthal's interrogation.

Put simply, Rosenthal had been sitting on dynamite.

First, he had known the composition of Majestic-12:

The Chairman: Randolph Loch, military industrialist, 70 years old, head of Loch-Mann Industries, the defence contractor. L-M Industries manufactured spare parts for military aircraft like the Huey and Black Hawk helicopters. It had made a fortune out of Vietnam and Desert Storm.

The Vice-Chair: Cornelius Kopassus, the legendary Greek container-shipping magnate.

Arthur Quandt, patriarch of the Quandt family steel empire.

Warren Shusett, the world's most successful investor.

J. D. Cairnton, chairman of the colossal Astronox Pharmaceutical Company.

Jonathan Killian, chairman and CEO of Axon Corp, the vast missile and warship-building conglomerate.

The list went on.

Apart from the absence of a few retail fortunes—like the Walton family in America, the Albrechts in Germany or the Mattencourts in France—it could have been a list of the Top Ten Richest People on Earth.

And as Major Benjamin Rosenthal had discovered, they were all men whose fortunes would be considerably enlarged by one thing.

Rosenthal on the screen: '*Their fortunes are based on military action. War. World War II was the foundation of the Quandt steel empire. In the '60s, Randolph Loch was one of the most vocal supporters of the US going to Vietnam. Warfare consumes oil. Warfare consumes steel. Warfare calls for the construction of thousands of new ships, helicopters, guns, bombs, pharmaceutical kits. In a world of big business, global warfare is the biggest business of them all.*'

And at another time:

'*Look at the "War on Terror". The United States dropped over four thousand bombs on the mountains of Afghanistan, and for what result? They didn't destroy bridges or supply routes, or military nerve centres. But when four thousand bombs are used, four thousand bombs must be replenished. And that means buying them. And what happened after Afghanistan? Surprise, surprise: another fight was found, this time with Iraq.*'

Another cut:

'*Do not underestimate the influence these men wield. They make Presidents, and they break them. From Bill Clinton's impeachment to the rise of a former KGB agent named Vladimir Putin to the Presidency of Russia, Majestic-12 always has a say in who sits in the seats of world power and for how long. Even if it doesn't directly bankroll a given President's campaign, it always maintains the ability to bring him down at any given moment.*

'*To this end Majestic-12 has forged strong links with leading figures in the world's major intelligence agencies. The Director of the CIA: a former business partner of Randolph Loch. The head of MI-6: Cornelius Kopassus's brother-in-law. That Killian fellow has been a regular visitor to the Paris home of the Director of the DGSE.*

'*After all,*' the Mossad agent smiled, '*who knows more about a country's leaders than that country's own intelligence service?*'

On the TV screen, Rosenthal became serious:

'*More than anything else, though, the war that M-12 loved the most, the war that garnered them more wealth than they ever dreamed of, was the one war that was never actually fought: the US–Soviet Cold War.*

'*Desert Storm. Bosnia. Somalia. Afghanistan. Iraqi Freedom. They pale in comparison to the absolute goldmine that was the Cold War. For as the US–Soviet arms race continued apace and indirect Cold War clashes occurred in Korea and Vietnam, the members of M-12 amassed fortunes of monstrous proportions.*

'*But then in 1991 the impossible happened: the Soviet Union collapsed and it all disappeared.*

'*The Berlin Wall fell and like a dam breaking, American consumerism flooded the globe. And the biggest winners in the globalised world were no longer American military manufacturers. They were American consumer goods retailers: Nike, Coca-Cola, Microsoft. Or European companies like BMW and L'Oreal. I mean, honestly, make-up retailers!*

'*And so ever since, the members of Majestic-12 have been looking for the one thing that will, without question, restore them to their former glory . . .*'

At that moment, with a flourish, Rosenthal extracted another document from one of his files and held it to the camera.

'*. . . a new Cold War.*'

Book II now held that very same document in his hands.

The TV screen in front of him was paused, the image of Rosenthal frozen.

Book scanned the document. It read:

Source	Delivery Sys.	W-H	Origin	Target	Time
Talbot	Shahab-5	TN76	35702.90	00001.65	1145
			5001.00	5239.10	
	Shahab-5	TN76	35702.90	00420.02	1145
			5001.00	4900.25	
	Shahab-5	TN76	35702.90	01312.15	1145
			5001.00	5358.75	
Ambrose	Shahab-5	TN76	28743.05	28743.98	1200
			4104.55	4104.64	
	Shahab-5	TN76	28743.05	28231.05	1200
			4104.55	3835.70	
Jewel	Taep'o-Dong-2	N-8	23222.62	23222.70	1215
			3745.75	3745.80	
	Taep'o-Dong-2	N-8	23222.62	24230.50	1215
			3745.75	3533.02	
	Taep'o-Dong-2	N-8	23222.62	23157.05	1215
			3745.75	4930.52	
Hopewell	Taep'o-Dong-2	N-8	11900.00	11622.50	1230
			2327.00	4000.00	
	Taep'o-Dong-2	N-8	11900.00	11445.80	1230
			2327.00	2243.25	

```
Whale   Shahab-5      TN76   07040.45   07725.05 1245
                             2327.00    2958.65
        Shahab-5      TN76   07040.45   07332.60 1245
                             2327.00    3230.55
```

Names and numbers leapt out at Book, and at first he couldn't make head or tail of it.

But then, slowly, parts of it began to make sense. He recognised the two most repeated names.

`Shahab-5` and `Taep'o-Dong-2`.

The *Shahab-5* and the *Taep'o-Dong*-2 were missiles.

Long-range intercontinental ballistic missiles.

The Shahab-5 was built by Iran. The Taep'o-Dong-2 by North Korea.

If international terrorist organisations like Al-Qaeda or Global Jihad were to ever get their hands on missiles that could deliver nuclear strikes against the West, it would be the Shahab and the Taep'o-Dong.

And each of the missiles was nuclear-tipped, as evidenced by the notations: `TN-76` and `N-8`. The TN-76 was a French-made nuclear warhead; the N-8 was North Korean.

But this list didn't belong to any terrorist organisation.

It belonged to Majestic-12.

And then it hit Book.

Could this be Majestic-12 impersonating a terrorist organisation?

He turned quickly, unpaused the image of Rosenthal on the screen.

The Israeli agent spoke again: 'This new Cold War is an enhanced War against Terrorism. A 50-year War on Terror.

'Majestic-12 are utilising two US projects to execute their plan: one is called "Kormoran", the other "Chameleon". Kormoran encompasses the launch vessels: missile-launching warships disguised as container ships or supertankers. These supertanker shells are built by the Kopassus Shipping Group, while the missile-launch systems are inserted into those shells at Axon plants in Norfolk, Virginia and Guam. These ships—ordinary-looking supertankers and container ships—can sit in harbours and ports around the world and yet never be noticed. That is Kormoran.

'The "Chameleon" project, however, is far more sinister. Indeed, it is perhaps the most sinister program ever devised by the United States. It centres on the missiles themselves. You see, the missiles mentioned in the document are not pure Shahabs or Taep'o-Dongs.

'Rather, they are US-built clones of those missiles. What you have to understand is that every major missile in the world has its own personal characteristics: flight signature, contrail wake, even the blast signature left after an impact. Chameleon is designed to exploit these differences. It is a deep-black US project under which America is building intercontinental ballistic missiles that mimic the characteristics of ICBMs built by other countries.

'Clone missiles.

'But Chameleon isn't limited to Iranian Shahabs and North Korean Taep'o-Dongs. Other missiles that have been cloned include the Indian Agni-II, the Pakistani Ghauri-II, the Taiwanese Sky Horse, the UK Trident-II D-5, the French M-5, the Israeli Jericho 2B, and of course the Russian SS-18.

'They are designed to start wars, but to make it look like someone else fired the first shot. If ever the US needs an excuse to wage war, it simply fires a clone of whichever country it seeks to blame.

'The thing is, just as the Chameleon Project has been contracted to the Axon Corporation, the Kormoran supertanker shells are built by Kopassus Shipping. And that is the key. Both projects are contracted to companies owned by M-12 members.'

'At 11.45 on October 26 we are going to see a rain of nuclear missiles. A rain such as the world has never seen. Co-ordinated. Precise. Missiles falling in fifteen-minute intervals, to accommodate the global news media. One missile hit is reported just as another lands, then another—striking major cities around the world. London, New York, Paris, Berlin. The world is plunged into chaos, wondering which major city will be next.

'And when it is over, the investigation begins, and the missiles—by their flight characteristics and blast signatures—are determined to be Iranian and North Korean.

'Terrorist weapons.

'The world is aghast. Then, naturally, horror turns to anger. The War on Terror must be expanded. It has already been going for two years. Now it runs for another fifty. A new Cold War has begun and the military–industrial complex is mobilised like never before. And Majestic-12 makes billions.'

Book's mind raced.

Disguised supertankers. Cloned missiles. And all of it created by his own government. He couldn't believe it. He knew the US Government could do terrible things, but setting up other nations with false missiles?

And now these cloned missiles were to be fired—not by the US Government, but by the missiles' builders, the men of Majestic-12— on major cities around the world: New York, London, Paris and Berlin . . .

New York, London, Paris . . .

And now Book saw the decimalised numbers on the list in a new light.

They were co-ordinates.

GPS co-ordinates of both the launch boats and the targeted cities.

It was then that he noticed the names of the Kormoran supertankers—*Ambrose, Talbot, Jewel Hopewell, Whale.* Cute joke. They were all named after ships from the *Mayflower* fleet, the ships that had seeded the New World. Just as Majestic-12 was now attempting to create a new world.

But what did all this have to do with Shane Schofield and a bounty hunt requiring his death by 12 noon today? Book thought.

And then he recalled Rosenthal himself, shouting in the rain on the roof of the King's Tower in London:

'It's all about reflexes. Superfast reflexes. The reflexes of the men on that list are the best in the world. *They passed the Cobra tests,* and only someone who passed the Cobra tests can disarm the

CincLock-VII missile security system, and CincLock-VII is at the core of Majestic-12's plan.'

CincLock-VII . . . Book thought.

He flicked through the many folders in front of him, searching for those words.

It didn't take him long to find them.

There was a whole file marked 'AXON CORP—PATENTED CINCLOCK SECURITY SYSTEM'.

It was filled with documents belonging to Axon Corp and the US Department of Defense. The first document's cover sheet was marked:

```
        PROJECT: CHAMELEON-042
          (VARIANT INCORPORATING
    CINCLOCK-VII LAUNCH SECURITY SYSTEM)


           US DEPARTMENT OF DEFENSE
            SECURITY LEVEL: 009


                 TOP SECRET


     Contractor: Axon Corporation LLC
        Progress Report: May, 2002
```

Book flicked to the section marked 'SECURITY', read the lead paragraph:

DISARM SYSTEM—CINCLOCK VII
In keeping with the high level of security necessary for such a weapon, the *Chameleon* series of missiles has been equipped with Axon's patented CincLock-VII disarm system. The most secure anti-tamper mechanism in the world today, CincLock-VII employs three unique defensive protocols. Unless all three protocols are applied in the prescribed sequence, system activation (or de-activation) is impossible.

The key to the system is the second protocol. It is based on the well-established principles of pattern-recognition (Haynes & Simpson, MIT 1994, 1997, 2001), whereby only a person who is familiar with, and well-practised in, an established sequential pattern can enter it on demand. A stranger to the system, unless he or she is possessed of abnormally quick motor-neural reflexes, cannot hope to overcome such a system (op. cit. Oliphant & Nicholson, USAMRMC, 1996, NATO MNRR study).

Employing these principles, field tests have shown the CincLock VII system to be 99.94% secure against unauthorised use. No other security system in the military can boast such a success rate.

PROTOCOLS

The three protocols of the CincLock VII unit are as follows:

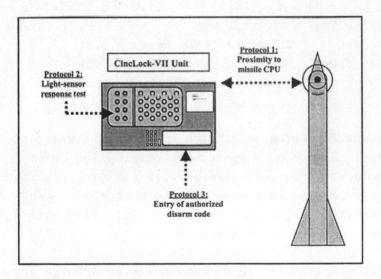

1. *Proximity*. To ensure against unauthorised arming/disarming, the CincLock unit is *not* attached to the delivery system. It is a portable disarming unit. The first protocol, then, is proximity to the delivery system. CincLock will only operate within sixty (60) feet of a Chameleon missile's central processing unit.

2. *Light-sensor response unit.* Once inside the proximity perimeter, the user must establish a wireless modem connection with the disarm system. This is effected by satisfying Axon's patented light-sensor interface. It is here that the principles of pattern recognition play their crucial part. (See NATO MNRR Research Program results, USAMRMC, 1996.)

3. *Security code.* Entry of the relevant disarm or override code.

To this last line Rosenthal had added: *'Universal Disarm Code insertion was supervised by subject Weitzman. Latest intelligence suggests use of a yet-to-be-determined Mersenne Prime.'*

Another page, however, was clipped to this protocol section. It was a Mossad telephone intercept transcript:

```
Trans log:    B2-3-001-889
Date:         25 April, 1515 hours E.S.T.
Rec from:     Axon Corp, Norfolk, VA, USA
Katsa:        ROSENTHAL, Benjamin Y (452-7621)
```

```
VOICE 1 (DALTON, P.J. AXON CHIEF OF ENGINEERING):
Sir, the D.O.D. inspection report is in. It's
good. They're very pleased with our progress. And
they particularly loved CincLock. Couldn't get
enough of it. Christ, they were like kids with a
new toy, trying to crack it.

VOICE 2 (KILLIAN, J.J. AXON CHAIR AND CEO):
Excellent, Peter. Excellent. Anything else?

VOICE 1: (DALTON) The next oversight inspection.
D.O.D asked if we had a preferred date.

VOICE 2: (KILLIAN) Why don't we make it October 26.
```

I believe that date would suit some of our partners
on this project very nicely.

Book II leaned back in his chair.

So there was the significance of the date.

October 26.

Killian had set it as the date for a Department of Defense oversight team to examine his installation plants.

But then Book saw the next document, and suddenly the meaning of the bounty hunt became clear.

Ironically, it was the most innocuous of all the documents he had
seen so far. An internal email from Axon Corp:

From:	**Peter Dalton**
To:	**All Engineering Staff, Project 'C-042'**
Date:	**26 April, 2003, 7:58 p.m.**
Subject:	**NEXT D.O.D. INSPECTION**

**Ladies and gentlemen, I am pleased to announce that last week's
six-monthly inspection by the Department of Defense Oversight
Committee went spectacularly well. I thank you all for your hard
work, especially over the past few months.**

**They were impressed with our progress and amazed by our
technological gains.**

**The next six-monthly inspection is slated for 26 October at the
Norfolk installation plant, to commence at 12 noon, department
heads only. As usual, strict security clearance provisions will
apply for the week preceding the inspection.**

Regards,

PD

And that was it.

At 12 noon today, October 26, the Department of Defense would be sending an inspection team into Axon's missile construction facility in Norfolk, Virginia.

And presumably at that time, they were going to discover that something was amiss at the plant, that the missiles had been tampered with in some way, or perhaps even gone—stolen—at which point . . .

. . . the US Government would go searching for the only men in the world who were able to disarm the CincLock system.

Men with abnormally quick reflexes.

The men on the list.

And then it dawned on Book—for some reason, Jonathan Killian and Majestic-12 *wanted* the US Government to carry out that inspection today. Although he didn't know why yet, somehow today's inspection was an integral part of their plan.

Which made him understand something else more clearly. It had always bothered Book that this bounty hunt might only serve to *warn* the very men who could foil M-12's plans.

But now this explained it.

At 12 noon today, the US Government was going to discover *something* at Axon's Norfolk plant, something about the state of the Chameleon missiles and the Kormoran launch ships. Something which was crucial to Majestic-12's plan to start a new Cold War.

'We have to get to that plant,' Book said aloud.

He turned to Scott Moseley. 'Mr Moseley. Call the Department of Defense. Tell them to send their Kormoran–Chameleon inspection team in early. And get on the horn to our people in Guam. Get someone to check out Axon's plant there as well.'

'Got it,' Moseley said.

Book then turned his attention to the stream of decimalised numbers on the launch list: the GPS co-ordinates of the launch sites and

the targets. 'Better find out where these missiles are going to be fired from and what they're aiming at.'

As he booted up a GPS plotting program on his computer, he keyed his satellite radio. 'Scarecrow! It's Book! Come in! I've got some big news for you . . .'

NEAR THE FORTERESSE DE VALOIS
BRITTANY, FRANCE
26 OCTOBER, 1500 HOURS LOCAL TIME
(0900 HOURS E.S.T USA)

The Axon chopper that had swung to a halt in front of Aloysius Knight and Libby Gant could be seen zooming away along the coastline, getting smaller and smaller, heading back toward the Forteresse de Valois—with Knight and Gant now inside it.

A lone figure treading water in the ocean waves at the base of the cliffs watched it fly away.

Schofield.

Naturally, when his blazing Mack had launched itself off the roadway and smashed into the hovering Mirage fighter jet, Schofield hadn't been in it.

As soon as his truck's tyres had left the road, he had bailed out the driver's side door, dropping into the air beneath the flying rig.

The truck hit the fighter.

Gigantic explosion. Colossal noise. Metal flying everywhere.

But Schofield had been *under* the blast when it had happened—well below the fireball, but also out of Gant or Knight's sight—and he fell like a bullet through the air.

His first thought had been: *Maghook.*

Not this time. Out of propellant.

Damn.

He kept falling—not vertically, but at a slanting angle thanks to the inertia of the truck—the cliff-face streaking past him at phenomenal speed. He saw the ocean waves below him, rushing upwards. If he hit the water from this height, his body would explode against the surface and burst like a tomato.

Do something! his mind screamed.

Like what!

And then he remembered—

—and quickly yanked the ripcord on his chest webbing. The ripcord that was attached to the attack parachute still on his back. He'd been wearing it ever since the battle on board the Hercules. It had been so compact that he'd almost forgotten it was there.

The attack parachute blossomed above him, a bare 80 feet above the water.

It didn't slow his fall completely, but it did enough.

He lurched in the air about 20 feet above the waves, his downward speed significantly reduced, before—*shoom*—he entered the water feet-first and disengaged the parachute, allowing himself to shoot into the ocean trailing a finger of bubbles above him.

And not a second too soon.

For a moment later, the Mack rig and the Mirage fighter crashed down in a flaming metal heap into the waves nearby.

Schofield surfaced a short distance out from the cliffs, amid some of the burning remains of the fighter jet.

Careful to stay out of sight, he trod water amid the floating debris and sure enough, a minute later, he saw the Axon chopper swing around a nearby cliff-bend and zoom back toward the castle.

Had Gant and Knight got away? Or were they in that chopper?

'Fox! Fox! Come in! This is Scarecrow,' he whispered into his throat-mike. 'For what it's worth, I'm still alive. Are you okay?'

A single laboured cough answered him. It was an old technique—she was up there but she obviously couldn't talk. They'd caught her.

'One for yes, two for no. Are you in that Axon chopper I just saw?'

Single cough.

'Are you wounded badly?'

Single cough.

'Really badly?'

Single cough.

Shit, Schofield thought.

'Is Knight with you?'

Single cough.

'Are they taking you back to the castle?'

Single cough.

'Hang in there, Libby. I'm coming for you.'

Schofield looked around himself and was about to start swimming for the shore when abruptly he saw the French destroyer surging to a halt 200 yards away from him off the coast.

On the side of the great ship, he saw a small patrol boat being lowered into the water, with at least a dozen men on board it.

The patrol boat dropped into the ocean and immediately zipped away from the destroyer, heading directly for him.

Schofield could do nothing except watch the French patrol boat approach him.

'I'm sure the French have forgotten about that thing in Antarctica,' he muttered to himself.

Then his earpiece burst to life.

'*Scarecrow! It's Book! Come in! I've got some big news for you.*'

'Hey, Book, I'm here.'

'*Can you talk?*'

Schofield rose and fell with the waves of the Atlantic. 'Yeah, sure, why not.' He eyed the patrol boat, now only 150 yards away. 'Although I have to warn you, I think I'm about to die.'

'*Yes, but I know why,*' Book II said.

★ ★ ★

'Book, patch Gant and Knight in on this transmission,' Schofield said. 'They can't talk, but I want them to hear this, too.'

Book did so.

Then he told them all about the Kormoran 'supertankers' and the Chameleon clone missiles, and Majestic-12's plan to start a new Cold War—on Terror—by firing those missiles on the major cities of the world. He also told them about the CincLock VII security system which only Schofield and those on the list could disarm, and the incorporation by Ronson Weitzman of the US Universal Disarm Code into it, a code which Rosenthal had described as 'a yet-to-be-determined Mersenne Prime'.

Schofield frowned.

'A Mersenne Prime . . .' he said. 'A Mersenne prime number. It's a *number* . . .'

The image of General Ronson Weitzman in the Hercules flashed across his mind, babbling incoherently under the influence of the British truth drug: 'It wasn't just Kormoran. It was Chameleon, too . . . oh God, Kormoran and Chameleon together. Boats and missiles. All disguised. *Christ* . . . But the Universal Disarm Code, it changes every week. At the moment, it's . . . the sixth . . . oh my God, the sixth m . . . m . . . mercen . . . mercen—'

Mercen . . .

Mersenne.

At the time, Schofield had thought Weitzman was just mixing up his sentences, trying to say the word 'mercenary'.

But he wasn't.

Under the influence of the drug, Weitzman had been telling the truth. He had been naming the code.

The Universal Disarm Code was the sixth Mersenne prime number.

As Book relayed his tale to Schofield and the others, behind him Scott Moseley was busy inserting the GPS co-ordinates from the launch list into the plotting program.

'I've got the first three boats,' Moseley said. 'The first co-ordinate must be the location of the Kormoran launch boat, the second is the target.'

He handed Book the document: now with place names added to it and highlighted:

Source	Delivery Sys.	W-H	Origin	Target	Time
Talbot	Shahab-5	TN76	35702.90 5001.00	00001.65 5239.10	1145
			(E. Channel)	(London)	
	Shahab-5	TN76	35702.90 5001.00	00420.02 4900.25	1145
			(E. Channel)	(Paris)	
	Shahab-5	TN76	35702.90 5001.00	01312.15 5358.75	1145
			(E. Channel)	(Berlin)	
Ambrose	Shahab-5	TN76	28743.05 4104.55	28743.98 4104.64	1200
			(New York)	(New York)	
	Shahab-5	TN76	28743.05 4104.55	28231.05 3835.70	1200
			(New York)	(Washington, D.C.)	
Jewel	Taep'o-Dong-2	N-8	23222.62 3745.75	23222.70 3745.80	1215
			(San Fran)	(San Fran)	
	Taep'o-Dong-2	N-8	23222.62 3745.75	24230.50 3533.02	1215
			(San Fran)	(Los Angeles)	
	Taep'o-Dong-2	N-8	23222.62 3745.75	23157.05 4930.52	1215
			(San Fran)	(Seattle)	

Moseley plotted the points on a map. 'The first boat is in the English Channel—off Cherbourg, France, up near the Normandy beaches.'

Book relayed this to Schofield, 'The first boat is in the English Channel, near Cherbourg, off the Normandy beaches. It'll fire on London, Paris and Berlin. The next two boats are in New York and San Francisco, each set to take out multiple cities.'

'Christ,' Schofield said as he hovered in the water.

The patrol boat was 50 yards away, almost on him now.

'Okay, Book. Listen,' he said, just as a low wave smacked him in the face. He spat out a mouthful of salt water. 'Submarine interdiction. Those missile boats can't launch if they're on the bottom of the ocean. Decode the GPS locations of all the Kormoran super-tankers and contact any attack subs we have nearby. 688Is, boomers, I don't care. Anything with a torpedo on board. Then send them to take out those Kormoran launch boats.'

'That might work for some of the tankers, Scarecrow, but it won't work for all of them.'

'I know,' Schofield said. 'I know. If we can't destroy a launch vessel, then we'll have to board it and disarm the missiles in their silos.

'The thing is, a light-signal response unit would require the disarmer—me—to be reacting to a disarm program on the unit's screen. Which means I'd have to be sitting within sixty feet of *each missile's control console* to disarm them, but I can't be everywhere around the world at the same time. Which means I'll need people on each launch boat connecting me via satellite to that boat's missiles.'

'You need people on each boat?'

'That's right, Book. If there are no subs in the area, someone's going to have get on board each Kormoran boat, get within sixty feet of its missile console, attach a satellite uplink to that console and then patch me in via satellite. Only then can I use a CincLock unit to personally stop *all* the missile launches.'

'Holy shit,' Book said. 'So what do you want me to do?'

Another wave splashed over Schofield's head. 'Let's tackle the first three boats first. Get yourself to New York, Book. And call

David Fairfax. Send him to San Francisco. I want people I know on those tankers. If I get out of this alive, I'll try for the tanker in the English Channel. Oh, and ask Fairfax what the sixth Mersenne prime number is. If he doesn't know, tell him to find out.

'And last, send that Department of Defense inspection team in early—the one that was going to visit Axon's missile-construction plant in Norfolk, Virginia, at 12 noon. I want to know what's happened at that plant.'

'Already done that,' Book II said.

'Nice work.'

'What about you?' Book said.

At that exact moment, the French patrol boat swung to a halt above Schofield. Angry-looking sailors on its deck eyed him down the barrels of FAMAS assault rifles.

'They haven't killed me yet,' Schofield said. 'Which means someone wants to talk with me. It also means I'm still in the game. Scarecrow, out.'

And with that Schofield was hauled out of the water at gunpoint.

THE WHITE HOUSE, WASHINGTON, USA
26 OCTOBER, 0915 HOURS LOCAL TIME
(1515 HOURS IN FRANCE)

The White House Situation Room buzzed with activity.

Aides hustled left and right. Generals and Admirals spoke into secure phones. The words on everyone's lips were 'Kormoran', 'Chameleon' and 'Shane Schofield'.

The President strode into the room just as one of the Navy men, an Admiral named Gaines, pressed his phone to his shoulder.

'Mr President,' Gaines said, 'I've got Moseley in London on the line. He's saying that this Schofield character wants me to deploy attack submarines against various surface targets around the world. Sir, please, I'm not seriously supposed to let a thirty-year-old Marine *captain* control the entire United States Navy, am I?'

'You'll do exactly as Captain Schofield says, Admiral,' the President said. 'Whatever he wants, he gets. If he says deploy our subs, you deploy the subs. If he says blockade North Korea, you blockade North Korea. People! I thought I was clear about this! I don't want you coming to me to check on everything Schofield asks for. The fate of the world could be resting on that man's shoulders. I know him and I trust him. Hell, I'd trust him with my life. Anything short of a nuclear strike, you do it and advise me later. Now do as the man says and dispatch those subs!'

OFFICES OF THE DEFENSE INTELLIGENCE AGENCY,
SUB-LEVEL 3, THE PENTAGON
26 OCTOBER, 0930 HOURS LOCAL TIME
(1530 HOURS IN FRANCE)

A battered and bruised David Fairfax trudged back into his office on the bottom floor of the Pentagon, flanked by a pair of policemen.

Wendel Hogg was waiting for him, with Audrey by his side.

'Fairfax!' Hogg roared. 'Where in all hell and damnation have you been!'

'I'm going home for the day,' Fairfax said wearily.

'Bull*shit* you are,' Hogg said. 'You are going on report! Then you are going upstairs to face a disciplinary hearing under Pentagon Security Regulations 402 and 403 . . .'

Too tired to care, Fairfax could only stand there and take it.

'. . . and then, *then*, you're going to be outta here for good, you little wise-ass. And you're finally gonna learn that you ain't special, that you ain't untouchable, and—' Hogg shot a look at Audrey— 'that this country's security is best left to men like me, men who can fight, men who are prepared to hold a weapon and put their lives on the—'

He never finished his sentence.

For at that moment a squad of twelve Force Reconnaissance Marines stomped into the doorway behind Fairfax. They wore full battle dress uniforms and were *heavily* armed—Colt Commando assault rifles, MP-7s, deadly eyes.

Fairfax's eyes widened in surprise.

The Marine leader stepped forward. 'Gentlemen. My name is Captain Andrew Trent, United States Marine Corps. I'm looking for Mr David Fairfax.'

Fairfax swallowed.

Audrey gasped.

Hogg just went bug-eyed. 'What in cotton-pickin' hell is going on here?'

The Marine named Trent stepped forward. He was a big guy, all muscle, and in his full battle dress uniform, a seriously imposing figure.

'You must be Hogg,' Trent said. 'Mr Hogg, my orders come direct from the President of the United States. There is a serious international incident afoot and at this critical time, Mr Fairfax is perhaps the fourth most important person in the country. My orders state that I am to escort him on a mission of the highest importance and guard him with my life. So if you don't mind, Mr Hogg, *get out of the man's way.*'

Hogg just stood there, stunned.

Audrey just gazed at Fairfax, amazed.

Fairfax himself hesitated. After this morning's events, he didn't know who to trust.

'Mr Fairfax,' Trent said. 'I've been sent by Shane Schofield. He says he needs your help again. If you still don't believe me, here . . .'

Trent held out his radio. Fairfax took it.

At the other end was Book II.

Within twenty-two minutes, Dave Fairfax was sitting on board a chartered Concorde jet, heading west across the country at supersonic speed, his destination: San Francisco.

On the way to the airport, Book had briefed him on what Schofield needed him to do. Book had also asked him a maths question: what was the sixth Mersenne prime number.

'The sixth Mersenne?' Fairfax had said. 'I'm going to need a pen, some paper and a scientific calculator.'

And so now he sat in the passenger cabin of the Concorde—head bent over a pad, writing furiously, concentrating intensely—shooting across the country all alone.

Alone, that is, except for the team of twelve United States Marines protecting him.

AXON CORPORATION SHIPBUILDING AND MISSILE ATTACHMENT PLANT, NORFOLK, VIRGINIA, USA 26 OCTOBER, 0935 HOURS LOCAL TIME (1535 HOURS IN FRANCE)

Surrounded by two teams of United States Marines, the Department of Defense inspection team in charge of the Kormoran–Chameleon Joint Project approached the missile installation facility in Norfolk, Virginia.

The Axon plant loomed above them—a giant industrial landscape comprising a dozen interconnected buildings, eight enormous dry-docks and innumerable cranes lancing into the sky.

This was where Axon Corp installed its cutting-edge missile systems onto US naval vessels. Sometimes Axon even built the vessels here as well.

At the moment, a lone mammoth supertanker sat in one of the plant's dry-docks, covered by gantry cranes, towering above the industrial shoreline.

But strangely, at 9.30 in the morning, there was not a sign of life anywhere.

The Marines stormed the plant.

There was no firefight.

No battle.

Within minutes, the area was declared secure, the Marine

commander declaring over the radio:

'*You can let those D.O.D. boys in now. But let me warn you, it ain't pretty in here.*'

The smell was overwhelming.

The stench of rotting human flesh.

The main office area was bathed in blood. It was smeared on the walls, caked on benchtops, some of it had even dried as it had dripped down steel staircases, forming gruesome maroon stalactites.

Fortunately for Axon's legions of construction workers, the plant had been in security lockdown for the week preceding the official inspection, so they had been spared.

The company's senior engineers and department heads, however, hadn't been so lucky. They lay slumped in a neat row in the main lab side-by-side, having been executed on their knees, one after the other. Foul starbursts of blood stained the wall behind their fallen bodies.

Over the past week, rats had feasted on their remains.

Five bodies, however, stood out amid the carnage—they had quite obviously not been Axon employees.

The men of Axon, it seemed, had not gone down without a fight. Their small security force had nailed some of the intruders.

The five suspicious bodies lay at several locations around the plant, variously shot in the head or in the body, AK-47 machine-guns lying on the ground beside their corpses.

All were dressed in black military gear, but all also wore black Arab howlis, or headcloths, to cover their faces.

And despite the sorry state of their vermin-ravaged bodies, one other thing about them was clear: they all bore on their shoulders the distinctive double-scimitar tattoo of the terrorist organisation, Global Jihad.

★ ★ ★

The Department of Defense inspection team assessed the damage quickly, aided by agents from the ISS and FBI.

They also took a call from a secondary team checking out Axon's Pacific plant in Guam. A similar massacre, it seemed, had happened there as well.

When this news came in, one of the D.O.D. men got on the phone, dialling a secure line at the White House.

'It's bad,' he said. 'In Norfolk: we have fifteen dead—nine engineers, six security staff. Enemy casualties: five terrorists, all dead. Forensics indicate that the bodies have been decomposing for about eight days. Actual time of death is impossible to tell. Same story in Guam, except only one terrorist was killed there.

'All the terrorists here have been identified by the FBI as known members of Global Jihad—including one pretty big fish, a guy named Shoab Riis. But sir, the worst thing is this: there must have been more terrorists involved. Three of the Kormoran supertankers are missing from the Norfolk plant, and two more from the Guam facility . . . and all of them are armed with Chameleon missiles.'

AIRSPACE ABOVE THE FRENCH COAST
26 OCTOBER, 1540 HOURS LOCAL TIME
(0940 HOURS E.S.T USA)

The *Black Raven* rocketed down the French coastline heading toward the Forteresse de Valois.

'So, Rufus,' Mother said, 'there's something I've got to know. What's the story with your boss? I mean, what's an honest grunt like you doing with a murderous bastard like this Knight guy?'

In the front seat of the Sukhoi, Rufus tilted his head.

'Captain Knight ain't a bad man,' he said in his drawling Southern accent. 'And definitely not as bad as everyone says he is. Sure, he can kill a man cold—and believe me, I seen him do it— but he weren't born that way. He was *made* that way. He ain't no saint, for sure, but he isn't an evil man. And he's always looked after me.'

'Right . . .' Mother said. She was worried about this bounty hunter who was supposedly protecting Schofield.

'So what about all that stuff in his file then? How he betrayed his Delta unit in the Sudan, warned Al-Qaeda of the attack and let his own guys walk into a trap. Thirteen men, wasn't it? All killed because of him.'

Rufus nodded sadly.

'Yeah, I seen that file, too,' he said, 'and let me tell you, all that stuff about Sudan, it's horseshit. I know because I was there. Captain Knight never betrayed no-one. And he sure as hell never left thirteen men to die.'

'He never left them there?' Mother asked.

'No ma'am,' Rufus said, 'Knight killed those cocksuckers himself.'

'I was a chopper pilot back then,' Rufus said, 'with the NightStalkers, flying D-boys like Knight in on black ops. We were doing night raids into Sudan, taking out terrorist training camps after the embassy bombings in Kenya and Tanzania in '98. We were flying out of Yemen, skimming into Sudan from across the Red Sea.

'I got to know Knight at the base in Aden. He was kinda quiet, kept to himself most of the time. He read books, you know, thick ones, with no pictures. And he was always writing letters to his young wife back home.

'He was different to most of the guys in my unit, the chopper pilots. They weren't so nice to me. See, I'm kinda smart, but in my own way—I can do maths and physics easy as pie, and because of that I can fly a plane or a helicopter better than any man alive. Thing is, I ain't so good in social environments. Sometimes I just don't get the humour in jokes, especially dirty ones. That kinda thing.

'And the other NightStalker pilots, well, they liked to joke with me—like sending one of the hospital nurses over to my table in the mess hall to talk all sexy with me. Or putting me down for briefings that I wasn't meant to attend. Stuff like that. Instead of calling me Rufus, they called me "Doofus".

'Then some of the Rangers at the base started calling me that, too. I hated it. But Captain Knight, he never called me that. Never once. He always called me by my name.

'Anyway, one time, he was walking past my dorm just after some of them pilot bastards had taken all my bedside books while I was sleeping and switched 'em with some dirty magazines. They was all laughing at me when Captain Knight asked what was going on.

'A pilot named Harry Hartley told him to fuck off, mind his own business. Knight just stood there in the doorway, dead still. Again Hartley told him to beat it. Knight didn't move. So Hartley approached him angrily and took a swing at him. Knight dropped the asshole using only his legs, then he pressed a knee to Hartley's throat and said that my pilot skills were very much his business and that I was to be left alone . . . or else he'd come back.

'No-one ever played a joke on me again.'

Mother said, 'So what happened with the thirteen soldiers who died in Sudan then?'

'When he went out on a mission,' Rufus said, 'Knight often worked alone. Delta guys are allowed to do that, run solo. One man acting alone can often do more damage than an entire platoon.

'Anyway, one night, he's in Port Sudan, staking out an old warehouse. Place is a ghost town, deserted, run-down to all hell. Which is why Al-Qaeda had a training camp there, inside a big old warehouse.

'So Knight gets inside the warehouse and waits. That night, there's a big meeting there but this ain't your usual backstreets-of-Sudan meeting between Al-Qaeda buyers and Russian arms dealers. No, it's fucking Bin Laden himself and three CIA spooks, and they're talking about the Embassy bombings.

'Knight sends a silent digital signal out, giving his location, calling for back-up, and indicating that OBL himself is there. He offers to liquidate OBL, but command tells him to stand down. They're sending a Delta hit team in on his signal.

'The Delta team is sent from Aden, sixteen men in a Black Hawk, flown by me. Of course, by the time we get to the warehouse in Port Sudan, Bin Laden is gone.

'We meet Knight at the rendezvous point on the coast—an abandoned lighthouse. He's pissed as hell. The leader of the Delta hit squad is a punk named Brandeis, Captain Wade Brandeis. He tells Knight that something bigger is at stake here. Something way over Knight's head.

'Knight turns on his heel, heads for the chopper in disgust. Then, behind him, that fucker Brandeis just nods to two of his guys and says, "The chopper pilot, too. He can't go back after seeing this." And so these Delta assholes raise their MP-5s at Knight's back *and* at me in my chopper.

'There was no time for me to shout, but I didn't have to. Knight

had heard 'em move. He told me later that he heard the sound of their sleeves brushing against their body armour—the sound of someone raising a gun.

'A second before they fired, Knight dashed forward and tackled me into my own helicopter's hold. The Delta guys rushed us, silenced guns blazin' away, hammering the chopper. But Knight is moving too fast. He pushes me out the other side of the chopper, yanks me across a patch of open ground and into the lighthouse.

'You wouldn't believe what happened inside that lighthouse after that. The Delta team came in after us, the *whole* Delta hit team. Sixteen men. Only three came out.

'Knight killed nine Delta commandos inside that lighthouse before Brandeis and two other guys cut their losses and headed out-side. Then, knowing that Knight was still inside fighting with four of his own men, Brandeis planted a Thermite-Amatol demolition charge at the front door.

'Don't know if you've ever seen a Thermite charge go off before, but they are mighty big blasters. Well, that charge went off and that old lighthouse fell like a big old California redwood. The whole area shook like an earthquake when it hit the ground.

'When the dust settled, there was nothing left—*nothing*—just a pile of rubble. Nobody inside could have survived. Not us. Not the four Delta guys Brandeis had left in there.

'So Brandeis and the other two took off in my chopper and headed back to Aden.

'As it turned out, the building's collapse did kill the last four D-boys. Squashed 'em like flapjacks. But not Knight and me. Knight had seen Brandeis leave the lighthouse, and guessed that he'd blow the building. So Knight zip-lined us down the hollow well-shaft of the lighthouse—past the four Delta guys on the stairs—and bundled us both into a storm cellar at the base of the building.

'The lighthouse fell, but that storm cellar held. It was strong, concrete-walled. Took the pair of us two whole days to dig our-selves out of the rubble.'

'Man . . .' Mother said.

'Turned out Brandeis was working for some group inside the US military called the Intelligence Convergence Group, or ICG. Heard of them?'

'Yeah. Once or twice,' Mother said grimly.

'Don't hear about the ICG much anymore,' Rufus said. 'They say it was a bad-ass government agency that infiltrated military units, big companies and universities with its agents and then reported back to the government. But there was a purge a couple of years back that wiped it out. But some members like Brandeis survived. Turned out the ICG had been behind the attacks on the US embassies in Africa—they were liquidating some spies in those offices and had got Al-Qaeda to do their dirty work.

'To cover itself for the lighthouse bloodbath, though, the ICG blamed the whole thing on Knight. Said that he'd been taking millions from Al-Qaeda. Attributed all thirteen Delta deaths to Knight by saying that he pre-warned Al-Qaeda of their arrival. Knight was placed at the top of the Department of Defense's Most Wanted Persons List. His file was marked Classification Zebra: shoot on sight. And the US Government put a price on his head: two million dollars, dead or alive.'

'A bounty hunter with a price on his head. Nice,' Mother said.

Rufus said, 'But then the ICG did the worst thing of all. Remember I told you that Knight had a young wife. He also had a baby. ICG had them killed. Set it up as a home invasion gone wrong. Killed the woman and the baby.

'And now, now the ICG is dead and Knight's family is dead, but the price on Knight's head remains. The US Government occasionally sends a hit squad after him, like they did in Brazil a few years ago. And, of course, Wade Brandeis is still on active duty with Delta. I think he's a major now, still based in Yemen.'

'And so Knight became a bounty hunter,' Mother said.

'That's right. And I went with him. He saved my life, and he's always been good to me, always respected me. And he ain't never forgot Brandeis. Got a tattoo on his arm just to remind himself. Boy, is he waiting for the chance to meet that cat again.'

Mother took this all in.

She found herself reliving the mission she'd endured with Schofield and Gant at that remote ice station in Antarctica a few years back, an adventure which had involved their own battle with the ICG.

Fortunately for them, they had won. But at around the same time, Aloysius Knight had also been doing battle with the ICG—and he'd lost. Badly.

'He sounds like a Shane Schofield gone wrong,' she whispered.

'What?'

'Nothing.'

Mother gazed out at the horizon, a peculiar thought entering her mind. She found herself wondering: what would happen to Shane Schofield if he ever *lost* such a contest?

A few minutes later, the *Black Raven* hit the coast of Brittany.

Rufus and Mother saw the cliff-side roadway winding away from the Forteresse de Valois—saw the exploded-open craters in the road, the shell impacts on the cliffs, saw the crashed and smoking remains of trailer rigs, rally cars and helicopters strewn all over the place.

'What the hell happened here?' Rufus gaped.

'The Scarecrow happened here,' Mother said. 'The big question is, where is he now?'

THE FRENCH AIRCRAFT CARRIER, *RICHELIEU*, ATLANTIC OCEAN, OFF THE FRENCH COAST 26 OCTOBER, 1545 HOURS LOCAL TIME (0945 HOURS E.S.T USA)

The giant French Super Puma naval helicopter landed on the flight deck of the aircraft carrier—with Shane Schofield in it, handcuffed and disarmed and covered by no fewer than six armed sailors.

After the patrol boat had picked him up near the cliffs, Schofield had been taken to the French destroyer. From there he had been whisked by helicopter to the colossal Charles de Gaulle-class carrier, *Richelieu,* hovering on the ocean farther out.

No sooner had the helicopter landed on the flight deck than the ground beneath it moved—downward. The Super Puma had landed on one of the carrier's gigantic side-mounted elevators, and now that elevator was descending.

The elevator lurched to a halt in front of a massive internal hangar bay situated directly underneath the flight deck. It was filled with Mirage fighters, anti-submarine planes, fuel trucks and jeeps.

And standing in the middle of it all, awaiting the arrival of the elevator containing the chopper, was a small group of four very senior French officials:

One Navy Admiral.

One Army General.

One Air Force Commodore.

And one man in a plain grey suit.

★ ★ ★

Schofield was shoved out of the Super Puma, his hands cuffed in front of him.

He was brought before the four French officials.

Apart from Schofield's half-dozen guards, the maintenance hangar had been cleared of personnel. It made for an odd sight: this cluster of tiny figures standing among the aeroplanes inside the cavernous but deserted hangar bay.

'So this is the Scarecrow,' the Army General snorted. 'The man who took out a team of my best paratroopers in Antarctica.'

The Admiral said, 'I also lost an entire submarine during that incident. To this day, it has not been accounted for.'

So much for forgetting about Antarctica, Schofield thought.

The man in the suit stepped forward. He seemed smoother than the others, more precise, more articulate. Which made him seem more dangerous. 'Monsieur Schofield, my name is Pierre Lefevre, I am from the Direction Générale de la Sécurité Extérieure.'

The DGSE, Schofield thought. *The French version of the CIA. And aside from the Mossad, the most ruthless intelligence agency in the world.*

Great.

'So, Pierre,' he said, 'what's the story? Is France in league with Majestic-12? Or just Jonathan Killian?'

'I do not know what you are talking about,' Lefevre said airily. 'All we know is what Monsieur Killian has told us, and the Republic of France sees a tactical advantage in allowing his organisation's plan to run its course.'

'So what do you want with me?'

The Army General said, 'I would like to rip your heart out.'

The Navy Admiral said, 'And I would like to show it to you.'

'*My* objective is somewhat more practical,' Lefevre said calmly. 'The Generals will get their wish, of course. But not before you answer some of my questions, or before we see for ourselves whether Monsieur Killian's plan is truly foolproof.'

Lefevre laid his briefcase on a nearby bench and opened it . . . to reveal a small metallic unit the size of a hardback book.

It looked like a mini-computer, but with two screens: one large touch-screen on the upper half, and a smaller elongated screen on the bottom right. The top screen glowed with a series of red and white circles. Next to the smaller screen was a 10-digit keypad, like on a telephone.

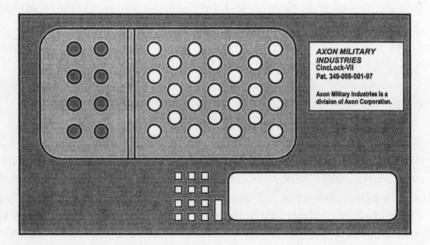

'Captain Schofield,' Lefevre said, 'allow me to introduce to you the CincLock-VII security system. We would like to see you disarm it.'

**FORTERESSE DE VALOIS
BRITTANY, FRANCE
26 OCTOBER, 1600 HOURS LOCAL TIME
(1000 HOURS E.S.T USA)**

They dragged Libby Gant into the dark underground pit.

Bloodied and wounded and teetering on the edge of consciousness, she noticed its circular stone walls, the pool of tidal seawater that filled most of its floor area. Seawater which contained two prowling sharks.

Thunk.

The upper half of the guillotine's wooden stocks came down over Gant's neck, pinning her head firmly in place.

The armed man covering her shot home the lock. Gant had never seen him before: he had carrot-red hair, vacant black eyes, and an exceedingly ugly rat-like face.

The imposing frame of the guillotine loomed above her—her head now fastened twelve feet beneath its suspended blade.

Gant grimaced. She could barely even kneel. The tracer wound to her chest burned with pain.

Next to Rat Face stood one of the bounty hunters—Cedric Wexley's No. 2, a psychotic ex-Royal Marine named Drake. He covered Gant with a Steyr-AUG assault rifle.

Gant noticed that Drake was wearing a strange-looking flak vest—a black utility vest equipped with all manner of odd-looking devices, like a Pony Bottle and some mountaineering pitons.

It was Knight's vest.

That made her look up.

And she saw him.

There, fifteen feet in front of her—standing on a stone platform which was itself two inches under the waterline, his eyes squeezed painfully shut since his amber glasses had been removed, his back pressed against the curved stone wall of the pit, his wrists manacled and his holsters glaringly empty—was Aloysius Knight.

A voice echoed across the watery dungeon.

'"Turning and turning in the widening gyre, the falcon cannot hear the falconer. Things fall apart, the centre cannot hold. Mere anarchy is loosed upon the world." Yeats, I believe.'

Jonathan Killian appeared in the viewing balcony—with the bounty hunter Cedric Wexley at his side.

Killian gazed out over the Shark Pit like an emperor at the Colosseum, his eyes falling on Gant, fifty yards away, on the other side of the pit.

'Anarchy is loosed upon the world, Lieutenant Gant,' he said pleasantly. 'I must say I like the sound of that. Don't you?'

'No,' Gant groaned with pain.

They didn't have to raise their voices; their words echoed across the dungeon.

Killian said, 'And Captain Knight. I find your actions most disturbing. A bounty hunter of your fame *hindering* a hunt. There can be only one conclusion: you are being paid to do so.'

Knight just stared back at the young billionaire, said nothing.

'It concerns me to think that someone wishes to foil the plans of the Council. Who is paying you to save Schofield, Captain Knight?'

Knight said nothing.

'Noble silence. How predictable,' Killian said. 'Perhaps when I have your tongue wrenched from your mouth, you will wish you had spoken sooner.'

'We know your plan, Killian,' Gant said through clenched teeth.

'Start a new Cold War to make *money*. It won't work. We'll blow the lid on it, inform the US Government.'

Killian snorted.

'My dear Lieutenant Gant. Do you honestly think I fear *governments*? The modern Western government is but a gathering of overweight middle-aged men trying to gloss over their own mediocrity with the attainment of high office. Presidential planes, Prime Ministerial offices, they are but the *illusion* of power.

'As for a new Cold War,' Killian mused, 'well, that is more the Council's plan than my own. My plan would embody somewhat more *vision*.

'Consider that poem by Yeats. I particularly love the notion of the falconer no longer being able to command his falcon. It suggests a nation that is no longer capable of controlling its most deadly weapon. The weapon has developed a mind of its own, realised its own deadly potential. It has outgrown its owner and attained dangerous independence.

'Now place that in the context of the US defence industry. What happens when the missile builders no longer choose to obey their masters? What happens when the military–industrial complex decides it no longer needs the United States Government?'

'The Scarecrow will stop you,' Gant said defiantly.

'Yes. Yes. The Scarecrow,' Killian said. 'Our mutual friend. He is a special one, isn't he? Did you know that the Council was so concerned about his presence on the list that they went to the trouble of arranging a sham mission to Siberia just to trap him? Needless to say, it didn't work.'

'No shit.'

'But if he is still alive,' Killian said, 'then, yes, it is something of a problem.'

Killian locked eyes with Gant . . .

. . . and she felt her spine turn completely to ice. There was something in his glare that she had never seen before, something truly terrifying.

Aloysius Knight saw it, too, and he immediately became concerned.

This was happening too fast. He shifted in his stance, strained against his manacles.

'Now,' Killian said, 'in any standard story, a villain like me would seek to draw out the troublesome Schofield by holding his beloved Lieutenant Gant hostage. I believe this was exactly Demon Larkham's thinking earlier today.'

'Yes,' Gant said warily. 'It was.'

'But it didn't work, did it?' Killian said.

'No.'

'Which is why, Lieutenant Gant, I must do something *more* to flush Shane Schofield out. Something that will make *finding me* far more important to him than disrupting the Council's plan. Mister Noonan.'

At that moment Rat Face—Noonan—grasped the release lever on the guillotine and Gant swallowed in horror.

Then she looked over at Knight, locking eyes with him.

'Knight,' she said. 'When you get out of here, tell Schofield something for me. Tell him I would have said yes.'

Then, without pause or patience, Rat Face pulled the lever and the guillotine's terrible blade dropped from its perch and rushed down its guide-rails toward Gant's exposed neck.

Chunk.

Libby Gant's headless body dropped to the ground at the base of the guillotine.

A hideous waterfall of blood gushed out from its open neck, spilling across the stone stage before flowing off it into the seawater at the platform's edge.

The blood in the water quickly attracted the sharks. Two pointed grey shadows appeared at the edge of the guillotine's stage, searching for the source of the blood.

'Jesus, *no*!' Aloysius Knight yelled, straining at his chains, staring at the gruesome sight in total apoplectic shock.

It had happened so fast.

So quickly.

Without any hesitation.

Libby Gant was dead.

Despite the pain of the light hitting them, Knight's eyes were wide, his face white. 'Oh God, no . . .' he gasped again.

He snapped to glare up at Jonathan Killian—but Killian's face was a mask. His cool hard stare had not changed at all.

And then suddenly one of the men in the pit was coming towards Knight.

It was Drake, the ExSol mercenary, carrying one of Knight's Remington shotguns and wearing his utility vest. The other man, Rat Face, was leaving the pit via a steel door over by the guillotine.

'What about this one?' Drake asked Killian.

Killian waved a hand. 'No guillotines for the Black Knight. No games that might permit him to escape. Shoot him in the head and then feed him to the sharks.'

'Yes, sir,' Drake said.

The giant mercenary strode across a narrow stone bridge between the guillotine's stage and Knight's wall-platform, each step kicking up a shallow splash.

As Drake approached him, the squinting Knight assessed his options.

There weren't many.

He could barely see.

His hands were manacled.

Drake was coming closer.

Thinking furiously, Knight bit his lip so hard that he drew blood. He spat the gob of bloody saliva away in disgust.

Drake halted about six feet from him, out of range from anything Knight could do—like strangle him with his legs, or kick him in the crotch.

Drake raised Knight's silver Remington, aimed it at Knight's head. 'Heard you were better than this, Knight.'

At which point, Knight nodded down at Drake's feet and said, 'I am.'

Drake frowned.

And looked down—to see one of the tiger sharks in the water *right next to his boots*, drawn to the edge of the platform by Knight's blood-laced saliva.

Just as Knight had hoped.

'Ah—' Drake took an involuntary step back from the big ten-foot shark at his feet . . .

. . . and walked into the strike zone of a far more dangerous predator.

What Knight did next, he did very *very* fast.

First, he whip-snapped his body upwards, lashing out with his legs, and grabbed Drake hard around the ribs from behind. Knight squeezed and there came a hideous *snap-snap-snap*, the sound of Drake's ribs breaking.

Drake roared with pain.

Then Knight yanked the mercenary closer so that he could reach

something hanging from the utility vest—*his* utility vest—that Drake was wearing.

Knight pulled a mountaineering piton from the vest and one-handed, jammed the piton into his left-hand manacle and pressed its release.

With a powerful spring-loaded *thwack*, the piton expanded in an instant—

—and the old iron manacle around Knight's wrist cracked open and suddenly his left hand was free.

Up on the viewing balcony, Cedric Wexley saw what was happening and immediately whipped up his gun, but Knight was holding Drake in the way with his legs.

And he wasn't finished with Drake either.

He used his now-free left hand to grab a second item from the vest: the miniature blowtorch.

Knight yanked the blowtorch from its pouch and immediately pulled the trigger, firing it at point-blank range *into Drake's back.*

The mini-blowtorch burst to life, emitting a superheated blue flame.

Drake roared.

The spike-like blue flame lanced right through his body, emerging from the other side—the front side—like the blade of a luminescent sword.

Drake's face, shocked and dying, fell back against Knight's chest.

'You got off lightly,' Knight growled, applying more power, blasting the insides of Drake's body to nothing.

Then the body went limp, and fell, and as it did so, Knight unclasped his utility vest from it, at the same time using his piton to break open his other manacle.

As Drake fell, however, Knight became exposed to Cedric Wexley up in the viewing balcony, who started firing.

But now Knight was completely free.

He dived behind Drake's corpse, let bullet after bullet hit it before, without warning, he rolled Drake's body into the blood-stained water, right in front of the nearest tiger shark, and then, to everyone's surprise . . .

. . . leapt into the water after it himself!

The shark lunged at Drake's corpse, bit into it with an almighty crunch, started tearing it to shreds. The second shark came over quickly and joined in the frenzy.

A churning bloody foam spilled out across the pool. Waves sloshed every which way.

After a few minutes, however, the frenzy died down and the water was calm once more.

But there was no sign of Knight.

Indeed, Aloysius Knight never surfaced again inside the deadly pool.

He did surface, however, *outside* the Forteresse de Valois, amid the waves of the Atlantic Ocean.

Exactly six minutes after he'd dived underneath the sharks feeding on Drake's body, he breached the surface of the ocean, still holding his Pony Bottle to his lips.

The mini-scuba bottle had only just had enough air in it to get him through the long underwater passage that connected the Shark Pit to the open sea.

Knight didn't bob in the water for long. A homing transponder on his vest took care of that.

In a matter of minutes, the hawk-shaped shadow of his Sukhoi S-37 swung into place above him, blasting the water around him with its thrusters.

Then a harness fell out of the plane's bomb bay and slapped into the water beside him, and within moments, Aloysius Knight was sitting inside the *Black Raven*, back with Mother and Rufus.

'You all right, Boss?' Rufus said, throwing him a new pair of yellow-lensed glasses.

Knight caught them as he slumped to the floor of the *Raven*'s rear holding cell, put them on. He didn't answer Rufus's question. Just nodded. He was still shell-shocked by the horrific execution he had just witnessed in the Shark Pit.

Mother said, 'What about the Scarecrow? And my little Chickadee?'

Knight looked up at her sharply.

Behind his yellow glasses, his eyes were the picture of horror. He gazed at Mother, wondering what to say.

Then abruptly he stood. 'Rufus. Do you have a fix on Schofield? Those MicroDots I put on his Palm Pilot should have rubbed off on his hand.'

'I've got him, Boss. And he's still moving. Looks like someone took him to that French carrier off the coast.'

Knight turned to Mother, took a deep, deep breath. 'Schofield's alive, but'—he swallowed—'there could be a problem with the girl.'

'Oh dear God, no . . .' Mother said.

'I can't talk about it now,' Knight said. 'We have to rescue Schofield.'

THE FRENCH AIRCRAFT CARRIER *RICHELIEU*, ATLANTIC OCEAN, OFF THE FRENCH COAST

Shane Schofield was thrown into a small steel-walled room adjoining the below-decks hangar. The door slammed shut behind him.

There was nothing in the room but a table and a chair.

On the table sat Lefevre's CincLock-VII disarming unit. Next to the unit, with a little red pilot light burning brightly on its top, was:

A phosphorus grenade.

High in the corner of the room, hidden behind a dark glass plate, Schofield heard a camera whirring.

'*Captain Schofield,*' the DGSE agent's voice came over some speakers. '*A simple test. The phosphorus grenade you see before you is connected by shortwave radio to the CincLock unit on the table. The only way to disarm the grenade is through the CincLock unit. For the purposes of this exercise, the final disarm code is 123. The grenade will go off in one minute. Your time starts . . . now.*'

'Holy shit,' Schofield said, sitting down quickly.

He examined the CincLock unit up close.

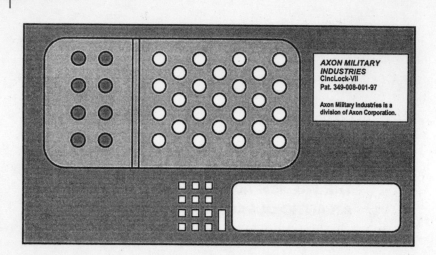

White and red circles filled the main screen—red on the left, white on the right.

Bing.

A message appeared on the lower screen:

FIRST PROTOCOL (PROXIMITY): SATISFIED.
INITIATE SECOND PROTOCOL.

Immediately, the white circles on the main screen began to flash—each one blinking for a brief instant, one at a time, in a slow random sequence.

The screen squealed in protest.

SECOND PROTOCOL (RESPONSE PATTERN): FAILED DISARM ATTEMPT RECORDED.
THREE FAILED DISARM ATTEMPTS WILL RESULT IN DEFAULT DETONATION.
SECOND PROTOCOL (RESPONSE PATTERN): RE-ACTIVATED.

'What?' Schofield said to the screen.

'*Fifty seconds, Captain,*' Lefevre's voice said. '*You have to touch the illuminated circles in the prescribed order.*'

'Oh. Right.'

The white circles began to flash again, one after the other.

And now Schofield began pressing them—just after they flashed.

'*Forty seconds . . .*'

The white circles' sequence became faster. Schofield's hands began to move faster with them, touching the circles on the screen.

Then, abruptly, one of the red circles on the *left* side of the display illuminated.

Schofield wasn't ready for it. But hit it anyway, and got it in time. The white circles resumed their sequence, now blinking very quickly. Schofield's fingers increased their pace, too.

'*Thirty seconds . . . you're doing well . . .*'

Then another red circle flashed.

And this time Schofield was too slow.

The screen beeped angrily.

SECOND PROTOCOL (RESPONSE PATTERN): FAILED DISARM ATTEMPT RECORDED.

THREE FAILED DISARM ATTEMPTS WILL RESULT IN DEFAULT DETONATION.

SECOND PROTOCOL (RESPONSE PATTERN): RE-ACTIVATED.

'Damn it!' Schofield yelled, eyeing the grenade on the table beside him.

And the white circles began their blinking sequence for a third and final time.

'*Twenty-five seconds left . . .*'

But this time Schofield was prepared, knowing what he had to do. His hands now moved fluidly across the screen, punching the white circles as they blinked, breaking left every so often as a red circle flashed.

'*Ten seconds, nine . . .*'

The sequence became faster. The darting moves to the reds became more frequent—to the point, Schofield thought, where it became a test of his reflexes.

'*Eight, seven . . .*'

His eyes stayed focused on the display. His fingers kept dancing. Sweat trickled into his eyes.

'*Six, five . . .*'

The lights kept blinking: white-white-red-white-red-white.

'*Four, three . . .*'

Bing—a message sprang up on the screen:

SECOND PROTOCOL (RESPONSE PATTERN): SATISFIED.

THIRD PROTOCOL (CODE ENTRY): ACTIVE.

PLEASE ENTER AUTHORIZED DISARM CODE.

'*Two . . .*'

Schofield typed '1-2-3-ENTER' on the keypad. The numbers appeared on the smaller screen.

'*One . . .*'

Bing.

THIRD PROTOCOL (CODE ENTRY): SATISFIED.

DEVICE DISARMED.

Schofield exhaled, slumped back in his chair.

The door to the room opened. Lefevre entered, dove-clapping.

'Oh, très bien! Très bien!' he said. 'Very good, Captain.'

Two burly French naval commandos covered Schofield on either side.

Lefevre smiled. 'That was most impressive. *Most* impressive. Thank you, Captain. You've just reassured us of the verity of Majestic-12's claims. Not to mention the merit of this disarm system. I'm sure the Republic of France will find many uses for it. It really is such a shame that we have to kill you now. Gentlemen, take Captain Schofield back up to the hangar and string him up with the other one.'

Schofield rose into the air, his legs and arms spread wide, star-like.

He stood on the forward lifting prongs of a forklift, one foot on each horizontal prong, while his wrists were handcuffed to the vehicle's vertical steel runners.

The forklift was parked in a corner of the *Richelieu*'s deserted main hangar bay, behind the exhausts of several Rafale fighter jets. Seated in a semi-circle in front of it were the three French military officers and the DGSE agent, Lefevre.

'Bring in the British spy,' Lefevre said to one of Schofield's guards.

The guard hit a button on the wall nearby and the steel wall beside Schofield suddenly began to rise—it was in fact a door, a great fighter-sized steel door—revealing darkness beyond it.

Out from the darkness came a second forklift, on which stood another captured individual, crucified in the same manner as Schofield.

There was only one difference.

The man on this second forklift had been thoroughly tortured. His face, his shirt, his arms—they were all covered with blood. His head hung limply over his chest.

Lefevre said, 'Captain Schofield, I'm not sure if you have met Agent Alec Christie of British Intelligence.'

Christie. From MI-6. And the bounty list.

So this was where Christie had got to.

'Over the last two days, Mr Christie has been a fountain of information for us regarding Majestic-12,' Lefevre said. 'It seems that for the last eighteen months, he has been well placed in Loch-

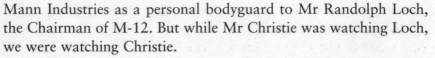

Mann Industries as a personal bodyguard to Mr Randolph Loch, the Chairman of M-12. But while Mr Christie was watching Loch, we were watching Christie.

'However, in one of his more lucid moments last night, Mr Christie told us something of concern. He stated that Randolph Loch has been most displeased of late with one of the younger members of M-12, our friend Jonathan Killian.

'According to Mr Christie, Randolph Loch commented several times that Killian was quote, "pestering him with this follow-up idea". It appears that Mr Killian does not think Majestic-12's plan goes far enough. In light of your own investigations, Captain Schofield, do you know anything about this "follow-up idea"?'

Schofield said, 'Killian's *your* friend. Why don't you ask him?'

'The Republic of France does not have friends.'

'I can see why.'

'We have useful acquaintances,' Lefevre said. 'But sometimes, one must watch one's acquaintances as closely as one's enemies.'

'You don't trust him,' Schofield said.

'Not an inch.'

'But you give him protection, sanctuary.'

'For as long as it suits us. It may no longer suit us.'

Schofield said, 'But now you're worried he's playing you.'

'Yes.'

Schofield thought about that for a moment.

Then he said, 'One of M-12's Chameleon missiles is aimed at Paris.'

'Oh, please. We know that. We are *prepared* for that. That is the very idea behind my country's involvement with Majestic-12. That was why we provided them with the bodies of the Global Jihad terrorists. For while America, Germany and Britain suffer catastrophic losses, France will be seen as the only Western nation to have defeated this threat.

'Where New York, Berlin and London will be lost, Paris will stand tall. France will be the only nation to have successfully shot down one of these terrible terrorist missiles.

'It took America three whole months to retaliate for September 11. Imagine how shell-shocked they will be when they lose *five entire cities*. But France, France will be the nation who beat off these heinous attacks. The only Western nation who moved fast enough. It will make us—strong and capable and completely unhurt—the world's leader in this new Cold War period.

'Captain Schofield, our friends in Majestic-12 want money out of all of this, because for them money is power. The Republic of France does not want that kind of power—we want something far more important than that. We want a global power shift. We want to lead the world.

'The 20th century was the American century. A sad bankrupt time in the history of this planet. The 21st century will be the French century.'

Schofield just stared at Lefevre and the generals.

'You guys are really messed up, you know that,' he said.

Lefevre pulled some photos out of his briefcase, showed them to the elevated Schofield.

'Back to Killian. These are photos of Monsieur Killian during his tour of Africa last year.'

Schofield saw standard newspaper pics: Killian standing with African leaders, opening factories, waving to crowds.

'A goodwill tour to promote his charitable activities,' Lefevre said. 'During that tour, however, Killian attended meetings with the leaders and defence ministers of several strategically significant African nations: notably Nigeria, Eritrea, Chad, Angola and Libya.'

'Yes . . .' Schofield said expectantly.

Lefevre paused, delivered the punch. 'Over the last eleven hours, the Air Forces of Nigeria, Eritrea, Chad and Angola have all scrambled, with over two hundred fighter planes converging on airfields in eastern Libya. Now, taken individually, these air forces are relatively small. Taken together, however, they make up a veritable aerial armada. My final question for you, Captain, is *what are they doing*?'

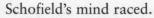

Schofield's mind raced.

'Captain Schofield?'

But Schofield wasn't listening. He could only hear Jonathan Killian's voice in his head, saying: 'Although many don't know it, the future of the world lies in Africa.'

Africa . . .

'Captain Schofield?' Lefevre said.

Schofield blinked. Came back.

'I don't know,' he answered honestly. 'I wish I did, but I honestly don't.'

'Hmmm,' Lefevre said. 'That is exactly what Mr Christie said, too. Which might mean you are both speaking the truth. Of course, it might also mean that you need some more persuasion.'

Lefevre nodded to the driver of Christie's forklift.

The driver fired up the engine and drove the vehicle a few yards to the left, so that Christie—raised up on the forklift's prongs—was positioned right behind the thrusters of a nearby Rafale fighter jet. The driver then quickly jumped out of his seat and ran away.

A moment later, Schofield saw why.

ROOOOAAAARRRRR!

The fighter's engines rumbled to life. Schofield saw another French soldier standing in its cockpit.

The battered and ragged Alec Christie looked up at the sound of the colossal noise, and found himself staring into the yawning rear thruster of the Rafale fighter. He didn't seem to care. He was too beaten, too weary to bother straining at his bonds.

Lefevre nodded to the man in the cockpit.

The man hit the plane's thrust controls.

Instantly, a shocking tongue of white-hot fire blasted out from the rear thruster of the Rafale, engulfing the immobile Christie.

The heat-blast battered the British agent's body like a wind-fan—the piping-hot air blasted his hair backwards, ripped the skin off his face, burned his clothes in a nanosecond—until ultimately it tore his body to pieces.

Then, abruptly, the burst stopped and the hangar was silent again.

All that remained of Alec Christie were four grisly quarters, charred and disgusting, dangling from the forklift's prongs.

'This is very bad,' Schofield swallowed.

Lefevre turned to him. 'Does that refresh your memory at all?'

'I'm telling you, I don't know,' Schofield said. 'I don't know about Killian or the African countries, or if they have anything in common. This is the first I've heard of them.'

'Then I am afraid we have no further need for you,' Lefevre said. 'It is now time for the Admiral and the General to have their wish and watch you die.'

And with that, Lefevre nodded to Schofield's forklift driver. Schofield's vehicle moved forward, stopping alongside Christie's charred forklift, in front of the Rafale's second rear thruster.

Schofield gazed into the dark depths of the thruster.

'General?' Lefevre said to the old Army officer, the man who had lost an entire paratrooper unit to Schofield in Antarctica. 'Would you like to do the honours?'

'With pleasure.'

The General stood up from his chair, and climbed up into the Rafale's cockpit, glaring at Schofield all the way.

He leaned into the cockpit, reached for the flight stick, his thumb hovering over the 'AFTERBURN' switch.

'Good-bye, Captain Schofield,' Lefevre said matter-of-factly. 'World history will have to continue without you. Au revoir.'

The General's thumb came down on the 'BURN' switch.

Just as a gigantic explosion boomed out from somewhere above the main hangar.

Klaxons sounded.

Warning lights flashed to life.

And the entire aircraft carrier was suddenly awash with the red lighting of an emergency.

The General's thumb had frozen a millimetre above the burn switch.

An ensign ran up to the Navy Admiral. 'Sir! We're under attack!'

'*What?*' the Admiral yelled. 'By whom!'

'It looks like a Russian fighter, sir.'

'A Russian fighter? *One* Russian fighter! This is an aircraft carrier, for God's sake! Who in their right mind would attack an aircraft carrier with a single plane?'

The *Black Raven* hovered level with the flight deck of the *Richelieu*, raining gunfire and missiles down on the fighter planes parked there.

Four missile smoke-trails extended out from the Sukhoi's wings and then separated to pursue different targets.

One Rafale fighter on the deck was instantly blasted to pieces, while two anti-aircraft missile stations were obliterated. The fourth missile whizzed into the main hangar bay and rammed into an AWACS plane, destroying it in a billowing explosion.

★ ★ ★

Inside the *Raven*, Rufus flew brilliantly.

In the gunner's seat behind him sat Knight, swivelling around in the plane's 360-degree revolving rear chair, lining up targets and then blazing away with the *Raven*'s guns.

'Mother! You ready?' Knight called.

Mother stood in the converted bomb bay behind the cockpit—armed to the teeth: MP-7, M-16, Desert Eagle pistols; she even had one of Knight's rocket launcher packs strapped to her back.

'Fuckin'-A.'

'Then go!' Knight hit a button.

Whack!

The floor of the bomb bay/holding cell snapped open and Mother dropped down through it, whizzing down on her Maghook's rope.

Inside the French aircraft carrier's control tower, chaos reigned.

Comm-techs were shouting into their radio-mikes, relaying information to the captain.

'—damn thing got under our radars! Must have some sort of stealth mechanism—'

'—They've hit the anti-aircraft stations on the flight deck—'

'—Get those fighters to the catapults *now*!'

'Sir! The *Triomphe* says it has a clear shot . . .'

'Tell it to fire!'

In response to the order, an anti-aircraft missile streaked out from one of the destroyers in the carrier group—heading straight for the *Black Raven*.

'Rufus! I hope you fixed our electronic countermeasures when we were in Archangel!'

'Taken care of, Boss.'

The missile zoomed towards them at phenomenal speed.

But at the last possible moment, it hit the *Raven*'s electronic jamming shield and veered wildly away . . .

. . . and slammed into the outer hull of the aircraft carrier!

'Escorts! Cease fire! Cease fire!' the captain yelled. 'That plane is too close to us! You're hitting us! Electronics Department—find out what its jamming frequency is and neutralise it! We'll have to destroy it with fighters.'

Inside the main hangar bay of the carrier, Schofield was still quasi-crucified in front of the thrusters of the parked Rafale fighter.

Abruptly, the deck around him banked steeply as the immense carrier wheeled around in the face of the *Black Raven*'s surprise assault.

Lefevre and the French generals were now all on radios, looking for answers.

All, that is, except for the Army General in the cockpit of the Rafale.

After the initial distraction, he now glared back at Schofield. He wasn't going to miss this opportunity.

He reached for the 'AFTERBURN' switch again, gripped the control stick just as—*sprack!*—a bullet entered his ear and the cockpit around him was sprayed with his brains.

In all the confusion, no-one had noticed the shadowy figure that had landed on the open-air starboard elevator adjoining the main hangar, a figure that had whizzed to the bottom of a vertical rope like a spider on a thread, a figure bearing arms.

Mother.

Carrying an MP-7 in one hand and an M-16 in the other, Mother stormed through the hangar bay towards Schofield.

She was like an unstoppable force of nature.

The squad of French paratroopers that had been guarding Schofield came at her from all sides—from behind vehicles, from around parked fighter jets.

But Mother just strode forward, nailing them left, right and centre, never once losing her stride.

She loosed two shots to the left—hit two paratroopers in their faces. Swung right—firing her M-16 pistol-style—and another three bad guys went down.

A paratrooper rose from the wing of a Rafale above her and Mother just somersaulted, firing as she rolled, peppering him with bloody holes.

She threw two smoke grenades next, and in the haze that followed, she moved and hunted like a vengeful ghost.

Four French paratroopers went down, sucked into the smoke-haze—so, too, the French Admiral. Not even the spy, Lefevre, could escape her. A four-bladed shuriken throwing knife whistled out of the smoke near him and entered his Adam's apple. He would die slowly.

Then suddenly, Mother burst out of the cloud haze right next to Schofield on his forklift.

'Hey, Scarecrow. How's it hanging?' she said.

'Feeling much better now that you're here,' Schofield said.

Two of Knight's pitons made short work of his handcuffs. In seconds he was on solid ground again, free.

But before Mother could hand him some guns, Schofield dashed over to Lefevre's body lying on the ground nearby.

He picked up something from the ground beside the dying Frenchman, returned to Mother's side. She handed him an MP-7 and a Desert Eagle.

'Ready to do some damage?' she asked.

Schofield turned to her, his eyes catching the RPG pack on her back.

'I'm ready to do some serious damage,' he said.

They ran towards a jeep parked nearby.

In rapid two-by-two catapult launches, four state-of-the-art Rafale fighters shot down the runway of the *Richelieu* and took off.

They wheeled around in the sky above the carrier, turning back in deadly formation, heading for the hovering *Black Raven*.

'They're coming!' Rufus yelled.

'I see them!' Knight called.

He whirled around in his revolving seat, hammering on his triggers like a kid playing a video game.

Two Rafales shot toward them, cannons blazing.

A phalanx of orange tracer bullets sizzled through the air all around the *Raven*. The *Raven* banked and rolled in the sky, dodging the tracers, at the same time returning fire from its own revolving belly-mounted gun.

Then the first two planes overshot them—twin sonic booms. But that was only the first act, a distraction to hide the main show.

For the *other* two French fighters had swung around low, skimming over the ocean waves from the other direction, coming at the Sukhoi from below and behind.

Still hovering above the carrier's starboard elevator, the Sukhoi swivelled in mid-air, faced these two new planes head-on.

'Damn it,' Rufus said, eyeing his countermeasures screen. 'The bastards are screwing with our jamming frequency . . . it's flicking on and off. We're losing missile jam.'

The two new Rafales fired two missiles each.

Knight blasted away with his cannons at the missiles, hit two of them, but the other two missiles ducked and rose and swerved too well.

'Rufus . . . !'

The missiles roared toward them.

Rufus saw them coming, and a moment before it was too late, saw the answer.

The missiles rushed forward, zooming in for the kill . . .

. . . just as Rufus swung the *Black Raven* inside the massive doorway that opened off the aircraft carrier's starboard elevator, manoeuvring his airborne fighter *inside the ship's main hangar!*

The missiles—unlike the shots from the destroyer, *Le Triomphe*— were fitted with electronic detection systems that didn't allow them to strike their own carrier. As such, they ditched into the ocean, detonating in twin hundred-foot geysers.

Inside the carrier's tower, radar operators stared at their screens in confusion, shouted into their radio-mikes:

'—Where the fuck did it go?—'

'—*What?* Say again—'

'What happened?' the captain asked. 'Where are they?'

'Sir. They're inside us!'

The *Black Raven* now hovered *inside* the cavernous hangar of the French aircraft carrier.

'I like your style, Rufus,' Knight said as he started firing indiscriminately at the array of parked planes, helicopters and trucks.

Like a giant bird trapped inside a living room, the *Black Raven* powered over the interior of the hangar, overturning entire planes with its backwash, flinging fuel trucks into the walls.

It shoomed across the hangar causing untold mayhem and destruction, its two high tail fins even scraping against the ceiling once.

Knight called into his radio: 'Mother! Where are you?'

★ ★ ★

A lone jeep shot towards the aft end of the elongated hangar bay, driving at full speed, zooming under tilting planes and bouncing fuel trucks, with Mother at the wheel and Schofield crouched in the back.

Mother yelled. 'I'm at the other end of the hangar bay, trying to avoid your mess!'

'*Do you have Schofield?*'

'I've got him.'

'*Want us to pick you up while we're in here?*'

Mother turned to Schofield, bent over in the back with her—or rather, Knight's—RPG pack. 'You wanna be picked up in here?'

'No! Not yet!' he yelled. 'Tell Knight to get outside. He doesn't want to be in here in the next two minutes! In fact, he doesn't want to be anywhere near this ship! Tell him we'll meet him outside!'

'Copy that,' Knight said, moments later.

He turned. 'Rufus! Time to bail!'

'You got it, Boss!' Rufus said. 'Now, where is that other . . . ah,' Rufus said, spotting a second open-air elevator on the opposite side of the hangar bay.

He powered up the Sukhoi, brought her swooping across the interior of the hangar bay, the roar of her engines drowning out all other sound, before—*shoom*—the *Raven* blasted out through the port-side elevator and into blazing sunlight.

Meanwhile, in the back of his speeding jeep, Schofield rummaged through the RPG pack that Mother had brought.

It was indeed Knight's Russian-made RPG pack—which meant it contained a disposable rocket launcher and various explosive-tipped rocket charges.

He found the one he was looking for.

The notorious Soviet P-61 Palladium charge.

★ ★ ★

A Palladium charge—comprising a palladium outer shell around a liquid core of enhanced hydrofluoric acid—has only one purpose: to take out civilian nuclear power plants in a terrible, terrible way.

Nuclear *weapons* require a core consistency of 90% enhanced uranium. The nuclear *reactors* in civilian power plants, on the other hand, have a core consistency of around 5%; while reactors on nuclear-powered aircraft carriers hover at around 50%—as such, neither of these reactors can *ever* create a nuclear explosion. They can leak radiation—as happened at Chernobyl—but they will never create a mushroom cloud.

What they do release every single second, however, are massive quantities of hydrogen—highly flammable hydrogen—an action which is nullified by the use of 'recombiners' which turn the dangerous hydrogen (H) into very safe water (H_2O).

Mixing *palladium* with hydrogen, however, has the opposite effect. It multiplies the deadly hydrogen, producing *vast* quantities of the flammable gas which can then be triggered by the addition of a catalyst like hydrofluoric acid.

As such, the P-61 charge operates as a two-stage detonator.

The first stage—the initial blast—mixes Palladium with hydrogen, multiplying the gas at a phenomenal rate. The second stage of the weapon ignites that gas with the acid.

The result is a colossal explosion—not quite as big as a nuclear blast, but perhaps the only explosion in the world big enough to crack the reinforced hull of an aircraft carrier.

'There!' Schofield yelled, pointing at two gigantic cylindrical vents at the aft end of the hangar bay, fan-covered vents which expelled excess hydrogen out the rear port flank of the carrier. 'The reactor's exhaust vents!'

The jeep whipped through the hangar bay, weaving past flaming fighter jets.

Schofield stood up in the rear section of the jeep, hoisted the

RPG launcher onto his shoulder, aimed it at a gigantic fan set into the side of the exhaust stacks.

'As soon as I fire, Mother, hit the gas and head for the ascending ramp! We're gonna have about thirty seconds between the first stage and the second stage. That means thirty seconds to get off this boat!'

'Okay!'

Schofield peered down the sights of the launcher. 'Au revoir to you, assholes.'

Then he jammed his finger down on the trigger.

The launcher fired, sending its Palladium-tipped RPG rocketing into the upper reaches of the hangar, a dead-straight smoke-trail extending through the air behind it.

The Palladium charge smashed through the fan in the right-hand exhaust vent and disappeared inside it, heading downward, searching for heat.

No sooner was it away than Mother floored the jeep, wheeling it around in a tight circle before disappearing into the tunnel-like ascension ramp that allowed vehicle access from the hangar to the upper flight deck.

Round and round the jeep went, rising upwards.

As it circled higher, tyres squealing, there came an awesome muffled *boom* from deep within the bowels of the aircraft carrier.

The Palladium charge had hit its target.

Schofield hit his stopwatch: 00:01 . . . 00:02 . . .

In the air above the *Richelieu*, the *Black Raven* was still engaged in the dogfight of its life with the four French Rafale fighters.

It banked hard, screaming through the air, and took one of the Rafales out with its last remaining missile.

But then Rufus heard a shrill *beeeeeeeeep* from his console.

'They've fully hacked our countermeasure frequency!' he called.

'We just lost missile shield completely!'

At that moment, another of the Rafales got on their tail and the two planes roared over the ocean together, the Rafale trailing the Sukhoi, blazing away at it with orange tracers.

As the *Raven* rushed forward, Knight swung around in his revolving gunner's chair and opened fire on the trailing plane with the Raven's underslung revolving gun, raking the French fighter's cockpit with a withering rain of fire, shattering its canopy, ripping the pilot to bits, causing his plane to plough into the sea with a jarring explosive splash.

'Boss!' Rufus called suddenly. 'I need guns forward! Now!'

Knight spun. What he hadn't seen was that this trailing Rafale had been driving the *Raven* toward . . . the other two French fighters!

The two waiting Rafales launched one missile each—

—twin fingers of smoke lanced into the air, arcing in towards the *Black Raven*'s nose—

—but Rufus rolled the sleek black plane, flying it on its side just as he engaged his custom-fitted—and very rare—*secondary* countermeasures: a system known as 'Plasma Stealth' that enveloped the entire aircraft in a cloud of ionised gas particles.

The two missiles went berserk, splitting in a V-shape to avoid the ion cloud around the Sukhoi, and the *Raven* bisected them at blinding speed—leaving one missile to ditch wildly into the sea and the other to wheel around in the sky.

But the *Raven* was still on a collision course with the two incoming Rafales.

Knight swung forward, opened fire—and destroyed the left-hand wing of one Rafale a moment before the *Raven* overshot the two French fighters with a deafening roar.

There was only one Rafale left now, but not for long. A moment after it passed Knight's plane, the last French Rafale was hit by its own missile—the one that had gone rogue after being assailed by the Sukhoi's Plasma Stealth mechanism.

Knight and Rufus turned to see the final explosion, but as they

did so, there came another noise from across the waves—a deep ominous *boom* from within the aircraft carrier.

'Faster, Mother. Faster,' Schofield eyed his stopwatch:

00:09 . . .

00:10 . . .

The jeep shot up the circular ramp, kicking up sparks against the ramp's close steel walls.

Abruptly, the entire carrier banked sharply, turning to port, tilting the whole world thirty degrees.

'Keep going!' Schofield yelled.

The first-stage blast of the Palladium charge had knocked out the *Richelieu*'s hydrogen recombiners: that was the ominous boom.

Which meant that uncontrolled hydrogen was now building inside the carrier's cooling towers at an exponential rate. In exactly 30 seconds the second stage of the palladium charge would detonate, igniting the hydrogen and bringing about aircraft carrier Armageddon.

00:11

00:12

The jeep burst out from the ascension ramp into sunlight, bounced to a halt.

There was pandemonium on the flight deck.

Smoking planes, charred anti-aircraft guns, dead sailors. One Rafale fighter—nose down, its front wheels destroyed—blocked the *Richelieu*'s No. 2 take-off runway. The fighter must have been just about to take off when the *Black Raven* had hit it with a missile.

Schofield saw it instantly.

'Mother! Head for that broken fighter!'

'That thing ain't gonna fly, Scarecrow! Not even for you!' Mother yelled.

00:15

00;16

Amid the chaos, the jeep skidded to a halt beside the destroyed

Rafale fighter. Mother was right. With its nose down and its front wheels crumpled, it wasn't going anywhere.

00:17

00:18

'I don't want the plane,' Schofield said. 'I want this.'

He jumped out of the jeep, reached down and grabbed the catapult hook that lay on the runway in front of the destroyed plane. The small, trapezoidal catapult hook had formerly been attached to the front wheels of the plane. Normally you would attach it to the steam-driven catapult mechanism that ran for the length of the flight deck in order to get your plane to take-off speed in the space of 90 metres.

Schofield, however, wedged the catapult hook crudely under the front axle of his jeep and then clipped the other end of the hook to the deck catapult.

00:19

00:20

'Oh, you cannot be serious . . .' Mother said, eyeing the empty runway in front of their jeep—a runway that simply stopped at the bow horizon of the ship. The catapult's rails stretched away for the length of the flight deck like a pair of railway tracks heading toward a cliff edge.

00:21

00:22

Schofield jumped back into the jeep beside Mother.

'Put her into neutral and buckle up!' he said.

00:23

00:24

Mother snatched up her seatbelt, clicked it on. Schofield did the same.

00:25

Then he drew his MP-7 and levelled it at the nearby catapult controls, long since abandoned during the *Black Raven*'s attack . . .

00:26

. . . and fired.

00:27

Ping!

The bullet slammed into the launch lever, triggering the catapult.

And the jeep shot off the mark at a speed that no humble jeep had ever gone before.

Ninety metres in 2.2 seconds.

Schofield and Mother were thrust into their seats, felt their eye-balls ram into the backs of their sockets.

The jeep shot down the runway at *unbelievable* speed.

The deck blurred with motion.

The jeep's front tyres blew out after fifty metres.

But it still kept rocketing forward—like a cannonball out of a cannon—propelled by the tremendous force of the catapult.

Truth be told, they weren't travelling as fast as a fighter jet on take-off, since a fighter is also propelled by its own thrusters.

But Schofield didn't want to fly.

He just wanted to get off this aircraft carrier before she—

Blew.

The jeep hit the edge of the runway . . . and shoomed straight off it . . . blasting out into the sky . . . nose up, wheels spinning . . . *just as the entire aircraft carrier behind it shattered spontaneously.*

There was no fire.

No billowing clouds.

There was just a mighty, mighty BANG! as every exterior steel wall of the aircraft carrier *instantaneously* expanded outward—pushed out by the tremendous pressure of ignited hydrogen—bursting at the seams like the Incredible Hulk busting out of his clothes.

A starburst of a billion rivets was thrown high into the sky.

The rivets were thrown for miles, and rained down for the next whole minute. A helicopter that had just taken off from the rear of

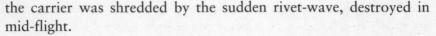

the carrier was shredded by the sudden rivet-wave, destroyed in mid-flight.

Dislodged pieces of the carrier—including entire plates of steel—flew out into the air and slammed down into the surrounding French destroyers, denting their sides, smashing their bridge windows.

The greatest damage to the *Richelieu* occurred at the aft end of the carrier, around the epicentre of the blast: the cooling vents.

The exterior walls there were simply ripped apart at the seams— at the vertical rivet joints—opening up wide gashes on both sides of the carrier, gashes into which the Atlantic Ocean flowed without mercy.

And the *Richelieu*—the largest and greatest aircraft carrier ever built by France—began to sink unceremoniously into the ocean.

Schofield and Mother's jeep, however, flew off the bow of the massive carrier.

As it soared through the air in front of the ship, they unclipped their seatbelts and pushed themselves up and out of the jeep, allowing themselves to sail through the sky above it.

The drop from the flight deck to the water level was about twenty-five metres.

The jeep hit the water first. A large foamy explosion of spray.

Schofield and Mother hit it next. Twin splashes.

It hurt, but they angled their bodies as they entered the water—so that they entered it boots-first and knifed under the surface not a moment before the carrier erupted and its storm of rivets blasted across the surface of the ocean like a rain of deadly shrapnel.

The mighty aircraft carrier was sinking fast, ass-end first.

It was a truly spectacular sight.

And then, as its hapless crew hurried for the lifeboats or simply

leapt for their lives into the ocean, the great warship went vertical—its bow rising high, its aft section completely submerged.

The rest of the French carrier group was frozen in shock.

Outside full-scale war, this sort of thing was unthinkable. No country had lost an aircraft carrier since World War II.

Which was probably why they were slow to react when, a minute after the explosion, the *Black Raven* swung into a hovering position ten feet above the waves of the Atlantic and plucked two tiny figures from the chop, raising them up on a cable-harness into its rear bomb bay.

Once the two figures were safely inside it, the sleek Sukhoi rose into the air and blasted off into the sky, away from the shattered remains of the *Richelieu* carrier group.

Aloysius Knight strode back into the holding cell of the *Black Raven*, saw Schofield and Mother lying there looking like a pair of drowned rats.

Schofield glanced up at Knight as he entered. 'Set a course for the English Channel, off Cherbourg. That's where the first Kormoran ship is. We have to find it before it launches its missiles on Europe.'

Knight nodded. 'I've already told Rufus to take us there.'

Schofield paused.

Knight appeared unusually sombre, almost . . . sensitive. What was going on?

Schofield looked around the tight confines of the holding cell, and it hit him.

'Where's Gant?' he asked.

It was then that, behind his amber-tinted glasses, Knight's eyes wavered—just slightly. Schofield saw it and at that moment, he felt something inside him that he had never felt before.

Absolute, total dread.

Aloysius Knight swallowed.

'Captain,' he said, 'we have to talk.'

SIXTH ATTACK

ENGLISH CHANNEL–USA
26 OCTOBER 1700 HOURS (E. CHANNEL)
E.S.T. (NEW YORK, USA) 1100 HOURS

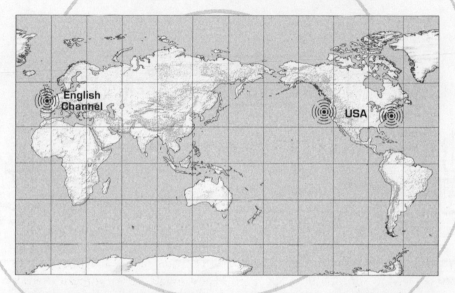

40 (a) (ii) In the event of a conflict involving the major global powers, it is highly likely that the poverty-stricken populations of Africa, the Middle East and Central America—some of which out-number the populations of their Western neighbours by a ratio of 100-to-1—will flood over Western borders and overwhelm Western city centres.

From: United States National Security Council Planning Paper Q-309, 28 October, 2000

(UN PRESS, NEW YORK)

'Who must do the hard things? He who can.'

Quote attributed to Confucius

KORMORAN-CLASS WARSHIP/SUPERTANKER

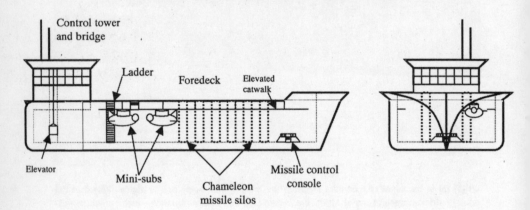

Control tower and bridge

Ladder

Foredeck

Elevated catwalk

Elevator

Mini-subs

Chameleon missile silos

Missile control console

ENGLISH CHANNEL COASTLINE, NORTHERN FRANCE
26 OCTOBER, 1700 HOURS LOCAL TIME
(1100 HOURS E.S.T USA)

With a burst from its thrusters, the *Black Raven* landed on a cliff-top overlooking the English Channel, lashed by driving rain.

Out of its cockpit stepped Shane Schofield. He dropped to the muddy ground and staggered away from the fighter, oblivious to the storm around him.

After Knight had finished telling him about what had happened in the Shark Pit with Gant and Jonathan Killian and the guillotine, Schofield had said only three words.

'Rufus. Land now.'

Schofield stopped at the edge of the cliff, jammed his eyes shut.

Tears mixed with the rain hammering against his face.

Gant was dead.

Dead.

And he hadn't been there. Hadn't been there to save her. In the past, no matter what happened, he'd *always* been able to save her.

But not this time.

He opened his eyes. Stared into space.

Then his legs gave way beneath him and he dropped to his knees in the mud, his shoulders heaving violently with every desperate sob.

★ ★ ★

Mother, Knight and Rufus watched him from the open cockpit of the *Raven*, twenty yards away.

'Fuck me . . .' Mother breathed. 'What the hell is he going to do now?'

Schofield's mind was a kaleidoscope of images.

He saw Gant—smiling at him, laughing, holding his hand as they strolled along the beach at Pearl, rolling up close against him in bed. God, he could almost feel the warmth of her body in his mind.

He saw her fighting in Antarctica and in Utah. Saving his life with a one-in-a-million Maghook shot inside Area 7.

And then—shocking himself—he saw Killian at the castle saying, 'I love to observe the look of pure horror that appears on a person's face when they realise that they are, without doubt, going to die.'

And he saw the world from now on . . .

Without her.

Empty.

Meaningless.

And with that, he looked down at the Desert Eagle pistol in his holster . . . and he drew it.

'Hey there, champ,' a voice said from behind him. 'Whatcha planning on doing with that gun?'

It was Mother.

Standing right behind him.

Schofield didn't turn around when he spoke. 'Nobody cares, Mother. We could save the world and nobody would give a shit. People would go on living their lives, completely unaware of soldiers like us. Like Gant.'

Mother's eyes were locked on the gun in his hand. Rain dripped off it.

'Scarecrow. Put the gun away.'

Schofield looked down at the Desert Eagle, seemed to notice it for the first time.

'Hey,' Mother said. Solely to distract him, she asked a question that she already knew the answer to. 'What did she mean when she said, "Tell him, I would have said yes"?'

Schofield looked away into the distance, spoke like an automaton.

'She could read me like a book. I could never keep anything secret from her. She knew I was going to propose in Tuscany. That's what she was gonna say yes to.'

He shifted his grip on the gun. Bit his lip. Another tear streaked down his face. 'Jesus, Mother. She's dead. She's fucking dead. There's nothing left for me now. Screw it. The world can fight its own battles.'

With a quick move, he placed the gun under his chin and pulled the—

But Mother moved faster.

She tackled him just as the gun went off and the two of them went rolling in the mud by the cliff edge.

And they fought—Mother trying to pin his gun-hand, Schofield trying to push her clear.

Taller, stronger and far bulkier, at first Mother had the jump on him. She pinned him underneath her great weight and punched his gun-wrist. The Desert Eagle dropped out of his hand. Then she smacked him hard in the face—

The blow had a strange effect on Schofield.

It seemed to focus him.

With almost disturbing ease, he grabbed Mother's left wrist with two fingers and twisted it. Mother roared with pain and Schofield—with perfect centre-of-gravity manipulation—threw her clear off him.

And they both stood.

Facing each other on the wind-lashed cliff, squaring off in the driving rain.

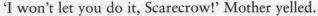

'I won't let you do it, Scarecrow!' Mother yelled.

'I'm sorry, Mother. It's too late.'

Mother moved.

She advanced quickly, unleashing a bone-crushing right, but Schofield ducked it, hit her back, square on the nose. Mother swung again, but Schofield—perfectly balanced in the mud—avoided that blow too, and hit her again.

Mother staggered back to a standing position. 'You're gonna have do more than that to get rid of me!'

She lunged at him again, driving into him with her shoulders, tackling him linebacker-style, lifting him off his feet and sending them both crashing to the earth.

Over by the *Black Raven*, Aloysius Knight and Rufus just stood there in the rain, watching the fight like stunned spectators.

Rufus took a step forward, making to intervene—but Knight stopped him with a light hand to the chest, never taking his eyes off the battle.

'No,' he said. 'This is for the two of them to sort out.'

Schofield and Mother rolled in the mud, struggling.

Mother seemed to have him pinned when suddenly Schofield landed a short sharp elbow to her jaw and—again with surprising strength—rolled her clear.

He stood.

She stood.

Both were dripping with mud.

Mother staggered slightly, tiring, but she re-engaged anyway, swinging blindly.

Schofield parried every blow easily now, martial-arts-style. Mother roared in frustration just as he spun on one knee and swept her legs out from under her, and Mother fell unceremoniously onto her butt in the mud.

Having won for himself the distance he needed, Schofield walked back over to his gun, picked it up.

'Scarecrow, no!' Mother called, tears welling in her eyes. 'Please, Shane, don't . . .'

And for some reason, that stopped him.

Schofield paused.

Then he realised what it was.

For as long as he could remember, Mother had never called him by his first name. Not even in situations outside the Marine Corps.

He lowered the gun an inch, gazed at her.

She looked pathetic: on her knees on the ground, covered in mud, tears streaking down her face.

'Shane,' she called, 'the world may not care. The world may not know that it needs people like you and Gant. But I care! And I know that I need you! Shane, I have a husband and some beautiful nieces—they're thirteen years old and they all dress like Britney fucking Spears—and I have a mother-in-law who hates my guts.

'But I love them all, love 'em to death, and I don't want to see them living in a world of suffering and death that is run by a bunch of billionaire motherfuckers. *But I can't stop that from happening.* I can't. No matter what I do, no matter how hard I try, in the end I'm just not smart enough, not quick enough, not good enough. But you are. You can beat them. And do you know why? I do. I've always known it. And my little Chickadee knew it, too, and that was why she loved you. *It's because you can do things that other people can't.*'

Mother was on her knees in the mud, eyes filled with tears.

'Shane, I ain't the smartest kid in the class, but I know this: people are people. They're selfish and they're self-centred, they do stupid things and they have absolutely no idea that there are heroes like you out there looking after them every day.'

Schofield didn't say a word.

The rain smacked against his cheeks.

But Mother had broken the spell.

Life was coming back into his eyes.

'I don't call you Shane,' she said. 'You probably know that. But do you know why?'

Schofield was rooted to the spot. Frozen.

'No. Why?'

'Cause you ain't a regular fucking fella. You ain't a "Brad" or a "Chad" or a "Warren". You're the Scarecrow. *The fucking Scarecrow.*

'You're more than just an ordinary guy. Which is why I've never treated you like an ordinary guy. You're better than all of them. But if you off yourself now, if you take the easy way out, then you're taking the path that Brad or Chad or Warren would take. That ain't you. That ain't the Scarecrow. The Scarecrow is made of tougher stuff than that. Now, I ain't saying living is going to be easy—I don't know if any normal person could bounce back after hearing what you just heard—but if anyone can, it's you.'

Schofield was silent for a long time.

Then at last he spoke.

'I'm going to kill them all, Mother,' he said. 'The bounty hunters who caught her. All the bounty hunters involved in this hunt. Plus everyone on Majestic-12 who made this happen. And when it's all over—however it turns out, whether the world survives this crisis intact or whether it goes to hell on a handcart—I'm going to find Jonathan Killian and I'm going to blow his fucking brains out.'

Mother smiled through her tears. 'Sounds good to me.'

'But Mother,' he added somewhat ominously, 'I won't guarantee what I'll do *after* that.'

'Then I guess I'll just have to fight you again,' Mother said.

And at that, Schofield blinked.

Life had fully returned.

Mother nodded. 'Scarecrow. Nobody else may ever say this, so

I'll just say it for me . . . and for Ralph, and for the six Britney clones and my bitch from hell mother-in-law. Thank you.'

Schofield came over to her, extended his hand. Mother clasped it and let him haul her up.

Before he could move off, however, she embraced him in a mighty hug, engulfing his body in her massive frame. Then she kissed him on the forehead and guided him back to the *Raven* with one arm around his shoulders.

'I miss her already,' she said as they walked.

'Me, too,' Schofield said. 'Me, too.'

They walked together.

'Mother, I'm sorry I hit you.'

'Hey, it's okay. I hit you first.'

'Thanks for fighting me. Thanks for not letting me go.'

UPPER NEW YORK BAY, USA
26 OCTOBER, 1125 HOURS LOCAL TIME

Exactly eleven minutes after his Concorde had touched down on the tarmac at JFK, Book II was sitting in the back of a Marine Corps CH-53E Super Stallion helicopter, blasting over the Statue of Liberty and Upper New York Bay, the mighty steel-and-glass mountain range of New York City spread out behind him.

Seated in the hold with him were twelve fully-armed Force Reconnaissance Marines.

'You found *terrorists* at the plant?' Book shouted into his mike, puzzled. He was talking to the leader of the Department of Defense team that had checked the Axon plant earlier, a man named Dodds.

'*Yes. All from Global Jihad, including—wait for it—Shoab Riis. Looks like it was a hell of a fight there,*' Dodds said.

'Global Jihad,' Book said. 'But that just doesn't make—' He cut himself off.

Suddenly he understood.

Majestic-12 needed someone to blame for all this. And who better than a terrorist organisation?

For, really, how could Axon Corp help it if Global Jihad terrorists stole their missiles and ships. But where could Majestic-12 find a team of genuine Global Jihad terrorists?

'France,' Book II said aloud. 'It's always fucking France.'

Dodds said, 'Book, what the hell is going on? Everyone here is

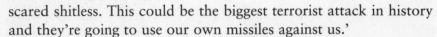

scared shitless. This could be the biggest terrorist attack in history and they're going to use our own missiles against us.'

'This isn't a terrorist thing, Dodds,' Book said. 'It's a business thing. Trust me, the terrorists were already dead when they got to that plant. I'm starting to think that the French Secret Service has been giving Majestic-12 some quiet assistance. I gotta go. Book, out.'

Book turned his gaze back toward the container ships and super-tankers resting at anchor off Staten Island—a pack of leviathans awaiting permission to enter the Hudson and East Rivers.

Thanks to the Kormoran project, each one of them was a potential missile launch vessel.

'So which one is it?' the pilot asked.

'Just go to GPS co-ordinates 28743.05—4104.55,' Book said. 'That's where it'll be.'

The pilot adjusted his dials, flew by his GPS locator.

Book checked the launch list on his hand-held computer for the hundredth time. After he had spoken with Schofield earlier, he and Scott Moseley had calculated the GPS locations of the last two Kormoran tanker-launchers:

Hopewell	Taep'o-Dong-2	N-8	11900.00	11622.50	1230
			2327.00	4000.00	
			(Taiwan Sts)	(Beijing)	
	Taep'o-Dong-2	N-8	11900.00	11445.80	1230
			2327.00	2243.25	
			(Taiwan Sts)	(Hong K)	
Whale	Shahab-5	TN76	07040.45	07725.05	1245
			2327.00	2958.65	
			(Arab'n Sea)	(New Delhi)	
	Shahab-5	TN76	07040.45	07332.60	1245
			2327.00	3230.55	
			(Arab'n Sea)	(Islamabad)	

After that, he and Moseley had then plotted *all* the boats on a map of the world:

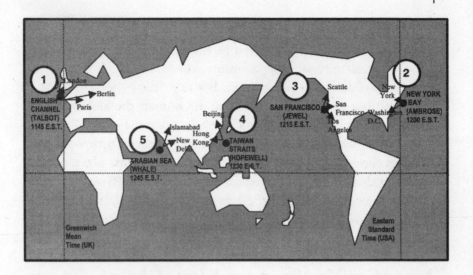

The sum of it all?

In addition to the three tankers set to fire their nuclear-tipped missiles on America, England, France and Germany, there were two extra Kormoran ships out there: one in the Arabian Sea, ready to fire on both India and Pakistan, and another in the Taiwan Straits, aiming cloned Taep'o-Dong ICBMs at Beijing and Hong Kong.

'Jesus H. Christ . . .' Book whispered.

He shook himself out of it, hit his satellite mike.

'Fairfax? You there? How you doing out West?'

PACIFIC OCEAN,
TWO MILES OFF SAN FRANCISCO BAY
0825 HOURS LOCAL TIME
(1125 HOURS E.S.T USA)

Dave Fairfax sat in a Super Stallion of his own, flanked by his own Marine Recon team, his right foot shaking incessantly—a nervous gesture that betrayed his rather extreme fear.

He wore a helmet that was too big and a bulletproof vest that was even bigger, and he held in his lap a real-time satellite uplink unit. He felt very small compared to the Marines all around him.

At the moment, his Super Stallion was powering low over the waves of the Pacific, heading toward—

A lone supertanker lying silently at anchor off the San Francisco coast.

'Hi, Book,' Fairfax yelled into his newly-acquired throat-mike. 'We have our tanker, and she's a big one, all right. She's exactly where she should be; her position matches the GPS co-ordinates you gave me. Tanker identified as the MV *Jewel,* registered in Norfolk, Virginia, to the Atlantic Shipping Company, a deep subsidiary of Axon Corporation.'

Fairfax's foot kept shaking. He wished it would stop.

'Oh, and I got that Mersenne prime for you,' he said. 'God, man, Mersennes are very cool mathematics. There are only thirty-nine that we know of, but some of those are, like, two million digits long. They're a very rare kind of prime number. You get them by applying a strict formula: Mersenne Prime = $2^p - 1$, where "p" is a prime number, but where the answer is also prime. Three is the first Mersenne Prime because $2^2 - 1 = 3$, and both 2 and 3 are prime. So they start small, but end up very big. The sixth Mersenne is 131071. It's based on the prime number, 17. That is, $2^{17} - 1 = 131071$, which is also prime—'

'*So the answer is 131071,*' Book said.

'Uh, yes,' Fairfax said.

'*I'll pass that on to the Scarecrow,*' Book said. '*Thanks, David. Out.*'

The signal went dead.

Fairfax scowled at his treacherous foot.

'Goes with the job, Mister Fairfax,' the Marine leader, Trent, said, nodding at Fairfax's foot. 'But if the Scarecrow trusts you to do this, then you must be up to the challenge.'

'I'm glad *he* thinks I'm up for it,' Fairfax muttered.

The Super Stallion roared toward the tanker.

★ ★ ★

ENGLISH CHANNEL, NORTH OF CHERBOURG, FRANCE
26 OCTOBER, 1725 HOURS LOCAL TIME
(1125 HOURS E.S.T USA)

The *Black Raven* shot like a bullet through the rain-driven sky, searchlights blazing, zooming high over a constellation of supertanker lights on the English Channel.

While Rufus, Mother and Knight searched the sea for their target, Schofield was talking on the radio with Book II.

'*Okay, I'm sending it all through now,*' Book's voice said.

Schofield's Palm Pilot pinged: it now had Book's plots of all the Kormoran ships on it. Schofield's eyes widened at the location names: the Arabian Sea, the Taiwan Straits . . .

'*And Fairfax figured out the sixth Mersenne for you,*' Book said. '*It's 131071.*'

'131071 . . .' Schofield wrote it down on his hand. 'Thanks, Book. Tell David I'll be in touch with him shortly. Scarecrow, out.'

He switched channels, patched in to the US Embassy in London. 'Mr Moseley. What's the word on our submarines?'

'I've got good news and bad news,' Scott Moseley's voice said.

'Give me the good news.'

'The good news is we have Los Angeles-class attack subs in both the Arabian Sea and the Taiwan Straits—close enough to take out the launch boats at those locations.'

'And the bad news.'

Moseley said, 'The bad news is the other three launch boats: the ones in New York, San Francisco and the English Channel. They're going to fire too soon. We don't have any 688s close enough to get to any of those launch vessels in time. Book and Fairfax are going to have to go in and disarm them *in situ*, on board.'

'Okay,' Schofield said.

'Found it!' Rufus pointed to a supertanker rolling at anchor in the raging sea, its deck illuminated by powerful floodlights—just another gigantic supertanker nestled in amongst all the others waiting off the French coast. 'Transponder signal identifies it as the MV *Talbot* and its location matches the GPS location perfectly.'

'Good work, Rufus,' Schofield said. 'Mr Moseley, thanks for your help. Now I have to get to work.'

Schofield turned to Knight and Mother. 'We take the launch tankers in the order that they'll fire. This one first. Then we high-tail it out of here and disarm the others by remote from a safe location. Good for you?'

'Good for me,' Knight said.

'Fuckin' dandy,' Mother said.

'Hold on, people,' Schofield said, his face deadly. 'We're going in.'

ENGLISH CHANNEL
1730 HOURS LOCAL TIME
(1130 HOURS IN NEW YORK)

The *Black Raven* swooped in low over the supertanker's main deck, cutting across the beams of the ship's floodlights.

Rain fell all around it—slanting, stinging rain.

Forks of lightning slashed the sky.

Then the bomb bay on the *Raven* opened and three figures rappelled down from it: Schofield, Knight and Mother.

They were all fully armed—MP-7s, Glock pistols, Remington shotguns—thanks to the *Raven*'s onboard arsenal. Schofield and Mother even wore two spare utility vests that Knight kept for himself aboard the *Raven*.

The three of them landed on the superlong foredeck of the *Talbot*, in front of its control tower, while above them the *Black Raven* peeled away into the rainy sky.

And not a moment too soon.

For no sooner were Schofield and the others on the deck than the entire area around them exploded with bullet sparks from a pair of snipers firing from the control tower.

NEW YORK BAY
EAST COAST, USA

At the exact same time on the other side of the Atlantic, Book II and his team of Marines were storming their supertanker—the *Ambrose*—in New York Bay.

Like Schofield, they rode ziplines from their chopper down to the tanker's elongated foredeck.

Like Schofield, they entered under fire.

Unlike Schofield, however, they didn't have the advantage of darkness and pouring rain. It was 11:30 a.m. on this side of the world. Broad daylight.

The two snipers waiting for them inside the bridge of the *Ambrose* opened fire before Book's men had reached the bottom of their ropes.

Two Marines fell immediately. Dead.

Book hit the deck hard, landing with a heavy thump, returned fire.

SAN FRANCISCO
WEST COAST, USA

It was the same on the West Coast.

Fairfax's team stormed their supertanker—the *Jewel*—under heavy sniper fire from its control tower.

But Trent's men saw it coming.

Their own crack shooter nailed both of the enemy snipers with two shots from the open door of their Super Stallion.

The Marines stormed the ship, landing on the roof of the super-tanker's control tower—with Dave Fairfax running in their midst.

They found the snipers' nest on the bridge: two snipers had been firing out through the supertanker's high-visibility bridge windows.

The two snipers had deep black skin, and wore khaki African military fatigues.

'What the hell?' Andrew Trent said when he saw their shoulder insignia.

Both snipers wore the badge of the Eritrean Army.

THE ENGLISH CHANNEL

Lightning lit up the sky—waves crashed against the side of the super-tanker—thunder roared—bullets banged down against the foredeck.

Knight and Mother nailed the two snipers up on the bridge of the *Talbot* with a blitzkrieg of fire.

'I should have known!' Schofield shouted as they charged across the foredeck toward a door at the base of the control tower. 'Killian wouldn't leave the ships unguarded!'

'So who are they? Who did he get to do the guarding?' Mother yelled.

On the way to the tower, they found a large access hatch sunk into the deck. Knight and Schofield opened it . . .

. . . to be met by the deafening *brack-a-brack!* of automatic gunfire and the sight of a long vertical ladder disappearing down into the ship's vast missile hold.

Of more immediate interest to Schofield and Knight, however, was what they saw at the base of the ladder.

The source of the gunfire.

To their utter amazement, they saw a team of black-clad commandos—brandishing Uzis and M-16s with clinical precision, and firing them ferociously at an unseen enemy.

Schofield jammed the hatch shut again.

'I think we interrupted someone's battle,' he said.

Mother yelled, 'What did you see down there?'

'We're not the first people to arrive at this tanker,' Schofield said.

'What! Who's down there?'

Schofield exchanged a look with Knight.

'Not many elite units use Uzis these days,' Knight said. 'Zemir. I'd say it's the Sayaret Tzanhim.'

'I agree,' Schofield said.

'Would someone *please* tell me what's going on!' Mother yelled in the rain.

'My guess,' Schofield called, 'is that we've been beaten to this ship by the only other man in the world who can disarm the CincLock security system. It's that Israeli Air Force guy from the list—Zemir—with a crack team of Israel's best troops, the Sayaret Tzanhim, protecting him.'

'Hey, this day has been so weird, I'd believe fucking anything,' Mother said. 'So where now?'

Schofield checked his watch.

1735 hours.

1135 in New York.

Ten minutes to launch.

He said, 'We let the Israelis do the dirty work downstairs. Hell, I'm happy to let Zemir be the hero and disarm those missiles. As for us: into the tower. I want to check those snipers. See who we're up against before we go running into that mess downstairs to help Zemir.'

They came to the door at the base of the tower, flung it open just as—

Bam!

—they were assaulted by the blinding white beam of a helicopter searchlight.

Schofield spun in the doorway, rain in his face.

'Oh, you have got to be joking . . .' he said.

There, landing on the long flat foredeck of the supertanker—a hundred yards away, its searchlight panning the area—was an obviously stolen Alouette helicopter.

It touched down on the deck.

And out of it stepped three men in Russian battle-dress uniforms and carrying Skorpion machine pistols . . .

Dmitri Zamanov and the last two remaining members of the Skorpions.

'Damn. I forgot,' Knight said, 'you've still got a price on your head. It's Zamanov. Run.'

Into the control tower. Up some ladder-stairs. Emerging onto the bridge.

1736.

Fairfax's voice in Schofield's ear: '*Scarecrow. We've taken the bridge of the San Francisco tanker. Found enemy snipers wearing the uniforms of the Eritrean Army . . .*'

Schofield went straight over to the bodies of his snipers.

African soldiers.

Commandos. Khaki fatigues. Black helmets.

And on their shoulders, a crest—but *not* the crest of Eritrea.

Rather, it was the badge of the Nigerian Army's elite commando unit: the Presidential Guard.

As veterans of Africa's many civil wars, the Nigerian Presidential Guard were CIA-trained killers who in the past had been used against their own citizens as much as against their nation's enemies. In the streets of Lagos and Abuja, the Presidential Guards were known by another name: the Death Squads.

Killian's protection team.

Two snipers up here. And more men downstairs, guarding the missile silos—the unseen enemy that the Israelis were fighting right now in the hold.

'Mr Fairfax. Did you say yours were Eritrean?'

'*That's right.*'

'Not Nigerian?'

'*Nope. My Marines confirm it. Definitely Eritrean insignia.*'

Eritrea? Schofield thought—

'Scarecrow,' Mother said, opening a storeroom door wide. Four

body bags lay on the floor of the storeroom. Mother quickly unzipped one—to reveal the stinking corpse of a Global Jihad terrorist.

'Ah, now I get it,' Schofield said. 'The whipping boys.'

He keyed his sat-mike: 'Mr Fairfax. Tell your Marines to stay sharp. There'll be more African troops down in the main hold, guarding the silos. Sorry, David. It's not over for you yet. You have to get past those troops and get your satellite uplink unit within sixty feet of the missiles' control console for me to disarm them.'

'*Ten-four*,' Fairfax's voice signed off. '*We're on the case.*'

Mother joined Knight at the windows of the bridge, searching the area outside for Zamanov.

'Do you see him?' Mother said.

'No, the little Russian ratbastard's disappeared,' Knight said. 'Probably gone after Zemir.'

Suddenly Rufus's voice exploded in their earpieces:

'*Boss. Scarecrow. I got a new contact closing in on your tanker. A large cutter of some kind. Looks like the French Coast Guard.*'

'Christ,' Schofield said, moving to the windows, seeing a large white boat approaching them on their starboard side.

Schofield couldn't believe it.

In addition to the Nigerian Death Squad, the Israeli shock troops and the Russian bounty hunters already on this supertanker, they now had a group of French maritime police on the way!

'That ain't the Coast Guard,' Knight said, peering through some night-vision binoculars.

Through them he could see a big white cutter, charging through the chop—could see its knife-like bow, its big foredeck gun, its glassed-in wheelhouse, and bloodbursts all over the wheelhouse's windows.

Armed men stood at its wheel.

'It's Demon Larkham and IG-88,' Knight said.

★ ★ ★

1738.

Seven minutes to launch.

'Damn it, more bounty hunters,' Schofield said. 'Rufus! Can you take them out?'

'*Sorry, Captain, I'm outta missiles. Used them all against that French carrier.*'

'Okay, okay . . .' Schofield said, thinking. 'All right, Rufus, you keep to your instructions, okay. If we can't disarm those missiles in time, we'll be needing your special help later.'

'*Got it.*'

Schofield spun, still thinking, thinking, thinking.

Everything was happening too fast. The situation was spiralling out of control. Missiles to disarm, the Israelis already on board, Nigerian troops, more bounty hunters . . .

'Focus!' he shouted aloud. 'Think, Scarecrow. What do you ultimately have to achieve?'

Disarm the missiles. I have to disarm the missiles by 1745 hours. Everything else is secondary.

His eyes flashed to an elevator at the back of the bridge.

'We're going down to the hold,' he said.

1739 hours.

 NEW YORK BAY
1139 HOURS

On the foredeck of their supertanker, in bright morning sunshine, Book's team of Marines dived for cover.

Book scrambled into a deck hatch, slid down a very long ladder into darkness, followed by his Marine escorts.

He hit the floor, looked around.

He stood in a cavernous hold, easily three hundred yards long. A dozen cylindrical missile silos stretched away into darkness, like colossal pillars holding up the ceiling.

And bunkered down in front of the farthest missile silo, taking cover behind a heavily fortified barricade of steel crates and fork-lifts, was a team of heavily-armed African commandos.

THE ENGLISH CHANNEL
1739 HOURS

The elevator doors opened to reveal the aft section of the super-tanker's main hold.

Schofield, Knight and Mother emerged, leading with their guns.

The missile hold was absolutely enormous—a massive interior space the size of three football fields stretched end-on-end. And in its forward half, the Chameleon missile silos: high reinforced titanium cylinders stretching all the way up to the underside of the supertanker's foredeck. Inside them: the most devastating weapons known to man.

And in that forward section of the ship, a *brutal* battle was underway.

A dozen Nigerian commandos were bunkered down beneath the farthest pair of missile silos, covering the missile control console—an elevated platform mounted ten feet off the ground on steel struts, and the place Schofield needed to be within sixty feet of in order to disarm the missiles.

The Nigerians were positioned behind a very well-prepared barricade, and they fired machine guns and hurled grenades at their Israeli attackers.

Bullets and grenades hit the silos, but did no damage—the walls of the silos were far too strong.

In between Schofield and this battle were all sorts of supply materials: shipping containers, missile spare parts; he even saw two yellow mini-submarines with hemispherical glass cockpits suspended from chains high up near the ceiling catwalks.

Schofield recognised the subs as heavily-modified ASDSs—

Advanced SEAL Delivery Systems. With their glass domes, these shallow-water mini-submarines were often used by the US Navy to visually inspect the exterior hull of an aircraft carrier or ballistic missile submarine for sabotage devices. It was a given that a project as important as Kormoran–Chameleon would be equipped with them.

1740.

Schofield, Knight and Mother dashed forward, ducking low, winding their way between the supply materials, observing the battle.

Just as the Israelis launched a ruthless offensive.

They sent a few men to the right to draw the Nigerian fire, then they hit the Nigerian barricade with three rocket-propelled grenades from the left.

The grenades shot down the length of the missile hold . . . three white smoke-trails, flying together . . . and hit the Nigerian barricade.

It was like a dam bursting.

The Nigerians flew into the air. Some screamed. Others burned.

And the Israelis stormed forward, killing the Nigerians where they fell, shooting them in the heads, at the same moment as . . .

. . . a gigantic steel loading door set into the starboard wall of the hold rumbled open, rising into the air on its runners.

The massive door opened fully and—*whump!*—a wide steel boarding plank clanged to the floor from *outside* the aperture and like a crew of 16th-century pirates boarding a galleon, the men of IG-88 flooded into the missile hold, charging into it from their stolen Coast Guard boat, their devastating MetalStorm guns blazing.

Schofield watched as—now under fire from at least twenty IG-88 men—the Israeli commandos, the crack Sayaret Tzanhim, seized the area around the missile control console.

They formed a tight semi-circle around the elevated console platform, all facing aft, firing their Uzis and M-16s at IG-88.

Under their protection, the Israelis' leader—a man who could only be Simon Zemir—climbed up onto the steel platform and went

straight over to the console, flipped open a briefcase and extracted a CincLock-VII disarm unit.

'Sneaky bastard Israelis,' Mother said. 'Is there any US technology that they haven't stolen?'

'Probably not,' Schofield said, 'but today they're our bestest buddies. We watch over them while they watch over Zemir.'

1741.

From behind his missile silo, Schofield watched as Zemir's CincLock unit illuminated like a laptop and Zemir stared at its touchscreen, flexing his fingers in anticipation of the disarm sequence he was about to face.

He's going to disarm the missile system, Schofield thought. *Excellent. We might get out of here without much hassle after all.*

But then, to his absolute horror, Schofield saw three shadowy figures descending by rope from the rafters of the missile hold *above and behind* Zemir's console platform.

None of the Sayaret Tzanhim saw them. They were too busy firing at Demon Larkham and his IG-88 bounty hunters.

'No,' Schofield whispered. '*No, no, no . . .*'

The three shadowy figures whizzed down their ropes at lightning speed.

Zamanov and his Skorpions.

Ziplining down from the ship's foredeck, from a hatch near the bow.

Schofield broke cover, yelled uselessly above the gunfire: '*Behind you!*'

Of course, the Israelis responded immediately.

By firing at him. Even Zemir himself looked up, about to start the disarm sequence.

Schofield dived back behind his silo, rolled to the ground, peered back out—

—just in time to see the three Skorpions land lightly on the elevated platform a few yards *behind* the preoccupied Zemir.

And Schofield could only watch, powerless, as in the strobe-like glare of the Israelis' muzzle-flashes, Zamanov crept silently forward, drew his Cossack fighting sword and swung the blade at Zemir's neck from behind in a brutal horizontal slashing motion.

And in that instant, Shane Schofield became the last person on the bounty list still alive.

And the only man on Earth capable of disarming the CincLock-VII missile security system.

Zemir's head dropped off his shoulders. He had not even been able to start the disarm sequence.

Schofield's mouth fell open. 'This cannot be happening.'

One of the Sayaret Tzanhim glanced over his shoulder—in time to see Zemir's headless corpse drop off the console platform and down to the floor, spilling blood; to see Zamanov stuff Zemir's ragged head into his rucksack and whiz back up his retractable zipline—

Blam!

Covering the fleeing Zamanov, the other two Skorpions shot the Israeli trooper in the face—just as two more Sayaret Tzanhim soldiers were blasted by IG-88 fire from the *other* direction.

Fire from both directions—twin forces of professional bounty hunters—assailed the Israeli commando team.

And as the remaining Sayaret Tzanhim noticed Zemir's fallen body and the fleeing Skorpions above it, they became confused and in the face of IG-88's superior firepower, lost formation.

They were decimated.

IG-88 overwhelmed them. Within moments, the entire Israeli force was dead.

1742.

IG-88 took control of the barricade. Demon Larkham strode like a conquering general into the enemy blockade. He pointed up at the ceiling, at Zamanov and his Skorpions fleeing on their retractable ziplines with Zemir's head in their possession.

★ ★ ★

The three Skorpions hit the ceiling next to a wide cargo hatch.

Zamanov's two companions climbed up through the hatch first, stepping up into the pouring rain on the foredeck, reached back down as Zamanov handed them the severed head of Simon Zemir.

Supermachine-gun fire riddled their bodies.

The two Skorpions on the foredeck convulsed violently, their chests exploding in bloody fountains.

A six-man subteam of IG-88 troopers stood in the rain waiting for them. Demon Larkham had anticipated this, and so had already dispatched a second team to the foredeck.

The rucksack containing Zemir's head dropped to the deck, and the IG-88 subteam ran forward, grabbed it.

Outnumbered and outgunned, Zamanov ducked below the floorline, swung over to a catwalk high above the missile hold and disappeared into the shadows.

Down in the missile hold itself, Schofield was speechless.

This was unbelievable.

With three minutes to go till the nuclear missiles fired, Zemir was dead and IG-88 held the control console. Twenty of them, with MetalStorm guns!

He needed some kind of distraction, a *really big* distraction.

'Call Rufus,' he said to Knight.

'You sure?'

'It's the only way.'

'Right,' Knight said. 'You're a truly crazy man, Captain Schofield.' Then Knight spoke into his throat-mike. 'Rufus. How is Plan B coming along?'

Rufus's voice came in. '*I got the nearest one for you! And she's one big momma! I'm a hundred yards out, engines running, and pointed straight at you!*'

★ ★ ★

One hundred yards away from the *Talbot*, a second supertanker was powering through the storm with Rufus at the helm.

Waiting its turn to unload its cargo at Cherbourg, the giant 110,000-ton container ship, the MV *Eindhoven*, had been sitting at rest in the Channel, its engines idling, when Rufus had landed the *Black Raven* on its foredeck.

Now, but for Rufus, it was empty, its sailing crew of six having wisely decided to depart on a lifeboat after Rufus had strafed their bridge windows with two M-16s.

'What do you want me to do!' Rufus shouted into his radio.

On the *Talbot*, Schofield assessed the situation.

The Rufus Plan was always meant to be a last resort—a means by which Schofield could *sink* the false supertanker if he failed to disarm its missiles.

He stole a glance at the control console and its barricade and suddenly his blood froze.

Demon Larkham was looking directly back at him. He'd spotted them.

The Demon smiled.

'Rufus,' Schofield said. 'Ram us.'

17:42:10.

Demon Larkham's men charged out from behind their barricade, winding their way between the missile silos, their MetalStorm rifles blazing.

Coming after Schofield.

Schofield led Mother and Knight over to a lifeboat positioned beside the open cargo door on the starboard side of the hold.

'Quickly,' he yelled. 'Get in!'

They all dived into the lifeboat, then snapped up to return fire.

The IG-88 men closed in.

Schofield fired hard. So did Mother and Knight, trying to hold them off until Rufus arrived.

But the IG-88 troopers kept advancing.

'Come on, Rufus,' Schofield said aloud. 'Where are you . . . ?'

And then—magnificently—Rufus arrived.

It sounded like the end of the world.

The shriek of rending metal, of steel striking steel.

The collision of the two supertankers on the surface of the English Channel, veiled in sleeting rain, was an awesome, *awesome* sight.

Two of the largest moving objects on the planet—each nearly a thousand feet long and each weighing more than 100,000 tons—collided at ramming speed.

Rufus's stolen tanker, the *Eindhoven*, ploughed bow-first right into the port flank of the *Talbot*, hitting it perfectly perpendicularly.

The sharpened bow of the *Eindhoven* drove like a knife into the side of the *Talbot*, smashing into it like a battering ram.

The port flank of the *Talbot* just crumpled inward. Seawater gushed in through the gigantic gash the *Eindhoven* created in its side.

And like a boxer recoiling from a blow, the entire supertanker rocked wildly in response to the impact.

At first, it rolled to starboard, so great was the force of Rufus's ramming strike. But then as seawater began to enter the *Talbot* en masse, the missile-firing supertanker tilted dramatically—and fatally—back to port.

At which point it rolled over onto its left-hand side and began to sink.

Fast.

The scene inside the missile hold of the *Talbot* would have made Noah gulp.

In here, the impact had been a thunderous experience.

Not even Schofield had been prepared for the sheer power of the blow, or the sudden appearance of the *Eindhoven*'s pointed bow thrusting unexpectedly *right through* the port-side wall of the missile hold.

In response, the entire hold had swayed to starboard, throwing everyone off their feet.

Then seawater began to enter the hold through the gigantic gash—in monumental proportions.

A tidal wave of water, ten feet high and utterly immense in its force, rushed into the hold, swallowing several members of IG-88 in an instant, lifting forklifts and cargo containers and missile parts clear into the air.

The water rushed underneath Schofield's lifeboat, lifting it off its mounts. Schofield immediately released the craft from its davits and gunned the engine.

Within seconds, the hold's floor was completely under water, the water level rising fast.

And as it filled, the *Talbot* rolled dramatically to port—toward the fatal gash, tilting at least 30 degrees—and Schofield, blasting forward in the motorised lifeboat on the level surface of the water, saw the whole hold all around him start to roll.

17:42:30

From outside, it all made for a very unusual sight.

The *Eindhoven* was still embedded in the side of the *Talbot*—while the *Talbot*, taking on water in incredible quantities, lay foundering half-tilted on its left-hand side, literally hanging off the bow of the *Eindhoven*.

But so great was the weight of the water rushing into its belly, the *Talbot* was actually driving the bow of the *Eindhoven* under the surface as well—as such, the *Talbot*'s long foredeck and bridge tower remained above the waterline, slanted at a steep 30-degree sideways angle, while its left-hand flank drove the *Eindhoven*'s bow relentlessly downward, toward the waves.

On board the *Eindhoven*, Rufus didn't need to be told what to do.

He raced for the *Raven*, still parked on the foredeck of his tanker, climbed into the cockpit and lifted off into the rain-swept sky.

17:43:30.

Inside the rapidly-filling *Talbot*, Schofield was moving fast.

In fact, very very fast.

His motorised lifeboat whipped across the surface, slicing in between the now-slanted missile silos with Mother and Knight positioned on its flanks, shooting at their enemies floating in the water. It was like speedboating through a forest of half-fallen trees.

After the impact, Demon Larkham and most of his men had all made for the starboard side of the hold—the high side—the only part of the hold still above water.

Schofield, however, cut a beeline for the control console at the forward end of the missile hold.

17:43:48

17:43:49

17:43:50

His lifeboat carved through the chop, his two loyal shooters blazing away, killing IG-88 men as they whistled by.

The lifeboat came alongside the elevated control console. The wire-frame control console was also tilted at a dramatic angle, barely a foot above the rising waterline.

'Cover me!' Schofield yelled. From where he stood in his lifeboat, he could see the console's illuminated display screen, saw stark red numerals on it ticking downward in hundredths of a second—the countdown to missile launch.

```
00:01:10.88
00:01:09.88
00:01:08.88
```

The digitised hundredths of a second whizzed by in such a blur that they looked like 8s.

Schofield pulled his CincLock-VII unit—the one he'd taken from the French—from a waterproof pouch on his vest and once again saw the unit's display.

White and red circles hovered on the touchscreen.

Bing.

A message appeared:

MISSILE LAUNCH SEQUENCE IN PROGRESS.
PRESS 'ENTER' TO INITIATE DISARM SEQUENCE.
FIRST PROTOCOL (PROXIMITY): SATISFIED.
INITIATE SECOND PROTOCOL.

Like before, the white circles on the screen began to blink slowly on and off.

Schofield punched them as they did so.

The countdown ticked ever-downward.

```
00:01:01
00:01:00
00:00:59
```

Then abruptly the *Talbot* lurched sharply. The entire super-tanker, still hanging off the bow of the *Eindhoven*, was now slowly slipping off it!

With the unexpected jolt, Schofield missed one of the white circles.

The display beeped:

SECOND PROTOCOL (RESPONSE PATTERN): FAILED DISARM ATTEMPT
RECORDED.
THREE FAILED DISARM ATTEMPTS WILL RESULT IN DEFAULT
DETONATION.
SECOND PROTOCOL (RESPONSE PATTERN): REACTIVATED.

'Shit,' Schofield said.

He started all over again.

The supertanker was still sinking.

He felt water lapping against his boots.

★ ★ ★

While Schofield punched at the touchscreen, Aloysius Knight fired at the IG-88 force on the high starboard side of the hold.

He loosed a new burst, before suddenly he saw it.

'Oh, no . . .' he breathed.

'What?' Mother called.

'The starboard-side cargo door,' Knight said. 'It's about to go under.'

He was right. Owing to the leftward tilt of the ship, the massive starboard-side cargo doorway had until now been well above the waterline.

But now the rising water was about to hit it. And that was very bad—because once it did, seawater would start entering the *Talbot* from *both* sides of the ship.

After that, the *Talbot* would go down with frightening speed—

'Knight!' Mother yelled. 'Check right!'

'Oh, crap,' Knight said.

Over to their right, six of Demon Larkham's men were climbing out of the water into two motorised lifeboats.

They were coming for them.

'Captain Schofield!' Knight called. 'Are you done yet?'

'Almost . . . !' Schofield yelled, his eyes locked on the screen.

```
00:00:51
00:00:50
00:00:49
```

The two IG-88 lifeboats swung over to the starboard side of the water-filled hold, picked up the Demon and the remaining IG-88 force—sixteen men in total.

Then they charged toward Schofield and the missile control console.

Knight and Mother fired.

The two IG-88 boats blasted across the water, skimming through the forest of slanted missile silos, firing as they sped.

In the meantime, Schofield was still in his own world, punching red and white circles.

```
00:00:41
00:00:40
00:00:39
```

Then he hit the final white circle and the screen changed to:

SECOND PROTOCOL (RESPONSE PATTERN): SATISFIED.
THIRD PROTOCOL (CODE ENTRY): ACTIVE.
PLEASE ENTER AUTHORIZED DISARM CODE.

'All *right*,' Schofield said. The Universal Disarm Code. The sixth Mersenne prime was still written on his hand: 131071.

He started punching the numerical keypad on the CincLock unit when without warning the lifeboat beneath him moved and—

Beep!

The screen squealed in protest.

FIRST PROTOCOL (PROXIMITY): FAILED.
ALL PROTOCOLS REACTIVATED.

'What!' Schofield snapped his eyes up to find Knight gunning their lifeboat *away* from the missile console, while Mother fired off their stern at two pursuing IG-88 boats.

They weaved in between the missile silos.

'Sorry, Captain!' Knight yelled. 'But we had to go! We were dead if we stayed there!'

'Yeah, well we have to get back within range of that console in about ten seconds! Because I need at least twenty-five seconds to complete the response pattern!'

Bullet geysers raked the water all around their speeding lifeboat.

```
00:00:35
00:00:34
00:00:33
```

Knight brought the lifeboat round. 'How close do you have to be!'

'Sixty feet!'
'All right!'
Bullets whizzed past their ears, pinged off the missile silos.
Knight swung their boat around and brought it into a wide circular path around the steel island that was the control console, a circle that included the occasional weaving run in amongst the forest of silos.

```
00:00:27
00:00:26
00:00:25
```

Schofield's screen beeped to life.

FIRST PROTOCOL (PROXIMITY): SATISFIED.
INITIATE SECOND PROTOCOL.

The light-response display began—which meant so did Schofield's screen-tapping.
Mother kept firing at the IG-88 boats behind them.
Knight drove with one hand, fired with the other, careful to keep their boat within sixty feet of the control console.

```
00:00:16
00:00:15
00:00:14
```

But then the IG-88 boats, now aware of the circular path Knight was taking, split up.
One of them pivoted in the water, and took off in the opposite circular direction: the effect being that the first IG-88 boat was now driving Schofield's boat toward the second one.
Oblivious to the chase, Schofield's hands moved more quickly now.
Red-white-white . . .
Tap-tap-tap . . .

```
00:00:11
00:00:10
00:00:09
```

Knight saw IG-88's plan. He fired at the oncoming boat's driver.
Blam!-blam!-blam! . . .
Miss-miss-miss . . .

00:00:08
00:00:07
00:00:06

Schofield's hands were a blur now, tapping smoothly left and right.
Mother hit one of their pursuers. But then roared as she took a sizzling-hot round to her shoulder.

00:00:05
00:00:04
00:00:03

They came on collision course with the second IG-88 boat, Knight still firing at its driver.
Blam!-blam!-blam! . . .
Miss-miss . . .
Hit.

00:00:02

The driver flopped and fell, dead. The IG-88 boat peeled away, and Knight kept his boat within the 60-foot zone of the console.

00:00:01

And Schofield's hand movements changed slightly. Instead of tapping circles, it looked as if he was entering a—

00:00:00

Too late.

None of the Chameleon missiles, however, fired.

The countdown timer on the console was frozen at:

```
00:00:00.05
```

The seconds may have hit zero, but the very last second—calculated in blurring digital hundredths—had yet to fully expire when Schofield had punched in the Universal Disarm Code and hit 'ENTER'.

The screen now read:

THIRD PROTOCOL (CODE ENTRY): SATISFIED.
AUTHORIZED DISARM CODE ENTERED.
MISSILE LAUNCH ABORTED.

Schofield breathed a sigh of relief.

No missiles had launched.

London, Paris and Berlin were safe.

It was then, however, that the open starboard side door of the MV *Talbot* went slowly under the waterline.

SHOOOOOOM!!!

The roar was absolutely deafening.

It was, literally, like the opening of the floodgates.

Like an invading army overwhelming its enemy's lines, an unimaginable quantity of seawater came gushing in over the threshold of the *Talbot*'s wide starboard-side doorway.

A *wall* of water—a super tidal wave of unstoppable, ravenous liquid.

The result was instantaneous.

The entire supertanker rolled dramatically, *righting itself* as the inrushing water from the starboard side began to balance off against the inflow from port.

This righting of the *Talbot*, however, had one very important side-effect: it served to disengage the *Talbot* from the bow of the *Eindhoven*. And with the loss of its grip on the other supertanker, the *Talbot* lost its only means of staying afloat.

And so it began to sink—at speed—into the depths of the English Channel.

For Schofield, Knight and Mother, in their lifeboat on the water's surface inside the missile hold, the noise was all-consuming.

The roar of the waterfall flooding into the hold echoed throughout the ship. Waves crashed against steel walls. Whirlpools formed.

And the water level rose at frightening speed.

Indeed, to Schofield, it seemed as if the ceiling was lowering itself toward them. Quickly.

Within moments, they found themselves speeding along the surface *halfway up* the gigantic missile silos, 20 feet below the steel catwalks suspended from the roof.

In addition to this, with the breaching of the starboard-side door, Demon Larkham and his IG-88 men broke away from their chase, heading instead for the various ladders that led to the hold's ceiling.

'Damn, he's good,' Knight said. 'The Demon's heading topside, for the foredeck. He's going to cover all the hatches. Then he just waits for us to come up—which we'll have to do eventually.'

'Then we have to find another way out,' Schofield said. 'All I need now is to get away from this ship and find a safe place to hole up while I disarm the missiles aimed at America.'

Schofield pulled out his Palm Pilot to see which was the next Kormoran ship to launch.

He called up the bundle of documents that he had seen on the Pilot before:

Source	Delivery Sys.	W-H	Origin	Target	Time
Talbot	Shahab-5	TN76	35702.90 5001.00	00001.65 5239.10	1145
	Shahab-5	TN76	35702.90 5001.00	00420.02 4900.25	1145
	Shahab-5	TN76	35702.90 5001.00	01312.15 5358.75	1145
Ambrose	Shahab-5	TN76	28743.05 4104.55	28743.98 4104.64	1200

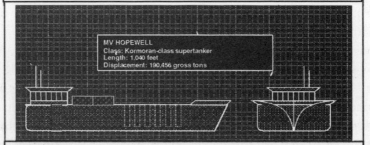

MV HOPEWELL
Class: Kormoran-class supertanker
Length: 1,040 feet
Displacement: 190,456 gross tons

SUBJECT: PAYMENT OF ASSESSOR'S COMMISSION

PAYMENT OF THE ASSESSOR'S COMMISSION WILL BE MADE BY INTERNAL ELECTRONIC FUNDS TRANSFER WITHIN AGM-SUISSE FROM ASTRAL-66 PTY LTD'S PRIVATE ACCOUNT.

Executive Itinerary

The proposed order of travel is as follows: Asmara (01/08), Luanda (01/08), Abuja (05/08), N'djamena (07/08) and Tobruk (09/08).

01/08—Asmara (embassy)
03/08—Luanda (stay with M. Loch, R's nephew)

	Name	Nat.	Org.
1.	ASHCROFT, William H.	UK	SAS
2.	CHRISTIE, Alec P.	UK	MI-6
3.	FARRELL, Gregory C.	USA	Delta
4.	KHALIF, Iman	AFGH	Al-Qaeda
5.	KINGSGATE, Nigel E.	UK	SAS
6.	McCABE, Dean P.	USA	Delta

He clicked on the abbreviated launch list. The full list came up:

Source	Delivery Sys.	W-H	Origin	Target	Time
Talbot	Shahab-5	TN76	35702.90 5001.00	00001.65 5239.10	1145
	Shahab-5	TN76	35702.90 5001.00	00420.02 4900.25	1145
	Shahab-5	TN76	35702.90 5001.00	01312.15 5358.75	1145
Ambrose	Shahab-5	TN76	28743.05 4104.55	28743.98 4104.64	1200
	Shahab-5	TN76	28743.05 4104.55	28231.05 3835.70	1200
Jewel	Taep'o-Dong-2	N-8	23222.62 3745.75	23222.70 3745.80	1215
	Taep'o-Dong-2	N-8	23222.62 3745.75	24230.50 3533.02	1215
	Taep'o-Dong-2	N-8	23222.62 3745.75	23157.05 4930.52	1215
Hopewell	Sky Horse-3	W-88	11900.00 2327.00	11622.50 4000.00	1230
	Sky Horse-3	W-88	11900.00 2327.00	11445.80 2243.25	1230
Whale	Ghauri-II	R-5	07040.45 2327.00	07725.05 2958.65	1245
	Agni-II	I-22	07040.45 2327.00	07332.60 3230.55	1245
Arbella	Jericho-2B	W-88	04402.25 1650.50	04145.10 2130.00	1400

He saw the familiar list.

It was the same as the one Book II had decrypted before. He saw the GPS locations of the first three boats: *Talbot, Ambrose* and *Jewel*.

The *Ambrose* was next: set to fire at 12 noon from GPS co-ordinates 28743.05,4104.55.

That's right, he remembered. *New York.*

Wait a second, his mind stopped short.

This list was different to Book's list.

He looked at it more closely.

Some of the missiles on the lower half of the list had been altered.

Book's list had featured only two varieties of missile: the Shahab and the Taep'o-Dong.

Yet this one featured several others in their place: the Sky Horse (from Taiwan), the Ghauri-II (Pakistan), the Agni-II (India) and the Jericho-2B (Israel).

It also, Schofield saw, had an *extra* launch vessel on it—the last entry, the *Arbella*—set to fire more than two hours after the first group of missiles.

This wasn't even mentioning another disturbing fact: the Taiwanese and Israeli missiles on this list were armed with *American* nuclear warheads, the powerful W-88—

A withering volley of bullets smacked the water next to Schofield. He hardly noticed.

When he looked up, he saw that Knight had brought their lifeboat alongside a ladder leading up to a ceiling catwalk. Once upon a time that catwalk had been suspended eighty feet above the floor of the hold. Now it was barely *eighteen* feet above the fast-rising water level.

On it, however, sixty yards away in *both* directions and closing fast, were two four-man teams of IG-88 troops. They had just burst down through hatches in the ceiling and were now charging down the length of the catwalk from either end, firing hard, their bullets hitting the girders all around Schofield's boat.

Ping!-ping!-ping!-ping!-ping!

'Bastard!' Knight yelled. 'He's not waiting for us to come up. He's forcing us up!'

Mother lifted Schofield up by the collar. 'Come on, handsome,

you can get back to your computer later.' She hauled him out of the lifeboat and up the ladder, covering him with her body.

They climbed the ladder quickly, shooting as they did so, reached the catwalk, where they were met by a million impact sparks.

Mother took up a covering position while Knight led Schofield aft.

Ping!-ping!-ping!-ping!-ping!

Bullets were spraying everywhere.

Knight and Schofield fired at the IG-88 men coming from the stern-end of the catwalk. Schofield went dry.

'Are we actually going anywhere in particular!' he yelled.

'Yes! To a safe place!' Knight called, still firing. 'A place where you can do your disarming thing, and where, at the same time, we can all get out of this sinking death-trap! Here!'

Knight cut sharply right, running past a small maintenance shack erected at a T-junction of this catwalk and another, emerging behind the shack to behold—

—the two yellow mini-submarines suspended on chains from the ceiling of the missile hold.

Like the catwalks, the subs weren't very high up anymore. Seventeen feet above the water level. A wide hood-like awning covered both the two subs and the catwalk between them. It now partially covered Schofield and Knight from the IG-88 teams.

Ping!-ping!-ping!-ping!-ping!

Trailing a dozen yards behind Knight and Schofield, Mother came to the maintenance shack at the T-junction, still returning fire at the IG-88 troops, now only twenty yards away from her on either side.

Schofield watched as she tried to make a break for the mini-subs, but the IG-88 troops blocked her way with a storm of bullets.

Mother ducked inside the shelter of the maintenance shack.

She was cut off.

'Mother!' Schofield yelled.

'*Get out of here, Scarecrow!*' she said over the radio.

The IG-88 men assaulted her shack with the most violent fusillade of MetalStorm rounds Schofield had seen yet.

The shack erupted in bullet impacts.

Mother ducked out of view—and Schofield feared that she'd been hit—but then she popped up again, firing and yelling, and took out two of the IG-88 men.

'*Scarecrow! I said, get out of here!*'

'I'm not leaving without you!'

'*Go!*' She loosed two more shots.

'I won't lose you and Gant in one day!'

Mother's voice became serious. '*Scarecrow. Go. You're more valuable than an old grunt like me.*' Mother looked over at him from the shack. '*You always were. My value comes in keeping you alive. At least let me do that. Now, go, you sexy little thing! Go! Go! Go!*'

And with that, Schofield saw Mother do something both courageous and suicidal.

She stood fully upright in the windows of the shack and, issuing a primal yell of 'Yaaaahhhhhhh!', started firing with two guns at *both* of the IG-88 forces.

Her sudden move stopped the two IG-88 teams in their tracks—each of them lost their front man in a gruesome fountain of blood—but crucially, it gave Schofield and Knight the opening they needed to escape.

'Get in!' Knight yelled, hitting the 'HATCH' button on one of the yellow submarines. With a quick iris-like motion, the circular hatch on top of the sub opened. 'Don't let her sacrifice count for nothing!'

Schofield took a half-step into the hatch, looked back at Mother—just as the two IG-88 forces overwhelmed her with their fire.

'Damn it, no . . .' he breathed.

A volley of MetalStorm bullets hit Mother, slamming into her chest armour . . .

Mother snapped upright, swaying, not firing anymore, her mouth open, her eyes suddenly blank—

—and then she fell and in the haze of smoke and flying glass,

Schofield lost sight of her as she dropped out of sight below the maintenance shack's window frames.

A moment later the two IG-88 forces put the issue beyond doubt.

At the exact same time, both IG-88 teams fired rocket launchers at the maintenance shack.

Two fingers of smoke lanced toward Mother's little shack from both fore and aft.

They hit it together and—*boom!*—the shed's four walls blasted outward, the whole structure exploding in an instant, its flat floor section just dropping through the air to the water sixteen feet below.

Schofield made to step out of the sub but Knight pushed him back in.

'No! We go! Now!' Knight yelled above the gunfire.

He shoved Schofield into the mini-sub, and Schofield landed inside it—

—only to discover that someone else was already there.

Schofield's feet hit the floor of the mini-sub, and he looked up to see a sword blade rushing directly at his face.

Reflex action.

He whipped up his empty H&K pistol and—*clang!*—the blade rushing at his throat hit the pistol's trigger-guard and stopped: one inch from Schofield's neck.

Dmitri Zamanov stood before him.

He held a short-bladed Cossack sword in his hands, and his eyes blazed with hatred.

'You chose the wrong hiding place,' the Russian bounty hunter growled.

Then before Schofield could move, he punched two buttons.

First, the internal 'HATCH' button.

The hatch whizzed shut, its steel door irising closed.

And second, the 'ASDS RELEASE' button, and suddenly Schofield felt his stomach turn as the entire mini-submarine dropped from its chains and fell sixteen feet straight down, landing with a massive splash in the rising body of seawater.

'Goddamn it!' Aloysius Knight couldn't believe it. 'What is this shit!'

One moment, he'd been shoving Schofield into the yellow ASDS and was about to climb in after him—the next, the sub's hatch closed right in front of him and then the whole fucking thing dropped down into the water below!

Hypercharged bullets hit the girders all around him as the IG-88

teams rushed past the destroyed maintenance shack and onto the submarine catwalk.

So Knight did the only thing he could do. He dived into the second mini-submarine, bullet-marks sizzling across the soles of his boots as he did so.

Schofield and Zamanov fought.

No style here. No graceful technique.

It was pure street-fight.

In the tight confines of the mini-sub, they rolled and punched—and punched and punched.

Schofield's empty gun was useless, but Zamanov's Cossack sword was the key.

Which was why the first thing Schofield had done after their sub had bounced with a splash into the water was hit Zamanov's wrist, causing him to drop the sword.

And then they wrestled—ferociously—Schofield because he was fuelled by Mother's recent sacrifice, Zamanov because he was a psychopath.

They hurled each other into the sub's walls, fighting with venom, drawing blood with every blow.

Schofield broke Zamanov's cheekbone.

Zamanov broke Schofield's nose, while another of his blows dislodged Schofield's earpiece.

Then Zamanov tackled Schofield, throwing him against the sub's control panel, and all of a sudden—*shoosh*—the mini-sub began to . . .

. . . submerge.

Schofield peeled himself off the instrument panel, saw that he'd knocked the 'BALLAST' switch. The ASDS was going under.

And suddenly they were underwater. Out through the sub's two hemispherical domes, Schofield saw the now-submerged world of the missile hold.

Everything was silent, tinged with blue—the floor, the missile

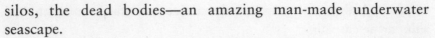

silos, the dead bodies—an amazing man-made underwater seascape.

The *Talbot* was now leaning slightly to starboard, the hold's floor tilted at least 20 degrees to that side.

Zamanov scooped up his sword.

The yellow mini-sub continued its slow-motion freefall through the watery hold.

And Zamanov and Schofield engaged—Zamanov swinging lustily, Schofield grabbing the bounty hunter's sword-hand as it came down.

But then, with a muffled crash, their ASDS hit the floor of the missile hold . . .

. . . and started to slide on its side *toward the open starboard cargo door*!

Schofield's world tilted crazily.

Both men were thrown sideways.

The sub slid down the sloping floor before, to Schofield's utter horror, it tipped off the edge of the doorway and fell out through it, into the open sea.

The little yellow sub fell quickly through the darkened water of the English Channel—beneath the gigantic hull of the MV *Talbot*.

The sheer size of the foundering supertanker above it dwarfed the ASDS. The mini-sub looked like an insect underneath a sinking blue whale.

But while the supertanker was sinking slowly and gradually, the mini-sub—its ballast tanks full—was descending at speed.

More than that.

It shot vertically down through the water, free-falling like an express elevator.

The average depth of the English Channel is about 120 metres. Here, off Cherbourg, it was 100 metres deep, and the ASDS was covering that depth quickly.

Inside it, Schofield and Zamanov fought in near darkness,

struggling in the ghostly blue glow of the mini-sub's instrument lights.

'After I *kill* you, I am going to cut your *fucking* American heart out!' Zamanov roared as he struggled to extract his sword-hand from Schofield's grasp.

Up until then, the fight had used more or less standard moves. But then Zamanov went for what Marines call 'the Lecter move'—a very uncivilised tactic.

He bared his teeth and tried to bite Schofield's face.

Schofield recoiled instantly, stretched his face out of range, and Zamanov got what he really wanted—his sword-hand back.

He made to swing, just as with a jarring thud, their sub hit the bottom of the Channel and both men fell to the floor.

They rose together, moving like lightning.

Zamanov leapt up and swung—just as Schofield lunged forward, ducking inside Zamanov's swing arc, at the same time whipping something metallic from his borrowed utility vest and *jamming it into the Russian's mouth!*

Zamanov didn't have time for shock, because Schofield didn't hesitate.

He activated the mountaineering piton—and turned his head away, not wanting to see this.

With a powerful *snap!* the piton's pincer-like arms expanded, shooting instantaneously outward, searching for something to wedge themselves against.

What they found were Zamanov's upper and lower jaws.

Schofield never saw the actual event, but he heard it.

Heard the foul *crack* of Zamanov's lower jaw being stretched far further than it ever was designed to go.

Schofield turned back to see the Russian's jaw hanging grotesquely from his face, dislocated and broken. The upper arm of the piton, however, had done more damage: it had bruised Zamanov's brain, leaving Zamanov frozen bolt upright in mid-stance, the shock having shut down his entire body.

The Russian fell to his knees.

Schofield seized his sword, stood over the fallen bounty hunter.

Zamanov's eyes blinked reflexively. The only sign that he was still conscious.

Schofield wanted to run him through, or even cut his head off, to do to Zamanov what he had done to others . . .

But he didn't.

He *couldn't*.

And so he just let the Russian waver where he knelt, and then he watched as a moment later Zamanov fell flat on his face with a final bloody splat.

The fight over, Schofield grabbed his dislodged earpiece, put it back in his ear—

'*Schofield! Schofield! Come in!*' Knight's voice blared in his ear. '*Are you alive out there!*'

'I'm here,' Schofield said. 'I'm on the bottom. Where are you?'

'*I'm in the other sub. Put your exterior lights on so I can see where you are.*'

Schofield did so.

At which moment Knight's voice said, '*Oh, fuck me . . .*'

'What?'

'*Do you have power?*' Knight said quickly.

Schofield tried his instrument panel. No response. 'I have air, but no propulsion. Why? What is it? Can't you just come and get me?'

'*There's no way I can make it in time.*'

'In time? In time for what? What's the problem?'

'*It's a . . . uh . . . very big one . . .*'

'What?'

'*Look up, Captain.*'

Schofield peered up through the top dome of his mini-submarine.

And saw the hull of the supertanker—impossibly huge—gliding steadily down through the water above him, freefalling through the Channel waters like the moon falling out of the sky . . . its colossal mass heading straight for him.

Schofield swallowed at the awesome sight: 100,000 tons of pure supertanker was about to land right on top of his tiny submarine.

Its bulk was so vast, so immense, that it generated a deep vibrating *rrmmmmmm* as it moved down through the water.

'Now you don't see that every day,' Schofield said to himself. 'Knight!'

'*I can't make it in time!*' Knight yelled in frustration.

'Shit,' Schofield said, looking left and right.

Options! his mind screamed. He couldn't swim away from the tanker. At 1000 feet long and 200 feet wide, it was just too big. He'd never get out from under it in time.

The only other alternative was to stay here and be crushed to death.

Some choice. Certain death or certain death.

But if that was all there was, then at least he might be able to achieve something before death came.

And so on the bottom of the English Channel, Shane Schofield keyed his satellite mike.

'Book! How are you doing over there in New York?'

'*We own the* Ambrose, *Scarecrow. All enemy troops are down. We're at the control console now, and I've plugged the satellite uplink into it. I have the time as 1152. You've got eight whole minutes to disarm this thing.*'

Schofield saw the supertanker falling through the water above him—a silent freefalling giant. At its current speed, it would hit the bottom in less than a minute.

'You might have eight minutes, Book, but I don't. I have to disarm those missiles now.'

And so he pulled his CincLock-VII unit from its waterproof pouch and hit its satellite uplink.

The unit came to life:

SAT-LINK: CONNECT 'AMBROSE-049'--UPLINK CONNECTION MADE.
ACTIVATE REMOTE SYSTEM.
MISSILE LAUNCH SEQUENCE IN PROGRESS.
PRESS 'ENTER' TO INITIATE DISARM SEQUENCE.
FIRST PROTOCOL (PROXIMITY): SATISFIED.
INITIATE SECOND PROTOCOL.

The red and white circles from the New York launch ship's missile control console appeared on Schofield's screen.

And with the mighty hull of the *Talbot* thundering down through the great blue void above him, Schofield started the disarm sequence.

The supertanker was gathering speed.

Falling, falling . . .

Schofield's moves became faster.

The supertanker was eighty feet above him.

A red circle blinked, Schofield punched it.

Sixty feet . . .

Fifty feet . . .

The noise of the falling supertanker grew louder—*rrmmmmmm.*

Forty feet . . .

Thirty feet . . .

Schofield hit the last red circle. The display blinked:

SECOND PROTOCOL (RESPONSE PATTERN): SATISFIED.
THIRD PROTOCOL (CODE ENTRY): ACTIVE.
PLEASE ENTER AUTHORIZED DISARM CODE.

Twenty feet . . .

The water all around his little submarine darkened dramatically, consumed by the shadow of the supertanker.

Schofield entered the Universal Disarm Code: 131071.

Fifteen feet . . .

The screen beeped:

THIRD PROTOCOL (CODE ENTRY): SATISFIED.
AUTHORIZED DISARM CODE ENTERED.
MISSILE LAUNCH ABORTED.

And as he waited for the end—the true end; the end that he physically could not escape—Schofield closed his eyes and thought about his life and people who had been in it:

He saw Libby Gant smiling that thousand-watt smile, saw her kissing him tenderly—saw Mother Newman shooting hoops on her garage basketball court, saw her big wide grin on her big wide face—and tears welled in his eyes.

That there were still missiles to disarm somehow didn't bother Schofield. Someone else would have to solve that this time.

When it came, the end came swiftly.

Ten seconds later, the supertanker MV *Talbot* hit the bottom of the English Channel with an earth-shaking, earth-shuddering *boom*.

It landed right on top of Schofield's stricken ASDS and crushed it in a single pulverising instant.

The thing was, Schofield wasn't in the sub when it happened.

Seconds before the *Talbot* hit the bottom—when it was barely twelve feet off the seabed, its shadow looming over the mini-sub, and Schofield was lost in his thoughts—a dull metallic *clunk* was heard hitting the outside of his ASDS.

Schofield snapped to look out the windows and saw a *Maghook* attached to the metal exterior of his little submarine, its rope stretching away across the ocean floor, disappearing into the darkness to the side of the falling supertanker.

Knight's voice exploded in his ear: '*Schofield! Come on! Move! Move! Move!*'

Schofield was electrified into action.

He took a breath and hit the 'HATCH' button.

The hatch irised open and water *gushed* into the sunken mini-submarine. It took barely two seconds for it to completely fill the sub, and suddenly Schofield was outside, moving fast, grabbing the Maghook attached to the sub's flank.

No sooner had he clutched it than Knight—at the other end of the rope—hit the hook's demagnetise switch and the Maghook's rope began to reel itself in quickly.

Schofield was yanked across the ocean floor at phenomenal speed—the falling supertanker looming above him, its great endless hull hovering over his body like the underside of a planet, while a foot below him, the sandy ocean floor zoomed by at dizzying speed.

And then abruptly Schofield emerged from beneath the supertanker, his feet sliding out from under it just as the gigantic vessel

hit the bottom of the English Channel with a singular reverberating *boom* that sent sand and silt billowing out in every direction, consuming Schofield in a dense underwater cloud.

And waiting for him in that cloud—sitting atop the second ASDS, breathing from a new Pony Bottle and holding Gant's Maghook in his hands—was Aloysius Knight.

He handed Schofield the Pony Bottle and Schofield breathed its air in deeply.

Within a minute, the two of them were inside Knight's mini-sub. Knight repressurised the sub, expunged it of seawater.

And then the two warriors rose through the depths of the English Channel, a short silent journey that ended with their little yellow sub breaching the storm-riddled surface—where it was assaulted by crashing waves and the blinding glare of brilliant halogen spotlights: spotlights that belonged to the *Black Raven* hovering low over the water, waiting for them.

'Killian,' Schofield said.

'Why?'

But now Schofield understood.

'There must have been another computer in that office. In a drawer or on a side table,' he said. 'You said it yourself. Your Pilot would retrieve documents from *any computer* in the room. When you initiated the wireless hack, you picked up documents from *another* computer in that office. Killian's computer.'

'Yeah, so?'

Schofield held up the new list. 'This isn't Majestic-12's plan. *Their* plan involves starting a global Cold War on Terror. M-12 wants *terrorist* missiles striking major centres—Shahabs and Taep'o-Dongs. Which was why they left the bodies of the Global Jihad guys at the Axon plant and on the supertankers: to make the world think that terrorists stole the Kormoran ships.

'But this list shows something else entirely. It shows that Killian's company installed *different* Chameleon missiles on the Kormoran ships—not the ones Majestic-12 was expecting. Killian is planning something much worse than a global war on terrorism. He's set it up so that each of the world's major powers is *seemingly* hit by its most-hated enemy.

'The West is hit by terrorist strikes. India and Pakistan are hit by each other. China is hit by what appear to be Taiwanese missiles.'

Schofield's eyes widened at the realisation.

'It's Killian's extra step. This isn't M-12's plan at all. This is Killian's own plan. And it won't produce any kind of Cold War at all. It'll produce something much much worse. It'll produce total global warfare. It'll produce *total global anarchy*.'

Rufus said, 'You're saying that Killian has been deceiving his rich buddies on Majestic-12?'

'Exactly,' Schofield said.

But then, again, he remembered Killian's words from the Forteresse de Valois: 'Although many don't know it yet, the future of the world lies in Africa.'

'The future of the world lies in Africa,' Schofield said. 'There

were African guard squads on each of the boats. Eritreans. Nigerians. Oh, shit. *Shit!* Why didn't I see it before . . .'

Schofield brought up one of the other documents on his Palm Pilot:

Executive Itinerary

The proposed order of travel is as follows: Asmara (01/08), Luanda (01/08), Abuja (05/08), N'djamena (07/08) and Tobruk (09/08).

01/08—Asmara (embassy)
03/08—Luanda (stay with M. Loch, R's nephew)

This was the itinerary of Killian's tour of Africa the previous year.

Asmara: the capital of Eritrea.

Luanda: the capital of Angola.

Abuja: Nigeria.

N'djamena: Chad.

And Tobruk: the site of Libya's largest Air Force base.

Killian hadn't been opening factories—he had been forging alliances with five key African nations.

But why?

Schofield spoke: 'What would happen if the major powers of the world descended into anarchic warfare? What would happen elsewhere in the world?'

'You'd see some old scores settled, that's for sure,' Knight said. 'Ethnic wars would reignite. The Serbs would go after the Croats, the Russians would wipe out the Chechens, and that's not even mentioning everybody who wants to nail the Kurds. Then there'd be the opportunists, like the Japanese in WWII. Countries seizing the opportunity to grab resources or territory: Indonesia would snatch East Timor back . . .'

'What about Africa?' Schofield said. 'I'm thinking of National Security Council Planning Paper Q-309.'

'*Whoa,*' Knight said.

Schofield remembered the policy word for word. 'In the event of a conflict involving the major global powers, it is highly likely that the poverty-stricken populations of Africa, the Middle East and Central America—some of which outnumber the populations of their Western neighbours by a ratio of 100-to-1—will flood over Western borders and overwhelm Western city centres.'

Q-309 was a policy based on history—the long history of wealthy self-indulgent elites falling to impoverished but numerically overwhelming underclasses: the fall of Rome to the barbarians, the French Revolution, and now the wealthy Western world succumbing to the sheer numbers of the Third World.

Jesus, Schofield thought.

Anarchic global warfare would provide just such an opportunity for the Third World to rise up.

And if Killian had given forewarning to a few key African nations, then . . .

No, it's not possible, Schofield's mind protested. *For the simple reason that Killian's plan just didn't seem big enough.*

It didn't guarantee *total* global anarchy.

And then Schofield saw the final entry on the missile list—the entry that had not been on Book II's list at all, an entry describing a missile to be fired nearly two hours after all the others.

He brought it up on his screen:

```
Arbella Jericho-2B     W-88   04402.25   04145.10 1400
                              1650.50    2130.00
```

A *Jericho-2B clone*, Schofield thought. *The Jericho was a long-range ballistic missile belonging to Israel; and this one was armed with an American W-88 warhead.*

And the target?

Using Book II's map, Schofield plotted the GPS co-ordinates of the target.

His finger came down on the map . . . and as it did so, Schofield felt a bolt of ice-cold blood shoot through his entire body.

'God save us all,' he breathed as he saw the target.

The last clone missile—ostensibly Israeli in origin, with an American nuclear warhead on it—was aimed at a target in Saudi Arabia.

It was aimed at the holy city of Mecca.

The cockpit fell silent.

The sheer idea of it was just too great, too *shocking*, to contemplate. An Israeli missile armed with an American warhead striking the most sacred Muslim site on the planet on one of the most holy Muslim days of the year.

In the post-September 11 world, there could be no more provocative act.

It would ignite global chaos—no American citizen or embassy or business would be safe. In every city in every country, enraged Muslims would seek vengeance.

It would create a worldwide Muslim–American war. The first truly global conflict between a religion and a nation. Which would itself become the precursor for total global revolution—the rise of the Third World.

'God, October 26, it's been staring me in the face all day,' Schofield said. 'The first day of Ramadan. I hadn't even thought about the significance of the date. Killian even chose the most provocative day.'

'So where's it going to fire from?' Knight asked.

Schofield quickly plotted the GPS co-ordinates of the last Chameleon missile's launch location . . . and he frowned.

'It's not coming from a boat,' he said. 'The launch location is *on land*. Somewhere inside Yemen.'

'Yemen?' Rufus said.

'It borders Saudi Arabia to the south. Very close to Mecca,' Knight said.

'Yemen . . .' Schofield said, thinking fast. 'Yemen . . .'

At some time today, he had been told about Yemen, had heard of something *inside* Yemen—

He remembered.

'There's a Krask-8 clone in Yemen,' he said.

He'd heard it right at the start of all this, during his briefing on Krask-8. During the Cold War, the Soviets had constructed land-based ICBM facilities identical to Krask-8 in their client states—states like Syria, the Sudan, and Yemen.

Schofield's mind raced.

Krask-8 had been owned by the Atlantic Shipping Company. David Fairfax had discovered that earlier today.

And the Atlantic Shipping Company—he now knew—*was a subsidiary of Axon Corp.*

'Goddamn,' Schofield breathed. 'Rufus: set a course heading due south-east and give it everything you've got. Afterburners all the way.'

Rufus looked doubtful. 'Captain, I don't mean to be rude, but even flying at full speed, there's no way we can get from here to Yemen inside of two hours. That's a 6,000-kilometre trip, which is at least four hours travel time. Besides, on full burn, we'll chew up all our gas before we even reach the French Alps.'

'Don't worry about that,' Schofield said. 'I can arrange for fuel to be delivered in flight. And we're not going all the way to Yemen in *this* bird.'

'Whatever you say,' Rufus said. He banked the *Raven*, directed her south-east, and hit the afterburners.

While this was happening, Schofield keyed his satellite mike. 'Mr Moseley. You still with us?'

'*Sure am,*' came the reply from London.

'I need you to do an asset search on a company for me. It's called the Atlantic Shipping Company. Search for any land holdings that it has in Yemen, especially old Soviet sites.

'I also need two more things. First, I need express passage across Europe, including several mid-air refuellings. I'll send you our transponder signal.'

'*Okay. And the second thing?*'

'I need you to fuel up a couple of very special American planes for me. Planes that are currently at the Aerostadia Italia Airshow in Milan, Italy.'

The next thirty minutes went by in a blur.

Around the world, an array of forces sprang into action.

THE ARABIAN SEA
OFF THE COAST OF INDIA
26 OCTOBER, 2105 HOURS LOCAL TIME
(1205 HOURS E.S.T USA)

The supertanker MV *Whale* hovered off the coast of India on a languid sea, the giant vessel seemingly gazing at the shared coastline of India and Pakistan, its missiles ready to fire.

It never saw the Los Angeles-class attack submarine approach it from behind, two miles away.

Likewise, the African commandos in its control tower never saw the sub's torpedoes on their scopes until it was too late.

The two Mark 48 torpedoes hit the *Whale* together, blasting open its flanks with simultaneous explosions, sinking it.

THE TAIWAN STRAITS
INTERNATIONAL WATERS BETWEEN
CHINA AND TAIWAN
0110 HOURS (27 OCT) LOCAL TIME
(1210 HOURS E.S.T USA, 26 OCT)

The MV *Hopewell* suffered a similar fate.

Parked inconspicuously in a sealane in the middle of the Taiwan

Straits, not far from a long line of supertankers and cargo freighters, it was hit by a pair of wire-guided American Mark 48 torpedoes.

Some night-watchmen on other ships claimed to see the explosion on the horizon.

Radio calls to the *Hopewell* went unanswered and by the time anyone got to its last known location, there was nothing there.

The *Hopewell* was gone.

No-one ever laid eyes on the submarine that sank it. Indeed, the US Government would later deny that it had any 688Is in the area at the time.

WEST COAST, USA
NEAR SAN FRANCISCO
26 OCTOBER, 0912 HOURS LOCAL TIME
(1212 HOURS IN NEW YORK)

Inside the vast missile hold of the Kormoran-class supertanker *Jewel*, covered by twelve United States Marines and standing over the bodies of a dozen dead African commandos, David Fairfax plugged his satellite uplink into the vessel's missile control console.

The satellite signal shot up into the sky and bounced over to Schofield in the *Black Raven*, flying over France, heading for Italy.

And while Schofield disarmed the CincLock system from afar, Fairfax held the console—at times protecting the uplink with his body, shielding it from two Eritrean commandos who had survived his Marine-enhanced entry.

He was scared out of his mind, but in the midst of bullets and gunfire and exploding grenades, he held that console.

Within a couple of minutes, the last two Eritrean soldiers were dead—nailed by the Marines—and the MV *Jewel*'s launch system was neutralised by Schofield in the *Raven* and David Fairfax fell to the floor with a deep sigh of relief.

With a blast from its retros, the *Black Raven* landed vertically on the tarmac of the Aerostadia Airfield in Milan.

It was evening already in northern Italy, but the US Air Force contingent at the airshow had been working overtime for the last forty-five minutes, fuelling two very special aeroplanes at the express orders of the State Department.

The *Raven* landed a hundred yards from a spectacular-looking B-52 bomber, parked on the runway.

Two small black bullet-shaped planes hung from the big bomber's wings, looking like a pair of oversized missiles.

But these weren't missiles.

They were X-15s.

Many people believe that with a top speed of Mach 3, the SR-71 'Blackbird' is the fastest plane in the world.

This is not entirely true. The SR-71 is the fastest *operational* plane in the world.

One plane, however, has gone faster than it has—a lot faster, in fact—attaining speeds of over 7,000 km/h, more than Mach 6. That plane, though, never made operational status.

That plane was the NASA-built X-15.

Most aeroplanes use jet engines to propel them through the sky, but jet power has a limit and the SR-71 has found that limit: Mach 3.

The X-15, however, is *rocket*-powered. It has few moving parts. Instead of shooting ignited compressed air out behind it, an X-15 ignites solid hydrogen fuel. Which makes it less like a jet plane, and more like a missile. Indeed, the X-15 has been described by some observers as a missile with a pilot strapped to it.

Only five X-15s were ever built, and two of those—as Schofield knew—were making an appearance at the Aerostadia Italia Airshow, scheduled to start in a few days.

Schofield leapt out of the *Raven*, crossed the tarmac with Knight and Rufus by his side.

He gazed at the two X-15s slung from the wings of the B-52.

They weren't big planes. And not exactly pretty either. Just functional—designed to cut through the air at astronomical velocity.

Speed-slanted letters on their tailfins read: NASA. Along the side of each black plane were the words US AIR FORCE.

Two colonels met Schofield: one American, one Italian.

'Captain Schofield,' the American colonel said, 'the X-15s are ready, fully fuelled and ready to fly. But we have a problem. One of our pilots broke his ribs in a training accident yesterday. There's no way he can handle the G-forces of these things in his condition.'

'I was hoping I could use my own pilot anyway,' Schofield said. He turned to Rufus. 'Think you can handle Mach 6, Big Man?'

A grin cracked Rufus's hairy face. 'Does the Pope shit in the woods?'

The Air Force colonel guided them to the planes. 'We've also received some satellite radar scans from the National Reconnaissance Office. Could be a problem.'

He held up a portable viewscreen the size of a clipboard.

On it were two infra-red snapshots of the south-eastern Mediterranean, the Suez Canal and the Red Sea. One wider shot, the other zoomed in.

On the first image, Schofield saw a large cloud of red dots that seemed to be hovering over the Suez Canal area:

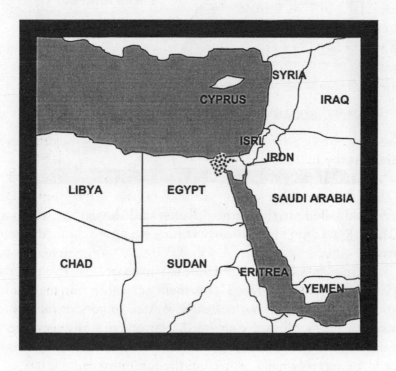

On the second satellite photo, the image became clearer.

There were about *one hundred and fifty* dots in the 'cloud'.

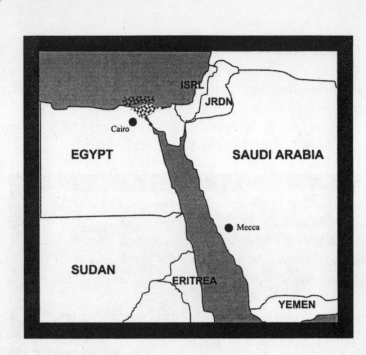

'What the hell are those dots?' Rufus said slowly.

The colonel didn't have to answer him, because Schofield already knew.

'They're planes,' he said. 'Fighter jets from at least five different African nations. The French saw them scramble but they didn't know why. Now I do. They're from five African nations that would like to see the world order changed. Nations that do *not* want to see us stop that last missile hitting Mecca. It's Killian's last safe-guard. An aerial armada protecting the final missile.'

The B-52 bomber thundered down the runway with the two X-15s hanging from its outstretched wings.

It soared into the sky, rising steadily to its release height.

Schofield sat with Rufus inside the two-man cockpit of the right-hand X-15. It was a tight fit for Rufus, but he managed. Knight was in the other plane, with a NASA pilot.

Schofield had his CincLock-VII disarm unit strapped to his utility vest, next to the array of other weapons in its pouches. The plan was a long shot—since no-one else in the world could disarm the Chameleon missile aimed at Mecca, he would have to go into the Krask-8 clone in Yemen with only Knight by his side.

They expected resistance to be waiting for them—probably in the form of an African commando unit—so Schofield had requested a Marine team be dispatched from Aden to meet them there. But whether it would arrive in time was another question.

Scott Moseley called in from London.

'*Captain, I think I've found what you're looking for,*' he said. '*The Atlantic Shipping Company owns two thousand acres of desert in Yemen, about two hundred miles south-west of Aden, right on the mouth of the Red Sea. On that land are the remains of an old Soviet submarine repair facility. Our satellite pics are from the '80s, but it looks like a big warehouse surrounded by some support buildings—*'

'That's it,' Schofield said. 'Send me the co-ordinates.'

Moseley did so.

Schofield punched them into his plane's trip computer.

Flight distance to southern Yemen: **5,602 KILOMETRES.**

Flight time in an X-15 travelling at 7,000 km/h: **48 MINUTES**.

Time till the Mecca ICBM launched: **ONE HOUR**.

It was going to be close.

'You ready, Rufus?' he said.

'Yeah, baby,' Rufus replied.

When the B-52 reached release height, its pilot came over the comms: '*X-15s, we just got word from the USS* Nimitz *in the Med. She's the only carrier within range of your attack route. She's sending every plane she has to escort you: F-14s, F/A-18s, even five Prowlers have volunteered to ride shotgun for you. You must be one important man, Captain Schofield. Prepare for flight systems check. Release in one minute—*'

As the pilot signed off, Knight's voice came over Schofield and Rufus's earpieces. His voice was low, even.

'Hey, Ruf. Good luck, buddy. Remember, you're the best. The *best*. Stay low. Stay focused. Trust your instincts.'

'Will do, Boss,' Rufus said. 'Thanks.'

'And Schofield,' Knight said.

'Yes?'

'Bring my friend back alive.'

'I'll try,' Schofield said softly.

The B-52 pilot spoke again. '*Flight systems check is complete. We are go for launch. Gentlemen, prepare for release. On my mark, in five, four . . .*'

Schofield stared forward, took a deep, deep breath.

'*Three . . .*'

Rufus gripped his control stick firmly.

'*Two . . .*'

Over in his plane, Knight looked over at Schofield and Rufus on the other wing.

'*One . . . mark.*'

CLUNK-CLUNK!

The two X-15s dropped from the wings of the B-52 bomber, swooping briefly before—

'Engaging rocket thrusters . . . *now!*' Rufus said.

He hit the thrust controls.

The X-15's tail cone ignited, hurling its afterburner flame a full hundred feet into the air behind it.

Schofield was thrown back into his seat with a force he had never even *imagined*.

His X-15 shot off into the sky—*cracking* the air with sonic booms, literally ripping the fabric of the sky—its flight signature just one continuous roar that would be heard all the way across the Mediterranean Sea.

And so the two X-15s rocketed to the south-east, toward the Suez Canal and the Red Sea and a small decrepit base in Yemen from which a Chameleon missile would soon be launched, a missile that would shatter the existing world order.

In their way: the greatest aerial armada ever assembled by man.

After only twenty minutes of flying, Rufus caught sight of it.

'Oh my *Lord* . . .' he breathed.

They hung in the orange evening sky like a swarm of insects: the squadron of African fighters.

It was an incredible sight—a veritable *wall* of moving pinpoints spread out across the Egyptian coastline, guarding the airspace over the Suez Canal.

One hundred and fifty warplanes.

All manner of fighter planes made up the aerial armada.

Old planes, new planes, red planes, blue planes—anything that could carry a missile—a motley collection of once-great fighters purchased from First World nations after their First World use-by dates had expired.

The Sukhoi Su-17—built in 1966 and long since discarded by the Russians.

The MiG-25 Foxbat—superseded in the 1980s by more modern variants, but which could still hold its own against all but the best American planes.

The French-made Mirage V/50—one of France's biggest military exports, which they sell to anyone: Libya, Zaire, Iraq.

There were even a few feisty Czech L-59 Albatrosses, a favourite among African nations.

Performance-wise, all these fighters lost ground to more modern planes like the F-22 Raptor and the F-15E. But when they came equipped with top-of-the-line air-to-air missiles—Sidewinders, Phoenixes, Russian R-60Ts and R-27s, missiles that were easily obtainable at the arms bazaars of Romania and the Ukraine—this older force of fighters could match it with the best of them. Fighters may be expensive and hard to get, but good-quality

missiles can be bought by the dozen.

And if nothing else, Schofield thought, *these guys have the advantage of sheer numbers.*

The best-equipped F-22 in the world could not hold off a force of this size forever. Ultimately, sheer force of numbers would overwhelm even the best technology.

'What do you think, Rufus?'

'This baby wasn't built to fight, Captain,' Rufus said. 'She was built for speed. So that's what we're gonna do with her—we're gonna fly her low and fast and we're gonna do what no pilot has ever done before: we're gonna *outrun* any missiles those bastards throw at us.'

'Missiles chasing us,' Schofield said. 'Nice.'

Rufus said, 'For what it's worth, Captain, we've got exactly one piddly little single-barrel gun pointing out from our nose. I think it's there for decoration.'

Just then, a new voice came over their headsets: '*American X-15s, this is Captain Harold Marshall of the USS* Nimitz. *We have you on our scopes. The Jolly Rogers are en route. They will intercept you as you reach the enemy force. Five Prowlers have been sent ahead at hundred-mile intervals to provide electronic jamming for you. It's going to get hot in there, gentlemen, but hopefully we can punch a hole big enough for you guys to shoot through.*' There was a pause. '*Oh, and Captain Schofield, I've been informed of the situation. Good luck. We're all right behind you.*'

'Thank you, Captain,' Schofield said softly. 'Okay, Rufus. Let's rock.'

Speed.

Pure, unadulterated speed. 7,000 km/h is about 2,000 metres per second. Seven times supersonic is super super fast.

The two X-15s ripped through the sky toward the swarm of enemy aircraft.

As they came within twenty miles of the African planes, a phalanx

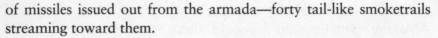

of missiles issued out from the armada—forty tail-like smoketrails streaming toward them.

But no sooner had the first missile been loosed, than its firer—a Russian MiG-25 Foxbat—erupted in a burst of orange flames.

Six other African planes exploded, hit by AIM-120 AMRAAM air-to-air missiles, while twenty of the missiles loosed by the African armada exploded harmlessly in mid-air, hitting chaff-deploying dummy missiles that had been fired from—

—an incoming force of American F-14 fighters bearing ominous skull-and-crossbones symbols on their tailfins.

The famous 'Jolly Rogers' from the *Nimitz*. About a dozen F-14 Tomcats, flanked by nimble F/A-18 Hornets.

And suddenly a gigantic aerial battle, unheard of in modern warfare, was underway.

The two X-15s banked and swerved as they shot through the ranks of the African armada, avoiding mid-air explosions, dive-bombing fighters, waves of tracer bullets and superfast missile smoketrails.

All manner of fighter planes whipped through the twilight sky—MiGs, Mirages, Tomcats and Hornets, rolling, diving, engaging, exploding.

At one point, Schofield's X-15 swooped upside-down to avoid one African fighter, only to come on a head-on collision course with another African bogey—a Mirage—but just as the two planes were about to slam nose-to-nose into each other, the African plane exploded—hit from underneath by a brilliant AMRAAM shot—and Schofield's X-15 just blasted *right through* its flaming remains, sheets of burning metal scraping against the X-15's flanks, the severed hand of the enemy plane's dead pilot smearing a streak of blood across the X-15's canopy right next to Rufus's eyes.

And yet the African missiles never hit the NASA rocket planes.

They would get close, and then the missiles would just swerve wildly around the X-15s as if the two NASA planes were protected by some kind of invisible bubble.

In actual fact, they were.

Care of the five US Navy EA-6B Prowlers—with their directional AN/ALQ-99F electronic jamming pods—that were flying parallel to the X-15s, ten miles away.

Nuggetty and tough, the Prowlers knew that they could never keep up with the superfast X-15s, so they had cleverly placed themselves parallel to Schofield's flight path but spaced out, each Prowler protecting the rocket planes with its jamming signal before passing the X-15s onto the next Prowler, like relay runners passing a baton.

'*American X-15s, this is Prowler Leader,*' a voice said in Schofield's headset. '*We can cover you up to the Canal, but we just ain't fast enough to keep up. You'll be on your own from there.*'

'You've done more than enough already,' Schofield said.

'Christ! Look out!' Rufus yelled.

For right then, in the face of the Prowlers' long-range electronic protection, the African planes embarked on a new strategy.

They started doing kamikaze dives at the X-15s.

Suicide runs.

Electronic countermeasures may be able to disrupt the homing systems of a missile, but no matter how good they are, they cannot stop a man wilfully flying his plane into another.

A half-dozen fighter jets rained down on the two X-15s, screaming through the sky, loosing withering waves of tracer bullets as they did so.

The two X-15s split up.

Rufus rolled his plane right and down, while the other X-15 banked left, avoiding its dive-bomber by a bare foot, but not before a lone tracer bullet from one of the kamikazes entered its canopy from the side and exited out the other side: a flight path that also entailed a short trip through the head of Knight's pilot.

Blood and brains splattered the interior of the X-15.

The plane peeled away into the sky, out of control, heading eastward, away from the battle.

Knight scrambled into the front seat—where he quickly unbuckled the dead pilot and hurled his body into the back. Then Knight himself took the controls, trying desperately to bring the plane up before she ploughed into the Mediterranean Sea.

The sea rushed up before him—faster, faster, faster . . .

Boom.

For their part, Schofield and Rufus had swung their plane low over the sea—so low in fact that they were now rushing barely twenty feet above the waves, kicking up a continuous whitewater geyser

behind them at the same time as criss-crossing missiles blasted into the water all around them.

'I see the Canal!' Rufus yelled above the din.

It lay about twenty miles ahead of them, the mouth of the Suez Canal—a modern-day marvel of engineering; two colossal concrete pillars flanking the entry to the mighty sealane that gave access to the Red Sea.

And above it, more planes from the African armada.

'Rufus! Bank left!' Schofield yelled, peering up through their canopy.

Rufus did so—rolling them on their side just as two Czech L-59s went screaming past them on either side and buried themselves in the sea.

And then all of a sudden they hit the confines of the Canal—

—and lost the electronic protection of the Prowlers.

Schofield's X-15 blasted down the length of the Suez Canal, flying low, banking around anchored ships, turning the mighty concrete-walled canal into little more than an obstacle-filled trench—but effectively flying *under* the main body of the aerial armada.

They had run the blockade.

But then into the Canal behind them shot two American-made Phoenix missiles that had somehow found their way onto the wing-mounts of an African fighter jet.

The X-15 rushed down the water-filled trench.

The two Phoenix missiles gained on it.

Two suicide fighters rained down—coming at the X-15 from either side in a scissor formation—but Rufus rolled the rocket plane and the two fighters missed it by inches—blasting instead into the sandy banks of the Canal, exploding in twin geysers of sand and fire.

And then the two Phoenix missiles came *alongside* the X-15's tail and Schofield saw an amazing thing: he could *read* the stencilled lettering on their sides: 'XAIM-54A—HUGHES MISSILE SYSTEMS.'

'Rufus . . . !' he yelled.

'I know!' Rufus called back.

'Please do something!'

'Was just about to!'

And suddenly Rufus swung them to the right, up over the bank of the Canal, swinging them around in a wide wide circle, heading *back* towards the Mediterranean.

The two missiles followed, swooping around in identical semi-circles, unaffected by the incredible G-forces.

Since the bulk of the African armada had been protecting the Egyptian coastline, only about six African fighter planes remained back here.

These planes saw the X-15 swoop around in its wide circle, coming back toward them, and thought that this was their lucky day.

Wrong.

The X-15—circling, circling—shot through their midst like a bullet through a stand of trees, blasting between two African MiGs with barely 10 feet to spare on either side . . .

. . . but leaving the MiGs in the path of the two Phoenix missiles.

Boom-boom!

The MiGs exploded and the X-15 continued its wide circle until it was back in the trench of the Canal, back on its south-easterly course.

However, its wide circle—easily two hundred kilometres wide—had allowed one of the African planes to loose a last-ditch missile, its finest: a single stolen American AIM-120 AMRAAM, the best air-to-air missile in the world.

The AMRAAM shot through the air behind the speeding X-15, closing in on it like a hungry hawk.

'I can't shake it!' Rufus yelled.

'How long will it stay on our tail?' Schofield asked. 'Doesn't it have a cut-out switch if the chase goes too long?'

'No! That's the thing about AMRAAMs! They just chase you all day and all night! Wear you down and then kill you.'

'Well, no AMRAAM has ever chased one of these planes before! Keep going! Full throttle! Maybe we can outrun it—'

A voice in his earpiece cut him off.

It was Scott Moseley, and his voice sounded dead, shocked.

'*Uh, Captain Schofield. I have some really bad news.*'

'What?'

'*Our early warning satellites just picked up an ICBM launch signature from south-central Yemen. Flight characteristics indicate that it is a Jericho-2B intercontinental ballistic missile, heading north toward Mecca. Captain, Killian knows you're coming. He's fired the missile early.*'

'Oh, no way!' Schofield yelled, staring off into the sky. 'You have got to be kidding. That is not fair. That is not fucking fair!'

He looked at the weapons strapped to his chest, guns that he had planned to use to storm the missile base in Yemen. All useless now.

He held up the CincLock-VII disarm unit and just shook his head . . .

Then he froze.

Staring at the CincLock unit.

'Mr Moseley. Do you have telemetry on that missile signal?'

'*Sure.*'

'Send it through.'

'*You got it.*'

A moment later, Schofield's trip computer beeped and a map similar to the one he had seen earlier appeared on its screen. An arrow-like icon representing the Chameleon missile approaching Mecca tracked northwards up the screen.

Schofield punched in his own transponder signal into the computer and a second icon appeared on the screen, tracking southward:

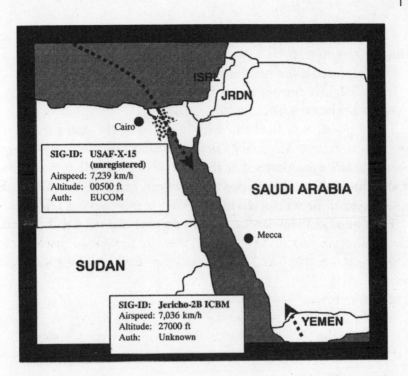

Schofield saw the flight data on the screen: signal IDs, airspeeds, altitudes.

He almost didn't need to do the math.

The picture said it all.

Two aircraft were converging on Mecca: his X-15 and the Chameleon missile, labelled by the satellite's automated recognition system as a Jericho-2B intercontinental ballistic missile.

Both aircraft were travelling at practically the same speed and were roughly equidistant from Mecca.

'Rufus,' Schofield said flatly.

'Yeah?'

'We're not going to Yemen anymore.'

'I kinda figured that,' Rufus said, defeat in his voice. 'What are we going to do now?'

But Schofield was hitting buttons on his computer, doing rapid calculations. It would be absolutely incredible if this worked.

He and Rufus were still about 1,000 kilometres from Mecca. Time to target: **8:30**.

He did the calculations for the Chameleon missile.

It was slightly further away. Its countdown read:

TIME TO TARGET: 9:01 . . . 9:00 . . . 8:59 . . .

That's good, Schofield thought. *We'll need the extra thirty seconds to overshoot Mecca and swing around . . .*

Schofield's eyes gleamed at the very idea of it. He looked down at the CincLock unit strapped to his chest, gripped it in his hands.

'Sixty feet,' he whispered aloud.

Then he said, 'Hey Rufus. Have you ever chased a missile?'

Schofield's X-15 shot through the darkening sky at bullet speed—still pursued by the AMRAAM missile.

'You want me to fly *alongside* it?' Rufus said, dumbstruck.

'That's exactly what I want you to do. We can still disarm that ICBM, we just have to be within sixty feet of it,' Schofield said.

'Yeah, but *in flight*? Nobody can keep a plane side-by-side with a missile at Mach 6.'

'I think you can,' Schofield said.

From where he was sitting, Schofield didn't see the grin cross Rufus's broad bearded face.

'What do you need me to do?' the big pilot said.

Schofield said, 'ICBMs fly high and then come down vertically on their targets. This Chameleon is currently at 27,000 feet. She should stay at that altitude until she's practically over Mecca, and then she'll start her dive. At Mach 6, it'll take her about five seconds to make that vertical run. But I need at least twenty-five seconds to disarm her. Which means we have to get alongside her while she's flying level at 27,000 feet. Once she goes vertical, it's all over. We're screwed. Think you can bring us around so that we're travelling beside her?'

'You know, Captain,' Rufus said softly, 'you're a lot like Aloysius. When you talk to me, you make me feel like I could do anything. Consider it *done*.'

The X-15 blasted into the sky, chased by the AMRAAM, shooting down the length of the Red Sea while at the same time rising—rising, rising—to an altitude of 27,000 feet.

'We just passed Mecca!' Rufus yelled. 'I'm going to start our turn now. Keep an eye out, we should be able to see that Chameleon any minute now . . .'

Rufus banked the speeding rocket plane, bringing it round in a *wiiiide* 180-degree arc that would hopefully end with the X-15 coming alongside the nuclear missile, joining it on its flight path toward Mecca.

The X-15 rolled onto its side, shot through the air, banking left in its gigantic turn.

The sudden course-change allowed the AMRAAM missile behind it—ever-closing, ever-ravenous—to reel them in even more. It was only a hundred yards behind the X-15 now, and still closing.

TIME TO TARGET: 1:20 . . . 1:19 . . . 1:18 . . .

'There it is!' Rufus yelled. 'Dead ahead!'

Schofield strained against the G-forces to peer out over Rufus's shoulder, out at the twilight Arabian sky.

And he saw it.

The mere sight of the intercontinental ballistic missile took his breath away.

It was incredible.

The Jericho-2B clone ICBM looked like a spaceship from a science fiction movie—something that was far too big, far too sleek, and moving far too fast to exist on Earth.

The 70-foot-long cylinder shot like a spear through the sky, a white-hot tailflame blazing from its base like a magnesium flare, leaving an impossibly long smoketrail in its wake. The smoketrail extended, snakelike, a God-sized python, *over* the distant horizon, streaking away toward the missile's source, Yemen.

And the sound it made.

A single, continuous *BOOOOOOOOOOOOOOM!*

If Schofield's X-15 was ripping the fabric of the sky, then this baby was shredding it to pieces.

The banking X-15 roared round in a giant semi-circle, careering

in toward the moving ICBM, while itself trailed by the dogged AMRAAM.

TIME TO TARGET: 1:00 . . . 0:59 . . . 0:58 . . .

One minute.

And then, like the arms of a flattened Y converging to meet at the stem, the X-15 rocket plane and the Chameleon missile came alongside each other.

But they weren't level yet.

The X-15 was just behind and to the left of the ICBM—parallelling the horizontal column of smoke shooting out of the ICBM's base.

TIME TO TARGET: 0:50 . . . 0:49 . . . 0:48 . . .

But the rocket plane was moving slightly faster than the missile, so it was gradually hauling the ICBM in.

Noise was everywhere. The roar of supersonic speed.

BOOOOOOOOOOOOOOOOOOOOOOOOM!

TIME TO TARGET: 0:40 . . . 0:39 . . . 0:38 . . .

'Get me closer, Rufus!' Schofield called.

Rufus did so—and the nose-cone of the X-15 came alongside the tail of the roaring ICBM.

The CincLock VII unit didn't respond. They still weren't close enough to the missile's CPU.

The X-15 crept forward, edging up the length of the Chameleon missile.

'Closer!'

TIME TO TARGET: 0:33 . . . 0:32 . . . 0:31 . . .

Out through the cockpit canopy, Schofield saw the lights of a city down in the evening darkness below.

The holy city of Mecca.

TIME TO TARGET: 0:28 . . . 0:27 . . . 0:26 . . .

And the X-15 came level with the mid-point of the missile and Schofield's disarm unit beeped:

FIRST PROTOCOL (PROXIMITY): SATISFIED.
INITIATE SECOND PROTOCOL.

'I'm gonna get you,' Schofield said to the ICBM.

The reflex response pattern on his unit began its sequence, and Schofield began hitting its touchscreen.

The two rocket-propelled aircraft carved a sonic tear through the sky, travelling side-by-side at astronomical speed.

And then the AMRAAM behind the X-15 made its move.

Rufus saw it on his scopes. 'Come *on*, Captain . . . !'

'I just . . . have . . . to do . . . this first . . .' Schofield grimaced, concentrating on the reflex-response test.

TIME TO TARGET: 0:19 . . . 0:18 . . . 0:17 . . .

The AMRAAM powered forward, closing in on the tailflame of the X-15.

'It's approaching lethal range!' Rufus yelled. Lethal range for an AMRAAM was twenty yards. It didn't have to actually hit you, only explode close to you. 'You've got maybe five seconds!'

'We don't have five seconds!' Schofield shouted, not taking his eyes off the screen, his fingers moving quickly over it.

TIME TO TARGET: 0:16 . . . 0:15 . . . 0:14 . . .

'I can't take evasive action!' Rufus yelled desperately. 'I'll move us out of proximity! Jesus Christ! We can't come this far to lose now! Two seconds!'

Schofield kept hitting the touchscreen.

TIME TO TARGET: 0:13 . . . 0:12 . . .

'One second!'

And the AMRAAM entered lethal range—20 yards from the X-15's tailpipe.

'No!' Rufus yelled. 'Too late—!'

'*Not if I can help it,*' a voice said suddenly in their earpieces.

Then, in a supersonic blur, something black and fast shot side-ways *across the wake of the X-15*—cutting in between the AMRAAM and Schofield's X-15, so that the AMRAAM hit it and not Schofield's plane.

An explosion rocked the sky and Rufus whirled around in his seat to see the front half of *another* X-15 rocket plane go tumbling through the air, its rear-end vaporised, destroyed by the AMRAAM.

Knight's X-15.

He must have survived the death of his pilot and then stayed on their trail, catching up with them while they'd made their two time-consuming circling manoeuvres. And now he had flown himself into the path of the AMRAAM missile that had been about to take them out!

The shattered front half of Knight's X-15 fell through the sky, nose-first, before abruptly, its canopy jettisoned and a flight seat blasted out from the falling wreckage, a parachute blossoming above it a moment later.

TIME TO TARGET: 0:11 . . . 0:10 . . .

Schofield hardly even noticed the explosion. He was consumed with the reflex pattern on his touchscreen: white, red, white, white, red . . .

TIME TO TARGET: 0:09 . . .

'Whoa, shit! It's going vertical!' Rufus yelled.

With a sickening roll, the Chameleon missile abruptly changed course, banking *downward*, pointing its nose directly down at Mother Earth.

Rufus manoeuvred his control stick and the X-15 copied the move—and went vertical with the ICBM—and suddenly the two rocketcraft were travelling supersonically, side-by-side, heading *straight down!*

'Aaaaaaaaahhh!' Rufus yelled.

Schofield's eyes remained fixed to the touchscreen, focused, his fingers moving quickly.

TIME TO TARGET: 0:08 . . .

The X-15 and the ICBM raced toward the Earth like two vertical bullets.

TIME TO TARGET: 0:07 . . .

The lights of Mecca rushed up toward Rufus's eyes.

TIME TO TARGET: 0:06 . . .

Schofield's fingers danced.

And the CincLock disarm unit beeped.

SECOND PROTOCOL (RESPONSE PATTERN): SATISFIED.
THIRD PROTOCOL (CODE ENTRY): ACTIVE.
PLEASE ENTER AUTHORIZED DISARM CODE.

TIME TO TARGET: 0:05 . . .

Schofield punched in the Universal Disarm Code and the screen beeped again:

THIRD PROTOCOL (CODE ENTRY): SATISFIED.
AUTHORIZED DISARM CODE ENTERED.

At which point the crucial line appeared:

MISSILE FLIGHT ABORTED.

What happened next happened in a blur.

High above the minarets of Mecca, the supersonically-travelling Chameleon missile self-destructed in a spectacular explosion. It looked like a gigantic firecracker—a spectacular starburst of sparks spraying out in every direction.

It was moving so amazingly fast, however, that its blasted-apart pieces were just stripped away by the onslaught of uprushing wind. The charred remains of the cloned Jericho-2B would later be found over an area 100 miles in diameter.

Schofield's X-15, on the other hand, suffered a far different fate.

The shock wave from the Chameleon's blast sent it spiralling away from the explosion, completely out of control, rocketing toward the Earth.

Rufus fought heroically with his stick and by doing so managed one single thing: to avoid crashing into any of the inhabited parts of Mecca.

But that was all he achieved. For a bare second later, the X-15 slammed into the desert like a meteor from outer space, smashing vertically into the sandy landscape in a thumping, slamming, earth-shuddering impact that could be heard more than fifty miles away.

And for a moment its fiery explosion lit up the dark desert sky as if it were midday.

The X-15 hit the desert floor doing Mach 3.

It hit the ground hard and in a single flashing, blinding instant, the rocket plane transformed into a ball of fire.

Nothing could have survived the crash.

A split second before the impact, however, two ejection seats could be seen catapulting clear of the crashing plane's cockpit, shooting diagonally out into the sky—seats that contained Schofield and Rufus.

The two flight seats floated back down to earth on their parachutes, landing a mile away from the flaming crater that marked the final resting place of the X-15.

The two seats hit the dusty ground, rocked onto their sides.

There was no movement in them.

For there, lying slumped against their seatbacks, sat Shane Schofield and Rufus, both unconscious, both knocked out by the colossal G-forces of their supersonic ejection.

After a time, Schofield awoke—to the sound of voices.

His vision was blurry, blood seeped down his face, and his head throbbed with a terrible ache. Bruises were forming around his eyes—the natural by-product of ejecting.

He saw shadows surrounding his flight seat. Some men were trying to unbuckle his seatbelts.

He heard their voices again.

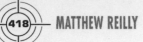

'Crazy sons of bitches, ejecting at that speed.'

'Come on, man, hurry up, before the fucking boy scouts from the Marines arrive.'

At the edge of his consciousness, Schofield noted that they were speaking English.

With American accents.

He sighed with relief. It was over.

Then, with the whistling cut of a knife, his seatbelt came free and Schofield tumbled out of his seat onto the sand.

A man appeared at the rim of his vision. A Westerner, wearing military gear. Through the haze of his mind, Schofield recognised the man's uniform: the customised battle outfit of the US Special Forces' Delta Detachment.

'Captain Schofield . . .' the man said gently, his voice blurry to Schofield's slow mind. 'Captain Schofield. It's okay. You're safe now. We're from Delta. We're on your side. We've also picked up your friend, Captain Knight, a few miles from here.'

'Who—' Schofield stammered. 'Who are you?'

The Delta man smiled, but it wasn't a friendly smile. 'My name is Wade Brandeis. From Delta. We've come from Aden. Don't worry, Captain Schofield. You're perfectly safe with me.'

SEVENTH ATTACK

FRANCE
27 OCTOBER 0700 HOURS (FRANCE)
E.S.T. (NEW YORK, USA) 0100 HOURS

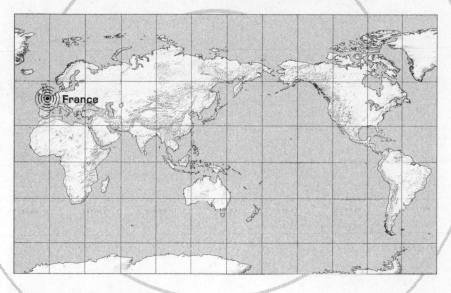

Beware the fury of a patient man.

—John Dryden

Schofield dreamed.

Dreamed of being lifted out of his crashed flight seat . . . and flex-cuffed . . . then being loaded into the back of a private Lear jet . . . and the jet taking off . . .

Voices in the haze.

Brandeis saying, 'I heard it first from a couple of guys in the 'Stan. They said he turned up at a cave-hunting site and bolted inside. Said it had something to do with a bounty hunt.

'Then I get a call a few hours ago from a guy I know in ISS—he's one of those background guys, real old-school CIA, knows everything about everyone, so he's fucking *untouchable*. He's also ex-ICG. Good man. Ugly fuck, though. Looks like a goddamned rat. Name's Noonan, Cal Noonan, but everyone I know just calls him the Rat.

'As always, the Rat knows everything. For instance, he knows I'm working out of Aden. He confirms that there's a price on Schofield's head: eighteen million bucks. He also says that Schofield is on his way to Yemen. If I'm interested, he says, he can arrange leave for me and a few trusted men.

'He also says, wait for it, that *Aloysius Knight* is with Schofield, and that there's a price on Knight's head, too: two million dollars. Hell, I'd bring Knight in for fucking free. But if someone wants to give me two million bucks to do it, that's even better.'

★ ★ ★

The plane flew on. Schofield slept.

He woke briefly, uncomfortable. He was still wearing his utility flak vest, but all the weapons on it had been removed. The only thing they hadn't taken was the tightly-rolled Soviet chemical body bag. Not much of a weapon.

He shifted—and caught a glimpse of Knight and Rufus, also flex-cuffed, sitting a few rows back, covered by armed Delta operators. Rufus was asleep, but Knight was wide awake. He seemed to see Schofield rouse, but Schofield couldn't keep his eyes open.

He dropped back to sleep.

Another waking moment.

The sky outside the window next to him had changed from black to pale blue.

Dawn.

And then the voices came again.

'So where are we taking them?'

'Some castle,' Brandeis said. 'Some castle in France.'

**FORTERESSE DE VALOIS
BRITTANY, FRANCE
27 OCTOBER, 0700 HOURS**

It was raining heavily when Schofield's jet landed at Jonathan Killian's private airstrip on the coast of Brittany.

A quick transfer to a covered truck and soon—under the watchful eye of Brandeis and his five-man Delta team—Schofield, Knight and Rufus were taken down a steep cliff-side road, heading toward the familiar castle built on its rocky mount just off the coastal cliffs.

The mighty Forteresse de Valois.

The lone truck crossed the massive drawbridge connecting the castle to the mainland, shrouded by rain and lightning.

During the short trip, Knight told Schofield about his history with Wade Brandeis: about that night in Sudan and Brandeis's treacherous ICG links.

'Believe me, I know about the ICG,' Schofield said.

'I've been meaning to catch up with Brandeis for a long time,' Knight said.

As he spoke, Schofield saw the two tattoos on Knight's arm again: 'SLEEP WITH ONE EYE OPEN' and 'BRANDEIS' and suddenly realised that they were in truth a single tattoo: 'SLEEP WITH ONE EYE OPEN BRANDEIS'.

'The thing is,' Knight said, 'Brandeis isn't a bounty hunter, and it shows.'

'How?'

'He's just broken the first rule of bounty hunting.'

'Which is?'

'If you have a choice between bringing someone in dead or alive,' Knight said, 'dead is better.'

At that moment, the truck entered the gravel courtyard inside the castle and crunched to a halt.

Schofield, Knight and Rufus were all shoved out of it, covered by Brandeis and his Delta men.

Monsieur Delacroix was waiting for them.

The Swiss banker stood at the entrance to the classic-car garage, prim and proper as ever.

He was flanked by Cedric Wexley and ten mercenaries from Executive Solutions, Jonathan Killian's private security force.

'Major Brandeis,' Delacroix said. 'Welcome to the Forteresse de Valois. We've been expecting you. Come this way, please.'

Delacroix guided them into the garage and then down some stone stairs to the ante-room that Schofield had seen before—but instead of turning *left* toward the long forbidding tunnel that took you to the verification office, he turned *right*, through a small stone doorway that opened onto a tight medieval stairwell that spiralled downwards.

Lit by flaming torches, the stairwell went down and down, round and round, descending deep into the bowels of the castle.

It ended at a thick steel door set into a solid stone frame.

Delacroix hit a switch and with an ominous rumble the steel door rose into the ceiling. Then the dapper Swiss banker stood aside, allowing Brandeis and his prisoners to enter first.

They passed through the doorway—

—and emerged inside a wide circular pit, a dungeon in which sloshing seawater wended its way between an irregular series of elevated stone platforms. In the laneways of water, Schofield saw two sharks, prowling. And on the nearest elevated stage he saw . . .

. . . a 12-foot-tall guillotine.

He froze, caught his breath.

This was the dungeon that Knight had told him about before. The terrible dungeon in which Libby Gant had met her end.

This was the Shark Pit.

Once they had all stepped out into the Shark Pit, the steel door behind them slid back into place, sealing them all inside.

Monsieur Delacroix, wisely, had remained outside.

Someone else, however, was waiting for them inside the Pit.

A man with carrot-red hair and a sinister rat-like face.

'Hey, Noonan,' Brandeis said, stepping forward, taking the man's hand.

Schofield remembered Knight's horrifying description of Gant's death, and how a man with red hair and a rat face had pulled the lever that had ended her life.

Schofield glared at the murderer.

For his part, Rat Face turned and glared insolently back at him.

'So this is the Scarecrow,' Rat Face said. 'Resilient little fucker, aren't you. I went to a lot of trouble to arrange that little mission in Siberia yesterday. Set the scene. Sent ExSol to wait for you. Then made sure that it was McCabe and Farrell and you who were sent into the trap. Then I cut your comms from Alaska. McCabe and Farrell weren't good enough. But not you. You survived.

'But not now. Now, there's no escape. In fact, you're gonna buy it the same way your girlfriend did.' Rat Face turned to the Delta men holding Schofield. 'Put him in the guillotine.'

Schofield was shoved over to the guillotine by two of Brandeis's D-boys. His head was thrust into the stocks, while his hands stayed out, flex-cuffed behind his back.

'No!' a voice called from across the Pit.

Everyone turned.

Jonathan Killian appeared on a balcony overlooking the Pit,

flanked by Cedric Wexley and the ten men from Executive Solutions, plus the just-arrived Monsieur Delacroix.

'Put him in face up,' Killian said. 'I want Captain Schofield to see the blade coming.'

The Delta men did as they were told, and rolled Schofield over so that his face was pointed upwards. The 12-foot guide rails of the wooden guillotine stretched away from him to the stone ceiling. At their peak he saw the glistening blade, suspended high above him.

'Captain,' Killian said. 'Through courage and audacity, you have saved the existing world order. Spared the lives of millions of people who will never even know your name. You are, in the true sense of the word, a hero. But your victory is at best temporary. Because I will continue to live—continue to rule—and ultimately my time will come. You, on the other hand, are about to discover what really happens to heroes. Mr Noonan. Drop the blade, and then shoot Captain Schofield's protectors in the head—'

'Killian!' Schofield called.

Everyone froze.

Schofield's voice was even, cold. 'I'll be coming for you.'

Killian smiled. 'Not in this life, Captain. Drop the blade.'

Rat Face strode to the side of the guillotine, and looking down at Schofield, gripped the lever.

At the same time, Wade Brandeis raised his Colt .45 to Knight's head.

'I'll see you in hell, Scarecrow,' Rat Face said.

Then he yanked the lever, releasing the blade.

The guillotine's blade thundered down its guide rails.

And Schofield could do nothing but watch it rush down toward his face.

He shut his eyes and waited for the end.

Chunk!

But the end didn't come.

Schofield felt nothing.

He opened his eyes—

—to see that the guillotine's diagonal blade had been stopped a foot above his neck, its deadly downward rush halted by a five-bladed shuriken throwing knife that had lodged itself with a loud *chunk* in the vertical wooden guide rail of the guillotine.

So recently had it been thrown, the shuriken was still quivering.

Aloysius Knight was also saved as—a split-second after the shuriken had hit the guillotine—a bullet slammed into Wade Brandeis's gun-hand, sending his pistol splashing into the water, blood gushing from his hand.

Schofield turned . . . to see an unexpected but very welcome apparition emerge from the waters of the Shark Pit.

It was a fearsome image—a warrior in grey battle uniform, scuba gear and bearing shuriken throwing knives and guns. Lots and lots of guns.

If Death exists, he's afraid of one person.

Mother.

Mother exploded from the water, now with an MP-7 in each hand, firing them hard. Two of the five Delta men dropped immediately, hit in their chests.

Then things started happening everywhere.

For Knight and Rufus, Mother's entry had been distraction enough to allow them to king-hit their captors and, together, leap over their bound hands jump-rope style—bringing their wrists in front of their bodies—and hold up their plastic flex-cuffs.

Mother didn't need instructions.

Two shots—and the flex-cuffs were history. Knight and Rufus were free.

Over on the viewing balcony, Cedric Wexley quickly threw his ten-man team into action—he sent four over the balcony into the Pit, while he ordered the other six out through the back door of the balcony, into a corridor.

Then he himself whipped up his M-16 and hustled Jonathan Killian out of the dungeon.

Down in the Pit, Knight snatched up a Colt Commando rifle from one of the fallen D-boys and started firing at the four ExSol men leaping down into the Pit from the balcony.

Beside him, Rufus—still unarmed—whirled and killed a third Delta man with a driving flat-palmed blow to the nose.

'Rufus!' Knight yelled. 'Get Schofield out of those stocks!'

Rufus scrambled for the guillotine.

Over by the guillotine, the rat-faced man named Noonan was ducking ricochets, a short distance from the still-pinned Schofield.

When he spotted a brief gap in the gunfire, he reached up for the shuriken throwing knife holding the guillotine blade suspended above Schofield's head. If he could remove it, the blade would fall, decapitating Schofield.

Noonan's hand gripped the shuriken knife—

—just as a diving backhand punch from Rufus sent him flying.

Noonan landed on his stomach near the edge of the stone platform, and found himself eye-to-eye with one of the tiger sharks in the water. He recoiled instantly, clambered to his feet.

Rufus, however, landed next to Schofield, and now covered by the rifle-firing Knight, yanked up the guillotine's stocks and pulled Schofield free.

One shot from Knight severed Schofield's flex-cuffs, but then suddenly, inexplicably, Rufus hurled Schofield around and covered him with his own body.

An instant later, the big man was assailed in the back by several rapid-fire bullets.

'Ah!' he roared, his body jolting with three hits.

The volley had come from Wade Brandeis—standing nearby on one of the stone islands, nursing his bloodied right hand while firing a Colt Commando wildly with his unnatural left.

'No!' Aloysius Knight yelled.

He turned his own gun on Brandeis—but the rifle went dry, so instead he just hurled himself across the slick platform, sliding on his chest, and slammed into Brandeis's legs, tackling the Delta man and sending both of them tumbling into the shark-infested pool.

Free from the guillotine, Schofield turned to see Noonan staggering toward the steel door that led out from the Shark Pit.

As he ran, Noonan pulled a remote from his jacket and hit a button.

The thick steel door rose, opening. Noonan bolted for it.

'Damn it, shit!' Schofield yelled, taking off after him. 'Mother!'

Mother was on a nearby stage, taking cover behind one of the random stone objects in the Pit and firing at the two remaining D-boys with a pistol when she heard Schofield's shout.

She turned fast and loosed a volley at the fleeing Noonan. She didn't hit him, but her burst did cut him off from the exit, forcing him to stop and take cover behind a stone block.

She didn't get to see if this actually helped Schofield, though,

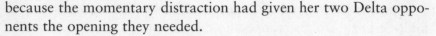

because the momentary distraction had given her two Delta opponents the opening they needed.

One of them nailed her in the chest with a dozen rapid-fire shots from his Colt. Of course, her borrowed flak vest was bulletproof, so the shots just jolted her backwards, shot after shot after shot.

Under the weight of heavy fire, Mother staggered backwards, and just as the D-boy firing at her raised his aim for the kill-shot to her head—

—she dropped abruptly—

—into the water, and the kill-shot went high.

Mother sank underwater.

Brief merciful silence.

Then she came up—knowing what would be waiting—breaching the surface with her pistol extended, and nailed the two D-boys just as they themselves fired at her.

The two Delta men dropped, their faces bloody messes.

Mother sighed with relief.

It was then that she felt an odd swell in the water around her.

She turned . . .

. . . and saw a large bow-wave *surging* through the water toward her, the high dorsal fin of a tiger shark scything through the waves, charging at her.

'Oh, no way!' she yelled. 'No fucking way! I've survived far too much today to end up as fish food!'

She fired her pistol at the inrushing shark—*blam!-blam!-blam!-blam!-blam!-blam!*

The shark didn't slow down.

Mother's shots hit it, but the big shark just powered through the waves.

Blam!-blam!-blam!

The shark *still* didn't slow down.

It rose out of the frothing water, jaws wide—

—just as Mother, still firing, raised one of her legs instinctively and—

—*chomp!*

The shark clamped down on her left leg.

And Mother didn't react at all.

Her left leg was her artificial leg, made of titanium. A replacement for an injury from a previous adventure.

Two of the shark's teeth broke. Shattered into fragments.

'Try eating this, motherfucker,' Mother said, levelling her pistol at the tiger shark's brain.

Blam.

The shark bucked violently in the water, but when it came down, it was stilled, dead, its jaws clamped around Mother's left leg, as if even in its last moment of life, it had been unwilling to let go of its prize.

For her part, Mother just kicked the 10-foot shark away from her and leapt out of the pool to get back into the action.

While Mother had been firing at the shark, on the other side of the Pit, Schofield had chased after Noonan and caught him—tackling him—just as he had arrived at the open doorway to the dungeon.

The ISS man tried to kick Schofield clear, but Schofield just flung Noonan back into the dungeon and started hitting him—with venom.

One punch, and Noonan staggered backwards.

'I know you pulled the lever . . .' Schofield said grimly.

Second punch, and Noonan's nose broke, spraying blood.

'I know she died in pain . . .'

The third punch, and Noonan's jaw broke. He slipped, lost his footing.

'You killed a beautiful thing . . .'

Schofield grabbed Noonan two-handed and hurled him head-first *into* the guillotine. Noonan's head slid into the stocks underneath the razor-sharp blade, which itself was still held up by the shuriken.

'So now you're gonna die in pain . . .' Schofield said.

And with that Schofield yanked the shuriken out of the guillotine's wooden guide rails—causing the blade to drop the final two feet.

'No!' Noonan screamed. 'Noooo—!'

Chunk.

Noonan's rat-like head hit the stone floor like a bouncing ball, his eyelids blinking rapidly in those first moments after decapitation before they settled into a blank stare, forever frozen in a final look of absolute utter horror.

Ten yards away from the guillotine, floating in the shark-infested water, Aloysius Knight was engaged in the fight of his life with Wade Brandeis.

With their equal Delta training, they were perfectly matched, and as such, they traded punches and tactics, splashing and ducking under the surface in a fight that could only be to the death.

Then suddenly both men rose above the surface, nose-to-nose. Only now Brandeis had a small gun pressed up against Knight's chin. He had him.

'I always had the wood on you, Knight!'

Knight spoke through clenched teeth:

'You know, Brandeis, ever since that night in Sudan, I've thought of a thousand ways to kill you. But until right now, I'd never thought of this one.'

'Huh?' Brandeis grunted.

And with that, Knight yanked Brandeis around in the water and brought him right into the path of the inrushing second tiger shark.

The big 10-foot shark *rammed* into Brandeis at full speed, taking him in its mouth, its gnashing chomping teeth inches away from Knight's own body. But the shark only had eyes for Brandeis, drawn by his bleeding right hand.

'Sleep with one eye open, you fuck,' Knight said.

Caught in the grip of the massive shark, Brandeis could only stare back at him—and scream as he was eaten alive.

Knight clambered out of the water, out of the bloody froth that had once been Wade Brandeis, and headed back to join Schofield.

Knight rejoined Schofield behind the guillotine—at the spot where Schofield had just pulled the wounded Rufus out of the line of fire of the four ExSol men now traversing across the Pit's stone islands.

Schofield had also collected some weapons—two Colt Commando assault rifles, one MP-7, one of Knight's H&K 9mm pistols, plus Knight's own fully-loaded utility vest, taken from one of the dead Delta men.

Mother joined them.

'Hey, Mother,' Knight said. 'Last time I saw you, you were inside that maintenance shack in the *Talbot*, just before it was RPG'd by the Demon's boys. What'd you do, hide in the floor?'

'Screw the floor,' Mother said. 'That damn shack was hanging from the roof of the hold. It had a hatch in the ceiling. That was where I went. But then, of course, the whole fucking boat sank . . .'

Knight said, 'So how did you know we were here?'

Mother pulled out a Palm Pilot from a waterproof pouch in her vest. 'You've got a lot of nice toys, Mr Knight. And *you*,' Mother turned to Schofield, 'have got MicroDots all over your hands, young man.'

'Nice to see you, Mother,' Schofield said. 'It's good to have you back.'

A volley of bullets from the ExSol men hit the guillotine.

Schofield turned quickly, eyeing the open doorway ten yards away.

'I'm going upstairs now,' he said abruptly, 'to get Killian. Mother, stay with Rufus, and take care of these assholes. Knight, you can come or you can stay. It's your choice.'

Knight held his gaze. 'I'm coming.'

Schofield—still wearing his stripped utility vest—gave Knight one of the rifles, the 9mm pistol and the full utility vest he had picked up. 'Here. You can use these things better than I can. Let's move. Mother, cover fire, please.'

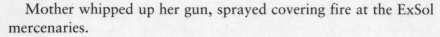

Mother whipped up her gun, sprayed covering fire at the ExSol mercenaries.

Schofield dashed for the door. Knight took off after him . . . but not before quickly grabbing something from Mother.

'What are you taking that for?' Mother shouted after him.

'I've got a feeling I'm gonna be needing it,' was all Knight said before he disappeared through the stone doorway after Schofield.

The Knight and the Scarecrow.

Storming up the spiralling stone stairwell—illuminated by fire-light, rising from the depths of the dungeon—two warriors of equal awesome skill, covering each other, moving in tandem, their Colt Commando machine-guns blazing.

Like the six ExSol men guarding the stairwell had a chance.

As Schofield had suspected, Cedric Wexley had dispatched his six remaining mercenaries to this side of the Pit, to cut off their escape.

The ExSol mercs had divided themselves into three pairs stationed at regular intervals up the stairwell, firing from alcoves in the walls.

The first two mercenaries were ripped to shreds by fire from the uprushing warriors.

The second pair never even heard it coming as two shuriken throwing knives whipped *around* the corner of the curving stairwell—banking through the air like boomerangs—and lodged in their skulls.

The third pair were cleverer.

They'd set a trap.

They had waited at the top of the stairwell, inside the long stone tunnel beyond the ante-room—the tunnel with the boiling-oil gutters—the same tunnel that led to the verification office, where Wexley himself now stood with Killian and Delacroix.

Schofield and Knight arrived at the top of the stairwell, saw the two mercenaries in the tunnel, and the others beyond them.

But this time when Schofield moved, Knight didn't.

Schofield dashed through the ante-room, firing at the two

mercenaries in the tunnel, taking them down just as they tried to do the same to him.

Knight leapt up after him shouting, 'No, wait! It's a tra—'

Too late.

The three large steel doors came thundering down from the ceilings of the tunnel and the ante-room. A fourth sealed off the stairwell leading down from the ante-room.

Wham! Wham! Wham! Wham!

And Schofield and Knight were separated.

Schofield: trapped in the tunnel with the two fallen ExSol mercenaries.

Knight: caught in the ante-room.

Schofield froze in the sealed-off tunnel.

He'd hit both of the mercenaries in here—they now lay sprawled on the floor, one dead, the other whimpering.

Killian's voice came over the speakers: '*Captain Schofield. Captain Knight. It was a pleasure to know you both—*'

Knight spun in the ante-room, saw the six microwave emitters arrayed in a circle around the ceiling, embedded in the rock.

'Deep shit . . .' he breathed.

Killian's voice boomed: '*—but the game ends now. It seems only fitting that your deaths be hard-won.*'

Inside the office, Killian peered through the small perspex window that allowed him to see into the boiling-oil tunnel. He saw Schofield there, trapped like a rat.

'Good-bye, gentlemen.'

And Killian hit the two buttons on his remote that triggered each chamber's booby trap: the microwave emitters in Knight's ante-room, and the boiling-oil gutters in Schofield's tunnel.

★ ★ ★

First, Killian heard the humming vibrations from the ante-room, quickly followed by the sound of repeated gunshots.

This had happened before.

People had sometimes tried to shoot their way out through the ante-room's steel doors. It had never worked. On a couple of occasions, some had attempted to shoot the microwave emitters themselves, but bullets weren't powerful enough to penetrate the emitters in their reinforced stone emplacements.

Then with an explosive spurt, steaming yellow oil sprayed across the tiny perspex window separating Killian from the tunnel holding Schofield, blotting out his view of Shane Schofield.

But he didn't need to see Schofield to know what was happening.

As the superheated boiling oil sprayed its way down the length of the tunnel, Killian could hear Schofield's screams.

A minute later, after both the screaming and the gunshots had ceased, Killian opened the steel doors—

—to be confronted by a surprising sight.

He saw the bodies of the two ExSol men lying in the tunnel, blistered and scorched by the boiling oil. One of them had his arms frozen in a defensive cowering posture—he had died screaming in agony, trying to fend off the oil.

Schofield, however, was nowhere to be seen.

In his place, standing at the ante-room end of the tunnel was a dark man-sized shape.

A body bag, standing upright.

It was a black polymer-plastic body bag. A Markov Type-III, to be precise. The best the Soviets had ever built—and the only item that Wade Brandeis had *not* taken from Schofield's vest. Capable of keeping *in* any kind of chemical contamination, now it seemed that it had successfully kept boiling oil *out*.

In a flash the zipper on the body bag whizzed open from the inside and Schofield emerged from it, leading with his MP-7.

His first shot hit Killian's hand—sending the remote flying from his grip—thus keeping the tunnel's doors open.

His second shot blew off Killian's left earlobe. Seeing the gun in Schofield's hand, Killian had ducked reflexively behind the doorframe. A nanosecond slower and the shot would have taken off his head.

Schofield stormed down the narrow tunnel toward the office, his MP-7 blazing.

Cedric Wexley returned fire from the cover of the office doorway. Bullets flew every which way.

Chunks of stone fell off the wall-columns that lined the tunnel.

The floor-to-ceiling panoramic window in the office behind Wexley shattered completely.

But the key question in a stand-off like this was simple: who would run out of ammunition first? Schofield or Wexley?

Schofield did.

Ten feet short of the office doorway.

'Shit!' he yelled, ducking behind a stone column that barely concealed him.

Wexley smiled. He had him.

But then, strangely, *another* source of gunfire assailed Wexley's position—gunfire that came from behind Schofield, from the ante-room end of the tunnel.

Schofield was also perplexed by this and he turned . . .

. . . to see Aloysius Knight charging down the length of the tunnel, his Colt Commando raised and firing.

Schofield caught a fleeting glimpse of the ante-room in the distance behind Knight.

On its stone floor were 9mm shell casings—a dozen of them—relics of Knight's shooting spree during the activation of the microwave emitters.

But they weren't regular shell casings.

These shell casings had orange bands around them.

The emplacements of the six microwave emitters in the ante-room may have been able to withstand regular bullets. But they'd been no match for Knight's gas-expanding bull-stoppers.

Knight's fire was all that Schofield needed.

Wexley was forced to return fire and within moments he was dry too. Unfortunately, so was Knight.

Schofield sprang.

He flew into the office at speed, striking Wexley in his already

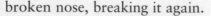

broken nose, breaking it again.

Wexley roared with pain.

And Wexley and Schofield engaged. Brutal hand-to-hand combat. South African Reccondo vs United States Marine.

But as they came together in a flurry of moves and parries, Monsieur Delacroix stepped forward, a glistening knife appearing from his right sleeve-cuff and he lunged at Schofield with it.

The blade got within an inch of Schofield's back before Delacroix's wrist was clutched from the side by an exceedingly strong grip and suddenly Delacroix found himself staring into the eyes of Aloysius Knight.

'Now that just isn't fair,' Knight said, a moment before he was stabbed deep in the thigh by a second knife that had appeared from Delacroix's other cuff.

Delacroix's knife-wielding hands moved like lightning, forcing the now-limping Knight to step back across the floor.

The blades were the sharpest things Knight had ever seen. Or felt. One of them slashed across his face, carving a line of blood across his cheek.

What had previously been all dapper-Swiss-banker was now a perfectly-balanced bladesman exhibiting the exquisite knife skills only associated with the—

'Swiss Guards, hey, Delacroix?' Knight said as he moved. 'You never told me that. Nice. Very nice.'

'In my trade,' Delacroix sneered, 'a man must know how to handle himself.'

Schofield and Wexley traded blows by the doorway.

Wexley was bigger and stronger than Schofield, skilful, too.

Schofield, however, was quicker, his now-famous reflexes allowing him to evade Wexley's more lethal blows.

But after the exertions of the previous twenty-four hours and the crash of the X-15 and the trip as a captive to France, his energy levels were low.

As such, he over-extended with one punch.

Wexley nailed him for the error—a withering blow to the nose that would have killed any other man—and Schofield staggered, but as he fell, he managed to unleash a ruthless blow of his own to Wexley's Adam's apple.

Both men fell, dropping to the floor together—Wexley went sprawling across the open doorway, gasping, while Schofield slumped against the doorframe beside him.

Wexley groaned, and rising to his knees, drew a Warlock hunting knife from his boot.

'Too late, asshole,' Schofield said.

The strange thing was, he had no weapon in his hands. He had something better. He had Killian's remote.

'This is for McCabe and Farrell,' he said, hitting a button on the remote.

Immediately, the steel door above Wexley came thundering down out of its recess, slamming into Wexley's head like a pile-driver, driving it down into the stone floor where—*sprack!*—it cracked Wexley's head in an instant, flattening it.

With Wexley dead, Schofield turned to find the man he really wanted.

He saw him standing behind the desk.

Jonathan Killian.

Knight was still fighting Delacroix when he saw Schofield approach Killian over by the desk.

It wasn't that Knight was worried about Killian. Far from it. He was worried about what Schofield was going to do.

But he couldn't get away from Delacroix . . .

Schofield stopped in front of Killian.

The contrast couldn't have been more marked. Schofield was covered in dirt and grime, bloodied and beaten and worn. Apart from his bullet-nicked ear and wounded hand Killian was relatively neat and tidy, his clothes perfectly pressed.

The shattered floor-to-ceiling panoramic window overlooking the Atlantic yawned beside them.

The thunderstorm outside raged. Lightning forks tore the sky. Rain lanced in through the broken window.

Schofield gazed at Killian without emotion.

When he didn't speak, Killian just smirked.

'So, Captain Schofield. What are your intentions now? To kill me? I am a defenceless civilian. I have no military skills. I am unarmed.' Killian's eyes narrowed. 'But then, I don't think you could kill me. Because if you killed me now in rank cold blood, it would be my final victory, and perhaps my greatest achievement. For it would only prove one thing: *that I broke you*. I turned the last good man in the world into a cold-hearted murderer. And all I did was kill your girl.'

Schofield's eyes never wavered.

His whole appearance was unnaturally still.

When he finally spoke, his voice was low, dangerous.

'You once told me that Westerners don't understand suicide bombers,' he said slowly. 'Because suicide bombers don't fight fair. That the battle is meaningless to a suicide bomber, because he wants to win a far more important war: a psychological war in which the man who dies in a state of terror or fear—the man who dies *against his will*—loses.' Schofield paused. 'While the man who dies when he is emotionally ready, wins.'

Killian frowned.

Schofield never flinched, not even when a totally fatalistic, nihilistic smile washed across his face.

Then he grabbed Killian roughly by the throat and brought the billionaire right up close to his face and growled, 'You're not emotionally ready to die, Killian. But I am. Which means I win.'

'Jesus Christ, no . . .' Killian stammered, realising what was about to happen. 'No!!!'

And with those words, hauling the screaming Jonathan Killian with him, Shane Schofield stepped out through the shattered panoramic window beside them, out into the storm, and the two of them—hero and villain—fell together through 400 feet of sky down to the jagged rocks below.

At the very same moment that Schofield pulled Killian right up close to his face, Aloysius Knight had got the jump on Delacroix.

A quick sidestep to the left had caused Delacroix to stab one of his knives deep into the wood-panelled wall of the office—and allowed Knight to whip his blowtorch out from his utility vest and jam it into Delacroix's mouth and pull the trigger.

The blue flame from the blowtorch blasted out the back of Delacroix's head, spiking right through his skull, sending burnt brains flying across the room. The Swiss banker slumped instantly, dead, a char-rimmed hole driven right through his head.

Knight emerged from behind the fallen Delacroix just in time to see Shane Schofield step out into the storm, taking the screaming Killian with him.

Schofield fell through the rain with Jonathan Killian at his side.

The rocky mount rushed past them, while directly below them, Schofield saw the rocks, assaulted by the waves of the Atlantic, that would end his life.

And as he fell, a strange peace came over him. This was the end, and he was ready for it.

Then suddenly, from out of nowhere, something struck him hard in the back and he jolted sickeningly and without warning . . .

. . . stopped falling.

Jonathan Killian shrank away from him—falling, falling, falling—disappearing with the rain, before slamming into the rocks at the base of the mount where he bent at an obscene angle and

then vanished in a foul explosion of his own blood. He screamed all the way down.

And yet Schofield did not fall.

He just hung from the panoramic window at the end of a Maghook rope—from the Maghook that had just been fired by Aloysius Knight, the Maghook he had taken from Mother before—a desperate last-gasp shot that he had fired as he leaned out the window a second after Schofield had jumped—the bulbous magnetic head of the Maghook having attached itself to the metal plate inside the back section of Schofield's borrowed flak vest.

Schofield allowed himself to be reeled back up to the office like a fish on a line. When he got there, Knight hauled him back inside.

'I'm sorry, buddy,' Knight said. 'But I just couldn't let you go like that. That said, I still think you made your point to Killian.'

Ten minutes later, as the sun appeared on the horizon, a lone Aston Martin sped away from the Forteresse de Valois with Aloysius Knight at the wheel and Shane Schofield, Mother and Rufus inside it.

The car took the side-road leading up to the castle's airfield. There, after a very one-sided gunbattle, its occupants stole an Axon helicopter and flew off toward the rising sun.

Over the next few months, a strange variety of incidents took place around the world.

Just a week later, in Milan, Italy, it was claimed that there had been a break-in at the Aerostadia Italia Airshow, and that an aircraft had been stolen from one of the airshow's outlying hangars.

After the disappointing non-appearance of the fabled US X-15 rocket planes already, this was not the kind of publicity that the airshow needed.

Witnesses claimed that the aircraft taken was a sleek, black fighter which—so they said—took off vertically. While this description matched the description of the experimental Russian Sukhoi S-37, airshow and Italian Air Force officials were quick to point out that no such plane had been slated to appear at the show.

In the lead-up to Christmas, there was also a spate of unfortunate deaths among some of the world's richest families.

Randolph Loch disappeared while on safari in southern Africa. His entire private hunting party was never found.

In March, the Greek shipping magnate Cornelius Kopassus suffered a fatal heart attack in his sleep.

Arthur Quandt was found dead with his mistress in the spa of his Aspen lodge.

Warren Shusett was murdered in his isolated country mansion.

J. D. Cairnton, the pharmaceutical tycoon, was hit and killed by a speeding truck outside his company's New York headquarters. The driver of the truck was never found.

Heirs took over their empires.

The world kept turning.

The only connection made to their deaths was in a confidential memo to the President of the United States.

It read simply: 'SIR, IT IS OVER. MAJESTIC-12 IS NO MORE.'

The hired Volkswagen circled the charming cobblestoned piazza on the Spanish island of Majorca, the famed luxury hideaway for the rich and reclusive.

'So where are we going again?' Rufus asked.

'We're going to meet our employer,' Knight said. 'The person who engaged us to keep Captain Schofield alive.'

Knight parked the car outside a streetside café.

Their employer was already there.

She sat at one of the sidewalk tables, smoking a cigarette, her eyes hidden behind a pair of opaque Dior sunglasses.

She was a very distinguished-looking woman—late forties, dark hair, high cheekbones, porcelain skin, her posture all at once refined and cultured and confident.

Her name was Lillian Mattencourt.

Billionaire owner of the Mattencourt cosmetics empire.

The richest woman in the world.

'Why if it isn't my knight in shining armour,' she said as they approached her table. 'Aloysius, my dear. Do sit down.'

Over tea, Mattencourt smiled warmly.

'Oh, Aloysius, you have done well. And you shall be rewarded handsomely.'

'Why?' Knight said. 'Why didn't you want him killed?'

'Oh, my dashing young knight,' Lillian Mattencourt said. 'Is it not obvious?'

Knight had thought about this. 'Majestic-12 wanted to start a new Cold War. And Jonathan Killian wanted global anarchy. But your fortune is based on the opposite of that. You want people to feel safe, secure, to be happy little consumers. Your fortune rests on the maintenance of global peace and prosperity. And nobody buys make-up during wartime. Warfare would ruin you.'

Mattencourt waved his answer away. 'My dear boy, are you always so cynical? Of course, what you say is absolutely true. But it was only one small part of my reasoning.'

'What was it then?'

Mattencourt smiled. Then her tone became deadly. 'Aloysius. Despite the fact that I have a greater net wealth than all but a few of them, and despite the fact that my father was once a member of their little club, for many years now, for the sole and single reason that I am a woman, Randolph Loch and his friends have consistently refused to let me join their Council.

'Put simply, after years of suffering their various innuendos and sexual taunts, I decided that I'd had enough. So when I learned of their bounty hunt through sources of my own within the French government, I decided that the time was right to teach them a lesson. I decided, Aloysius, *to hurt them.*

'And the best way to achieve that was to take from them that which they desired most—their precious plan. If they wanted certain people dead, then I wanted them alive. If they wanted to destroy the existing global order, then I did not.

'I had heard of Captain Schofield. His reputation is well known. Like yourself, he is a rather resilient young man. If anyone could defeat Majestic-12 it was him, with you by his side. As such, he became the man you would protect.'

Lillian Mattencourt raised her nose and inhaled the fresh Mediterranean air, a sign that this meeting was over.

'Now, run along my brave little foot soldier. Run along. You

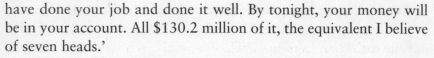

have done your job and done it well. By tonight, your money will be in your account. All $130.2 million of it, the equivalent I believe of seven heads.'

And with that she stood, donned her hat, and left the café, making for her 500 Series Mercedes Benz on the far side of the piazza.

She was inside the car and about to start it when Knight saw the shadowy figure standing in an alleyway not far from it.

'Oh, you cunning bastard,' Knight said a split second before Lillian Mattencourt keyed the ignition.

The explosion rocked the piazza.

Potted plants were thrown across the cobblestones. Table umbrellas were blown inside-out. Bystanders started running toward the flaming ruins of Lillian Mattencourt's Mercedes.

And the man who had been standing in the alleyway walked casually over to Knight's table and sat down beside him.

His flame-scarred face and bald head were covered by sunglasses and a cap.

'Well, if it isn't the Demon,' Knight said flatly.

'Hello, Captain Knight,' Demon Larkham said. 'Two weeks ago, you stole something from me. From a cargo plane travelling between Afghanistan and France. Three heads, if I recall. $55.8 million worth of bounty.'

Knight saw three other members of IG-88 standing nearby, guns under their jackets, flanking him and Rufus.

No escape.

'Oh yeah, that.'

Demon Larkham's voice was low. 'Others would kill you for what you did, but I'm not like that. The way I see it, things like this happen in our profession. It is the nature of the game and I enjoy that game. Ultimately, however, I believe that what happens on the field, stays on the field. That said, considering this unfortunate incident'—Demon waved at the smoking remains of Lillian Mattencourt's car—'and the amount of money that you have just seen go up in smoke, what do you say we consider the debt settled.'

'I'd say that would be a good idea,' Knight said evenly, his lips tight.

'Until we meet again then, Captain,' the Demon said, standing. 'See you on the next safari.'

And with that, Demon Larkham and his men were gone, and all Aloysius Knight could do was gaze after them ruefully and shake his head.

The sun shone brightly over the BBQ underway in Mother's backyard.

It was a Sunday and a small but very close crowd had gathered for a casual get-together.

Mother's trucker husband Ralph was there—tending to the sausages with an oversized spatula. Their nieces were inside, miming to Britney Spears's latest hit.

David Fairfax sat in a deck chair under the clothesline, nursing a beer, swapping stories with Book II and Mother about their adventures the previous October: tales of chases in parking lots near the Pentagon, office towers in London, Zulu bounty hunters, British bounty hunters, and their mirror-image assaults on super-tankers on either side of the United States.

They also talked about Aloysius Knight.

'I heard the government cleared his record, cancelled the bounty and took him off the Most Wanted List,' Fairfax said. 'They even said he could come back to Special Forces if he wanted to.'

'So has he?' Book II asked.

'I don't even think he's come back to the States,' Fairfax said. 'Mother? What do you know about Knight?'

'He phones every now and then,' she said, 'but no, he hasn't come back to the States. If I were him, I don't know if I would

either. As far as Special Forces is concerned, I don't think Knight is a soldier anymore. I think he's a bounty hunter now.'

Thinking about Knight made Mother look over her shoulder.

Over in a corner of the yard, by himself, sat Schofield—clean-shaven and wearing jeans and a T-shirt and a pair of reflective Oakleys. He sipped on a Coke, staring up into the sky.

He had hardly spoken to anyone since he had arrived, which was not unusual these days. Gant's death in France had hit him hard. He'd been on indefinite leave ever since, and didn't look like coming back to active duty any time soon.

Everyone gave him a bit of space.

But just then, as Ralph was sizzling the onions, the doorbell rang.

Courier delivery. For the attention of Shane Schofield. Care of Mother's address.

A large cardboard envelope.

Mother took it to Schofield in the yard. He opened it. Inside the envelope was a lone gift-shop card with a cheesy cartoon of a cowboy that read: 'YOUR NEW LIFE BEGINS TODAY, BUCKAROO!'

Inside it was a handwritten message:

SCARECROW,

I'M SORRY I COULDN'T MAKE IT TODAY, BUT A NEW JOB CAME UP.

HAVING SPOKEN WITH MOTHER RECENTLY, I REALISED THAT THERE IS SOMETHING I SHOULD HAVE TOLD YOU FOUR MONTHS AGO.

DID YOU KNOW THAT, STRICTLY SPEAKING, MY CONTRACTUAL COMMITMENT TO MY EMPLOYER TO KEEP YOU ALIVE EXPIRED WHEN YOU DISARMED THAT MISSILE OVER MECCA. MY TASK WAS TO KEEP YOU ALIVE 'UNTIL 12 NOON, 26 OCTOBER OR UNTIL SUCH TIME AS CAPTAIN SCHOFIELD'S REASON FOR ELIMINATION HAS BEEN UTILISED TO ITS FULLEST POTENTIAL.'

I HAVE NEVER GONE BEYOND THE LETTER OF A CONTRACT

BEFORE. TO BE HONEST, I ACTUALLY THOUGHT ABOUT LEAVING YOU IN THAT DUNGEON—AFTER ALL, BY THEN, YOUR REASON FOR ELIMINATION HAD INDEED BEEN UTILISED TO THE FULLEST.

BUT AFTER WATCHING THE WAY YOUR MEN—AND YOUR WOMEN—STOOD BY YOU OVER THE COURSE OF THAT AWFUL DAY, AFTER OBSERVING THE LOYALTY THEY HAD TO YOU, I CHOSE TO STAY AND FIGHT BY YOUR SIDE.

LOYALTY IS NOT SOMETHING THAT SIMPLY HAPPENS, CAPTAIN. IT IS ALWAYS PREDICATED BY AN INDEPENDENT SELFLESS ACT: A SUPPORTIVE WORD, A KINDLY GESTURE, AN UNPROVOKED ACT OF GOODNESS. YOUR MEN ARE LOYAL TO YOU, CAPTAIN, BECAUSE YOU ARE THAT RAREST OF MEN: A GOOD MAN.

PLEASE LIVE AGAIN. IT WILL TAKE TIME. BELIEVE ME, I KNOW. BUT DO NOT ABANDON THE WORLD JUST YET—IT CAN BE A TERRIBLE PLACE, BUT IT CAN ALSO BE A BEAUTIFUL PLACE, AND NOW MORE THAN EVER IT NEEDS MEN LIKE YOU.

AND KNOW THIS, SHANE 'SCARECROW' SCHOFIELD. YOU HAVE WON <u>MY</u> LOYALTY, A FEAT WHICH NO MAN HAS ACHIEVED FOR A VERY LONG TIME.

ANYTIME, ANYWHERE, IF YOU NEED HELP, JUST MAKE THE CALL AND I'LL BE THERE.

YOUR FRIEND,

THE BLACK KNIGHT

P.S. I AM SURE SHE IS WATCHING OVER YOU RIGHT NOW.

Schofield folded up the card.
And stood up.

And started walking out of the yard and down the driveway, heading for his car out on the street.

'Hey!' Mother called, concerned. 'Where are you going, champ?'

Schofield turned to her and smiled—a sad but genuine smile. 'Thank you, Mother. Thank you for worrying about me. I promise, you won't have to do it for too much longer.'

'What are you doing?'

'What am I doing?' he said. 'I'm going to try and start living again.'

The next morning he appeared at the personnel offices of Marine Headquarters in the Navy Annex building in Arlington.

'Good morning, sir,' he said to the Colonel in charge. 'My name is Captain Shane Schofield. The Scarecrow. I'm ready to get back to work.'

AN INTERVIEW WITH MATTHEW REILLY

THE WRITING OF *SCARECROW*

[WARNING—Some of the later questions in this interview address plot points in *Scarecrow*. Be careful if you are reading them before you read the book!]

What were you trying to achieve with this new novel?

From the very beginning, I was aware that *Scarecrow* would be closely compared to my other books. This is natural—hey, as soon as you write *two* books, people automatically compare them and decide which is their favourite. With that in mind, what I really wanted was for *Scarecrow* to be seen as a new *kind* of Matthew Reilly novel, a faster book, a book that was more densely packed with plot: a book that was a stylistic leap forward from my previous efforts. I'm hoping people will see *Contest, Ice Station, Temple* and *Area 7* as 'Matthew Reilly Version 1.0' and *Scarecrow* as the beginning of 'Matthew Reilly Version 2.0'.

It's funny, in the interview at the back of *Area 7*, I mentioned that I wanted to create a new level of speed and pace in my next book—and then I'd meet people at book signings and they'd say 'How are you possibly going to make it *faster*?' I like to think that *Scarecrow* has lived up to the promise of being faster and completely out-of-control!

How have you tried to achieve this?

Mainly by combining action and exposition—I wanted my characters to be running away from the bad guys *while* they were figuring stuff out. A lot of thrillers have rest breaks between the action scenes during which the author spells out the plot. I wanted to fuse the action and the plot advancement together. The result is that

Scarecrow is about the same length as *Area 7*, but has a lot more happening in it.

What was the inspiration for the bounty hunters in Scarecrow?

It's odd, you know, but for me bounty hunters have only ever appeared in two storytelling spheres: westerns and the original *Star Wars* trilogy (I haven't read any of Janet Evanovich's books, but I believe her lead character is a bounty hunter).

The idea of international bounty hunters, with their own planes and units and even submarines, was something I adapted from the (real-life) concept of mercenary forces: private armies that sell themselves and their hardware to the highest bidder. In Australia, such forces got a lot of press when Papua New Guinea engaged a mercenary army a few years ago; I also read about them operating in Sierra Leone, helping the government stay in power in exchange for diamonds.

In addition to this, I have always been intrigued by the concept of the Wild West freelance bounty hunter, a concept which was adapted to a sci-fi environment in the *Star Wars* trilogy, in particular *The Empire Strikes Back*. Indeed, this is why Demon Larkham's gang—the InterContinental Guards, Unit 88, or 'IG-88'—is proudly named after the obscure bounty hunter of the same name in *The Empire Strikes Back*. (For those who don't know, IG-88 was the very tall robot bounty hunter who stands in the background as Darth Vader offers a reward for the bounty hunter who finds the *Millennium Falcon*. IG-88 utters no dialogue, nor does he actually move, but he became one of those cult *Star Wars* action figures— probably because he was always the one left on the shelf!).

In any case, the idea of these elite hunters-of-men really appealed to me, and I wanted to fashion a story whereby my hero, Shane Schofield—an able warrior himself—was being pursued by the best manhunters on the planet. And thus *Scarecrow* was born.

Speaking of bounty hunters, you introduce in Scarecrow *a character named Aloysius Knight, a.k.a. the Black Knight. What lay behind his creation?*

I had a lot of fun creating Aloysius Knight. From the start, he was designed to be Schofield's darker shadow, his amoral twin (he even has an eye dysfunction to match Schofield's). I wanted him to be the equal of Schofield in battle skills, but darker, more ruthless—as shown, for example, when we first meet him at Krask-8, when he kills the pleading mercenary in cold blood.

But most of all, I wanted Knight to be a guy whose reputation preceded him. The men of ExSol are worried that he's coming to Siberia. David Fairfax discovers that he's the second-best bounty hunter in the world—at a time when Knight is standing right in front of Schofield.

As a writer, it's very liberating to create characters such as Knight—it's the same with Mother—because you can do all sorts of things with him. For the simple reason that there are no boundaries. Characters like Knight and Mother are not governed by socially acceptable norms, and so are fun to write about. They swear, they kill bad people, they do crazy things. But having said that, there is one special thing common to both Mother and Knight: their loyalty to their friends—Mother to Schofield, and Knight to his pilot, Rufus. However wild and crazy they may be, they stand by their friends.

As an interesting aside, Knight is named after St Aloysius (pronounced *allo-wishus*) Gonzaga, a Jesuit saint and the namesake of my old high school, St Aloysius' College, in Sydney.

[THIS QUESTION CONTAINS PLOT SPOILERS]

Okay. To the big question: how could you kill Gant! Seriously,
Scarecrow *sees some of the biggest 'character moments' you've*
written. What made you make those choices?

You cannot believe how hard that scene was for me to write. Unlike
other characters who have met their end in my previous books,
Gant had been with me for two-and-a-half books, and I virtually
considered her a member of the family. I've never considered myself
to be an emotional, fall-in-love-with-my-characters kind of writer,
but I remember vividly the day I wrote that terrible scene—I recall
physically standing up from my computer and saying (aloud, to my
empty office) 'Can I really do this?'

And so I thought about it. A lot. But then I said to myself 'No. This
is what makes my novels different to other kinds of books. No
character is safe. I've got to hold my nerve.'

It took me another day before I could sit down and actually type
the scene, but I did. In the end, though, this is the essential feature
of the action-thriller novel—the reader must believe that the hero
and his friends *might not make it.*

Ultimately, however, it was a 'character motivation' thing that
made me go through with killing Libby Gant. I decided that I
wanted to see what would happen to the hero, Schofield, if such a
terrible thing happened. What that led to was one of my favourite
scenes in all of my books: the fistfight between Schofield and
Mother (I don't know about you, but ever since I created them, I
have wondered who would win a fight between Schofield and
Mother: in the end, the answer is Schofield).

How do you interact with your military advisors?

This is a good question. My two military guys, Paul Woods and Kris Hankison, are two of the most knowledgable men I've ever known. And their input into my books has been beyond value, for the simple reason that no matter how much research you do on a given topic, someone 'in the industry' will always be able to give you that little bit of nuance, that little bit extra. That is what Paul and Kris do for me on military matters.

That said, sometimes the dictates of my story mean that I have to say to them, 'Sorry, guys, but I'll have to invoke poetic licence on this point.' A good example is the big MOAB bomb in *Scarecrow*. MOABs are actually satellite-guided, but my story required Gant to place a laser inside the Karpalov Coalmine. So, despite the protests of the guys, I made the MOAB laser-guided.

The best thing about my military advisors is that they have a keen sense of the tone of my books—they know that my novels are outrageous and over-the-top. So they accept that I sometimes have to bend the truth (and, hell, the laws of physics!) for the sake of a roller-coaster story.

Matthew. The French. They were the bad guys in Ice Station. *And now* Scarecrow. *What have you got against the French?*

Ha! Er, yes, the French do cop a bit of a pasting in *Scarecrow*. You have to understand, though, that I don't dislike France. Not at all!

What it boils down to is this: I write fiction. And I'm always looking for new dastardly villains. Back in the days of the Cold War, authors could just make the Soviet Union the evil bad guy. But that doesn't apply anymore. The world has changed. The way I see it— and as I suggested in *Ice Station*—international alliances are more fickle than we imagine. And France, more than any other major

Western nation, has been a vocal and active opponent of United States hegemony. Since Shane Schofield is American, France is often at cross-purposes with him.

Add to that France's chequered geopolitical history—the sinking of the *Rainbow Warrior*, her nuclear testing in the Pacific Ocean, and her outspoken opposition to the US invasion of Iraq—and you have a nation that could, in the world of fiction, have nefarious anti-US plans.

But I stress: it's fiction!

So what else have you been doing?

Since finishing *Scarecrow*, I have completed two screenplays. I enjoy writing scripts in between my books—a novel takes me a year to write, whereas a screenplay takes me about two months. I adapted my own short story, *Altitude Rush*, into a full-length screenplay, and have finished the first part of an epic science fiction trilogy that I think will rock the world one day!

Any more books on the way?

Yes indeed. Earlier this year I signed a new two-book deal with my publishers, Pan Macmillan, so there will be at least two more books from me. I have now moved to producing one book every two years—I would love to be able to produce a book every year, but I fear the quality would suffer and I just don't want to end up churning out books simply to keep to a timetable.

Not sure what they'll be about at this stage. One will probably be a Schofield book, although maybe Aloysius Knight could get a novel of his own. And I keep getting asked at book signings if I will be writing a sequel to *Temple*!

Any final words?

As always, I just hope you enjoyed the book. Keep reading and take care.

Matthew Reilly
Sydney, Australia
November 2003

Matthew Reilly
Contest

The New York State Library. A brooding labyrinth of towering
bookcases, narrow aisles and spiralling staircases. For Doctor Stephen
Swain and his daughter, Holly, it is the site of a nightmare. For one
night this historic building is to be the venue for a contest. A contest
in which Swain is to compete – whether he likes it or not.

The rules are simple. Seven contestants will enter. Only one will leave.
With his daughter in his arms, Swain is plunged into a terrifying fight
for survival. He can choose to run, hide or to fight – but if he wants to
live, he has to win. For in this contest, unless you leave as the victor,
you do not leave at all.

'Matt Reilly, genius . . . the arrival of a rare talent'
John Birmingham, THE SYDNEY MORNING HERALD

'An electrifying . . . novel for the *X-Files* generation'
Jessica Adams, CLEO

'Matthew Reilly is our Michael Crichton'
DAILY TELEGRAPH

Matthew Reilly
Ice Station

At a remote ice station in Antarctica, a team of US scientists has made an amazing discovery. They have found something buried deep within a 100-million-year-old layer of ice. Something made of METAL.

Led by the enigmatic Lieutenant Shane Schofield, a team of crack United States Marines is sent to the station to secure this discovery for their country. They are a tight unit, tough and fearless. They would follow their leader into hell. They just did . . .

'The pace is frantic, the writing snappy, the research thorough. Unputdownable . . .'
WEEKEND AUSTRALIAN

'It never slows down . . . it is unlike any other new Australian novel'
DAILY TELEGRAPH

'There is enough technological wizardry, military know-how, plot convolution and sheer non-stop mayhem to place it in the premier league of international bestsellers'
THE WEST AUSTRALIAN

'His publisher compares him to Grisham and Crichton, but I reckon the 23-year-old is a cut above'
RALPH

'This is Indiana Jones goes to Antarctica . . . backed by good research about weaponry, science and international jealousies'
NW

Matthew Reilly
Temple

Deep in the jungles of Peru, the hunt for a legendary Incan idol is underway – an idol that in the present day could be used as the basis for a terrifying new weapon.

Guiding a US Army team is Professor William Race, a young linguist who must translate an ancient manuscript which contains the location of the idol.

What they find is an ominous stone temple, sealed tight. They open it – and soon discover that some doors are meant to remain unopened . . .

'There is no denying it. Matthew Reilly has really arrived'
DAILY TELEGRAPH

'Like *Ice Station*, *Temple* is well researched and technically adept. Diehard action buffs will enjoy'
WHO WEEKLY

'Probably the most breathless read in the history of airport fiction'
AUSTRALIAN BOOKSELLER & PUBLISHER

Matthew Reilly
Area 7

It is America's most secret base, hidden deep in the Utah desert, an Air Force installation known only as Area 7.

And today it has a visitor: the President of the United States. He has come to inspect Area 7, to examine its secrets for himself. But he's going to get more than he bargained for on this trip. Because hostile forces are waiting inside . . .

Among the President's helicopter crew, however, is a young Marine. He is quiet, enigmatic, and he hides his eyes behind a pair of silver sunglasses.

His name is Schofield. Call-sign: *Scarecrow*.

Rumour has it he's a good man in a storm.

Judging by what the President has just walked into, he'd better be . . .

THE AUTHOR OF *ICE STATION* IS BACK AND THRILLERS JUST GOT A WHOLE LOT FASTER.

'Buckle up, put the seat back, adjust the headrest and hang on'
THE SUNDAY AGE

'Australia's new master of action'
DAILY TELEGRAPH